ALICE LECCESE POWERS

FRANCE IN MIND

Alice Leccese Powers is the editor of the anthologies *Italy in Mind* and *Ireland in Mind*, and coeditor of *The Brooklyn Reader: Thirty Writers Celebrate America's Favorite Borough*. A freelance writer and editor, she has been published in *The Washington Post*, *The Baltimore Sun*, *Newsday*, and many other newspapers and magazines. Ms. Powers also teaches writing at the Corcoran College of Art and Design. She lives in Washington, D.C., with her husband.

ALSO BY
ALICE LECCESE POWERS

Italy in Mind
Ireland in Mind
The Brooklyn Reader

FRANCE IN MIND

FRANCE IN MIND

A N   A N T H O L O G Y

Edited and with an Introduction by
Alice Leccese Powers

V I N T A G E   D E P A R T U R E S
Vintage Books
A Division of Random House, Inc.
New York

Library of Congress Cataloging-in-Publication Data

France in mind : an anthology / edited and with an introduction
by Alice Leccese Powers.
p. cm.—(Vintage departures)
ISBN 0-375-71435-9
1. France—Literary collections. 2. English literature.
3. American literature. I. Powers, Alice Leccese.
PR1111.F7 F73 2003
820.8'03244—dc21   2002028800

Book design by Matt Songer

www.vintagebooks.com

To my parents Vito and Gaetana Leccese

Acknowledgments

With grateful acknowledgment to my editors LuAnn Walther and Diana Secker Larson, and my agent, Jane Dystel; to my fellow writers Erich Parker, Kem Sawyer, Jane Vandenburgh, Michael Leccese and Michael Dolan; to my colleagues and students at the Corcoran College of Art and Design who taught me how to see; to my daughters Alison, Christina and Brenna who were with us in Paris; and of course—as always—to Brian.

"It isn't so much about what France gives you as what it doesn't take away."

GERTRUDE STEIN

Contents

Introduction

"Here before me now is my picture, my map, of a place and therefore of myself, and much that can never be said adds to its reality for me, just as much of its reality is based on my own shadows, my inventions."

M.F.K. FISHER

This is France—not seen through the eyes of the French, but from the perspective of thirty-three British and American writers who are seduced, confounded, appalled and delighted with France—often at once. The subject of *France in Mind* (as in my previous anthologies *Italy in Mind* and *Ireland in Mind*) is filtered through the authors' prejudices and preconceptions. A portrait of the country emerges, but so does an impression of the writers and of their "shadows and inventions."

Nearly a third of the entries in *France in Mind* are identified with Paris. The focus of France has always been its capital. In his 1926 book *The European Tour*, the travel writer Grant Allen wrote, "Americans, accustomed to a great decentralized community, can hardly understand the absolute centralization of everything French in Paris . . . In France *Paris is everything*. You are Parisian, or else you are provincial." Allen exhorts his readers, "*Paris first*, very much first, and the provinces nowhere."

Travelers have often gone to France with Allen's bias, assuming that there is nothing worth seeing beyond the St. Germain. Undeniably, Paris is Paris. But to concentrate only on the capital denies the complexity of the rest of France, with topography as extreme as Mediterranean beaches and Alpine mountains and country people whose lives are as simple as the Parisian's life is complex. Even Allen allowed that there were other places to visit besides Paris, if the tourist absolutely insisted. The Loire towns, Avignon, Normandy and Brittany. Of the Riviera he added, "Intrinsically, it has no claims save those of beautiful natural scenery, lush southern vegetation, charming sunny sea and fine shapes of mountains." Only that.

In contrast to Allen, I include literary selections from every area in France and most genres, both fiction and nonfiction. The venerable travel writers are here, of course, like Paul Theroux, Calvin Trillin, M.F.K. Fisher and Jan Morris, as are the famous expatriates such as Ernest Hemingway, Gertrude Stein, James Baldwin, Henry James and Edith Wharton. But it is the less well-known who delight me (and, I hope, the reader). Richard Wilbur's poem "Place Pigalle" was discovered rummaging through a secondhand bookstore in Washington, D.C. The shop had not one right angle and an assortment of shelves that bowed under the weight of the books, cataloged under the broadest headings: "Fiction, Poetry, Travel." The owner wore a huge beret, lived in a loft above his wares, seemed indifferent to his clientele and loath to part with even one volume in his collection. I could have been on the Left Bank. *Smollett's Travels,* found in a local library, had not been checked out in almost twenty years. I hesitated to include Tobias Smollett because his writing was caustic and devoid of self-censorship. But I decided he was the perfect antidote to modern, sometimes saccharine, memoirs of French village life.

James Fenimore Cooper and Washington Irving are so strongly identified with upstate New York that I was surprised to find that they both lived in and wrote about France. Shortly after his arrival in Paris, Cooper's entire family came down with scarlet fever, his writing was going slowly and he had a falling-out with his publisher. Yet, the man's enthusiasm never flagged. He wrote to a friend, "We are rather comfortably lodged for

Paris—Dirt, Bugs and Fleas, of course, but still a good deal of comfort."

Ezra Pound's *A Walking Tour of Southern France*—fragmentary and allusive—reveals a part of France seldom written about and a part of the poet's life that is seldom seen. Pound, still in his twenties, had yet to be buffeted by Fascism, his trial for treason and the years spent in a mental institution. He had not begun his famous Cantos (although their antecedents can be found in this early work), and he simply walked through the countryside, recording his impressions in school notebooks that were not rediscovered for decades.

Pound toured in the most primitive way—by foot. Robert Louis Stevenson had his donkey Modestine on his trip in 1879. Stevenson struggled loading Modestine's pack. "I had a common donkey packsaddle—a *barde,* as they call it—fitted upon Modestine, and once more loaded her with my effects. The double sack, my pilot-coat (for it was warm and I was to walk in my waistcoat), a great bar of black bread, and an open basket containing the white bread, the mutton and the bottles, were all corded together in a very elaborate system of knots, and I looked on the result with fatuous content." With the advice of several French grooms, Stevenson set out, unconvinced that he was sufficiently prepared. He wrote, "I went forth from the stable door as an ox goeth to the slaughter." Tobias Smollett rented a post chaise in the 1700s, a complicated arrangement where the visitor hired not only the coach, guides, drivers, servants, but paid for the use of the road. Naturally, Smollett found the terms disagreeable and the whole thing easier to do in England. Edith Wharton and Henry James toured France in her 1904 Panhard-Levassor. James and Wharton often motored together, Wharton at the wheel, and she wrote a travel book about their journey, *A Motor-Flight Through Southern France.* Paul Theroux, author of *The Great Railway Bazaar,* of course traveled by train, as did Mark Twain.

But for most travelers the mode of travel was not important; the sensation of simply being in France was momentous. In 1776 a young tourist named Mary Hamilton described her arrival in France after a crossing from Dover to Calais. "It seems strange that in the space of five hours, every object should appear so different—from building to language, to dress." There are many filters, of course, to the writers' impressions: nationality, social class, race, sex. Yet irresistible to almost every author is the compulsion to compare France to home. The dyspeptic Smollett wrote, "The wine commonly used in Burgundy is so weak and thin, that you would not drink it in England." James Baldwin complained that post–World War II Paris contained "no doughnuts, no milk shakes, no Coca-Cola, no dry Martinis, nothing resembling, for people on our economic level, an American toilet; as for toilet paper, it was yesterday's newspaper." David Sedaris came upon two Texans on the Paris Metro discussing which is a better city, Paris or Houston. Houston won hands down, scoring points for "ice cubes, tacos, plenty of free parking and something called a Sonic Burger." Like Stevenson's donkey Modestine, travelers in France are heavily freighted with the weight of home.

The earliest travelers in *France in Mind* are Smollett and Thomas Jefferson, who visited in the late 1700s. Jefferson, a widower, succeeded Benjamin Franklin as Ambassador to France and brought his two daughters and a slave, Sally Hemmings, to his post. He also found love in Maria Cosway, an Englishwoman. The five years that he spent in France bound him to the country, and he declared it his favorite, next to America. At the time, travel to France by British or Americans was limited to a wealthy few.

Large numbers of middle- and upper-middle-class tourists came with the Grand Tours of the 1800s, and it became almost obligatory for young people of means to travel to the Continent to complete their education. The clash between old money and new, between European sensibilities and Anglo-Saxon manners became fodder for many writers, including Edith Wharton and Henry James. The travelers, chaperones in tow, were wealthy and naive in comparison to their European hosts, a combination that often ended badly. Part of the dissonance was religious. Although American and British parents thought it imperative that their children experience French culture, they worried about exposure to so much Catholicism. As a tour of one cathedral was followed by yet another cathedral, some Protestant clerics warned that the impressionable children might be coerced into becoming Romanists.

A far greater risk was seduction by French life: the appreciation of food and drink, the looser social and moral structure, and the general freedom the Anglo-Saxon feels in France, away from social roots set in America or Britain. This was certainly the lure for the post–World War I Lost Generation of writers and artists—Hemingway, Fitzgerald, Janet Flanner, Ezra Pound, T. S. Eliot, Man Ray, Lee Miller, Berenice Abbott. Many were bound to each other by friendships, but also by their allegiance to Sylvia Beach, owner of the bookstore Shakespeare and Company, and Gertrude Stein, host of a salon for writers and artists. Beach operated a lending library—unusual for a bookshop—and was a "martyr and heroine" (according to Janet Flanner) to many writers and artists, even venturing into publishing. When English typesetters refused to set parts of Joyce's *Ulysses,* Beach had the work done in Dijon where the French typographers did not understand, and were not offended by, what they were printing. Gertrude Stein and her partner Alice B. Toklas had evening salons at their apartment at 27 rue de Fleurus. Toklas would be relegated to "the wives" while Stein held court with the husbands. Stein (in Toklas's voice) wrote, "Anybody could come in, however, there was the formula. Miss Stein once in opening the door said as she usually did by whose invitation do you come and we heard an aggrieved voice reply, but by yours, madame . . . They were always there, all sizes and shapes, all degrees of wealth and poverty, some very charming, some simply rough and every now and then a very beautiful young peasant." By 1940 most of the Lost Generation had left France, dispersed by illness, alcohol, ill fortune and the prospect of war. Stein and Toklas remained, eventually forced to sell some of their paintings simply to survive.

Following World War II, a second wave of émigrés arrived. Many had already gotten a free trip to France, courtesy of the

United States Army, and they returned, financed by the GI bill. Lawrence Ferlinghetti studied for his Ph.D. at the Sorbonne; Stanley Karnow also came to study and ended up writing for *Time* as a special correspondent. James Baldwin moved to France only to find racism in a different form against the thousands of African students, children of the French colonies, who crowded into Paris. "Voyagers discover that the world can never be larger than the person that is in the world," he wrote. "But it is impossible to foresee this, it is impossible to be warned."

As the middle class traveled more, a second, more egalitarian rendition of the Grand Tour evolved—the junior year abroad. Mary McCarthy in *Birds of America* created her own Candide: Peter Levi, spending his junior year at the Sorbonne. Peter grapples with his politics while looking for an apartment in Paris that has *une seule clef* and the barest amenities. "A lot of kids rent in the mansards of old buildings," he wrote to his mother. "You ought to see those rooms, like a series of doghouses under the eaves, where the maids used to be kept."

If the Grand Tour was the precursor for the junior year abroad, the prolonged stay of the families of Henry James, James Fenimore Cooper, Mark Twain and Henry Adams was later replicated, on a much reduced scale, in the European family vacation. Parents rented a house for a month in the French countryside to "expose" children to French culture. Calvin Trillin, his wife Alice and their daughters Sarah and Abigail took a house in Uzès, a small village in the south of France. Each had an agenda: Trillin wanted to eat, Alice wanted to see scenery and the children wanted to retain as much of their American routine and cuisine as possible. Like all family vacations, French or not, the month involved negotiations worthy of the Paris Peace Accords, and in the end "Alice had got her share of scenic drives and the girls had got their share of swims and I had got my share of fish soup."

Once travelers have gotten their taste of France, the next logical step is to colonize it. And swarms have, following the blueprint of Peter Mayle and *A Year in Provence*. A whole new literary genre, dubbed French Quaint (or even the more egregious French Cute) follows a predictable pattern. A British or American couple moves to France, buys a house in a terrible state of disrepair and proceeds to improve it by making it as much like England or the United States as possible. Their foils are those "wily rustics," necessary comprimarios to their tenors. The homeowners always think that the renovation will be done in X time, and it always takes X squared. Tiles are ordered and reordered, pipes are fitted and refitted correctly, a window should be placed facing south and—horrors—it faces north. And yet readers devour these fantasies, perhaps because a broken toilet in France, fixed by a French plumber, seems infinitely more interesting than a broken toilet in New York, fixed by Tony from Bensonhurst.

So, what is the draw of France to Anglo-Saxons? It is the romantic possibilities. The manners, the body language, the cuisine, the religion hold the promise of another life away from the ordinary. Writing is hard work; writing done in a café seems less hard. (The British equivalent, a pub, and the American equivalent, a bar, are just not conducive to writing. They are places to go after the writing is finished.) Renovating a house is grueling; renovating a farmhouse in Provence is passionate. And a crepe eaten outside of France is merely a flat pancake.

Writers are drawn to the anticipation of romance. Except Smollett, of course, who saw it as a peril, a force that renders Anglo-Saxons powerless. Even a casual friendship with a Frenchman, he warned, endangers all female members of the family, for he will attempt to debauch, in order, your wife, daughter, sister, niece and even your grandmother. In France, Smollett declared, this is what passes as gallantry. And perhaps there is something to Smollett's claim, for many have simultaneously fallen in love with France and fallen in love in France. James Baldwin wrote, "Everyone loses his head, and his morals, lives through at least one histoire d'amour." Adam Gopnik theorized that the French encourage love and sex; it is simply the desirable norm. He and his wife, expecting their second child, were instructed to return to "normal" as soon as possible after the birth. Pregnancy is the result of sex, and the best thing is to get over it and have more sex.

I sifted through all the ingredients that make writers—all travelers, in fact—go to France. The food and wine. The cafés. The tranquil village life and the vivaciousness of its cities. The architecture and history. The language. The French sense of style and fashion. (Why is it that Americans insist on wearing white sneakers and shorts in Paris? According to David Sedaris, "Comfort has its place, but it seems rude to visit another country dressed as if you've come to mow its lawns.") M.F.K. Fisher wrote that "often in the sketch for a portrait, the invisible lines that bridge one stroke of the pencil or brush to another are what really make it live. This is probably true in a word picture too." It is those invisible lines that I am trying to identify in my word picture of France.

And I come up with only one thing: the promise of love in all of its forms. Love manifested in the precision of the cathedral at Chartres, in the preparation of a perfect meal or in a good wine, prepared from grapes grown in a family vineyard. But above all it is human love that dominates *France in Mind*. The friendship of that unlikely duo Edith Wharton and Henry James, the family camaraderie of Alice and Calvin Trillin and their daughters, happily eating French fries and playing endless games of table soccer in their village of Uzès, the relationship between Gillian Tindall and the peasant Bernardet who, unasked, maintained her vegetable garden, the combustible combination of Zelda and Scott Fitzgerald (all the more heartbreaking because we already know its sad end), the lifelong companionship of Alice B. Toklas and Gertrude Stein in their salon at 27 rue de Fleurus. Not all of the writers in this book found love in France, for no country, event or person can always live up to the promise of an ideal. But *France in Mind* is a testament to their quest.

FRANCE IN MIND

HENRY ADAMS

(1838–1918)

The great-grandson of President John Adams and the grandson of President John Quincy Adams, Henry Adams was born into American political aristocracy. Like many of his class, the Harvard graduate embarked on the European Grand Tour in 1858—and stayed on the Continent for ten years, writing travel and scholarly articles about his experiences. Eventually, Adams returned to Washington, D.C., and set up a salon in a mansion near the White House. He and his wife, Marian (nicknamed Clover), were the most sought-after invitation in the post–Civil War capital. Their inner circle, called The Five of Hearts, included John and Clara Hay and Clarence King. Adams was shattered by Clover's suicide in 1885, and he resumed his restless traveling—through the Far East, the Caribbean, Mexico, Australia and Europe.

In 1895 Henry Adams made his first systematic study of the architecture of Mont St. Michel and Chartres. The result, Mont St. Michel and Chartres, *was published privately in 1904 and again (in a slightly revised form) in 1912.* Chartres *came out as a trade edition published by the American Institute of Architects in 1913—and broke sales records. A stroke in 1913 ended Adams's travels, but he resumed the political salon in his Washington home. He died in 1918, shortly before the publication of his autobiography* The Education of Henry Adams, *for which he posthumously received the Pulitzer Prize. Henry Adams is buried in Washington next to his beloved Clover.*

Towers and Portals

from MONT ST. MICHEL
AND CHARTRES

For a first visit to Chartres, choose some pleasant morning when the lights are soft, for one wants to be welcome, and the Cathedral has moods, at times severe. At best, the Beauce is a country none too gay.

The first glimpse that is caught, and the first that was meant to be caught, is that of the two spires. With all the education that Normandy and the Isle de France can give, one is still ignorant. The spire is the simplest part of the Romanesque or Gothic architecture, and needs least study in order to be felt. It is a bit of sentiment almost pure of practical purpose. It tells the whole of its story at a glance, and its story is the best that architecture had to tell, for it typified the aspirations of man at the moment when man's aspirations were highest. Yet nine persons out of ten,— perhaps ninety-nine in a hundred,—who come within sight of the two spires of Chartres will think it a jest if they are told that the smaller of the two, the simpler, the one that impresses them least, is the one which they are expected to recognise as the most perfect piece of architecture in the world. Perhaps the French critics might deny that they make any such absolute claim; in that case you can ask them what their exact claim is; it will always be high enough to astonish the tourist.

Astonished or not, we have got to take this southern spire of the Chartres Cathedral as the object of serious study, and before taking it as art, must take it as history. The foundations of this tower—always to be known as the old tower,—are supposed to have been laid in 1091, before the first crusade. The *flèche* was probably half a century later (1145–1170). The foundations of the new tower, opposite, were laid not before 1110, when also the Portal, which stands between them, was begun with the three lancet windows above it, but not the Rose. For convenience, this old façade, including the Portal and the two towers, but not the *flèches,* and the three lancet windows, but not the Rose, may be dated as complete about 1150.

Originally the whole Portal,—the three doors and the three lancets—stood nearly forty feet back, on the line of the interior foundation, or rear wall of the towers. This arrangement threw the towers forward, free on three sides, as at Poitiers, and gave room for a Parvis, before the Portal,—a Porch, roofed over, to protect the pilgrims who always stopped there to pray before entering the church. When the church was rebuilt after the great fire of 1194, and the architect was required to enlarge the interior, the old Portal and lancets were moved bodily forward, to be flush with the front walls of the two towers, as you see the façade today; and the façade itself was heightened, to give room for the Rose, and to cover the loftier *pignon* and vaulting behind. Finally, the wooden roof, above the stone vault, was masked by the Arcade of Kings and its railing, completed in the taste of Philip the Hardy, who reigned from 1270 to 1285.

These changes have of course altered the values of all the parts. The Portal is injured by being thrown into a glare of light, when it was intended to stand in shadow, as you will see in the north and south Porches over the transept-portals. The towers are hurt by losing relief and shadow; but the old *flèche* is obliged to suffer the cruelest wrong of all by having its right shoulder hunched up by half of a huge Rose and the whole of a row of kings, when it was built to stand free, and to soar above the whole façade from the top of its second storey. One can easily figure it so, and replace the lost parts of the old façade, more or less at haphazard, from the front of Noyon.

What an outrage it was, you can see by a single glance at the new *flèche* opposite. The architect of 1500 has flatly refused to submit to such conditions, and has insisted, with very proper self-respect, on starting from the balustrade of the arcade of kings, as his level. Not even content with that, he has carried up his square tower another lofty storey before he would consent to touch the heart of his problem, the conversion of the square tower into the octagon *flèche*. In doing this, he has sacrificed once more the old *flèche*; but his own tower stands free as it should.

At Vendome, when you go there, you will be in a way to appreciate still better what happened to the Chartres *flèche*; for the *clocher* at Vendome, which is of the same date,—Viollet-le-Duc says earlier, and Enlart, "after 1130,"—stood, and still stands, free, like an Italian campanile, which gives it a vast advantage. The tower of St. Leu d'Esserent, also after 1130, stands free, above the second storey. Indeed, you will hardly find, in the long list of famous French spires, another which has been treated with so much indignity as this, the greatest and most famous of all; and perhaps the most annoying part of it is that you must be grateful to the architect of 1195 for doing no worse. He has on the contrary, done his best to show respect for the work of his predecessor, and has done so well that, handicapped as it is, the old tower still defies rivalry. Nearly three hundred and fifty feet high, or, to be exact, 106.50 metres from the church floor, it is built up with an amount of intelligence and refinement that leaves to unprofessional visitors no chance to think a criticism,—much less to express one. Perhaps—when we have seen more—and feel less—who knows? but certainly not now!

"The greatest, and surely the most beautiful monument of this kind that we possess in France," says Viollet-le-Duc; but although an ignorant spectator must accept the architect's decision on a point of relative merit, no one is compelled to accept his reasons as final. "There is no need to dwell," he continues, "upon the beauty and the grandeur of composition in which the artist has given proof of rare sobriety where all the effects are obtained not by ornaments but by the just and skilful proportion of the different parts. The transition, so hard to adjust, between the square base and the octagon of the *flèche*, is managed and carried out with an address which has not been surpassed in similar monuments."

One stumbles a little at the word "adresse." One never caught oneself using the word in Norman churches. Your photographs of Bayeux or Boscherville or Secqueville will show you at a glance whether the term "adresse" applies to them. Even Vendome would rather be praised for "droiture" than for "adresse." Whether the word address means cleverness, dexterity, adroitness, or simple technical skill, the thing itself is something which the French have always admired more than the Normans ever did. Viollet-le-Duc himself seems to be a little uncertain whether to lay most stress on the one or the other quality:—

"If one tries to appreciate the conception of this tower," quotes the Abbé Bulteau (II, 84.), "one will see that it is as frank as the execution is simple and skilful. Starting from the bottom, one reaches the summit of the *flèche* without marked break; without anything to interrupt the general form of the building. This *clocher,* whose base is broad *(pleine),* massive and free from ornament, transforms itself, as it springs, into a sharp spire with eight faces, without its being possible to say where the massive construction ends and the light construction begins."

Granting, as one must, that this concealment of the transition is a beauty, one would still like to be quite sure that the Chartres scheme is the best. The Norman *clochers* being thrown out, and that at Vendome being admittedly simple, the *clocher de Saint Jean* on the church of Saint Germain at Auxerre seems to be thought among the next in importance, although it is only about one hundred and sixty feet in height (49 metres), and therefore hardly in the same class with Chartres. Any photograph shows that the Auxerre spire is also simple; and that at Etampes you have seen already to be of the Vendome rather than of the Chartres type. The *clocher* at Senlis is more "habile"; it shows an effort to be clever, and offers a standard of comparison; but the mediæval architects seem to have thought that none of them bore rivalry with Laon for technical skill. One of these professional experts, named Villard de Honnecourt, who lived between 1200 and

1250, left a note-book which you can see in the *vitrines* of the Bibliothèque Nationale in the Rue Richelieu, and which is the source of most that is known about the practical ideas of mediæ-val architects. He came to Chartres, and, standing here before the doors, where we are standing, he made a rough drawing, not of the tower but of the Rose, which was then probably new, since it must have been planned between 1195 and 1200. Apparently the tower did not impress him strongly, for he made no note of it; but on the other hand, when he went to Laon, he became vehe-ment in praise of the cathedral tower there, which must have been then quite new: "I have been in many countries, as you can find in this book. In no place have I ever such a tower seen as that of Laon.—*J'ai esté en mult de tieres, si cum vus porés trover en cest livre. En aucun liu onques tel tor ne vi com est cele de Loon.*" The rea-son for this admiration is the same that Viollet-le-Duc gives for admiring the tower of Chartres,—the "adresse" with which the square is changed into the octagon. Not only is the tower itself changed into the *flèche* without visible junction, under cover of four corner *tourelles,* of open work, on slender columns, which start as squares; but the *tourelles* also convert themselves into octa-gons in the very act of rising, and end in octagon *flèches* that carry up—or once carried up—the lines of profile to the central *flèches* that soared above them. Clearly this device far surpassed in cleverness the scheme of Chartres, which was comparatively heavy and structural, the weights being adjusted for their intended work, while the transformation at Laon takes place in the air, and challenges discovery in defiance of one's keenest eye-sight. "Regard . . . how the *tourelles* pass from one disposition to another, in rising! Meditate on it!"

The *flèche* of Laon is gone, but the tower and *tourelles* are still there to show what the architects of the thirteenth century thought their most brilliant achievement. One cannot compare Chartres directly with any of its contemporary rivals, but one can at least compare the old spire with the new one which stands opposite and rises above it. Perhaps you will like the new best. Built at a time which is commonly agreed to have had the highest standard of taste, it does not encourage tourist or artist to insist on setting up standards of their own against it. Begun in 1507, it was finished in 1517. The dome of St. Peter's at Rome, over which Bramante and Rafael and Michael Angelo toiled, was building at the same time; Leonardo da Vinci was working at Amboise; Jean Bullant, Pierre Lescot, and their patron Francis the First, were beginning their architectural careers. Four hundred years, or thereabouts, separated the old spire from the new one; and four hundred more separate the new one from us. If Viollet-le-Duc, who himself built Gothic spires, had cared to compare his *flèches* at Clermont-Ferrand with the new *flèche* at Chartres, he might perhaps have given us a rule where "adresse" ceases to have charm, and where detail becomes tiresome; but in the want of a schoolmaster to lay down a law of taste, you can admire the new *flèche* as much as you please. Of course one sees that the lines of the new tower are not clean, like those of the old; the devices that cover the transition from the square to the octagon are rather too obvious; the proportion of the *flèche* to the tower quite alters the values of the parts; a rigid classical taste might even go so far as to hint that the new tower, in comparison with the old, showed signs of a certain tendency towards a dim and distant vulgarity. There can be no harm in admitting that the new tower is a little wanting in repose for a tower whose business is to counterpoise the very classic lines of the old one; but no law compels you to insist on absolute repose in any form of art; if such a law existed, it would have to deal with Michael Angelo before it dealt with us. The new tower has many faults, but it has great beauties, as you can prove by comparing it with other late Gothic spires including those of Viollet-le-Duc. Its chief fault is to be where it is. As a companion to the crusades and to Saint Bernard, it lacks austerity. As a companion to the Virgin of Chartres, it recalls Diane de Poitiers.

In fact, the new tower, which in years is four centuries younger than its neighbor, is in feeling fully four hundred years older. It is self-conscious if not vain; its coiffure is elaborately arranged to cover the effects of age, and its neck and shoulders are covered with lace and jewels to hide a certain sharpness of skeleton. Yet it may be beautiful, still; the poets derided the wrinkles of Diane de Poitiers at the very moment when King Henry II idealised her with the homage of a Don Quijote; an atmosphere of physical beauty and decay hangs about the whole renaissance.

One cannot push these resemblances too far, even for the twelfth century and the old tower. Exactly what date the old tower represents, as a social symbol, is a question that might be as much disputed as the beauty of Diane de Poitiers, and yet half the interest of architecture consists in the sincerity of its reflexion of the society that builds. In mere time, by actual date, the old tower represents the second crusade, and when, in 1150, Saint Bernard was elected chief of that crusade in this very Cathedral,— or rather, in the Cathedral of 1120, which was burned,—the workmen were probably setting in mortar the stones of the *flèche* as we now see them; yet the *flèche* does not represent Saint Bernard in feeling, for Saint Bernard held the whole array of church towers in horror as signs merely of display, wealth and pride. The *flèche* rather represents Abbot Suger of Saint Denis, Abbot Peter the Venerable of Cluny, Abbot Abélard of Saint Gildas de Rhuys, and Queen Eleanor of Guienne, who had married Louis le Jeune in 1137; who had taken the cross from Saint Bernard in 1147; who returned from the Holy Land in 1149; and who compelled Saint Bernard to approve her divorce in 1152. Eleanor and Saint Bernard were centuries apart, yet they lived at the same time and in the same church. Speaking exactly, the old tower represents neither of them; the new tower itself is hardly more florid than Eleanor was; perhaps less so, if one can judge from the fashions of the court-dress of her time. The old tower is almost Norman, while Eleanor was wholly Gascon, and Gascony was always florid without being always correct. The new tower, if it had been built in 1150, like the old one, would have expressed Eleanor perfectly, even in height and apparent effort to dwarf its mate, except that Eleanor dwarfed her husband without an effort, and both in art and in history the result lacked harmony.

Be the contrast what it may, it does not affect the fact that no other church in France has two spires that need be discussed in comparison with these. Indeed no other Cathedral of the same class has any spires at all, and this superiority of Chartres gave most of its point to a saying that "with the spires of Chartres, the choir of Beauvais, the nave of Amiens, and the façade of Reims," one could make a perfect church—for us tourists.

JAMES BALDWIN
(1924–1987)

"By the time I was twenty-four," wrote James Baldwin, "I had decided to stop reviewing books about the Negro problem—which, by this time, was only slightly less horrible in print than it was in life—and I packed my bags and went to France, where I finished, God knows how, Go Tell It to the Mountain." It was 1948. Baldwin—black, homosexual and alienated from American culture—was one of the many American writers in postwar Paris who lived in cheap hotels and wrote in cafés. "The moment I began living in French hotels, I understood the necessity of French cafés. This made it rather difficult to look me up. For as soon as I was out of bed, I hopefully took notebook and fountain pen off to the upstairs room of the Flore, where I consumed rather a lot of coffee and, as evening approached, rather a lot of alcohol, but did not get much writing done." In Notes of a Native Son, *Baldwin wrote of his life in France, of the ex-GIs and the students and (in the essay "Equal in Paris") of his own eight-day imprisonment in a French jail for stealing a hotel bedsheet.*

In the early 1950s, James Baldwin returned to his native New York. "In America the color of my skin had stood between myself and me," he wrote. "In Europe that barrier was down . . . The world was enormous, and I could go anywhere in it I chose—including America." For the next thirty-five years, Baldwin traveled to Europe and Africa, writing essays, plays and novels. By the early 1960s, Baldwin became increasingly involved in the Civil Rights Movement and published the acclaimed The Fire Next Time, *a collection of essays.*

Near the end of his life, Baldwin had second thoughts about his decision to leave America for Europe. "I think I'd probably go to Africa, to some part of Asia—the Third World . . . I still love France. I do not want to repudiate a former mistress." Baldwin died in France, was waked in both France and Harlem, and was buried in New York.

The New Lost Generation

Voyagers discover that the world can never be larger than the person that is in the world; but it is impossible to foresee this, it is impossible to be warned. It is only when time has begun spilling through his fingers like water or sand—carrying away with it, forever, dreams, possibilities, challenges, and hopes— that the young man realizes that he will not be young forever. If he wishes to paint a picture, raise a family, write a book, design a building, start a war—well, he does not have forever in which to do it. He has only a certain amount of time, and half of that time is probably gone already. As long as his aspirations are in the realm of the dream, he is safe; when he must bring them back into the world, he is in danger.

Precisely for this reason, Paris was a devastating shock. It was easily recognizable as Paris from across the ocean: that was what the letters on the map spelled out. This was not the same thing as finding oneself in a large, inconvenient, indifferent city. Paris, from across the ocean, looked like a refuge from the American madness; now it was a city four thousand miles from home. It contained—in those days—no doughnuts, no milk shakes, no Coca-Cola, no dry Martinis; nothing resembling, for people on our economic level, an American toilet; as for toilet paper, it was yesterday's newspaper. The concierge of the hotel did not appear to find your presence in France a reason for rejoicing; rather, she found your presence, and in particular your ability to pay the rent, a matter for the profoundest suspicion. The policemen, with their revolvers, clubs, and (as it turned out) weighted capes, appeared to be convinced of your legality only after the most vindictive scrutiny of your passport; and it became clear very soon that they were not kidding about the three-month period during which every foreigner had to buy a new visa or leave the country. Not a few astounded Americans, unable to call their embassy, spent the night in jail, and steady offenders were escorted to the border. After the first street riot, or its aftermath, one witnessed in Paris, one took a new attitude toward the Paris paving stones, and toward the café tables and chairs, and toward the Parisians, indeed, who showed no signs, at such moments, of being among the earth's most cerebral or civilized people. Paris hotels had never heard of central heating or hot baths or showers or clean towels and sheets or ham and eggs; their attitude toward electricity was demonic—once one had seen what they thought of as wiring one wondered why the city had not, long ago, vanished in flame; and it soon became clear that Paris hospitals had never heard of Pasteur. Once, in short, one found oneself divested of all the things that one had fled from, one wondered how people, meaning, above all, oneself, could possibly do without them.

And yet one did, of course, and in the beginning, and sporadically, thereafter, found these privations a subject for mirth. One soon ceased expecting to be warm in one's hotel room, and read and worked in the cafés. The French, at least insofar as student hotels are concerned, do not appear to understand the idea of a social visit. They expect one's callers to be vastly more intimate, if not utilitarian, than that, and much prefer that they register and spend the night. This aspect of Parisian life would seem vastly to simplify matters, but this, alas, is not the case. It merely makes it all but impossible to invite anyone to your hotel room. Americans do not cease to be Puritans when they have crossed the ocean; French girls, on the other hand, contrary to legend, tend, preponderantly, to be the marrying kind; thus, it was not long before we brave voyagers rather felt that we had been turned loose in a fair in which there was not a damn thing we could buy, and still less that we could sell.

And I think that when we began to be frightened in Paris, to feel baffled and betrayed, it was because we had failed, after all, somehow, and once again, to make the longed-for, magical human contact. It was on this connection with another human being that we had felt that our lives and our work depended. It had failed at home. We had thought we knew why. Everyone at home was too dry and too frightened, mercilessly pinned beneath the thumb of the Puritan God. Yet, here we were, surrounded by quite beautiful and sensual people, who did not, however, appear to find us beautiful or sensual. They said so. By the time we had been abroad two years, each of us, in one way or another, had received this message. It was one of the things that was meant when we were referred to as children. We had been perfectly willing to refer to all the other Americans as children—in the beginning; we had not known what it meant; we had not known that we were included.

By 1950 some of us had already left Paris for more promising ports of call, Tangiers for some, or Italy, or Spain; Sweden or Denmark or Germany for others. Some girls had got married and vanished; some had got married and vanished and reappeared—minus their husbands. Some people got jobs with the ECA and began a slow retreat back into the cocoon from which they had never quite succeeded in emerging. Some of us were going to pieces—spectacularly, as in my own case, quietly, in others. One boy, for example, had embarked on the career which I believe still engages him, that of laboriously writing extremely literary plays in English, translating them—laboriously—into French and Spanish, reading the trilingual results to a coterie of friends who were, even then, beginning to diminish, and then locking them in his trunk. Magazines were popping up like toadstools and vanishing like fog. Painters and poets of thin talent and no industry began to feel abused by the lack of attention their efforts elicited from the French, and made outrageously obvious—and successful—bids for the attention of visiting literary figures from the States, of whose industry, in any case, there could be no doubt. And a certain real malice now began to make itself felt in our attitudes toward the French, as well as a certain defensiveness concerning whatever it was we had come to Paris to do, and clearly were not doing. We were edgy with each other, too. Going, going, going, gone—were the days when we walked through Les Halles, singing, loving every inch of France, and loving each other; gone were the jam sessions in Pigalle, and our stories about the whores there; gone were the nights spent smoking hashish in Arab cafés; gone were the mornings which found us telling dirty stories, true stories, sad, and earnest stories, in grey, workingmen's cafés. It was all gone. We were secretive with each other. I no longer talked about my novel. We no longer talked about our love affairs, for either they had failed, were failing, or were serious. Above all, they were private—how can love be talked about? It is probably the most awful of all the revelations this little life affords. We no longer walked about, as a friend of mine once put it, in a not too dissimilar context, in "friendly groups of five thousand." We were splitting up, and each of us was going for himself. Or, if not precisely for himself, his own way: some of us took to the needle, some returned to the family business, some made loveless marriages, some ceased fleeing and turned to face the demons that had been on the trail so long. The luckiest among us were these last, for they managed to go to pieces and then put themselves back together with whatever was left. This may take away one's dreams, but it delivers one to oneself. Without this coming together, the longed-for love is never possible, for the confused personality can neither give nor take.

In my own case, I think my exile saved my life, for it inexorably confirmed something which Americans appear to have great difficulty accepting. Which is, simply, this: a man is not a man until he's able and willing to accept his own vision of the world, no matter how radically this vision departs from that of others.

(When I say "vision," I do not mean "dream.") There are long moments when this country resembles nothing so much as the grimmest of popularity contests. The best thing that happened to the "new" expatriates was their liberation, finally, from any need to be smothered by what is really nothing more (though it may be something less) than mother love. It need scarcely, I hope, be said that I have no interest in hurling gratuitous insults at American mothers; they are certainly helpless, if not entirely blameless; and my point has nothing to do with them. My point is involved with the great emphasis placed on public approval here, and the resulting and quite insane system of penalties and rewards. It puts a premium on mediocrity and has all but slaughtered any concept of excellence. This corruption begins in the private life and unfailingly flowers in the public life. Europeans refer to Americans as children in the same way that American Negroes refer to them as children, and for the same reason: they mean that Americans have so little experience—experience referring not to *what* happens, but to *who*—that they have no key to the experience of others. Our current relations with the world forcibly suggest that there is more than a little truth to this. What Europe still gives an American—or gave us—is the sanction, if one can accept it, to become oneself. No artist can survive without this acceptance. But rare indeed is the American artist who achieved this without first becoming a wanderer, and then, upon his return to his own country, the loneliest and most blackly distrusted of men.

ELIZABETH BISHOP
(1911–1979)

*Born in Massachusetts, young Elizabeth Bishop was sent to live with her
Canadian grandparents after her mother's nervous breakdown and her
father's death.* She returned to the United States for boarding school and
then Vassar College, where she founded a literary magazine, Con Spir-
ito, with classmates Mary McCarthy, Eleanor Clark and Muriel Rukeyser.
*Independently wealthy, she set off on a life of travel. In the late 1930s,
Bishop went throughout Europe, North Africa and finally settled, for a
time, in Key West, Florida. After World War II, she spent sixteen years
in Brazil and only communicated with her editors and other writers
through letters. A product of her life in South America was the transla-
tion from the Portuguese of* The Diary of Helena Morley. *That
period of her life ended with the suicide of her lover, Lota de Macedo
Soares. Bishop returned to the United States and taught at several uni-
versities including Harvard, New York University and MIT, but her later
years were plagued by ill health and alcoholism.*

*Geography was an essential element of Bishop's poetry as her decep-
tively simple poems were often ruminations on places remembered. She
also wrote several travel books including* Questions of Travel *(1965)*
and Brazil *(1967). Elizabeth Bishop won the Pulitzer Prize for* Poems:
North and South—A Cold Spring *(1955) and the National Book
Award for* The Complete Poems *(1969). It was not until the end of
her life that she was recognized as a brilliant "poet's poet."*

Paris, 7 A.M.

I make a trip to each clock in the apartment:
some hands point histrionically one way
and some point others, from the ignorant faces.
Time is an Etoile; the hours diverge
so much that days are journeys round the suburbs,
circles surrounding stars, overlapping circles.
The short, half-tone scale of winter weathers
is a spread pigeon's wing.
Winter lives under a pigeon's wing, a dead wing with
    damp feathers.

Look down into the courtyard. All the houses
are built that way, with ornamental urns
set on the mansard roof-tops where the pigeons
take their walks. It is like introspection
to stare inside, or retrospection,
a star inside a rectangle, a recollection:
this hollow square could easily have been there.
—The childish snow-forts, built in flashier winters,
could have reached these proportions and been houses;
the mighty snow-forts, four, five, stories high,
withstanding spring as sand-forts do the tide,
their walls, their shape, could not dissolve and die,
only be overlapping in a strong chain, turned to stone,
and grayed and yellowed now like these.

Where is the ammunition, the piled-up balls
with the star-splintered hearts of ice?

This sky is no carrier-warrior-pigeon
escaping endless intersecting circles.
It is a dead one, or the sky from which a dead one fell.
The urns have caught his ashes or his feathers.
When did the star dissolve, or was it captured
by the sequence of squares and squares and circles, circles?
Can the clocks say; is it there below,
about to tumble in snow?

MARY BLUME

A freshly minted college graduate with a major in English, Mary Blume arrived in Paris in 1960. The city was still scarred from both World Wars; de Gaulle was in power; The Lost Generation was gone. Blume looked for work and, discouraged, was about to book a flight to return to the United States. Her final job application was to the International Herald Tribune. *To her surprise, they called and asked her to write articles and fashion copy for one hundred francs a week. That was the beginning of Blume's more than thirty-year tenure at the newspaper.*

The International Herald Tribune *is a staple for Americans living abroad, but the paper has changed greatly since the beginning of Blume's regular column in the mid-1960s. She recalled, "It was a quirky little paper. Unusual. Unpredictable. It is less so now . . . (a former editor) called it 'an international paper that speaks with American accents . . .' Now we've become an international paper with no accent." The change is reflected in the* Herald Tribune's *readership: several decades ago it was almost all Americans, now it is only 40 percent Americans.*

Mary Blume sees parallel changes in the French themselves. "They used to condemn American culture, shoes and food. Now they deconstruct Disney, jog in Nikes, consume 274,000 hamburgers a day, and put fish between slices of bread." Blume's essays are collected in A French Affair: 1965–1998 *from which this is taken.*

Money Speaks in France

Paris—The *Wall Street Journal* may be forgiven—although not, apparently, by the French government—for suggesting that France's new anti-inflation plan will, to the contrary, increase the rate of inflation. The *Wall Street Journal* should be forgiven because no economic theory that makes sense elsewhere can be applied to France, where money is a different substance from anywhere else.

The French say Americans are always talking about money. It could with equal truth be said that the French are always thinking about it. The materialism of each country is different. Each French franc, each centime seems to have a palpable existence. In America, money has a more abstract quality: It is thought of in terms of what it will buy. A man will be said in the United States to be worth x amount of dollars; in French one says "his surface" is x amount of francs, a phrase dating back to the days when wealth was measured in acres.

The American phrase "She looks like a million dollars" makes no sense to the French, although they rightly find it repellent. In America, money is something that will grow. In France, it is something to hold on to. Americans want money to move; the French are afraid it will move out of their grasp. Americans invest; the French tuck away. Wars and financial crises have made the ideal French investment a gold bar buried on a piece of one's own land; there have been too many property busts for land in the United States to have the absolute value it has here, and Americans are not salting away gold bars, although they do invest in gold-mine shares.

A French money manager, asked if he advised his clients to invest in French equities, replied, "Almost never." Americans boast about their salaries and investments. The Frenchman, remarks a Paris banker, would never boast of having made a killing, for it would let the world know he had money.

There is nothing more private than money. The singer Juliette Gréco was once interviewed at length on her love life. When the interviewer asked how much she earned, she bridled. "Some things," she said, "are private."

In France, the notion of money is invested with the anxiety of impermanence, a fear that it will be taken away. Gertrude Stein wrote, "Anyway the French people never take money very seriously, they save it certainly, they hoard it very carefully, but they know really that it has no very great permanence. That is the reason they all want a place in the country."

The French view of money seems even to affect the French seasons. The autumn, a rich and lush time in other places, is crabbed and pinched here because it is tax time and school-fee time and the time when the cost of having lived it up on summer holiday catches up. While in New York and London, September and October mark the crackling start of a new season, here it is known as the *rentée,* the return from vacation, the return to grim real life, a return made even more numbing this year by Prime Minister Raymond Barre's belt-tightening anti-inflation plan.

The Barre plan and its permutations have made this autumn especially morose and the subject of money even more overbearing than usual. The lively leftist weekly *Le Nouvel Observateur* (from which the above anecdote about Juliette Gréco was taken) has brought a certain freshness to the subject with a three-part series, "La Fortune des Français," directed by staff journalist Josette Alia (salary nine thousand francs per month).

The first issue in the series sold out immediately, for in it the journalists somehow persuaded France's leading political figures, from Gaullist to Communist, to list their assets (or *patrimoine* in French, a much richer-sounding word suggesting the accumulations of the years). As may be expected, the political leaders tumbled all over each other to show how little they possess.

In the second part of the series, the magazine asked, is the French attitude to money different from other people's? Yes.

Quoting an OECD report, the introductory article notes that France is the only country to combine republican egalitarianism with the utter inviolability of the strongbox.

Avarice is found to be peculiarly French and is traced by the sociologist Jean-Paul Aron in *Le Nouvel Observateur* to the revolution, when the peasant, who had been subservient to the landowner and the church, suddenly found himself free but still attached to his ancient reflex of hiding his possessions for fear that his masters might seize them. Even when the peasant became in time a salaried bourgeois, this atavism remained.

"Avarice," Mr. Aron continues, "is the contrary of exchanging and circulating wealth; it is accumulation pinning down. This avarice is the perfect explanation of an economy that is based on the value of real property, the earth."

The earth, like gold, is infinitely reassuring, according to another contributor to the series, the psychiatrist René Held. A miser, he adds, is still at the anal stage of development and he is likely to suffer from constipation.

Dr. Held's remarks make a rather jarring detail of the Barre anti-inflation plan fall into place. At the same time as major measures, it was announced that the government health service would no longer reimburse citizens for the purchase of laxatives. Why such a detail at such a time, one wondered. Dr. Held's theory makes the reason clear. The government is encouraging avarice, with its attendant constipation, as part of its tightening measures on consumer spending.

The *Wall Street Journal* thinks, of course, that money should be encouraged to circulate freely instead of being blocked up, but then it is not for them or for us to try to change the French. The Barre plan may lead to an explosion or it may be giving the French what they secretly want. To quote again from Gertrude Stein on the French attitude to money:

"Money to spend is not very welcome, if you have it and you

try to spend it, well spending money is an anxiety, saving money is a comfort and a pleasure, economy is not a duty it is a comfort, avarice is an excitement, but spending money is nothing, money spent is money nonexistent, money saved is money realized."

JAMES FENIMORE
COOPER
(1789–1851)

Novelist James Fenimore Cooper is inextricably linked with upstate New York. He was the son of the founder of Cooperstown, and his most famous novels, collectively known as The Leatherstocking Tales *and set on the shores of Lake Otsego, chronicle the life of social outcast Natty Bumppo, who followed the code of Native Americans.*

In 1826 Cooper and his family moved to Europe for almost a decade. He wrote to his publisher, "My object, is my own health, the instruction of my children in the French and Italian languages—perhaps there is also a little pleasure concealed in the bottom of the Cup." Their geographic base was Paris, although they traveled extensively throughout the rest of the Continent. Cooper supported his family by writing more novels and travel books.

Few travelers were more enthusiastic than Cooper. Despite his family's reoccurring illnesses and sometimes precarious living arrangements, he was effusive in his appreciation of the French. Unfortunately, Cooper's travel books (including France—*from which this excerpt was taken—and* Switzerland *and* The Rhine*) were not successful and reviewers urged Cooper to return to his American roots. Critic Thomas Philbrick wrote that the value of* France *and other travel writing is that "no other of Cooper's works, perhaps, brings us closer to his speaking voice or puts us more directly in contact with the man himself, with all his idiosyncratic preoccupation, his quick resentments, his restless curiosity, his surprising humor and his nobility of principle."*

Letter XVI

To James Stevenson, Esquire, Albany

We have been the residents of a French village ever since the first of June, and it is now drawing to the close of October. We had already passed the greater part of a summer, an entire autumn, winter and spring, within the walls of Paris, and then we thought we might indulge our tastes a little, by retreating to the fields, to catch a glimpse of country life. You will smile when I add that we are only a league from the *Barrière de Clichy*. This is the reason I have not before spoken of the removal, for we are in town three or four times every week, and never miss an occasion, when there is any thing to be seen. I shall now proceed, however, to let you into the secret of our actual situation.

I passed the month of May examining the environs of the capital in quest of a house. As this was an agreeable occupation, we were in no hurry, but having set up my *cabriolet,* we killed two birds with one stone, by making ourselves familiarly acquainted with nearly every village, or hamlet, within three leagues of Paris, a distance beyond which I did not wish to go.

On the side of St. Cloud, which embraces Passy, Auteuil, and all the places that encircle the *Bois de Boulogne,* the Hyde Park of Paris, there are very many pleasant residences, but, from one cause or another, no one suited us, exactly, and we finally took a house in the village of St. Ouen, the Runnymeade of France. When Louis XVIII came, in 1814, to his capital, in the rear of the allies, he stopped for a few days at St. Ouen, a league from the barriers, where there was a small *château* that was the property of the crown. Here he was met by M. de Talleyrand and others, and hence he issued the celebrated charter, that is to render France, forevermore, a constitutional country.

The *château* has since been razed, and a pavilion erected in its place, which has been presented to the Comtesse [du Cayla], a lady, who, reversing the ordinary lot of courtiers, is said to cause majesty to live in the sunshine of *her* smiles. What an appropriate and encouraging monument to rear on the birth-place of French liberty! At the opposite extremity of the village, is another considerable house, that was once the dwelling of M. Necker, and is now the property and country residence of M. Ternaux, or the *Baron* Ternaux, if it were polite to style him thus, the most celebrated manufacturer of France. I say polite, for the mere *fanfaronnade* of nobility is little in vogue here. The wags tell a story of some one, who was formally announced as *"Mons. le Marquis d'un tel,"* turning short round on the servant, and exclaiming with indignation, *"Marquis, toi-même!"* But this story savours of the Bonapartists, for, as the Emperor created neither *marquis* nor *vicomtes,* there was a sort of affectation of assuming these titles at the restoration, as proofs of belonging to the old *régime.*

St. Ouen is a cluster of small, mean, stone houses, stretched along the right bank of the Seine, which, after making a circuit of near twenty miles, winds round so close to the town, again, that they are actually constructing a basin, near the village, for the use of the capital; it being easier to wheel articles from this point to Paris, than to contend with the current and to thread its shoals. In addition to the two houses named, however, it has six or eight respectable abodes between the street and the river, one of which is our own.

This place became a princely residence about the year 1300, since which time it has been more or less frequented as such, down to the 4th June, 1814, the date of the memorable charter.*

---

*The *château* of St. Ouen, rather less than two centuries since, passed into the possession of the *Duc de Gesvre*. Dulaure gives the following, a part of a letter from this nobleman, as a specimen of the education of a *Duc*, in the seventeenth century. *"Monsieur, me trouvant obligé de randre une bonne party de largan*

Madame de Pompadour possessed the *château* in 1745, so you see it has been "dust to dust" with this place, as with all that is frail.

The village of St. Ouen, small, dirty, crowded and unsavoury as it is, has a *place,* like every other French village. When we drove into it, to look at the house, I confess to having laughed outright at the idea of inhabiting such a hole. Two large *portes cochères,* however, opened from the square, and we were admitted, through the best-looking of the two, into a spacious and an extremely neat court. On one side of the gate was a lodge for a porter, and, on the other, a building to contain gardener's tools, plants, &c. The walls that separate it from the square and the adjoining gardens are twelve or fourteen feet high, and once within them, the world is completely excluded. The width of the grounds does not exceed a hundred and fifty feet; the length, the form being that of a parallelogram, may be three hundred, or a little more; and yet in these narrow limits, which are planted *à l'Anglaise,* so well is every thing contrived, that we appear to have abundance of room. The garden terminates in a terrace that overhangs the river, and, from this point, the eye ranges over a wide extent of beautiful plain, that is bounded by fine bold hills which are teeming with gray villages and *bourgs.*

The house is of stone, and not without elegance. It may be ninety feet in length, by some forty in width. The entrance is into a vestibule, which has the offices on the right, and the great staircase on the left. The principal *salon* is in front. This is a good room, near thirty feet long, fifteen or sixteen high, and has three good windows, that open on the garden. The billiard-room communicates on one side, and the *salle à manger* on the other;

---

que mais enfant ont pris de peuis qu'il sont au campane, monsieur, cela moblige a vous suplier tres humblemant monsieur de me faire la grasse de commander monsieur quant il vous plera que lon me pay la capitenery de Monsaux monsieur vous asseurant que vous mobligeres fort sansiblement monsieur comme ausy de me croire avec toute sorte de respec, etc." This beats Jack Cade, out and out. The great *connétable Anne de Montmorency* could not write his name, and, as his signature became necessary, his secretary stood over his shoulder to tell him when he had made enough *pieds de mouche* to answer the purpose.

next to the latter come the offices again, and next to the billiard-
room is a very pretty little *boudoir.* Up stairs, are suites of bed-
rooms and dressing-rooms; every thing is neat, and the house is
in excellent order, and well furnished for a country residence.
Now, all this I get at a hundred dollars a month, for the five
summer months. There are also a carriage house, and stabling
for three horses. The gardener and porter are paid by the propri-
etor. The village, however, is not in much request, and the rent
is thought to be low.

One of the great advantages that is enjoyed by a residence in
Europe, are the facilities of this nature. Furnished apartments, or
furnished houses, can be had in almost every town of any size;
and, owning your own linen and plate, nearly every other neces-
sary is found you. It is true, that one sometimes misses comforts
to which he has been accustomed in his own house; but, in
France, many little things are found, it is not usual to meet with
elsewhere. Thus, no principal bed-room is considered properly
furnished in a good house, without a handsome secretary, and a
bureau. These two articles are as much matters of course, as are
the eternal two rooms and folding doors in New York.

This, then, has been our *Tusculum* since June. M. Ternaux
enlivens the scene, occasionally, by a dinner; and he has politely
granted us permission to walk in his grounds, which are exten-
sive and well laid out, for the old French style. We have a neigh-
bour on our left, name unknown, who gives suppers in his garden,
and concerts that really are worthy of the grand opera. Occa-
sionally, we get a song, in a female voice, that rivals the best of
Madame Malibran's. On our right lives a staid widow, whose
establishment is as tranquil as our own.

One of our great amusements is to watch the *living* life on the
river—there is no *still* life in France. All the washerwomen of
the village assemble, three days in the week, beneath our terrace,
and a merrier set of *grisettes* is not to be found in the neighbour-
hood of Paris. They chat, and joke, and splash, and scream from
morning to night, lightening the toil by never-ceasing good
humour. Occasionally an enormous scow-like barge is hauled

up against the current, by stout horses, loaded to the water's edge, or one, without freight, comes dropping down the stream, nearly filling the whole river as it floats broad-side to. There are three or four islands opposite, and, now and then, a small boat is seen paddling among them. We have even tried *punting* ourselves, but the amusement was soon exhausted.

Sunday is a great day with us, for then the shore is lined with Parisians, as thoroughly cockney as if Bow-bells could be heard in the *quartier Montmartre!* These good people visit us, in all sorts of ways; some on donkies, some in *cabriolets,* some in *fiacres,* and, by far the larger portion on foot. They are perfectly inoffensive and unobtrusive, being, in this respect, just as unlike an American inroad from a town, as can well be. These crowds pass vineyards on their way to us, unprotected by any fences. This point in the French character, however, about which so much has been said to our disadvantage, as well as to that of the English, is subject to some explanation. The statues, promenades, gardens, &c. &c. are, almost without exception, guarded by sentinels; and then there are agents of the police, in common clothes, scattered through the towns, in such numbers as to make depredations hazardous. In the country each *commune* has one, or more, *gardes champêtres,* whose sole business it is to detect and arrest trespassers. When to these are added the *gendarmes à pied* and *à cheval,* who are constantly in motion, one sees that the risk of breaking the laws, is attended with more hazard here, than with us. There is no doubt, on the other hand, that the training and habits, produced by such a system of watchfulness, enter so far into the character of the people, that they cease to think of doing that which is so strenuously denied them.

Some of our visitors make their appearance in a very quaint style. I met a party the other day, among whom the following family arrangement had obtained. The man was mounted on a donkey, with his feet just clear of the ground. The wife, a buxom brunette, was trudging afoot in the rear, accompanied by the two younger children, a boy and girl, between twelve and fourteen, led by a small dog, fastened to a string, like the guide of a blind mendicant; while the eldest daughter was mounted on the crupper, maintaining her equilibrium by a masculine disposition of her lower limbs. She was a fine, rosy cheeked *grisette,* of about seventeen; and, as they ambled along, just fast enough to keep the cur on a slow trot, her cap flared in the wind, her black eyes flashed with pleasure, and her dark ringlets streamed behind her, like so many silken pennants. She had a ready laugh for every one she met, and a sort of malicious pleasure in asking, by her countenance, if they did not wish they too had a donkey? As the seat was none of the most commodious, she had contrived to make a pair of stirrups of her petticoats. The gown was pinned up about her waist, leaving her knees instead of her feet, as the *points d'appui.* The well-turned legs, and the ankles, with such a *chaussure* as at once marks a *Parisienne,* were exposed to the admiration of a *parterre* of some hundreds of idle way-farers. Truly, it is no wonder that sculptors abound in this country, for capital models are to be found, even in the highways. The donkey was the only one who appeared displeased with this *monture,* and he only manifested dissatisfaction by lifting his hinder extremities a little, as the man occasionally touched his flanks with a nettle, that the ass would much rather have been eating.

Not long since I passed half an hour on the terrace, an amused witness of the perils of a voyage across the Seine, in a punt. The adventurers were a *bourgeois,* his wife, sister, and child. Honest Pierre, the waterman, had conditioned to take the whole party to the island opposite, and to return them safe to the main, for the modicum of five *sous.* The old fox invariably charged me a *franc,* for the same service. There was much demurring and many doubts about encountering the risks; and, more than once, the women would have receded, had not the man treated the matter as a trifle. He affirmed *parole d'honneur* that his father had crossed the Maine a dozen times, and no harm had come of it! This encouraged them, and with many pretty screams, *mes fois,* and *oh, dieus,* they finally embarked. The punt was a narrow scow, that a ton weight would not have disturbed, the river was so low and sluggish that it might have been forded two-thirds of the distance, and the width was not three hundred feet. Pierre protested that the danger was certainly not worth mentioning, and away he went, as philosophical in appearance as his punt. The voyage was made in safety, and the bows of the boat had actually touched the shore on its return, before any of the passengers ventured to smile. The excursion, like most travelling, was likely to be most productive of happiness by the recollections. But the women were no sooner landed, than that rash adventurer, the husband, brother, and father, seized an oar, and began to ply it with all his force. He merely wished to tell his *confrères* of the *rue Montmartre* how a punt might be rowed. Pierre had gallantly landed to assist the ladies, and the boat, relieved of its weight, slowly yielded to the impulse of the oar, and inclined its bows from the land. *"Oh! Edouard! mon mari! mon frère!—que fais-tu?"* exclaimed the ladies. *"Ce n'est rien,"* returned the man, puffing and giving another lusty sweep, by which he succeeded in forcing the punt fully twenty feet from the shore. *"Edouard! cher Edouard!"* *"Laisse-moi m'amuser. Je m'amuse—je m'amuse,"* cried the husband, in a tone of indignant remonstrance. But *Edouard,* a tight, sleek little *épicier,* of about five and thirty, had never heard that an oar on each side was necessary in a boat, and the harder he pulled, the less likely was he to regain the shore. Of this he began to be convinced, as he whirled more into the centre of the current; and his efforts now really became frantic, for his imagination probably painted the horrors of a distant voyage, in an unknown bark, to an unknown land, and all without food or compass. The women screamed, and the louder they cried, the more strenuously he persevered in saying, *"Laisse-moi m'amuser—je m'amuse, je m'amuse."* By this time the perspiration poured from the face of *Edouard,* and I called to the imperturbable Pierre, who stood in silent admiration of his punt while playing such antics, and desired him to tell the man to put his oar on the bottom, and to push the boat ashore. *"Oui, Monsieur,"* said the rogue, with a leer, for he remembered the francs, and we soon had our adventurer safe on *terra firma* again. Then began the tender expostulations, the affectionate reproaches, and the kind injunctions for the truant to remember that he was a husband and a father. *Edouard,* secretly cursing the punt and all rivers in his heart, made light of the matter, however, protesting to the last, that he had only been enjoying himself.

We have had a *fête,* too; for every village in the vicinity of Paris has its *fête.* The square was filled with whirligigs and flying-horses, and all the ingenious contrivances of the French to make and to spend a *sou* pleasantly. There was service in the parish church, at which our neighbours sang, in a style fit for St. Peter's; and the villagers danced *quadrilles* on the green, with an air that would be thought fine in many a country drawing-room.

I enjoy all this greatly; for, to own the truth, the crowds and mannered sameness of Paris began to weary me. Our friends occasionally come from town to see us, and we make good use of the *cabriolet.* As we are near neighbours to *St. Denis,* we have paid several visits to the tombs of the French kings, and returned, each time, less pleased with most of the unmeaning obsequies that are observed in their vaults. There was a ceremony, not long since, at which the royal family, and many of the great officers of the court assisted, and among others, M. de Talleyrand. The latter was in the body of the church, when a man rushed upon him, and actually struck him, or shoved him, to the earth, using, at the same time, language that left no doubt of the nature of the assault. There are strange rumours connected with the affair. The assailant was a *Marquis* [*d'Orsvault*], and it is reported that his wrongs, real or imaginary, are connected with a plot to rob one of the dethroned family of her jewels, or of some crown jewels, I cannot say which, at the epoch of the restoration. The journals said a good deal about it, at the time, but events occur so fast, here, that a quarrel of this sort produces little sensation. I pretend to no knowledge of the merits of this affair, and only give a general outline of what was current in the public prints, at the time.

We have also visited Enghien, and Montmorency. The latter, as you know already, stands on the side of a low mountain, in plain view of Paris. It is a town of some size, with very uneven streets, some of them being actually sharp acclivities, and a Gothic church that is seen from afar, and that is well worth viewing near by. These quaint edifices afford us deep delight, by their antiquity, architecture, size, and pious histories. What matters it to us how much or how little superstition may blend with the rites, when we know and feel that we are standing in a nave that has echoed with orisons to God, for a thousand years! This of Montmorency is not quite so old, however, having been rebuilt only three centuries since.

Dulaure, a severe judge of aristocracy, denounces the pretension of the *Montmorencies* to be the *Premiers Barons Chrétiens,* affirming that they were neither the first barons, nor the first Christians, by a great many. He says, that the extravagant title has most probably been a war-cry, in the time of the crusaders. According to his account of the family, it originated, about the year 1008, in a certain Burchard, who, proving a bad neighbour to the Abbey of St. Denis, the vassals of which he was in the habit of robbing, besides, now and then, despoiling a monk, the king caused his fortress in the *isle St. Denis* to be razed; after which, by a treaty, he was put in possession of the mountain hard by, with permission to erect another hold near a fountain, at a place called in the charters, *Montmorenciacum.* Hence the name, and the family. This writer thinks that the first castle must have been built of wood!

We took a road that led us up to a bluff on the mountain, behind the town, where we obtained a new and very peculiar view of Paris and its environs. I have said that the French towns have no straggling suburbs. A few wine-houses (to save the *octroi*) are built near the gates, compactly, as in the town itself, and there the buildings cease as suddenly as if pared down by a knife. The fields touch the walls, in many places, and between St. Ouen and the *guinguettes* and wine-houses, at the *barrière de Clichy,* a distance of quite two miles, there is but a solitary building. A wide plain separates Paris, on this side, from the mountains, and of course our view extended across it. The number of villages was absolutely astounding. Although I did not attempt counting them, I should think not fewer than a hundred were in sight, all gray, picturesque, and clustering round the high nave and church tower, like chickens gathering beneath the wing. The day was clouded, and the hamlets rose from their beds of verdure, sombre but distinct, with their faces of wall, now in subdued light, and now quite shaded, resembling the glorious *darks* of Rembrandt's pictures.

CHARLES DICKENS
(1812–1870)

"It was the best of times, it was the worst of times, it was the age of wisdom, it was the age of foolishness, it was the epoch of belief, it was the epoch of incredulity, it was the season of Light, it was the season of Darkness . . ." So begins Charles Dickens's A Tale of Two Cities. *The two cities are, of course, London and Paris.*

In his preface to the first edition, Dickens credits his knowledge of the political situation in France to the book French Revolution *by his friend Thomas Carlyle. However, the poverty that Dickens described in* A Tale of Two Cities *came firsthand. His father was imprisoned because of debt, and Charles was sent to work in a blacking factory when he was only twelve. Dickens also saw the bread riots in London's East End and drew parallels with the conditions of the French before the Revolution. "The people will not bear for any length of time what they bear now," he prophesied. He warned that unless the English government changed its priorities, there would be "such a shake in this country as was never seen on Earth since Samson pulled the Temple down upon his head."*

The following excerpt from A Tale of Two Cities *describes the desperation of Parisians before the Revolution.*

from **A Tale of Two Cities**

A large cask of wine had been dropped and broken, in the street. The accident had happened in getting it out of a cart; the cask had tumbled out with a run, the hoops had burst, and it lay on the stones just outside the door of the wine-shop, shattered like a walnut-shell.

All the people within reach had suspended their business, or their idleness, to run to the spot and drink the wine. The rough, irregular stones of the street, pointing every way, and designed, one might have thought, expressly to lame all living creatures that approached them, had dammed it into little pools; these were surrounded, each by its own jostling group or crowd, according to its size. Some men kneeled down, made scoops of their two hands joined, and sipped, or tried to help women, who bent over their shoulders, to sip, before the wine had all run out between their fingers. Others, men and women, dipped in the puddles with little mugs of mutilated earthenware, or even with handkerchiefs from women's heads, which were squeezed dry into infants' mouths; others made small mud embankments, to stem the wine as it ran; others, directed by lookers-on up at high windows, darted here and there, to cut off little streams of wine that started away in new directions; others devoted themselves to the sodden and lee-dyed pieces of the cask, licking, and even champing the moister wine-rotted fragments with eager relish. There was no drainage to carry off the wine, and not only did it all get taken up, but so much mud got taken up along with it, that there might have been a scavenger in the street, if anybody acquainted with it could have believed in such a miraculous presence.

A shrill sound of laughter and of amused voices—voices of men, women, and children—resounded in the street while this wine game lasted. There was little roughness in the sport, and much playfulness. There was a special companionship in it, an observable inclination on the part of every one to join some other one, which led, especially among the luckier or lighter-hearted, to frolicsome embraces, drinking of healths, shaking of hands, and even joining of hands and dancing, a dozen together. When the wine was gone, and the places where it had been most abundant were raked into a gridiron pattern by fingers, these demonstrations ceased, as suddenly as they had broken out. The man who had left his saw sticking in the firewood he was cutting, set it in motion again; the woman who had left on a doorstep the little pot of hot ashes, at which she had been trying to soften the pain in her own starved fingers and toes, or in those of her child, returned to it; men with bare arms, matted locks, and cadaverous faces, who had emerged into the winter light from cellars, moved away, to descend again; and a gloom gathered on the scene that appeared more natural to it than sunshine.

The wine was red wine, and had stained the ground of the narrow street in the suburb of Saint Antoine, in Paris, where it was spilled. It had stained many hands, too, and many faces, and many naked feet, and many wooden shoes. The hands of the man who sawed the wood left red marks on the billets; and the forehead of the woman who nursed her baby was stained with the stain of the old rag she wound about her head again. Those who had been greedy with the staves of the cask, had acquired a tigerish smear about the mouth; and one tall joker so besmirched, his head more out of a long squalid bag of a nightcap than in it, scrawled upon a wall with his finger dipped in muddy wine-lees— BLOOD.

The time was to come, when that wine too would be spilled on the street-stones, and when the stain of it would be red upon many there.

And now that the cloud settled on Saint Antoine, which a momentary gleam had driven from his sacred countenance, the darkness of it was heavy—cold, dirt, sickness, ignorance, and want, were the lords in waiting on the saintly presence—nobles of great power all of them; but, most especially, the last. Samples of a people that had undergone a terrible grinding and re-grinding in the mill, and certainly not in the fabulous mill which ground old people young, shivered at every corner, passed in and out at every doorway, looked from every window, fluttered in every vestige of a garment that the wind shook. The mill which had worked them down was the mill that grinds young people old; the children had ancient faces and grave voices; and upon them, and upon the grown faces, and ploughed into every furrow of age and coming up afresh, was the sign, Hunger. It was prevalent everywhere. Hunger was pushed out of the tall houses, in the wretched clothing that hung upon poles and lines; Hunger was patched into them with straw and rag and wood and paper; Hunger was repeated in every fragment of the small modicum of firewood that the man sawed off; Hunger stared down from the smokeless chimneys, and started up from the filthy street that had no offal, among its refuse, of anything to eat. Hunger was the inscription on the baker's shelves, written in every small loaf of his scanty stock of bad bread; at the sausage-shop, in every dead-dog preparation that was offered for sale. Hunger rattled its dry bones among the roasting chestnuts in the turned cylinder; Hunger was shred into atomies in every farthing porringer of husky chips of potato, fried with some reluctant drops of oil.

Its abiding place was in all things fitted to it. A narrow winding street, full of offence and stench, with other narrow winding streets diverging, all peopled by rags and nightcaps, and all smelling of rags and nightcaps, and all visible things with a brooding look upon them that looked ill. In the hunted air of the people there was yet some wild-beast thought of the possibility of turning at bay. Depressed and slinking though they were, eyes of fire were not wanting among them; nor compressed lips, white with what they suppressed; nor foreheads knitted into the likeness of the gallows-rope they mused about enduring, or inflicting. The trade signs (and they were almost as many as the shops) were, all, grim illustrations of Want. The butcher and the porkman painted up only the leanest scrags of meat; the baker, the coarsest of meagre loaves. The people rudely pictured as drinking in the wine-shops, croaked over their scanty measures of thin wine and beer, and were gloweringly confidential together. Nothing was represented in a flourishing condition, save tools and weapons; but, the cutler's knives and axes were sharp and bright, the smith's hammers were heavy, and the gunmaker's stock was murderous. The crippling stones of the pavement, with their many little reservoirs of mud and water, had no footways, but broke off abruptly at the doors. The kennel, to make amends, ran down the middle of the street—when it ran at all: which was only after heavy rains, and then it ran, by many eccentric fits, into the houses. Across the streets, at wide intervals, one clumsy lamp was slung by a rope and pulley; at night, when the lamplighter had let these down, and lighted, and hoisted them again, a feeble grove of dim wicks swung in a sickly manner overhead, as if they were at sea. Indeed they were at sea, and the ship and crew were in peril of tempest.

For, the time was to come, when the gaunt scarecrows of that region should have watched the lamplighter, in their idleness and hunger, so long as to conceive the idea of improving on his method, and hauling up men by those ropes and pulleys, to flare upon the darkness of their condition. But, the time was not come yet; and every wind that blew over France shook the rags of the scarecrows in vain, for the birds, fine of song and feather, took no warning.

LAWRENCE DURRELL
(1912–1990)

The Anglo-Irish poet, novelist and travel writer Lawrence Durrell epito-mized the life of the expatriate. He was born in India, educated in Dar-jeeling, went to boarding school in Canterbury and was employed by the British Foreign Office, posted in the Mediterranean. Durrell is probably best known for the four novels that form the Alexandria *Quartet:* Jus-tine, Balthazar, Montolive *and* Clea. *Each novel has the same set of international characters, but offers a different point of view—Durrell called the books "siblings" not "sequels." He wrote that "the whole was intended as a challenge to the serial form of the conventional novel . . ." Bridging the tetralogy is the ancient city of Alexandria, a place as multi-layered as the characters in Durrell's novels.*

The Mediterranean was often the background for Durrell's work. He became one of the region's best-known travel writers, illuminating not only the countries, but his fellow travelers with a sharp eye and keen wit. His books include Sicilian Carousel *about southern Italy,* Bitter Lemons *about Cyprus and* Prospero's Cell *about Greece.*

Durrell often wrote about France in his later life. Two novels, Mon-sieur *and* Livia or Buried Alive, *are set in the south of France. A travel book* Caesar's Vast Ghost: Aspects of Provence *was published in the year of his death.*

Avignon

Come, meet me in some dead café—
A puff of cognac or a sip of smoke
Will grant a more prolific light,
Say there is nothing to revoke.

A veteran with no arm will press
A phantom sorrow in his sleeve;
The aching stump may well insist
On memories it can't relieve.

Late cats, the city's thumbscrews twist.
Night falls in its profuse derision,
Brings candle-power to younger lives,
Cancels in me the primal vision.

Come, random with me in the rain,
In ghastly harness like a dream,
In rainwashed streets of saddened dark
Where nothing moves that does not seem.

LAWRENCE FERLINGHETTI
(1919–)

Shortly after Lawrence Ferlinghetti's birth in Yonkers, New York, his mother was committed to a mental institution. The child was sent to France to be raised by relatives, did not return to New York until he was five, and only then learned English. Discharged from the navy after World War II, Ferlinghetti went back to France. The GI bill allowed him to continue his education (he had an undergraduate degree from the University of North Carolina at Chapel Hill) at the Sorbonne. His doctoral dissertation was entitled, "The City as Symbol in Modern Poetry: In Search of Metropolitan Tradition."

Ferlinghetti is identified, not with France, but with San Francisco. He and Peter Martin, publisher of City Lights Magazine, *opened City Lights Bookstore, which became one of the centers of the Beat Movement. Ferlinghetti not only wrote poetry, including his most popular volume* Coney Island of the Mind *(1948), but also published other Beats in the Pocket Poets Series, books that were inexpensive, small and attractive. Allen Ginsberg's* Howl *was Pocket Books Number Four, and Ferlinghetti was tried for purveying obscenity.*

Today Ferlinghetti still owns City Lights Bookstore, is an active poet and one of the last surviving Beats.

Café Notre Dame

A sort of sexual trauma
has this couple in its thrall
He is holding both her hands
in both his hands
She is kissing his hands
They are looking
in each other's eyes
Up close
She has a fur coat
made of a hundred running rabbits
He
is wearing a formal
dark coat and dove grey trousers
Now they are inspecting the palms
of each other's hands
as if they were maps of Paris
or of the world
as if they were looking for the Metro
that would take them together
through subterranean ways
through the 'stations of desire'
to love's final terminals
at the ports of the city of light
It is a terminal case
But they are losing themselves
in the crisscrossing lines
of their intertwined palms

their head-lines and their heart-lines
their fate-lines and life-lines
illegibly entangled
in the *mons veneris*
of their passion

M.F.K. FISHER
(1908–1992)

*Mary Frances Kennedy Fisher first visited France in 1929 when her then-husband, Al Fisher, studied for his doctorate in Dijon. "It was there, I now understand, that I started to grow up, to study, to make love, to eat and drink, to be me and no one I was expected to be." During their three-year stay, M.F.K. learned about food, following the advice of her landlady, waiters and shopkeepers. Although she would not publish her first book of essays (*Serve It Forth, *1937*) for nearly ten years, her stay in France set M.F.K. on a gastronomical course.*

More than twenty years after her first visit to France, M.F.K. returned to Aix-en-Provence. She was the author of several now-classic books on food including How to Cook a Wolf, Consider the Oyster *and* The Gastronomical Me *and a single mother of two girls. "By letting my girls see-smell-touch outside our own borders I am helping them be thinking and good and loyal Americans." She rented an apartment above the stables of a château, and she and her daughters had an idyllic life. M.F.K. considered putting them in the local French school, but opted instead to forgo formal education altogether for a year. "We have three little bedrooms and an ancient beautiful kitchen where we'll eat . . . [The girls] get up when they want to, and either go down to the brook and wash some clothes with the farmer's wife and the shepherd's wife . . . or they go outside to the meadows, now blazing with scarlet poppies . . ." In 1955 the family returned to California, but France would always be a touchstone for M.F.K.*

In 1964 Fisher wrote Map of Another Town, *a memoir of Provence and in 1977,* A Considerable Town, *a memoir of Marseille, from which this excerpt is taken.*

The Place Where I Looked

One of the many tantalizing things about Marseille is that most people who describe it, whether or not they know much about either the place or the languages they are supposedly using, write the same things. For centuries this has been so, a typically modern opinion could have been given in 1550 as well as 1977.

Not long ago I read one, mercifully unsigned, in a San Francisco paper. It was full of logistical errors, faulty syntax, misspelled French words, but it hewed true to the familiar line that Marseille is doing its best to live up to a legendary reputation as world capital for "dope, whores, and street violence." It then went on to discuss, often erroneously, the essential ingredients of a true bouillabaisse! The familiar pitch had been made, and idle readers dreaming of a great seaport dedicated to heroin, prostitution, and rioting could easily skip the clumsy details of marketing for fresh fish. . . .

"Feature articles" like this one make it seem probable that many big newspapers, especially in English-reading countries, keep a few such mild shockers on hand in a back drawer, in case a few columns need filling on a rainy Sunday. Apparently people like to glance one more time at the same old words: evil, filthy, dangerous.

Sometimes such journalese is almost worth reading for its precociously obsolete views of a society too easy to forget. In 1929, for instance, shortly before the Wall Street Crash, a popular travel writer named Basil Woon published *A Guide to the Gay World of France: From Deauville to Monte Carlo* (Horace Liveright, New York). (By now even his use of the word "gay" is quaintly naïve enough for a small chuckle. . . .)

Of course Mr. Woon was most interested in the Côte d'Azur, in those far days teeming and staggering with rich English and even richer Americans, but while he could not actively recommend staying in Marseille, he did remain true to his journalistic background with an expectedly titillating mention of it:

> If you are interested in how the other side of the world lives, a trip through old Marseilles—by daylight—cannot fail to thrill, but it is not wise to venture into this district at night unless dressed like a stevedore and well armed. Thieves, cutthroats, and other undesirables throng the narrow alleys, and sisters of scarlet sit in the doorways of their places of business, catching you by the sleeve as you pass by. The dregs of the world are here, unsifted. It is Port Said, Shanghai, Barcelona, and Sidney combined. Now that San Francisco has reformed, Marseilles is the world's wickedest port.

(Mr. Woon's last sentence, written some fifty years ago, is more provocative today than it was then, to anyone interested in the shifting politics of the West Coast of America. . . .)

While I either accept or deplore what other people report about the French town, and even feel that I understand why they are obliged to use the words they do (Give the public what it wants, etc., etc. . . .), I myself have a different definition of the place, which is as indefinable as Marseille itself: *Insolite.*

There seems to be no proper twin for this word in English; one simply has to sense or feel what it means. Larousse says that it is somewhat like "contrary to what is usual and normal." Dictionaries such as the *Shorter Oxford* and *Webster's Third International* try words like *apart, unique, unusual.* This is not enough, though . . . not quite right. Inwardly I know that it means *mysterious, unknowable,* and in plain fact, *indefinable.*

And that is Marseille: indefinable, and therefore *insolite.* And the strange word is as good as any to explain why the place haunts me and draws me, with its phoenixlike vitality, its implacably realistic beauty and brutality. The formula is plain: Marseille = *insolite,* therefore *insolite* = Marseille.

This semantical conclusion on my part may sound quibbling, but it seems to help me try to explain what connection there could possibly, logically, be between the town and me . . . why I have returned there for so long: a night, ten nights, many weeks or months.

Of course it is necessary to recognize that there is a special karma about Marseille, a karmic force that is mostly translated as wicked, to be avoided by all clean and righteous people. Travellers have long been advised to shun it like the pesthole it has occasionally been, or at best to stay there as short a time as possible before their next ship sets sail.

A true karmic force is supposed to build up its strength through centuries of both evil and good, in order to prevent its transmigration into another and lesser form, and this may well explain why Marseille has always risen anew from the ashes of history. There seems to be no possible way to stamp it out. Julius Caesar tried to, and for a time felt almost sure that he had succeeded. Calamities caused by man's folly and the gods' wrath, from the plagues ending in 1720 to the invasions ending in the 1940s, have piled it with rotting bodies and blasted rubble, and the place has blanched and staggered, and then risen again. It has survived every kind of weapon known to European warfare, from the ax and arrow to sophisticated derivatives of old Chinese gunpowder, and it is hard not to surmise that if a nuclear blast finally leveled the place, some short dark-browed men and women might eventually emerge from a few deep places, to breed in the salt marshes that would gradually have revivified the dead waters around the Old Port. . . .

Meanwhile, Marseille lives, with a unique strength that plainly scares less virile breeds. Its people are proud of being "apart," and critics mock them for trying to sound even more Italianate than they are, trying to play roles for the tourists: fishermen ape Marcel Pagnol's *Marius* robustly; every fishwife is her own Honorine.

The Pinball Boys are thinner and more viperous there than any-
where in Europe, they assume as true Marseillais, and the tarts
are tarter and the old hags older and more haggish than any-
where in the world. . . .

Behind this almost infantile enjoyment of playing their parts
on a superb stage with changing backdrops that are certainly
insolite, and a full orchestration of every sound effect from the
ringings of great bells to the whine of the tramontane and
the vicious howl of the mistral, held together by sirens from
ambulances and ships, and the pinpricks of complaining sea-
gulls . . . behind this endlessly entertaining and absorbing melo-
drama, a secret life-source provides its inner nourishment to the
citizens.

There is a strong religious blood flowing in that corporate
body. Catholics and other Christians, Communists, Freethinkers,
Arabs, Gypsies, all admit to an acceptance of powers beyond their
questionings, whether or not they admit to *being* "believers." The
gigantic bell Marie-Joséphine, at the top of Notre Dame de la
Garde, rings for every soul that has ever lived there, no matter
how much a race-bound parishioner of St. Victor might deny
the right of a Moslem in the Panier across the Old Port to under-
stand its reassuring voice.

Naturally, in a place as old and *insolite* as Marseille, there is a
strong dependence on forces that are loosely called occult, or
mystical, or perhaps demonic. There are many fortune-tellers,
usually thriving in their chosen ways of neighborhood help or
prestigious social acclaim. The best known of the Tarot cards
were adapted to a special ritual that evolved there, and are called
by the town's name. Cabalistic signs are often in or on graffiti,
political or otherwise, and it is plain that the right people will
see and understand them. Why not? After all, the churches build
their altars over early Christian sepulchers laid in turn upon the
stones of temples built to Artemis and Adonis, who in turn . . .

There is a good description of the withdrawn side of the
noisy, rough-talking Marseillais in one of Simenon's books

about Inspector Maigret. It was written about another French
town, but it is Marseille to me:

> . . . a stone jungle, where you can disappear for months; where
> often you do not hear of a crime until weeks after it has been
> committed; where thousands of human beings . . . live on the
> fringes of the Law, in a world where they can find as many
> accomplices and hideouts as they need, and where the police put
> out their bait now and then and pull in a fish they were waiting
> for, all the while depending more for such luck on a telephone
> call from a jealous girl or an informer. . . .

This quasi-occult mutism is what has helped defeat the invaders
of Marseille, I think. Certainly it baffled the last militant "occu-
pants" in the 1940s. Many different stories are told about how
and why a large part of the ancient Greco-Roman bank of the
Old Port was destroyed by the Germans, but the basic reason for
this move was probably that they simply could not keep track of
what was going on in the deep warrens that went up from the
Quai du Port past Les Accoules toward La Vieille Charité and
the Place des Moulins. What was worse, they could not tell from
the flat black eyes, the blank unmoved faces of occupants of this
filthy old neighborhood, the pimps and bawds and small-time
gangsters who went there as a natural refuge when their other
ways of life were interrupted by war, which of them were work-
ing with what appointed or subterranean leaders, and even which
of them might be town fathers in false beards rather than black
marketeers dealing indirectly with the invaders.

The answer was to get rid of the whole infamous district, and
it was easy to have the German-appointed city council approve a
plan to blow up the mess from underground. It was done neatly,
with complete evacuation of the helpless residents and full warn-
ing to the numberless unknown invisibles who were using the
old tunnels for their special version of the Liberation. (Some
other destruction during that dubious time was less circumspect,
or course, and a few foul tricks were blamed on the invaders

when an orphanage, or a clinic, say, was without notice shattered from above and not below ground. . . .)

Soon after the dirty tunnels and gutters above the Quai du
Port were mined and hopefully wiped out, they were once more
in full swing, of course: rats and moles know how to dig again.
A lot of the diggers were summarily lined up and shot, but that
did not seem to impress the strange breed called Marseillais for
so many centuries. Some thirty-five years later, the whole quarter is threatened with a new demolition, to make way for high-
rise housing projects, but the people who live there, as elsewhere
in the big town, remain impassive and tough and sardonic . . .
that is to say, *insolite.*

This cannot be a guidebook, the kind that tells how, with a chart
to be got free from the driver of the tour, to follow a green line
from A to G and then switch to either the red or the yellow lines
to Z, depending on how weary or hungry one may feel. I am
not meant to tell anyone where to go in Marseille, nor even why
I myself went where I did there, and saw and smelled and felt
as I did. All I can do in this explanation about my being there
is to write something about the town itself, through my own
senses.

I first spent a night there in late 1929, and since then I have
returned even oftener than seems reasonable. Beginning in 1940,
there were wars, both worldwide and intramural, and then I
managed to regain my old rhythm. Each time I went back, I felt
younger: a chronological miracle, certainly!

One reason I now try to explain all this is that when I cannot
return, for physical or perhaps financial reasons, I will stay so
enriched and heartened by what I have known there that I
should be the envy of every crowned head of several worlds. I
boast, and rightly. Nobody who has lived as deeply for as long as
I have in Marseille-Insolite can be anything but blessed.

There is an almost impossible lot of things to see there, and
for one reason or another I know many of them, and have been

part of them with people I loved (another proud boast!). If I started to tell why I wished everybody in the world could do the same, it would make a whole book, a personal guide tour, and that is not what I am meant to write, according to my secret directives. I would say words like Longchamps, Borély, Cantini, Les Accoules, St. Victor, St. Nicolas, La Place des Moulins, La Vieille Charité, Notre Dame de la Garde, La Rue de Rome . . . and it would be for every unexpected reason known to human beings, from the smell of a sick lion in a zoo behind Longchamps to an obviously necrophilic guardian of the tombs in Borély to the cut of an exquisite tweed skirt in a Paris boutique on the Rome. Each reason I gave for wanting some people to know why I've been there would make the guide a long hymn, hopefully shot through with practical asides about how far Borély is from town, and how steep the walk is up through the Panier to the Vieille Charité, and how much to tip the elderly patient men at places like the Musée des Docks Romains . . . and yes, why did I not mention it before? Other places, other sounds: they tumble in my head like pebbles under a waterfall, and all I know is that I must try to understand why I myself go back to this strange beautiful town.

If I could be in only one part of it, I would go directly to the Old Port, and stay there. I know that a lot of people consider it hopelessly touristic or noisy or vulgar. I feel at ease there, perhaps more so than in any other populous place I have ever known. Most of the reasons for this escape me or were never even guessed, but the fact remains that if I could within the next three minutes go by teleportation to the Quai des Belges on the Vieux Port, I would know exactly what to do and say and eat, and would feel as welcome as any shadow. It is very nice to feel like this.

The Vieux Port has a narrow entrance, past the Pharo Palace that Napoleon III built for his Empress, so that from almost any part of its three quays it looks landlocked. Every Marseillais, though, and almost every stranger there, knows that out through the tumultuous inlet and past the jetties of the new port of La

Joliette lie several little bleak harsh islands, one of them crowned with the tomblike Château d'If that Dumas peopled with his noble ghosts.

Coming back from the Château, sometimes a very rough trip indeed, the Rive Neuve is on one's right, with the Abbey of St. Victor and then La Garde towering over it, and on the waterfront the façade of the Criée, the public auction house for fish. It looks something like a fragment of the Gare de Lyon in Paris, tall and with grimed glassy walls. It is said to be doomed, now that so much transportation is done by trucks and rail from all over Europe, with their mounting traffic problems, but I first heard this as an imminent fact some ten years ago, and it still hums and screams from late night until predawn, and then is as quiet as a church, except for the men who hose down the walls and trestle tables and floors for the next night's biddings. There are usually a few trawlers docked alongside to unload big catches or wait for cleanups.

The Rive Neuve is patchy and beautiful, architecturally, with some fine blocks of buildings that went up at the town end of the Port after the galleys stopped being built in the middle of the eighteenth century, a surprisingly short time ago. There is a dwindling number of good restaurants either on or just off the Quai, and the little fishhouses tacked onto the massive old blocks are tacky indeed to look at, and mostly evanescent. Portside there are private moorings for pleasure boats and larger yachts, a couple of clubs, generous moorings for small professional fishing boats. The feeling is lively, expert, no-nonsense, with several little cafés and chandleries and so on across the Quai.

Auto traffic is heavy and fast there, because of the cars that tear through the tunnel under the mouth of the Old Port from inland. Until the late 1940s, that end of the Port was hurdled by a strange thin loop of steel, referred to locally by several names, the most respectful being the "shore-to-shore hustler." Once Simenon wrote of it as a "gigantesque metal carcass, cutting across the horizon, on which one can make out, from a distance, tiny human beings." Raoul Dufy said it even better, with paint.

It seems odd to me that I never noticed the obtrusive *"pont transbordeur,"* until it was gone when I went back after the Occupation, in about 1951. It had always been there when I was, but since I had never seen the horizon any way but barred, I accepted it without question as part of the magic. It was no more gigantesque than any other man-made edifice: Notre Dame de la Garde, ugly but inspiring; St. Victor, ugly but reassuring; the aerial bridge, ugly but practical. Then when I returned to Marseille with my two small girls, I stood in a window in the old Hotel Beauvau on the Quai des Belges and felt a shock that made me gasp: the bridge was gone! The sky was free! Our eyes could look out over the boats, past the Pharo, which from the harbor always seemed more like a hospital than a palace, and then bend down as surely as any seagull's onto the tumble of rough water into La Joliette and our own Port! Perhaps it was the way a young sheep feels after its first shearing, very lightsome and cool suddenly.

The Quai des Belges is the shortest of the Port's three shores, at the head, the land end, of the little harbor. Like all centers of life past and present, it is concentrated, so that it has fine-to-sad restaurants and brasseries and commerce and mad traffic and a church and a bus terminal cramped onto the land side, with a subway station to open shortly, and then on the Port side docks for all the excursion boats to the Château d'If, and so on, with careful room for the fishermen to chug in six or seven mornings a week to set up their rickety tables in the casual market that strings out along the wide sidewalk.

For a long time in my Marseille life, the Quai des Belges had a sloping place where boats could be drawn up onto the pavement. When the wind was wild, water came onto the street, over the big plaque that tells how the Phoceans landed there. Then in perhaps the early sixties, some time after the *pont transbordeur* was taken down, the sloping pebbly pavement was made level with the rest of the Quai, and the edge went sharply down into the water so that it was uniformly convenient for the fishermen to put in with their catches for their wives to sell. Who dragged his craft up on shore, anymore, for a rest or some quick repairs? What fine ladies waited there to be rowed into mid-Port and then handed up to their sailing vessels?

One time, before the old beaching place was changed, I watched a small grey vessel of the American Navy swing delicately down the middle of the harbor, ease itself sideways within a few feet of the slope, and unload . . . disgorge . . . explode . . . what seemed like hundreds of sailors. I stood upstairs in my window, on that Christmas Eve, and it looked as if the young men flew onto the wet sloping pavement from their deck, without even touching the little boat alongside that was meant as a bridge. They gathered in knots on the windy Quai, and then melted fast in three directions, but mostly up the Can o' Beer.

Later a few strings of Christmas lights went on, looking pretty, but the next day there was almost no sign of life on the grim little vessel, and before the second dawn she slipped out of the harbor, presumably with her full crew. She was the last overtly military vessel I ever saw in the Vieux Port, although I suspect derring-do of international proportions in a few superpowerful-elegant-sleek-rich yachts I have watched there. (The whole district is more James Bond than Henry Kissinger!)

Around the north corner of the Quai des Belges, past the old church that is sinking slowly into the mouth of the Lacydon River (poetic justice, some infidels say!), the church that still shelters a few of the last of Marseille's infamous army of public beggars, there is a long ancient unequivocal stretch of wide street and wider portside pavement called the Quai du Port. Boats stretch from the Quai des Belges out to the Harbor Master's Quarters just before the Fort St. Jean and the entrance to the harbor. Near town they are small plain craft with oars, outboard motors and no masts, often scruffy, but looking as familiar as housecats. Until a few years ago, retired fishermen used to wait there to snag visitors, and take them jerking and bouncing on "tours" of La Joliette.

These self-styled tours were never the same, never dull. There were two or three little boats with awnings, I remember. They cost more, but were reassuring to visiting friends when we went over the bumps between the Vieux Port and the breakwater of the new port. One time in La Joliette we were putt-putting along under the prows of gigantic ships loading for Africa and Indo-China, and suddenly looked up into a beautiful Spanish or Italian vessel and its elegant Captain's Quarters, with mullioned windows and rich brocade curtains! It was a facsimile of one of Christopher Columbus's little toys, that had been made for movies and international fairs, and was being taken under motor power to Naples or Barcelona or some such coincidental port. The clean brutal outlines of a diesel freighter to Djakarta were almost a relief.

Farther along the Quai du Port, and especially in front of the little Town Hall that was saved from explosion by mutual agreement with the Invaders in 1943, there are dreamily beautiful yachts of every club and country. They come in and out. Usually they are in fine condition, at least to the eye, and now and then a lithe crewman polishes brass, but in general they are empty when we loiterers glance or stare at them. One time a "tall ship" with three masts, all painted a dull coal black, lay alongside the Town Hall for several weeks, and nobody seemed to know why, or what it was. It flew the French flag. And once in 1976 the ugliest hull I ever saw lay there, not attracting much notice.

It had fake anchors painted here and there near its prow, and was plainly some sort of mockery of everything beautiful about an ocean-going vessel, with almost no superstructure and yet without a single porthole that could be seen. It too was a flat ugly black, and was lettered minutely, *Club Méditerranée.* I knew about that so-called social corporation, or course, and asked a couple of Quai-watchers if it was going to be turned into a party ship. There was no answer, more than a shrug. It seemed strange, to look over from the Beauvau, too, and see that uncouth thing in front of the dainty little Town Hall.

Within a day or so, of course, when I was back in Aix and reading local interpretations of Marseille news instead of being there to garner the real truth of such matters (!), I learned that the ship was already famous, and would compete for the Atlantic International Cup on a solo voyage. It would be piloted mostly by electronics, and by a single Marseillais, alone in that dreadful carcass. I felt sick and fascinated and strangely embarrassed at my own unawareness, and I followed the log of the *Club Med* the whole way, and felt triumphant when it joined the "tall ships" in the great bicentennial parade on the Hudson River, July 4, 1976. I felt proud.

On the harbor water, which is somewhat cleaner as one goes along the Quai seaward, are docked the trawlers, the *chalutiers,* the vessels needing a deep draft for their enormous nets and, in port, their full hulls. They come into port to discharge their big fish across the harbor at the Criée, and then dock at the Quai du Port to keep their papers in order with the Harbor Master, and perhaps rest a few hours or days for the sakes of their crews. Drydocks mean going up the coast, although the smaller crafts have their own simple lifts along the Quai.

Most of the organizations of Vieux boat owners, professional and social, are housed portside on the ancient shore, and they are called Nautical Societies or Syndicates or Friendly Rowing Clubs or Lacydonian Brotherhoods or suchlike. They have simple clubhouses, firmly fenced off from the wide walk where people stroll and where nets are mended. Usually on weekends young couples chip at a small dangling hull, or paint seriously while the family dog or baby watches from the cobbles. Now and then a Sunday crowd on the Quai looks amiably over the fence as a group of amateur fishermen grill their catch of sardines and cool their fingers on plentiful bottles. The whole thing smells good: fish, wine, smoke from the burning driftwood; fresh paint from the next Société des Canotiers to the east; westward a whiff of tar from the modest drydock. On weekdays professionals take over the Quai, and watchers are fewer as men work hard on their boats or nets, and the air can be very salty.

Landside there are somber arcades almost hysterically lighted by countless thin deep espresso joints, and a few excellent restaurants that in fine weather flood their tables as far as possible out across the sidewalks toward the traffic, which is not quite as lethal as on the Rive Neuve. There seems no need for music, although now and then in summer a flameblower or a tumbler will pick up a few coins from the more sated diners.

As one moves back toward the Quai des Belges along the port, the gastronomy swings from pasta to bouillabaisse, and from Chianti to white house-wine, and the restaurants are more filled with tourists and with locals on a little weekend spree than they are with vacationing decorators and actors from "up North." It is pleasant, a good way to eat and talk, and behind, the pinball machines throb on, and the tiny espresso cups sit half-empty everywhere in the long bright bars.

And then behind the arcades and the pinball joints rise the graceful hills, where the Greeks and then the Romans built temples and theatres on the sites of older altars. Now the clock tower of Les Accoules rises sturdily, if off-time, as it did for other purposes in the thirteenth century, and leads up to the old Place des Moulins through streets that are cleaner than they have sometimes been, but still suspect to tidy travellers and even some City Fathers, who would like to get rid of them for high-rise condominiums.

And at the land's-end of the Port, high and straight behind the Quai des Belges to the west, new but lightsomely majestic, rises Longchamps, which cannot be suspected except from hilltops or out at sea. It is an astonishing public building, one that could never have been erected in France except in the mid-nineteenth century, when Napoleon III's taste was rampant. It spouts water in controlled extravagance from great carved mouths, down many churning basins toward the thirsty town, and on out along the course of the ancient Lacydon toward the open sea. It sweeps the Vieux Port cleaner than it has been since men started to pollute it some two thousand years ago, and then clogged it foully when they built over the mouth of the old river. Around this majestic waterworks that spews its blessings from the wicked river of the Durance, first curbed in 1838, is built a garishly wonderful palace that houses natural and manmade history, and that hides a relatively tiny little botanical garden and zoo. It is all almost nightmarish at close range, like being lost in a fetal Disneyland, but from afar, Longchamps is beautiful.

It is one of the reasons I want to say why I must return to its town. When I have tried to tell natives that I need to write about it, they are courteous in their own sardonic way. They do not mock too openly, but they manage to imply flatly that I am presumptuous: "Ah? You think that after a few visits here you can explain this place? Good luck!" Once a man who was repairing a typewriter for me lost some of his remoteness and said almost angrily that he was astounded at the effrontery of people who felt they could understand a subject or a race or a cult in a few minutes. I told him I felt humble about it, but undaunted, and we talked about how a model can sit in a room with ten painters and have ten different pictures of herself result. "Yes, your picture will not be mine," he said. I said, "I don't want to explain Marseille. I want to try to tell what it does about explaining myself," and we parted amicably, and not for the last time. Now and then taxi drivers have asked me why I stayed in Marseille, and I have told them that I did not want to leave until I had to, and they have either said I was a misguided sentimentalist or have indicated plainly that I should shut up.

The whole implication has been that nobody can understand anything about Marseille except the Massiliotes, as they used to be called. It is almost like the mystique of being a Gypsy. Either you are or you are damned, condemned, blasphemed, as *not*.

This is doubtless true, and in ways too mysterious to probe. But there is no reason why I cannot write about how I, an obvious Anglo-Saxon of American citizenship and birth, must accept the realization that I feel at ease in Marseille. Just as I can shrug off or laugh at the conditioned reactions of many of "us" to the place and its seething movement of people, all held in focus by the phoenix-race bred there since pre-Ségobridgian times, so I can enjoy an occasional soft voice, a reassuring pat on the shoulder. I felt pleased to have a wise old citizen of the town write directly to me in his *Evocations du Vieux Marseille:* "It is like no other town on earth." That is what I need to have him say, because I can never know as well as he does what we both still know.

And it is nice to read, in a letter Mme. de Sévigné wrote to her daughter in 1672,

> I am ecstatic about the peculiar beauty of this town. Yesterday, the weather was heavenly, and the place where I looked over the sea, the fortresses, the mountains, and the city is astonishing . . . I must apologize to Aix, but Marseille is lovelier and livelier than it, in proportion to Paris itself! There are at least a hundred thousand people here; and I cannot even try to count how many of them are beauties: the whole atmosphere makes me somewhat untrustworthy!

F. SCOTT FITZGERALD
(1896–1940)

*F. Scott Fitzgerald personified the Jazz Age, his own phrase for the
1920s. By the time Scott, Zelda and their daughter Scotty moved to Paris
in 1924, Fitzgerald had already had considerable literary success, but the
publication of* The Great Gatsby *in 1925 made him famous. The
Fitzgeralds became part of the circle that included Ernest Hemingway,
Gertrude Stein, and Gerald and Sara Murphy.*

Of Fitzgerald, Hemingway wrote in his memoir A Moveable Feast,
*"Scott was a man then who looked like a boy with a face between hand-
some and pretty. He had very fair wavy hair, a high forehead, excited
and friendly eyes and a delicate long-lipped Irish mouth that, on a girl,
would have been the mouth of a beauty." Hemingway remembered
Zelda as having "hawk's eyes and a thin mouth and deep-South man-
ners and accent." The Fitzgeralds' relationship was troubled even then
by their drinking and Zelda's mental instability. Zelda had her first
breakdown in 1930 and spent the rest of her life in and out of mental
institutions. Fitzgerald lapsed into alcoholism. By the 1930s the Fitzger-
alds' glittering promise had faded.*

In 1934 Scott Fitzgerald wrote Tender Is the Night *(from which
this excerpt it taken) based on their early years in France. Nicole and
Dick Diver are composites of Scott and Zelda and their friends the Mur-
phys. Although the book was well received, it did not sell. Pressed for
money, Fitzgerald turned to writing screenplays. He died in Hollywood
of a heart attack at the age of forty-four.*

from **Tender Is the Night**

On the pleasant shore of the French Riviera, about half way between Marseilles and the Italian border, stands a large, proud, rose-colored hotel. Deferential palms cool its flushed façade, and before it stretches a short dazzling beach. Lately it has become a summer resort of notable and fashionable people; a decade ago it was almost deserted after its English clientele went north in April. Now, many bungalows cluster near it, but when this story begins only the cupolas of a dozen old villas rotted like water lilies among the massed pines between Gausse's Hôtel des Étrangers and Cannes, five miles away.

The hotel and its bright tan prayer rug of a beach were one. In the early morning the distant image of Cannes, the pink and cream of old fortifications, the purple Alp that bounded Italy, were cast across the water and lay quavering in the ripples and rings sent up by sea-plants through the clear shallows. Before eight a man came down to the beach in a blue bathrobe and with much preliminary application to his person of the chilly water, and much grunting and loud breathing, floundered a minute in the sea. When he had gone, beach and bay were quiet for an hour. Merchantmen crawled westward on the horizon; bus boys shouted in the hotel court; the dew dried upon the pines. In another hour the horns of motors began to blow down from the winding road along the low range of the Maures, which separates the littoral from true Provençal France.

A mile from the sea, where pines give way to dusty poplars, is an isolated railroad stop, whence one June morning in 1925 a victoria brought a woman and her daughter down to Gausse's Hotel. The mother's face was of a fading prettiness that would soon be patted with broken veins; her expression was both tranquil and aware in a pleasant way. However, one's eye moved on quickly to her daughter, who had magic in her pink palms and her cheeks lit to a lovely flame, like the thrilling flush of children after their cold baths in the evening. Her fine forehead sloped gently up to where her hair, bordering it like an armorial shield, burst into lovelocks and waves and curlicues of ash blonde and gold. Her eyes were bright, big, clear, wet, and shining, the color of her cheeks was real, breaking close to the surface from the strong young pump of her heart. Her body hovered delicately on the last edge of childhood—she was almost eighteen, nearly complete, but the dew was still on her.

As sea and sky appeared below them in a thin, hot line the mother said:

"Something tells me we're not going to like this place."

"I want to go home anyhow," the girl answered.

They both spoke cheerfully but were obviously without direction and bored by the fact—moreover, just any direction would not do. They wanted high excitement, not from the necessity of stimulating jaded nerves but with the avidity of prize-winning schoolchildren who deserved their vacations.

"We'll stay three days and then go home. I'll wire right away for steamer tickets."

At the hotel the girl made the reservation in idiomatic but rather flat French, like something remembered. When they were installed on the ground floor she walked into the glare of the French windows and out a few steps onto the stone veranda that ran the length of the hotel. When she walked she carried herself like a ballet-dancer, not slumped down on her hips but held up in the small of her back. Out there the hot light clipped close her shadow and she retreated—it was too bright to see. Fifty yards away the Mediterranean yielded up its pigments, moment by moment, to the brutal sunshine; below the balustrade a faded Buick cooked on the hotel drive.

Indeed, of all the region only the beach stirred with activity.

Three British nannies sat knitting the slow pattern of Victorian England, the pattern of the forties, the sixties, and the eighties, into sweaters and socks, to the tune of gossip as formalized as incantation; closer to the sea a dozen persons kept house under striped umbrellas, while their dozen children pursued unintimidated fish through the shallows or lay naked and glistening with coconut oil out in the sun.

As Rosemary came onto the beach a boy of twelve ran past her and dashed into the sea with exultant cries. Feeling the impactive scrutiny of strange faces, she took off her bathrobe and followed. She floated face down for a few yards and finding it shallow staggered to her feet and plodded forward, dragging slim legs like weights against the resistance of the water. When it was about breast high, she glanced back toward shore: a bald man in a monocle and a pair of tights, his tufted chest thrown out, his brash navel sucked in, was regarding her attentively. As Rosemary returned the gaze the man dislodged the monocle, which went into hiding amid the facetious whiskers of his chest, and poured himself a glass of something from a bottle in his hand.

Rosemary laid her face on the water and swam a choppy little four-beat crawl out to the raft. The water reached up for her, pulled her down tenderly out of the heat, seeped in her hair and ran into the corners of her body. She turned round and round in it, embracing it, wallowing in it. Reaching the raft she was out of breath, but a tanned woman with very white teeth looked down at her, and Rosemary, suddenly conscious of the raw whiteness of her own body, turned on her back and drifted toward shore. The hairy man holding the bottle spoke to her as she came out.

"I say—they have sharks out behind the raft." He was of indeterminate nationality, but spoke English with a slow Oxford drawl. "Yesterday they devoured two British sailors from the flotte at Golfe Juan."

"Heavens!" exclaimed Rosemary.

"They come in for the refuse from the flotte."

Glazing his eyes to indicate that he had only spoken in order to warn her, he minced off two steps and poured himself another drink.

Not unpleasantly self-conscious, since there had been a slight sway of attention toward her during this conversation, Rosemary looked for a place to sit. Obviously each family possessed the strip of sand immediately in front of its umbrella; besides there was much visiting and talking back and forth—the atmosphere of a community upon which it would be presumptuous to intrude. Farther up, where the beach was strewn with pebbles and dead sea-weed, sat a group with flesh as white as her own. They lay under small hand-parasols instead of beach umbrellas and were obviously less indigenous to the place. Between the dark people and the light, Rosemary found room and spread out her peignoir on the sand.

Lying so, she first heard their voices and felt their feet skirt her body and their shapes pass between the sun and herself. The breath of an inquisitive dog blew warm and nervous on her neck; she could feel her skin broiling a little in the heat and hear the small exhausted wa-*waa* of the expiring waves. Presently her ear distinguished individual voices and she became aware that some one referred to scornfully as "that North guy" had kidnapped a waiter from a café in Cannes last night in order to saw him in two. The sponsor of the story was a white-haired woman in full evening dress, obviously a relic of the previous evening, for a tiara still clung to her head and a discouraged orchid expired from her shoulder. Rosemary, forming a vague antipathy to her and her companions, turned away.

Nearest her, on the other side, a young woman lay under a roof of umbrellas making out a list of things from a book open on the sand. Her bathing suit was pulled off her shoulders and her back, a ruddy, orange brown, set off by a string of creamy pearls, shone in the sun. Her face was hard and lovely and pitiful. Her eyes met Rosemary's but did not see her. Beyond her was a fine man in a jockey cap and red-striped tights; then the woman

Rosemary had seen on the raft, and who looked back at her, seeing her; then a man with a long face and a golden, leonine head, with blue tights and no hat, talking very seriously to an unmistakably Latin young man in black tights, both of them picking at little pieces of seaweed in the sand. She thought they were mostly Americans, but something made them unlike the Americans she had known of late.

After a while she realized that the man in the jockey cap was giving a quiet little performance for this group; he moved gravely about with a rake, ostensibly removing gravel and meanwhile developing some esoteric burlesque held in suspension by his grave face. Its faintest ramification had become hilarious, until whatever he said released a burst of laughter. Even those who, like herself, were too far away to hear, sent out antennae of attention until the only person on the beach not caught up in it was the young woman with the string of pearls. Perhaps from modesty of possession she responded to each salvo of amusement by bending closer over her list.

The man of the monocle and bottle spoke suddenly out of the sky above Rosemary.

"You are a ripping swimmer."

She demurred.

"Jolly good. My name is Campion. Here is a lady who says she saw you in Sorrento last week and knows who you are and would so like to meet you."

Glancing around with concealed annoyance Rosemary saw the untanned people were waiting. Reluctantly she got up and went over to them.

"Mrs. Abrams—Mrs. McKisco—Mr. McKisco—Mr. Dumphry—"

"We know who you are," spoke up the woman in evening dress. "You're Rosemary Hoyt and I recognized you in Sorrento and asked the hotel clerk and we all think you're perfectly marvellous and we want to know why you're not back in America making another marvellous moving picture."

They made a superfluous gesture of moving over for her. The

woman who had recognized her was not a Jewess, despite her name. She was one of those elderly "good sports" preserved by an imperviousness to experience and a good digestion into another generation.

"We wanted to warn you about getting burned the first day," she continued cheerily, "because *your* skin is important, but there seems to be so darn much formality on this beach that we didn't know whether you'd mind."

JANET FLANNER
(1892–1978)

For many New Yorker *readers, Janet Flanner was Paris. From 1925 through 1975 (with the exception of the war years from 1939–1944) she wrote a periodic column "Letter From Paris" for her friend and editor Harold Ross. Her pen name was Genêt. The entire city provided her material, and she wrote trenchantly of politics, art, theater, culture and people.*

Flanner's sensible, analytical style reflected, perhaps, her Midwestern roots. She was born in Indianapolis, the daughter of Quaker parents, attended the University of Chicago and became the first movie critic for the Indianapolis Star. *After a failed early marriage, she moved to New York and then to Europe, finally settling in Paris. She fell in with the American expatriates who were part of the post–World War I Lost Generation. Unlike Hemingway, Fitzgerald, Dos Passos, the Murphys and Ezra Pound, Flanner returned to her adopted city after World War II and remained until just three years before her death.*

Flanner's New Yorker *essays are collected in three volumes:* Men and Monuments *(1957),* Paris Journal 1965–1971 *(1971) and* Paris Was Yesterday 1925–1939 *(1972). Her letters to her longtime lover, Natalia Murray, were published in* Darlinghissima *(1975).*

March II

from PARIS JOURNAL

The retrospective exhibition called "The Twenties: American Writers in Paris and Their Friends," which has just opened in the St.-Germain-des-Prés quarter where they lived, is an act of recrudescence. It restores to life that memorable, far-back decade when talent and faces were fresh, when the young expatriates came here in numbers and in a united coincidence and founded what became the new contemporary school of American literature. The exhibition is under the aegis of the cultural wing of the American Embassy and is being held in the new United States Information Service Cultural Center on the Rue du Dragon, the narrow, short street just beyond the Brasserie Lipp and across and down from the Café des Deux Magots, those focal points in the old days. The exhibition's six hundred items, many rare, owe their presence almost entirely to the fact that Miss Sylvia Beach, of the Shakespeare and Company bookshop, on the Rue de l'Odéon, has never lost anything or thrown anything away. So now here it all is, gathered together with a few memorabilia from others of the epoch—the scribbled, jocose notes, the corrected page proofs, the photographs, the snapshots, the first editions dedicated "to Sylvia, with love" from Hem, Dos, Djuna, E.E., Ezra, Thornton, Gertrude, Scott, and others. As source material of literary and documentary importance, it is a miraculously complete show, with the first editions of the expatriates (often printed here in France on private presses by other expatriates, because no New York commercial editors had the faith to print them), and with examples of all the vital, struggling literary magazines from everywhere—splendid silken ragbags, sometimes backed by the rich—for which, in the early days, the poor-of-purse writers gladly wrote without remuneration, just to see their wonderful words in print. It is also a clearly, handsomely, and imaginatively arranged exhibition, using glass cases set upright against the walls, so that what is in them is easily visible and legible, with entire cases devoted to an outstanding writer—including his letters, manuscripts, photographs, snapshots of family increases, bullfights, fishing trips, and so on—so he can be studied all at once.

The expatriates' literary clubroom, the Shakespeare shop not only sold books in the English language but also rented them out as a lending library. Miss Gertrude Stein was Sylvia Beach's first subscriber, and early wrote a poem called "Rich and Poor in English to Subscribers in French and Other Latin Tongues," which Miss Alice B. Toklas typed off—there is a typescript copy in the show—and mailed to friends to encourage them to subscribe also. Robert McAlmon, who ran Contact Editions, a private press, published Miss Stein's enormous "Making of Americans" (shown along with one of her corrected page proofs), because Hemingway wanted him to and because no publisher in America would print it, and also printed Hemingway's first book, a small blue paperback called "Three Stories & Ten Poems." William Bird, who had the Three Mountains Press, published Hemingway's "In Our Time," a tall yellow book whose cover was ornamented with disjointed cuttings from newspapers, printed in red—phrases including "two billion dollars," "guidance from God," and "learn French." In the Hemingway showcase is a jovial note to "Madame Shakespeare," meaning Miss Beach, in which he remarked, "To hell with the book." In Scott Fitzgerald's showcase is a copy of "The Great Gatsby" dedicated to "Dear Sylvia, from Harold Bell Wright," which he crossed out, signing his own name. Bird also published "XVI Cantos," by Ezra Pound, who had brought Joyce and his "Ulysses" from Trieste to Paris in that almost willful concentration here of talented outlanders who were having trouble being published. Because English typesetters refused to set type for the bawdy parts of "Ulysses," Miss Beach and her Shakespeare shop became its publisher, the printing being done in Dijon by Frenchmen, ignorant of what the English words meant. In the Joyce showcase are order forms for the 1922 first edition of "Ulysses" sent in by Lawrence of Arabia, who ordered two copies of the most expensive edition—on Dutch paper, at three hundred and fifty francs—and by Yeats and Gide, who each ordered a copy of the cheapest edition, at a hundred and fifty francs. Also shown are some of Joyce's corrected page proofs. As the publisher of "Ulysses," Miss Beach became both martyr and heroine when its detractors and admirers began congregating, over the years, in her shop. Near the Joyce material, flanked by dashing photos of Margaret Anderson and Jane Heap, is the famous 1920 autumn number of the revolutionary *Little Review* in which they announced "our arrest" for having published sections of "Ulysses" in New York.

In the exhibition's photograph section, entitled "Portraits of a Generation," and mostly taken by Man Ray and Berenice Abbott, everyone is present who was attached, in one way or another, to the Shakespeare shop: T. S. Eliot; Eugene and Maria Jolas, of the intransigent magazine called *transition;* Archibald MacLeish; Katherine Anne Porter; Allen Tate; Virgil Thompson; Djuna Barnes, in profile in a cape; Kay Boyle, front-face in a beret; Dos Passos; Bryher; Arthur Moss, of *Gargoyle;* Louis Bromfield; Cummings; Sherwood Anderson; Wilder; Nathanael West; Caresse and Harry Crosby, of the Black Sun Press; Nancy Cunard, of the Hours Press; Alexander Calder; George Antheil; Edmund Wilson; Mary Reynolds; and others—plus the French writers and artists drawn to this new fire of foreign talent blazing in their own city, among them Gide, Valéry, Larbaud, Schlumberger, Chamson, and Marcel Duchamp.

In one corner of the exhibition room, the walls are covered with a photo-montage of the façade of the old Dingo café, in Montparnasse, where the St.-Germain talent spent many of its nights over the years. Real café chairs and tables are placed in front of the montage, and there, late in the afternoon of the exhibition's opening, sat Miss Alice B. Toklas and Thornton Wilder in literary reminiscence, while behind them a pianola beat out the rhythms of Antheil's "Ballet Mécanique," the shock music of that decade.

ADAM GOPNIK
(1956–)

"I've wanted to live in Paris since I was eight," said Adam Gopnik, a writer for the New Yorker since 1984. *"My first images of Paris had come from the book adaptation of* The Red Balloon, *the wonderful Albert Lamorisse movie about a small boy in the Parisian neighborhood of Menilmontant who gets a magic slightly overeager balloon, which follows him everywhere."* Gopnik first experienced France as a teenager in the early 1970s on a yearlong family sabbatical with his parents, both college professors. He returned two years later, this time with a girlfriend, Martha, who would later become his wife.

But living in Paris in the mid-1990s—actually living there—with a wife and young child (and eventually another child) was a different thing entirely. There was an apartment to be found—and then another when they had to vacate on short notice. Life was lived through a general strike that paralyzed not only the transit system, but postal deliveries. Child care had to be arranged. Computers and fax machines had to be adapted or figured out. Floating above the fray was Gopnik's son Luke who saw only the magic of Paris. He was enchanted by the carousel in the Luxembourg Gardens, ate crepes for snack, played soccer instead of baseball and spoke in unaccented French.

After five years Adam Gopnik and his wife decided to return to New York, with Luke (who preferred to be called Luca) and a new daughter, Olivia. Paris to the Moon *is a collection of Gopnik's "Paris Journal" articles from the* New Yorker.

Like a King

from PARIS TO THE MOON

When we discovered that the child we were going to have in Paris last fall would be a girl—we already have a boy—everybody told us that we had been blessed with the *choix du roi,* the king's choice. "Why, it's the *choix du roi!*" the technician said as she looked at the sonogram, more or less in the tone of the host on *Jeopardy!* announcing the Daily Double. "It's the *choix du roi!*" said the woman in the two-hour photo place on the rue du Bac when we told her. "A little girl coming after a little boy?" said my friend Pascal, the philosopher, with evident pleasure. "Why, then, it's the *choix du roi!*"

Martha was delighted to be having a girl, however the king felt about it. She had always wanted a son and a daughter, and as she only now explained to me, one of the reasons she had been so eager to leave New York four years earlier, just after the birth of our son, was that all her friends there who had two children had two boys, and she was starting to believe that two boys were just one of the things that happened to women in New York, "like high-intensity step classes and vanilla Edensoy," as she put it. Also, she said, she was worried about having to succumb to the New York social law that compels you nowadays to name your sons exclusively after the men your grandfather used to take a *shvitz* with. In our New York circle of under-tens we already had, in addition to the requisite Maxes, a Harry, a Joe, a Sam, an Otto, and a Charlie—the whole senior staff of Benny's Market: Lowest Prices in Town. "Even if I had had another boy, at least in Paris I wouldn't have had to call him Moe," she explained.

I was pleased by the news too, of course, but a little mystified by the expression. To be brutally frank, what mystified me was why a king would choose to have any girls at all. If I were a king, I would want only boys, so that the succession would never be challenged by the sinister uncle with a mustache lurking behind my throne. Or only girls and an immortality pill. What puzzled me even more was the way the phrase, though you heard it on Parisian lips, had a slightly disconcerting air of peasants-in-the-spring ecstasy about it, the kind of thing (*"C'est le choix du roi!"*) you would expect to hear set to a Trenet tune and sung by the villagers in a Pagnol film when the baker's daughter gives birth to little Lisette.

I soon sensed, though, that while people meant it, they also didn't mean it, that it was a thing you said both as a joke and not as a joke. After four years in Paris I have come to realize that this is where the true cultural differences reside: not in those famous moments when you think that a joke was meant straight ("My goodness, the *dessert grand-mère* is not made by Grandmother!"), or you misunderstood something that was meant straight as a joke ("The *tête de veau* is actually the head of a calf!"), but in those moments when you are confronted with something that is meant both as a joke and seriously. This zone of kidding overlaid with not kidding is one that we know at home. When a New Yorker passes out cigars in the office after the birth of his child, for instance, he is both making a joke about passing out cigars—with unspoken but quickly grasped reference to all the episodes of *Bewitched* and *I Love Lucy* in which Darrin or Desi or some other fifties-ish father passed out cigars—and sincerely celebrating the birth of his child. (The proof of this doubleness is that the cigars he passes out will actually be good to smoke, while mockery would make do with a bad or unsmokable cigar. Nobody tried to eat Warhol's soups.)

In Paris, the obstetricians all wear black. When your wife goes to be examined, the doctor who comes out into the waiting room is not a smart Jewish girl in a lab coat, as in New York, but a man with a day's growth of beard, who is wearing black jeans and a black silk shirt, like a character in a David Mamet play about Hollywood producers.

I first became aware of this when we went to get the first of many sonograms of the new baby. The sonogramist we had been sent to performs in a nineteenth-century apartment in the Sixth Arrondissement, with wainscoting and ceiling moldings and windows that open like doors. A curtain was drawn across one half of the living room, and couples sat on two sofas in the other half, turning the pages of *Elle* (*Elle* is a weekly in France) and waiting to be called.

After about ten minutes the curtain parted, and the sonogram specialist came into the room. He had on black jeans and a black silk shirt, open at the front and plunging down toward his navel, sleeves rolled up to the elbows. A day-old growth of beard covered his face. He smiled at us and asked us to come in. We sat down in front of a handsome Louis XV desk—the sonogram equipment was over in the other corner of the office—and he asked us when the baby had been conceived. My wife gave him the likely date.

"Was that at night or early the next day?" he asked. It took me a moment to realize that he was kidding, and then another moment to realize that he was not, and then still another moment—the crucial cultural gap moment—to realize that he was neither kidding nor not kidding. That is to say, he was kidding—he knew it didn't matter—but he was not kidding in the sense that he was genuinely interested, considered that it was part of his profession to view that precise moment of passion or lust with a special tenderness. The moment of conception, the sexual act, was, in his schema, not incidental information to be handled discreetly or pushed aside altogether, as American obstetricians do—all American "What to Expect" books begin with the test, not the act—but the prime moment, the hallowed moment, the first happy domino that, falling, caused all the other dominoes that had brought the three of us together to fall, and (his eyes implied) it was our special shared knowledge that that domino had not in fact fallen but had been nudged, deliberately, and by us. Then he asked Martha to get undressed. There was, to my surprise, no changing room or even a curtain, so she did, like that. (I was the only embarrassed person in the room.) The elaborate hospital rigmarole of American hygiene and American obstetrics—the white coats, the dressing rooms, the lab gowns—is dispensed with. They make no sense, since a pregnant woman is not only not sick but in a sense has doubled the sum of her health.

We looked at the baby on the sonar screen, as though she were a character in a Tom Clancy novel. "She's pretty," he said at last. Then we got a package of fifteen or so pictures of our daughter in embryo, full of allure, as the receptionist said. The pictures were stapled, in neat, ruffled rows, into a little wallet, with sans serif lowercase type, like an e. e. cummings poem.

"In New York the obstetricians all wear white, and they all have books out," Martha said to me one afternoon. She had called up an obstetrician in New York that day, before her appointment with her French doctor. "She covered me with congratulations, and then she told me all these tests I ought to take. Week ten the CVS, then in week fourteen an early amnio, and then in weeks eighteen to twenty a targeted ultrasound to test for neural tube defects, and then I'm supposed to get genetic carrier blood tests for all these other things."

"What did the French obstetrician say when you told her that?"

"She made that 'oh' face—you know, that lips-together, 'How naive can one be?' face— said that it was far too dangerous to do the CVS, and then she prescribed a lot of drugs for pain. I've got antispasmodics, antinausea drugs, painkillers, and some other ones too. Then she told me I could drink red wine and absolutely not to eat any raw vegetables. She keeps asking me if I've had any salad. She says 'salad' the way the doctors in New York say 'uninsured.'"

French doctors like to prescribe drugs as much as New York doctors like to publish books. I suppose that it fulfills a similar need for self-expression with a pen, without having to go to the trouble of having your photograph taken with a professional yet humane grin. You cannot go into a French doctor's office for a cinder in your eye and emerge without a six-part prescription, made up of pills of different sizes to be taken at irregular intervals.

I wanted to meet Martha's doctor, who would be delivering the baby while I "coached"—I am of the Phil Jackson school as a coach; you might not actually see me doing much, but I contribute a lot to the winning atmosphere—and so I accompanied her to the next appointment. We sat in the waiting room and read *Elle* some more. By now Martha was nervous. An American friend who lives in Normandy had gone into labor a few days before, only to find that all the anesthesiologists had gone out on strike that morning. She had delivered the baby, her second, without any epidural.

"I want to go to a place where the anesthesiologists are scabs," Martha said. "Or nuns or something. I don't want to go to a place where the man with the epidural is on a picket line."

While we were in the waiting room, a man in black jeans and a black silk shirt with the sleeves rolled up, and with a Pat Riley hairstyle, peeked in and mischievously summoned one of the women in the waiting room.

"Who's that?" I asked.

"The other obstetrician," Martha said.

"Does he always dress like that?" I demanded.

"Oh, yes. He's very nice. He examined me last time."

Martha's doctor was wearing black stretch slacks, a black tank top, and a handsome gold necklace. She was very exacting about appearances. "You have gained too much weight," she said to Martha, who had in fact gained less than with her first pregnancy. "Start swimming, stop eating." (Martha says that a friend who went for an appointment two months after the birth of her second baby was told by the same doctor, "You look terrible. And do something about your hair.") We did another sonogram. "Look at her, she's pretty," the doctor said as we looked at the sonogram. "There's her *fille,*" she said, pointing to the sex. Then she again counseled Martha to swim more and gave her a prescription for sleeping pills. We talked a bit about the approach of those hard, exhausting first weeks with a newborn. "Get a night nurse," she advised. "Go out with your husband. Be happy again."

In New York, in other words, pregnancy is a medical condition that, after proper care by people in white coats and a brief hospital stay, can have a "positive outcome." In Paris it is something that has happened because of sex, which, with help and counsel, can end with your being set free to go out and have more sex. In New York pregnancy is a ward in the house of medicine; in Paris it is a chapter in a sentimental education, a strange consequence of the pleasures of the body.

In America, we have managed to sexualize everything—cars, refrigerators, computers, Congress—except the natural consequences of sex. Though it is de rigueur for every pregnant supermodel to have her picture taken when she is full-bellied, it is always the same picture. She covers her breasts, she is swaddled below in some way, and she looks off into the middle distance, not dreamily, as she might when wearing lingerie, but slightly anxiously, as though she could not remember if she had left her husband's electric guitar turned on. The subject, the hidden subject, is not the apotheosis of sexuality but its transcendence into maternal instinct: babe into mother by way of baby.

In France, though, a pregnant woman is alive, since she has demonstrated both her availability and her fecundity: We Have a Winner. Though Lamaze method childbirth began here, it remains cultish and sectarian. Most women nurse for three months, no more. (It shrinks your breasts and gives you an uncomfortable accessory.) And when the anesthesiologists are not striking, they are, as our baby-sitter says, fully busy. (Two French friends of ours talk about natural childbirth: "What is the English for *accouchement sans douleur?*" one asks. "A lie," the other answers.)

The prohibition on uncooked vegetables, by the way, turns out to have a solid scientific basis. Toxoplasmosis—a mild parasitic infection that is devastating to unborn children—though it's rare in America (it's that thing you can get from cat litter), is common in France. Red wine is recommended, in turn, because it is high in iron and acts as an effective antispasmodic.

By law a French woman who is going to have a baby is guaranteed—not merely allowed but pretty much compelled—to stay four or five nights in a clinic or a hospital. In New York, when our son, Luke, was born—in the Klingenstein Pavilion of Mount Sinai Hospital—we had two days to have the baby, bond, and get out. French law is specific and protective about the rights of pregnant women. If you are a salaried employee, you get six weeks of prenatal leave and ten weeks of paid leave after the baby is born. For a third child, you get eight weeks off and eighteen more, and if you have three at once, you get, in all, forty-six weeks of paid leave. (The leave is paid, through a complicated formula, by your employer and the state.) The law is as finely tuned as a viola d'amore. There is even a beautiful added *remarque,* right there on the government document: *"Les artistes du spectacle, les mannequins des maisons de couture,"* and others who do work that is plainly incompatible with the state of pregnancy (i.e., a bigger belly) are assured of paid leave after the twenty-first week. In France, Cindy and Paulina and the rest would not just be having their pictures taken. They would already be on the dole.

The system, Martha's doctor observed once during a visit, is "royal for the users, good for the doctors, and expensive for the society." There are many rational arguments to be made about whether or not the outcomes justify the expenditures, and in any case, the level of care that the French have insisted on may be unsustainable. But the people who are being treated "royally" are ordinary people—everybody. For many, perhaps most, French people, life at the end of the century in the American imperium may look a bit like a typical transatlantic flight, with the airless, roomless, comfortless coach packed as tightly as possible, so that the maximum dollars can be squeezed out of every seat, with a few rich people up front. I am American enough to understand that this is, so to speak, one of the prices of mass travel—that there is no such thing as a free lunch, or clinic—and yet have become French enough to feel, stubbornly, that legroom and a little air should not be luxuries for the rich and that in a prosperous society all pregnant women should have three sonograms and four nights in a hospital, if they want to. It doesn't seem particularly royal to have four nights in a clinic when you have a baby or aristocratically spoiled to think that a woman should keep her job and have some paid leave afterward, even sixteen weeks, if she happens to be a mannequin in an haute couture house. All human desires short of simple survival are luxurious, and a mother's desire to have a slightly queenly experience of childbirth—a lying in rather than a pushing out and a going home—seems as well worth paying for as a tobacco subsidy or another tank.

In preparation for our own four-night stay we had first to search for the right clinic. Friends recommended two: the Clinique Sainte-Isabelle, in the leafy suburb of Neuilly, and the Clinique Belvedere, in Boulogne-Billancourt. We went to tour them. Both clinics had a pastoral, flower bed, medical but not quite hospital feel, like the sanitarium to which they pack off Nicole in *Tender Is the Night*. I liked the Belvedere best. The rooms there had a nice faded white and pale blue look, like the room in *Madeline* where she goes to have her appendix taken out and sees the crack in the ceiling that has a habit of sometimes looking like a rabbit. The cracks in the ceiling at the Belvedere were expressive too, and for a premium you could have a room with French doors leading out onto the garden. (The ordinary rooms were less grand, though they mostly had garden views too.) But what I really liked about the place were the clippings in the formal salon—the waiting room—downstairs, which was filled with dusty silk roses and blue and gold Louis XVI furniture. The clippings chronicled the birth of minor nobility in the halls of the Belvedere. A Bonapartist pretender had been born there, I remember, and also I think a prince of Yugoslavia. I liked the kingly company, particularly since it was such cheesy kingly company.

Martha, though, as we toured the clinics, kept asking gentle, pointed questions about labor relations with the anesthesiologists. Now, the anesthesiologists here—were they unionized? Did they have enough vacation time? Would the clinic manager say that they were happy with their working conditions? How long had it been since they signed a contract? Were there any, well, radicals among them, the kind of ex-Trotskyite *soixante-huitards* who might suddenly call for mass action by the workers? Eventually, we settled on the Clinique Sainte-Isabelle, which seemed to be the sensible, primly bourgeois choice of all our friends and which had a couple of full-time anesthesiologists on call, neither of whom looked like a sansculotte.

Everything was going along fine, in fact, until our meeting with the *sage-femme,* the wise woman, or, in American, the midwife. She was in yet another of the suburban clinics, an odd Jacques Tati modern place. This meeting was brisk, and it concentrated on two essential points: breathing and lying. The breathing bit we had heard about before—you are supposed to breathe from the diaphragm—but she emphasized that it was just as important, for a happy birth, to remember never to tell a taxi driver that you are in labor. Whatever you do, she said, don't say that you're in labor, or might be in labor, because no taxi driver in Paris will take a pregnant woman to her clinic, for fear of her having the baby in his car. (You can't call an ambulance because an ambulance won't go over the city line, and our clinic was out in Neuilly.)

Then how were we going to get to the clinic? Martha asked. (We don't have a car.) It's no problem, I interrupted, we'll simply walk over to the taxi stand. (You can't call a taxi, because there is a stand right across the street from our apartment.)

"I won't be able to stroll across the street and stand in line if I'm in labor," she objected. "I'll wait in the courtyard. Just get him to do the *demi-tour.*"

At these words my heart was stricken. *Demi-tour* means literally a U-turn, but in Paris it is also a half-metaphysical possibility that exists on the boulevard Saint-Germain just across the street from our apartment building. The boulevard itself runs one-way, from east to west. There is, however, a narrow lane carved out on it, for buses and taxis, that runs the other way, toward the place de la Concorde and the quai d'Orsay and, eventually, if you turn right over a bridge, toward Neuilly and the clinic too. Leading off this lane, at a single light about a hundred feet from our building, there is a small, discreet curved arrow marked on the asphalt. This arrow means that a taxicab—and only a taxicab—can make a U-turn there and go the other way, with the rest of the traffic. In principle, I could get a cab going against the traffic, have him do the *demi-tour*, pick up my pregnant wife, and then go back against the traffic. The trouble is that, though I have sometimes succeeded in persuading taxi drivers, when we arrive from the airport, to make the *demi-tour*, I have just as often failed. "It's impossible," the cabbie will tell you, when you ask him to do it.

"No, there is an arrow printed on the pavement that advertises the possibility of this maneuver," I will say. (When I'm under stress, my French becomes very abstract.)

"I've been driving a taxi for twenty years, and it doesn't exist," the cabbie will say. Then you either give up or get hot under the collar, and neither approach helps.

If I asked a Paris cabdriver to attempt the *demi-tour* at, say, five in the morning, to pick up a very pregnant-looking woman, he would know that the only reason was that she was in labor, and to the insult of being instructed would come the injury of being asked to ruin his cab.

For the next few weeks I became obsessed by the logic and strategies of the *demi-tour*. What if I couldn't pull it off? The only thing to do was to rehearse, just as we had done in New York in the Lamaze class. So I began walking over to the taxi station at all hours of the day and night, getting in a cab, asking the driver to make the *demi-tour*, and then going, well, someplace or other. Then I walked home. Sometimes the driver made the *demi-tour*, and sometimes he didn't. I was determined to keep practicing, until it felt as natural as breathing.

We still hadn't got to the bottom of the whole *choix du roi* thing. Martha had decided to give in to the obstetrician's insistence that she start swimming, and one day, with Luke, we got into a cab to go to the pool. The taxi driver was wearing a short-sleeved shirt, and had gray hair and a lot of metal teeth. Suddenly he chuckled and said, of Luke, "Why, he speaks so well. Tell me, is it a little sister or a brother?" A sister, we said, and I grimaced and tightened inside as I prepared myself for the response, which, of course, came on cue. "Ah," he said, slapping the steering wheel. *"C'est le choix du roi!"*

I was so fed up that I said, "Please explain it to me." It was an ironic, rhetorical question. But he didn't miss a beat.

"I will be happy to explain it," he said, and he actually pulled over to the curb, near the Crillon Hôtel, so that he could speak in peace. "In Latin countries we have what we call Salic law, which means that only your son can inherit the throne. You Anglo-Saxons, you don't follow Salic law." I let the Anglo-Saxon thing go by. "For your Anglo-Saxon royal families, it doesn't matter if the king has a *nana* or a *mec*." A *nana* is a doll, and a *mec* is a guy. "But you see, a French king, under Salic law, had to consolidate his hold on the throne by having a boy. And he had to have a girl, so that she could be offered in marriage to another king, and in this way the royal possessions would be expanded, since the daughter's son would be a king too. He," he said, gesturing toward Luke in the backseat, "is your strong piece, to be kept in reserve, while she"—he gestured toward Martha's belly—"is your pawn to build your empire. That's why it's the king's choice: first a boy to hold the throne, then a girl to get another. *Tendresse* has nothing to do with it. That is why it is the *choix du roi.*

"It is very odd," he went on expansively, "because in the Hundred Years' War the king of England, as duc de Guyenne, a title he had inherited from his grandfather, was subject to Salic law too. The story of how this worked itself out in the making of the two monarchies is a passionately interesting piece of history. I recommend the series *Les Rois Maudits* [the damned or cursed kings], which is a fascinating study of this history, particularly of the acts of John the Good and what he did as an act of policy to accommodate the Salic principle. The books are by Maurice Druon, of the Académie Française, and I heartily recommend them. Passionately interesting."

We sat in stunned silence.

"Ask him does he do *demi-tours*," said Martha.

"You're wearing stripes?" she asked. I had put on a striped shirt a few minutes before, in the excitement, but I quickly changed it. I put on a suit and tie, in fact—a nice maroon cotton number—thinking that though my New York child had been born with me watching in jeans and a collarless shirt, my French kid ought to see a dad who had a touch more finish.

The drama had begun a few hours earlier, in the middle of the night, and now it was five o'clock and we were on our way to the clinic. At five-thirty, with a baby-sitter for Luke and a suitcase in hand, we were out on the boulevard. I walked to the curb, held my breath, saw that there were cabs at the taxi stand, and, head down, told Martha to wait where she was while I started across the street, preparing to ask a taxi driver to make the *demi-tour,* my moment come at last.

Far down the boulevard, a single cab with a firelight light appeared. Martha stepped out into the street, just as though it were five-thirty in the evening on Sixth Avenue, got her right hand up in that weird New York Nazi taxi salute, and cried, "Taxi!" The guy came skidding to a stop. She got in, and I followed.

"Twenty-four boulevard du Château in Neuilly," I commanded, my voice pitched a little too high (as it also tends to get in French). "Just cross the street and make the *demi-tour,*" I added fairly casually, and docilely, at five-thirty in the morning, he swung the cab over to the taxi lane, on the other side of the street, and did a full U-turn. He flew along the boulevard. I took the hand of my queen.

"You've got him going the wrong way," she whispered.

He was too. I waited a few blocks and then told him that I had made a mistake, could he turn around and go the other way? He shrugged and did.

When we got to the clinic, it was shut tight, no light on at all. The advantages of a big hospital up on Madison Avenue became a little clearer. No one was answering the door, a thing I doubt happens much at Mount Sinai. We banged and cried out, "*Allô!* Is anybody there?" Finally, an incredibly weary-looking *sage-femme*—not our own—wearing sweater and slippers, sighed, let us in, hooked Martha up to an IV, and asked to see our papers. She shuffled through them.

"Where is your blood test for the dossier?" she asked at last.

"The doctor has it," I said. "She'll be here soon."

"That the doctor has it is of no consequence," the nurse said. "If your wife wishes to have an epidural, she must have that paper."

"It's all the way back home," I protested, but of course, nothing doing. It looked as though Martha's epidural, having escaped French syndicalism, was about to be done in by French bureaucracy. Having lived in France long enough to know there was no choice, I found another taxi, rushed all the way home, ran upstairs, tore open the filing cabinet, found the paper, and then took a taxi back, setting some kind of land speed record for trips from central Paris to Neuilly. The *sage-femme* slipped the paper into the dossier, yawned, put the dossier down on a radiator, and nobody ever looked at it or referred to it again.

The labor got complicated, for various reasons—basically the baby at the last moment decided to turn sideways—and Martha's doctor, acting with the quiet sureness that is the other side of Parisian insouciance, did an emergency cesarean. It turned out that behind a small, quaint-looking white door down in the basement there was a bloc—a warren of blindingly white-lit, state-of-the-art operating and recovery rooms. They hadn't shown it to us when we toured the clinic, of course. It seemed very French, the nuclear power plant hidden in the *bocage*.

The baby came out mad, yelling at the top of her lungs. In New York the nurses had snatched the baby and taken him off to be washed behind a big glass nursery window and then had dressed him in prison garb, the same white nightshirt and cap that the hundred other babies in the nursery had on. (The next day there was also an elaborate maximum security procedure of reading off the bracelet numbers of mother and child whenever either one wanted to nurse.) Here, after the *sage-femme* and I had given her a bath, and the *sage-femme* had taped her umbilical remnant, the *safe-femme* turned to me.

"Where are her clothes?" she asked. I said I didn't know, upstairs in the suitcase, I guessed, and she said, "You'd better get them," so I ran up, and came back down to the bloc with the white onesie and a lovely white-and-pink-trimmed baby-style cat suit, which her mother had bought at Bonpoint a few days before. All by myself I carefully dressed the five-minute-old squalling newborn and took her back to her mother, in the recovery room. A day later I would walk the six blocks to the *mairie,* the city hall, of Neuilly-sur-Seine and register her birth. The New York birth certificate had been a fill-in-the-blanks, choose-one-box business, which we had filled in on our way out of the hospital. The French birth certificate was like the first paragraph of a nineteenth-century novel, with the baby's parents' names, their occupations, the years of their births and of their emigration, their residence, and her number, baby number 2365 born in Neuilly in 1999. (It's got a big hospital too.) After that, of course, would come the weeks of exhaustion and 3:00 A.M. feedings, which are remarkably alike from place to place.

But just then, looking at the sleeping mom and the tiny newborn in her arms, I had a genuine moment of what I can only call revelation, religious vision. When people talk about what it is to have a baby, they usually talk about starting over, a clean slate, endless possibility, a new beginning, but I saw that that is

not it at all. A birth is not a rebirth. It's a weighty event. A baby is
an absolute object of nature *and* an absolute subject of civiliza-
tion, screaming in her new Bonpoint jumper. Life is nothing but
an unchanging sea of nature, the same endless and undifferenti-
ating human wave of lust and pain, and is still subject to a set of
tiny cultural articulations and antinomies and dualities and dis-
tinctions and hair-splittings so fine that they produce, in the
end, this single American baby lying in a French nursery in her
own fine new clothes, sipping her sugar bottle. In a telescopic
universe, we choose to see microscopically, and the blessing is
that what we see is not an illusion but what is really there: a sin-
gularity in the cosmos, another baby born in a Paris suburb. The
world is a meaningless place, and we are weird, replicating mam-
mals on its surface, yet the whole purpose of the universe since
it began was, in a way, to produce this baby, who is the tiny end
point of a funnel that goes back to the beginning of time, a sin-
gularity that history was pointing toward from the start. That
history didn't know it was pointing toward Olivia—and, of
course, toward Salome over in the other corner of the nursery
and little François just arrived, not to mention Max and Otto
and possibly even Moe, just now checking in at Mount Sinai—
doesn't change the fact that it was. We didn't know we were
pointing to her either, until she got here. The universe doesn't
need a purpose if life goes on. You sink back and hear the nurse
cooing in French to the mother and child (*"Ah, calme-toi, ma
biche, ma biche,"* she says, "Be calm, my doe, my doe," but which
one is she talking to?) and feel as completely useless as any other
male animal after a birth and, at the same time, somehow serenely
powerful, beyond care or criticism, since you have taken part in
the only really majestic choice we get to make in life, which is to
continue it.

JOANNE HARRIS

The child of a French mother and a British father, Joanne Harris, author of the novel Chocolat, *was raised above a sweetshop in her native Yorkshire. "It was called Shorts . . . My grandparents ran it. At the time, my mother had just come over from France and didn't speak English. And so we lived with my grandparents for some time." Harris's novels (including* Five Quarters of the Orange, *published in 2000) often have recipes woven into the plot. "Most of them are family recipes that I have made up . . . I come from a family where there is a long tradition of cooking and recipes are handed down from various parts of the family— usually down the French side."*

Influenced by magical realism, Chocolat *tells the story of Vianne Rocher who opens a chocolate shop in a French town near Agen. Her enterprise is met by suspicion and outright hostility by the close-minded villagers who suspect her a witch. The villagers are torn between the joyless teaching of the church and the sensuous pleasures of Vianne's chocolate shop. This excerpt describes the village at the time of Vianne's arrival.*

The success of Chocolat, *both the film and the book, allowed Joanne Harris to leave her teaching job at the Leeds Grammar School to write full-time. She lives in Yorkshire with her husband and young daughter.*

from Chocolat

The village is less strange to me now. Its inhabitants too. I am beginning to know faces, names; the first secret skeins of histories twisting together to form the umbilical that will eventually bind us. It is a more complex place than its geography at first suggests, the *rue principale* forking off into a hand-shaped branch of laterals—avenue des Poètes, rue des Francs Bourgeois, ruelle des Frères de la Révolution—someone among the town planners had a fierce republican streak. My own square, place St.-Jérôme, is the culmination of these reaching fingers, the church standing white and proud in an oblong of linden trees, the square of red shingle where the old men play *pétanque* on fine evenings. Behind it, the hill falls away sharply toward that region of narrow streets collectively called Les Marauds. This is Lansquenet's tiny slum, close half-timbered houses staggering down the uneven cobbles toward the Tannes. Even there it is some distance before the houses give way to marshland; some are built on the river itself on platforms of rotting wood, while dozens flank the stone embankment, long fingers of damp reaching toward their small high windows from the sluggish water. In a town like Agen, Les Marauds would attract tourists for its quaintness and rustic decay. But here there are no tourists. The people of Les Marauds are scavengers, living from what they can reclaim from the river. Many of their houses are derelict; elder trees grow from the sagging walls.

I closed La Praline for two hours at lunch, and Anouk and I went walking down toward the river. A couple of skinny children dabbled in the green mud by the waterside; even in February there was a mellow stink of sewage and rot. It was cold but sunny, and Anouk was wearing her red woolen coat and hat, racing along the stones and shouting to Pantoufle, scampering behind her. I have become so accustomed to Pantoufle—and to the rest of the strange menagerie that she trails in her bright wake—that at such times I can almost see him clearly, Pantoufle with his gray-whiskered face and wise eyes, the world suddenly brightening as if by a strange transference I have *become* Anouk, seeing with her eyes, following where she travels. At such times I feel I could die for love of her, my little stranger, my heart swelling dangerously so that the only release is to run too, my red coat flapping around my shoulders like wings, my hair a comet's tail in the patchy blue sky.

A black cat crossed my path, and I stopped to dance around it widdershins and to sing the rhyme,

> *Où va-ti, mistigri?*
> *Passe sans faire de mal ici.*

Anouk joined in, and the cat purred, rolling over into the dust to be stroked. I bent down and saw a tiny old woman watching me curiously from the angle of a house. Black skirt, black coat, gray hair coiled and plaited into a neat, complex bun. Her eyes were sharp and black as a bird's. I nodded to her.

"You're from the *chocolaterie*," she said. Despite her age— which I took to be eighty, maybe more—her voice was brisk and strongly accented with the rough lilt of the Midi.

"Yes, I am." I smiled.

"Armande Voizin," she said. "That's my house over there." She nodded toward one of the river houses, this one in better repair than the rest, freshly whitewashed and with scarlet geraniums in the window boxes. Then, with a smile that worked her apple-doll face into a million wrinkles, she said, "I've seen your shop. Pretty enough, I'll grant you that, but no good to folks like us. Much too fancy." There was no disapproval in her voice as she spoke, but a half-laughing fatalism. "I hear our *m'sieur le curé* already has it in for you," she added maliciously. "I suppose he thinks a chocolate shop is *inappropriate* in his square." She gave me another of those quizzical, mocking glances. "Does he know you're a witch?" she asked.

Witch, witch. It's the wrong word, but I knew what she meant.

"What makes you think that?"

"Oh, its obvious. Takes one to know one, I expect," and she laughed, a sound like violins gone wild. "*M'sieur le curé* doesn't believe in magic," she said. "Tell you the truth, I wouldn't be so sure he even believes in God." There was indulgent contempt in her voice. "He has a lot to learn, that man, even if he has got a degree in theology. And my silly daughter too. You don't get degrees in *life,* do you?" I agreed that you didn't, and inquired whether I knew her daughter.

"I expect so. Caro Clairmont. The most empty-headed piece of foolishness in all of Lansquenet. Talk, talk, talk, and not a particle of sense." She saw my smile and nodded cheerily. "Don't worry, dear, at my age nothing much offends me anymore. And she takes after her father, you know. That's a great consolation." She looked at me quizzically. "You don't get much entertainment around here," she observed. "Especially if you're old." She paused and peered at me again. "But with you I think maybe we're in for a little amusement." Her hand brushed mine like a cool breath. I tried to catch her thoughts, to see if she was making fun of me, but all I felt was humor and kindness.

"It's only a chocolate shop," I said with a smile.

Armande Voizin chuckled. "You really must think I was born yesterday," she observed.

"Really, Madame Voizin—"

"Call me Armande." The black eyes snapped with amusement. "It makes me feel young."

"All right. But I really don't see why—"

"I know what wind you blew in on," said Armande keenly. "I felt it. Mardi Gras, carnival day. Les Marauds is full of carnival people: gypsies, Spaniards, tinkers, *pieds-noirs,* and undesirables. I knew you at once, you and your little girl—what are you calling yourselves this time?"

"Vianne Rocher." I smiled. "And this is Anouk."

"Anouk," repeated Armande softly. "And the little gray friend—my eyes aren't as good as they used to be—what is it? A cat? A squirrel?"

Anouk shook her curly head. "He's a *rabbit*," she said with cheery scorn. "Called Pantoufle."

"Oh, a rabbit. Of course." Armande gave me a sly wink. "You see, I know what wind you blew in on. I've felt it myself once or twice. I may be old, but no one can pull the wool over my eyes. No one at all."

I nodded. "Maybe that's true," I said. "Come over to La Praline one day; I know everyone's favorite. I'll treat you to a big box of yours."

Armande laughed. "Oh, I'm not allowed *chocolate*. Caro and that idiot doctor won't allow it. Or anything else I might enjoy," she added wryly. "First smoking, then alcohol, now this . . . God knows, if I gave up breathing perhaps I might live forever." She gave a snort of laughter, but it had a tired sound, and I saw her raise a hand to her chest in a clutching gesture eerily reminiscent of Joséphine Muscat. "I'm not blaming them, exactly," she said. "It's just their way. Protection—from everything. From life. From death." She gave a grin that was suddenly very *gamine* in spite of the wrinkles.

"I might call in to see you anyway," she said. "If only to annoy the curé."

I pondered her last remark for some time after she disappeared behind the angle of the whitewashed house. Some distance away Anouk was throwing stones onto the mudflats at the riverbank.

The curé. It seemed his name was never far from the lips. For a moment I considered Francis Reynaud.

In a place like Lansquenet it sometimes happens that one person—schoolteacher, café proprietor, or priest—forms the linchpin of the community. That this single individual is the essential core of the machinery that turns lives, like the central pin of a clock mechanism, sending wheels to turn wheels, hammers to strike, needles to point the hour. If the pin slips or is damaged, the clock stops. Lansquenet is like that clock, needles perpetually frozen at a minute to midnight, wheels and cogs turning uselessly behind the bland, blank face. Set a church clock wrong to fool the devil, my mother always told me. But in this case I suspect the devil is not fooled.

Not for a minute.

ERNEST HEMINGWAY
(1898–1961)

"If you are lucky enough to live in Paris as a young man, then wherever you go for the rest of your life, it stays with you, for Paris is a moveable feast," wrote Ernest Hemingway to a friend in 1950. Hemingway came to Paris in the early 1920s with his first wife, Hadley, and their young son Bumby. Their friends included Scott and Zelda Fitzgerald, Gerald and Sara Murphy, Ezra Pound, Ford Maddox Ford, Gertrude Stein, and Sylvia Beach, owner of the bookstore Shakespeare and Company. Collectively, they were the postwar Lost Generation, depicted in Hemingway's The Sun Also Rises.

In Paris, Hemingway's marriage began to unravel. Hadley packed Hemingway's unpublished manuscripts in her suitcase—originals and carbons—to surprise her husband in Lausanne so that he could work during their holiday. She stowed her case on the train and left for a short while. It was gone when she returned and much of Hemingway's early work was lost. Hadley was devastated and, although Hemingway wrote that he forgave her, the pain of that loss is evident in A Moveable Feast, written nearly thirty years later.

The end of the Hemingways' Paris life was his affair with Pauline Pfeiffer, one of Hadley's friends. For a while, Hemingway was torn between Hadley and Pauline—and then he left his wife and young son. At the end of A Moveable Feast (which was written in 1950, but not published until 1964, three years after Hemingway's death) he wrote, "There is never any ending in Paris, and the memory of each person who has lived in it differs from that of any other . . . But this is how Paris was in the early days when we were very poor and very happy."

from **A Moveable Feast**

You got very hungry when you did not eat enough in Paris because all the bakery shops had such good things in the windows and people ate outside at tables on the sidewalk so that you saw and smelled the food. When you had given up journalism and were writing nothing that anyone in America would buy, explaining at home that you were lunching out with someone, the best place to go was the Luxembourg gardens where you saw and smelled nothing to eat all the way from the Place de l'Observatoire to the rue de Vaugirard. There you could always go into the Luxembourg museum and all the paintings were sharpened and clearer and more beautiful if you were belly-empty, hollow-hungry. I learned to understand Cézanne much better and to see truly how he made landscapes when I was hungry. I used to wonder if he were hungry too when he painted; but I thought possibly it was only that he had forgotten to eat. It was one of those unsound but illuminating thoughts you have when you have been sleepless or hungry. Later I thought Cézanne was probably hungry in a different way.

After you came out of the Luxembourg you could walk down the narrow rue Férou to the Place St.-Sulpice and there were still no restaurants, only the quiet square with its benches and trees. There was a fountain with lions, and pigeons walked on the pavement and perched on the statues of the bishops. There was the church and there were shops selling religious objects and vestments on the north side of the square.

From this square you could not go further toward the river without passing shops selling fruits, vegetables, wines, or bakery and pastry shops. But by choosing your way carefully you could work to your right around the grey and white stone church and reach the rue de l'Odéon and turn up to your right toward Sylvia Beach's bookshop and on your way you did not pass too many places where things to eat were sold. The rue de l'Odéon was bare of eating places until you reached the square where there were three restaurants.

By the time you reached 12 rue de l'Odéon your hunger was contained but all of your perceptions were heightened again. The photographs looked different and you saw books that you had never seen before.

"You're too thin, Hemingway," Sylvia would say. "Are you eating enough?"

"Sure."

"What did you eat for lunch?"

My stomach would turn over and I would say, "I'm going home for lunch now."

"At three o'clock?"

"I didn't know it was that late."

"Adrienne said the other night she wanted to have you and Hadley for dinner. We'd ask Fargue. You like Fargue, don't you? Or Larbaud. You like him. I know you like him. Or anyone you really like. Will you speak to Hadley?"

"I know she'd love to come."

"I'll send her a *pneu*. Don't you work so hard now that you don't eat properly."

"I won't."

"Get home now before it's too late for lunch."

"They'll save it."

"Don't eat cold food either. Eat a good hot lunch."

"Did I have any mail?"

"I don't think so. But let me look."

She looked and found a note and looked up happily and then opened a closed door in her desk.

"This came while I was out," she said. It was a letter and it felt as though it had money in it. "Wedderkop," Sylvia said.

"It must be from *Der Querschnitt.* Did you see Wedderkop?"

"No. But he was here with George. He'll see you. Don't worry. Perhaps he wanted to pay you first."

"It's six hundred francs. He says there will be more."

"I'm awfully glad you reminded me to look. Dear Mr. Awfully Nice."

"It's damned funny that Germany is the only place I can sell anything. To him and the *Frankfurter Zeitung.*"

"Isn't it? But don't you worry ever. You can sell stories to Ford," she teased me.

"Thirty francs a page. Say one story every three months in *the transatlantic.* Story five pages long made one hundred and fifty francs a quarter. Six hundred francs a year."

"But, Hemingway, don't worry about what they bring now. The point is that you can write them."

"I know. I can write them. But nobody will buy them. There is no money coming in since I quit journalism."

"They will sell. Look. You have the money for one right there."

"I'm sorry, Sylvia. Forgive me for speaking about it."

"Forgive you for what? Always talk about it or about anything. Don't you know all writers ever talk about is their troubles? But promise me you won't worry and that you'll eat enough."

"I promise."

"Then get home now and have lunch."

Outside on the rue de l'Odéon I was disgusted with myself for having complained about things. I was doing what I did of my own free will and I was doing it stupidly. I should have bought a large piece of bread and eaten it instead of skipping a meal. I could taste the brown lovely crust. But it is dry in your mouth without something to drink. You God damn complainer. You dirty phony saint and martyr, I said to myself. You quit journalism of your own accord. You have credit and Sylvia would have loaned you money. She has plenty of times. Sure. And then the next thing you would be compromising on something else. Hunger is healthy and the pictures do look better when you are hungry. Eating is wonderful too and do you know where you are going to eat right now?

Lipp's is where you are going to eat and drink too.

It was a quick walk to Lipp's and every place I passed that my stomach noticed as quickly as my eyes or my nose made the walk an added pleasure. There were few people in the *brasserie* and when I sat down on the bench against the wall with the mirror in back and a table in front and the waiter asked if I wanted beer I asked for a *distingué,* the big glass mug that held a liter, and for potato salad.

The beer was very cold and wonderful to drink. The *pommes à l'huile* were firm and marinated and the olive oil delicious. I ground black pepper over the potatoes and moistened the bread in the olive oil. After the first heavy draft of beer I drank and ate very slowly. When the *pommes à l'huile* were gone I ordered another serving and a *cervelas.* This was a sausage like a heavy, wide frankfurter split in two and covered with a special mustard sauce.

I mopped up all the oil and all of the sauce with bread and drank the beer slowly until it began to lose its coldness and then I finished it and ordered a *demi* and watched it drawn. It seemed colder than the *distingué* and I drank half of it.

WASHINGTON IRVING

(1783–1859)

The youngest of eight children, Washington Irving was the indulged favorite of a well-to-do New York family who named him after the first president. While his brothers were encouraged to pursue careers in law and commerce, Washington led the life of an intellectual. His family thought his health delicate and he was dispatched to Europe to recover. Although identified with the Catskill Mountains of New York, Irving spent much of his adulthood in Europe.

Irving was a restless traveler, often meeting up with members of his large extended family in different parts of the Continent. His Tales of a Traveller, *from which this excerpt is taken, was published in 1824. Irving made no claim that his stories were original. In most cases they were a retelling of an anecdote that he heard on the road. He wrote, "I have read somewhat, heard and seen more, and dreamt more than all. My brain is filled, therefore, with all kinds of odds and ends. In travelling, these heterogeneous matters have become shaken up in my mind, as the articles are apt to be in an ill-packed travelling trunk; so that when I attempt to draw forth a fact, I cannot determine whether I have heard, or dreamt it; and I am always at a loss to know how much to believe of my own stories." Washington Irving's travel writing was enormously popular among both Americans and Europeans.*

In old age, Irving retired to Sunnyside, his home in Tarrytown, New York, on the banks of the Hudson River. Of Irving's stories, one in particular has enduring appeal: The Legend of Sleepy Hollow, *the story of Katrina Van Tassel and her two suitors, the schoolmaster Ichabod Crane and Brom Bones, and the Headless Horseman.*

The Adventure of My Uncle

Many years since, some time before the French revolution, my uncle passed several months at Paris. The English and French were on better terms, in those days, than at present, and mingled cordially in society. The English went abroad to spend money then, and the French were always ready to help them: they go abroad to save money at present, and that they can do without French assistance. Perhaps the travelling English were fewer and choicer than at present, when the whole nation has broke loose, and inundated the continent. At any rate, they circulated more readily and currently in foreign society, and my uncle, during his residence at Paris, made many very intimate acquaintances among the French noblesse.

Some time afterwards, he was making a journey in the winter time, in that part of Normandy called the Pays de Caux, when, as evening was closing in, he perceived the turrets of an ancient chateau rising out of the trees of its walled park, each turret with its high conical roof of grey slate, like a candle with an extinguisher on it.

"To whom does that chateau belong, friend?" cried my uncle to a meagre but fiery postillion, who, with tremendous jack boots and cocked hat, was floundering on before him.

"To Monseigneur the Marquis de ———," said the postillion, touching his hat, partly out of respect to my uncle, and partly out of reverence to the noble name pronounced. My uncle recollected the Marquis for a particular friend in Paris, who had often expressed a wish to see him at his paternal chateau. My uncle was an old traveller, one who knew how to turn things to account. He revolved for a few moments in his mind how agreeable it would be to his friend the Marquis to be surprised in this sociable way by a pop visit; and how much more agreeable to himself to get into snug quarters in a chateau, and have a relish of the Marquis's well known kitchen, and a smack of his superior champagne and burgundy; rather than put up with the miserable lodgement, and miserable fare of a provincial inn. In a few minutes, therefore, the meagre postillion was cracking his whip like a very devil, or like a true Frenchman, up the long straight avenue that led to the chateau.

You have no doubt all seen French chateaus, as every body travels in France now adays. This was one of the oldest; standing naked and alone, in the midst of a desert of gravel walks and cold stone terraces; with a cold looking formal garden, cut into angles and rhomboids; and a cold leafless park, divided geometrically by straight alleys; and two or three cold looking noseless statues; and fountains spouting cold water enough to make one's teeth chatter. At least, such was the feeling they imparted on the wintry day of my uncle's visit; though, in hot summer weather, I'll warrant there was glare enough to scorch one's eyes out.

The smacking of the postillion's whip, which grew more and more intense the nearer they approached, frightened a flight of pigeons out of the dove cote, and rooks out of the roofs; and finally a crew of servants out of the chateau, with the Marquis at their head. He was enchanted to see my uncle; for his chateau, like the house of our worthy host, had not many more guests at the time than it could accommodate. So he kissed my uncle on each cheek, after the French fashion, and ushered him into the castle.

The Marquis did the honours of the house with the urbanity of his country. In fact, he was proud of his old family chateau; for part of it was extremely old. There was a tower and chapel which had been built almost before the memory of man; but the rest was more modern; the castle having been nearly demolished during the wars of the League. The Marquis dwelt upon this event with great satisfaction, and seemed really to entertain a grateful feeling towards Henry the Fourth, for having thought

his paternal mansion worth battering down. He had many sto-
ries to tell of the prowess of his ancestors, and several skull caps,
helmets and cross bows, and divers huge boots and buff jerkins,
to show, which had been worn by the Leaguers. Above all, there
was a two handled sword, which he could hardly wield; but
which he displayed as a proof that there had been giants in his
family.

In truth, he was but a small descendant from such great war-
riors. When you looked at their bluff visages and brawny limbs,
as depicted in their portraits, and then at the little Marquis, with
his spindle shanks, and his sallow lanthorn visage, flanked with a
pair of powdered ear locks, or *ailes de pigeon,* that seemed ready
to fly away with it; you could hardly believe him to be of the
same race. But when you looked at the eyes that sparkled out
like a beetle's from each side of his hooked nose, you saw at
once that he inherited all the fiery spirit of his forefathers. In
fact, a Frenchman's spirit never exhales, however his body may
dwindle. It rather rarifies, and grows more inflammable, as the
earthy particles diminish; and I have seen valour enough in a lit-
tle fiery hearted French dwarf, to have furnished out a tolerable
giant.

When once the Marquis, as he was wont, put on one of the
old helmets stuck up in his hall; though his head no more filled
it than a dry pea its pease cod; yet his eyes flashed from the bot-
tom of the iron cavern with the brilliancy of carbuncles; and
when he poised the ponderous two handled sword of his ances-
tors, you would have thought you saw the doughty little David
wielding the sword of Goliath, which was unto him like a
weaver's beam.

However, gentlemen, I am dwelling too long on this descrip-
tion of the Marquis and his chateau; but you must excuse me; he
was an old friend of my uncle's, and whenever my uncle told the
story, he was always fond of talking a great deal about his host.—
Poor little Marquis! He was one of that handful of gallant
courtiers, who made such a devoted, but hopeless stand in the
cause of their sovereign, in the chateau of the Tuilleries, against

the irruption of the mob, on the sad tenth of August. He displayed the valour of a preux French chevalier to the last; flourished feebly his little court sword with a sa-sa! in face of a whole legion of *sans culottes;* but was pinned to the wall like a butterfly, by the pike of a poissarde, and his heroic soul was borne up to heaven on his *ailes de pigeon.*

But all this has nothing to do with my story; to the point then:—When the hour arrived for retiring for the night, my uncle was shown to his room, in a venerable old tower. It was the oldest part of the chateau, and had in ancient times been the Donjon or strong hold; of course the chamber was none of the best. The Marquis had put him there, however, because he knew him to be a traveller of taste, and fond of antiquities; and also because the better apartments were already occupied. Indeed, he perfectly reconciled my uncle to his quarters by mentioning the great personages who had once inhabited them, all of whom were in some way or other connected with the family. If you would take his word for it, John Baliol, or as he called him Jean de Bailleul, had died of chagrin in this very chamber on hearing of the success of his rival, Robert the Bruce, at the battle of Bannockburn; and when he added that the Duke de Guise had slept in it, my uncle was fain to felicitate himself upon being honoured with such distinguished quarters.

The night was shrewd and windy, and the chamber none of the warmest. An old long faced, long bodied servant in quaint livery, who attended upon my uncle, threw down an armful of wood beside the fire place, gave a queer look about the room, and then wished him *bon repos,* with a grimace and a shrug that would have been suspicious from any other than an old French servant. The chamber had indeed a wild crazy look, enough to strike any one who had read romances with apprehension and foreboding. The windows were high and narrow, and had once been loop holes, but had been rudely enlarged, as well as the extreme thickness of the walls would permit; and the ill fitted casements rattled to every breeze. You would have thought, on a windy night, some of the old Leaguers were tramping and clanking about the apartment in their huge boots and rattling spurs. A door which stood ajar, and like a true French door would stand ajar, in spite of every reason and effort to the contrary, opened upon a long dark corridor, that led the Lord knows whither, and seemed just made for ghosts to air themselves in, when they turned out of their graves at midnight. The wind would spring up into a hoarse murmur through this passage, and creak the door to and fro, as if some dubious ghost were balancing in its mind whether to come in or not. In a word, it was precisely the kind of comfortless apartment that a ghost, if ghost there were in the chateau, would single out for its favourite lounge.

My uncle, however, though a man accustomed to meet with strange adventures, apprehended none at the time. He made several attempts to shut the door, but in vain. Not that he apprehended any thing, for he was too old a traveller to be daunted by a wild looking apartment; but the night, as I have said, was cold and gusty, and the wind howled about the old turret, pretty much as it does round this old mansion at this moment; and the breeze from the long dark corridor came in as damp and chilly as if from a dungeon. My uncle, therefore, since he could not close the door threw a quantity of wood on the fire, which soon sent up a flame in the great wide mouthed chimney that illumined the whole chamber, and made the shadow of the tongs, on the opposite wall, look like a long legged giant. My uncle now clambered on top of the half score of mattresses which form a French bed, and which stood in a deep recess; then tucking himself snugly in, and burying himself up to the chin in the bed clothes, he lay looking at the fire, and listening to the wind, and thinking how knowingly he had come over to his friend the Marquis for a night's lodging: and so he fell asleep.

He had not taken above half of his first nap, when he was awakened by the clock of the chateau, in the turret over his chamber, which struck midnight. It was just such an old clock as ghosts are fond of. It had a deep, dismal tone, and struck so slowly and tediously that my uncle thought it would never have done. He counted and counted till he was confident he counted thirteen, and then it stopped.

The fire had burnt low, and the blaze of the last faggot was almost expiring, burning in small blue flames, which now and then lengthened up into little white gleams. My uncle lay with his eyes half closed, and his nightcap drawn almost down to his nose. His fancy was already wandering, and began to mingle up the present scene with the crater of Vesuvius, the French opera, the Coliseum at Rome, Dolly's chop house in London, and all the farrago of noted places with which the brain of a traveller is crammed—in a word, he was just falling asleep.

Suddenly he was roused by the sound of footsteps slowly pacing along the corridor. My uncle, as I have often heard him say himself, was a man not easily frightened; so he lay quiet, supposing this some other guest, or some servant on his way to bed. The footsteps, however, approached the door; the door gently opened; whether of its own accord, or whether pushed open, my uncle could not distinguish:—a figure all in white glided in. It was a female, tall and stately, and of a commanding air. Her dress was of an ancient fashion, ample in volume and sweeping the floor. She walked up to the fire place without regarding my uncle; who raised his nightcap with one hand, and stared earnestly at her. She remained for some time standing by the fire, which flashing up at intervals cast blue and white gleams of light that enabled my uncle to remark her appearance minutely.

Her face was ghastly pale, and perhaps rendered still more so by the bluish light of the fire. It possessed beauty, but its beauty was saddened by care and anxiety. There was the look of one accustomed to trouble, but of one whom trouble could not cast down nor subdue; for there was still the predominating air of proud, unconquerable resolution. Such at least was the opinion formed by my uncle, and he considered himself a great physiognomist.

The figure remained, as I said, for some time by the fire, putting out first one hand, then the other, then each foot alternately, as if warming itself; for your ghosts, if ghost it really was, are apt to be cold. My uncle furthermore remarked that it wore high heeled shoes, after an ancient fashion, with paste or diamond buckles, that sparkled as though they were alive. At length the figure turned gently round, casting a glassy look about the apartment, which, as it passed over my uncle, made his blood run cold, and chilled the very marrow in his bones. It then stretched its arms towards heaven, clasped its hands, and wringing them in a supplicating manner, glided slowly out of the room.

My uncle lay for some time meditating on this visitation, for (as he remarked when he told me the story) though a man of firmness, he was also a man of reflection, and did not reject a thing because it was out of the regular course of events. However, being as I have before said, a great traveller and accustomed to strange adventures, he drew his nightcap resolutely over his eyes, turned his back to the door, hoisted the bed clothes high over his shoulders, and gradually fell asleep.

How long he slept he could not say, when he was awakened by the voice of some one at his bed side. He turned round and beheld the old French servant, with his ear locks in tight buckles on each side of a long, lanthorn face, on which habit had deeply wrinkled an everlasting smile. He made a thousand grimaces and asked a thousand pardons for disturbing Monsieur, but the morning was considerably advanced. While my uncle was dressing, he called vaguely to mind the visitor of the preceding night. He asked the ancient domestic what lady was in the habit of rambling about this part of the chateau at night. The old valet shrugged his shoulders as high as his head, laid one hand on his bosom, threw open the other with every finger extended; made a most whimsical grimace, which he meant to be complimentary, and replied, that it was not for him to know any thing of *les bonnes fortunes* of Monsieur.

My uncle saw there was nothing satisfactory to be learnt in this quarter.—After breakfast he was walking with the Marquis through the modern apartments of the chateau; sliding over the

well waxed floors of silken saloons, amidst furniture rich in gild-
ing and brocade; until they came to a long picture gallery, con-
taining many portraits, some in oil and some in chalks.

Here was an ample field for the eloquence of his host, who
had all the family pride of a nobleman of the *ancien regime.* There
was not a grand name in Normandy, and hardly one in France,
which was not, in some way or other, connected with his house.
My uncle stood listening with inward impatience, resting some-
times on one leg, sometimes on the other, as the little Marquis
descanted, with his usual fire and vivacity, on the achievements
of his ancestors, whose portraits hung along the wall; from the
martial deeds of the stern warriors in steel, to the gallantries and
intrigues of the blue eyed gentlemen, with fair smiling faces,
powdered ear locks, laced ruffles, and pink and blue silk coats
and breeches; not forgetting the conquests of the lovely shep-
herdesses, with hoop petticoats and waists no thicker than an
hour glass, who appeared ruling over their sheep and their
swains with dainty crooks decorated with fluttering ribbands.

In the midst of his friend's discourse my uncle was startled on
beholding a full length portrait, the very counterpart of his visi-
tor of the preceding night.

"Methinks," said he, pointing to it, "I have seen the original
of this portrait."

"Pardonnez moi," replied the Marquis politely, "that can
hardly be, as the lady has been dead more than a hundred years.
That was the beautiful Duchess de Longueville, who figured
during the minority of Louis the Fourteenth."

"And was there any thing remarkable in her history?"

Never was question more unlucky. The little Marquis imme-
diately threw himself into the attitude of a man about to tell a
long story. In fact, my uncle had pulled upon himself the whole
history of the civil war of the Fronde, in which the beautiful
Duchess had played so distinguished a part. Turenne, Coligni,
Mazarin, were called up from their graves to grace his narration;
nor were the affairs of the Barricadoes, nor the chivalry of the
Port Cocheres forgotten. My uncle began to wish himself a thou-

sand leagues off from the Marquis and his merciless memory, when suddenly the little man's recollections took a more interesting turn. He was relating the imprisonment of the Duke de Longueville, with the Princes Condé and Conti, in the chateau of Vincennes, and the ineffectual efforts of the Duchess to rouse the sturdy Normans to their rescue. He had come to that part where she was invested by the royal forces in the Castle of Dieppe.

"The spirit of the Duchess," proceeded the Marquis, "rose with her trials. It was astonishing to see so delicate and beautiful a being buffet so resolutely with hardships. She determined on a desperate means of escape. You may have seen the chateau in which she was mewed up; an old ragged wart of an edifice, standing on the knuckle of a hill, just above the rusty little town of Dieppe. One dark unruly night, she issued secretly out of a small postern gate of the castle, which the enemy had neglected to guard. The postern gate is there to this very day; opening upon a narrow bridge over a deep fosse between the castle and the brow of the hill. She was followed by her female attendants, a few domestics, and some gallant cavaliers who still remained faithful to her fortunes. Her object was to gain a small port about two leagues distant, where she had privately provided a vessel for her escape in case of emergency.

"The little band of fugitives were obliged to perform the distance on foot. When they arrived at the port the wind was high and stormy, the tide contrary, the vessel anchored far off in the road, and no means of getting on board, but by a fishing shallop which lay tossing like a cockle shell on the edge of the surf. The Duchess determined to risk the attempt. The seamen endeavoured to dissuade her, but the imminence of her danger on shore, and the magnanimity of her spirit urged her on. She had to be borne to the shallop in the arms of a mariner. Such was the violence of the wind and waves, that he faltered, lost his foothold, and let his precious burthen fall into the sea.

"The Duchess was nearly drowned; but partly through her own struggles, partly by the exertions of the seamen, she got to land. As soon as she had a little recovered strength, she insisted on renewing the attempt. The storm, however, had by this time become so violent as to set all efforts at defiance. To delay, was to be discovered and taken prisoner. As the only resource left, she procured horses; mounted with her female attendants *en croupe* behind the gallant gentlemen who accompanied her; and scoured the country to seek some temporary asylum.

"While the Duchess," continued the Marquis, laying his forefinger on my uncle's breast to arouse his flagging attention, "while the Duchess, poor lady, was wandering amid the tempest in this disconsolate manner, she arrived at this chateau. Her approach caused some uneasiness; for the clattering of a troop of horses, at dead of night, up the avenue of a lonely chateau, in those unsettled times, and in a troubled part of the country, was enough to occasion alarm.

"A tall, broad shouldered chasseur, armed to the teeth, galloped ahead, and announced the name of the visitor. All uneasiness was dispelled. The household turned out with flambeaux to receive her, and never did torches gleam on a more weather beaten, travel stained band than came tramping into the court. Such pale, careworn faces, such bedraggled dresses, as the poor Duchess and her females presented, each seated behind her cavalier; while half drenched, half drowsy pages and attendants seemed ready to fall from their horses with sleep and fatigue.

"The Duchess was received with a hearty welcome by my ancestor. She was ushered into the Hall of the chateau, and the fires soon crackled and blazed to cheer herself and her train; and every spit and stewpan was put in requisition to prepare ample refreshments for the wayfarers.

"She had a right to our hospitalities," continued the little Marquis, drawing himself up with a slight degree of stateliness, "for she was related to our family. I'll tell you how it was: Her father, Henry de Bourbon, Prince of Condé"——

"But did the Duchess pass the night in the chateau?" said my uncle rather abruptly, terrified at the idea of getting involved in one of the Marquis's genealogical discussions.

"Oh, as to the Duchess, she was put into the very apartment you occupied last night; which, at that time, was a kind of state apartment. Her followers were quartered in the chambers opening upon the neighbouring corridor, and her favourite page slept in an adjoining closet. Up and down the corridor walked the great chasseur, who had announced her arrival, and who acted as a kind of sentinel or guard. He was a dark, stern, powerful looking fellow, and as the light of a lamp in the corridor fell upon his deeply marked face and sinewy form, he seemed capable of defending the castle with his single arm.

"It was a rough, rude night; about this time of the year.—*Apropos*—now I think of it, last night was the anniversary of her visit. I may well remember the precise date, for it was a night not to be forgotten by our house. There is a singular tradition concerning it in our family." Here the Marquis hesitated, and a cloud seemed to gather about his bushy eyebrows. "There is a tradition—that a strange occurrence took place that night—a strange, mysterious, inexplicable occurrence."

Here he checked himself and paused.

"Did it relate to that Lady?" inquired my uncle, eagerly.

"It was past the hour of midnight," resumed the Marquis—"when the whole chateau———"

Here he paused again—my uncle made a movement of anxious curiosity.

"Excuse me," said the Marquis—a slight blush streaking his sallow visage. "There are some circumstances connected with our family history which I do not like to relate. That was a rude period. A time of great crimes among great men: for you know high blood, when it runs wrong, will not run tamely like blood of the *canaille*—poor lady!—But I have a little family pride, that—excuse me—we will change the subject if you please."—

My uncle's curiosity was piqued. The pompous and magnificent introduction had led him to expect something wonderful in the story to which it served as a kind of avenue. He had no idea of being cheated out of it by a sudden fit of unreasonable squeamishness. Besides, being a traveller, in quest of information, he considered it his duty to inquire into every thing.

The Marquis, however, evaded every question.

"Well," said my uncle, a little petulantly, "whatever you may think of it, I saw that lady last night."

The Marquis stepped back and gazed at him with surprise.

"She paid me a visit in my bed chamber."

The Marquis pulled out his snuff box with a shrug and a smile; taking this no doubt for an awkward piece of English pleasantry, which politeness required him to be charmed with. My uncle went on gravely, however, and related the whole circumstance. The Marquis heard him through with profound attention, holding his snuff box unopened in his hand. When the story was finished he tapped on the lid of his box deliberately; took a long sonorous pinch of snuff—

"Bah!" said the Marquis, and walked towards the other end of the gallery.——

Here the narrator paused. The company waited for some time for him to resume his narration; but he continued silent.

"Well," said the inquisitive gentleman, "and what did your uncle say then?"

"Nothing," replied the other.

"And what did the Marquis say further?"

"Nothing."

"And is that all?"

"That is all," said the narrator, filling a glass of wine.

"I surmise," said the shrewd old gentleman with the waggish nose—"I surmise the ghost must have been the old housekeeper walking her rounds to see that all was right."

"Bah!" said the narrator, "my uncle was too much accustomed to strange sights not to know a ghost from a housekeeper!"

There was a murmur round the table half of merriment half of disappointment. I was inclined to think the old gentleman had really an afterpart of his story in reserve; but he sipped his wine and said nothing more; and there was an odd expression about his dilapidated countenance which left me in doubt whether he were in drollery or earnest.

"Egad," said the knowing gentleman with the flexible nose, "this story of your uncle puts me in mind of one that used to be told of an aunt of mine, by the mother's side; though I don't know that it will bear a comparison; as the good lady was not so prone to meet with strange adventures. But at any rate, you shall have it."

HENRY JAMES
(1843–1916)

*Born in New York City, Henry James went to Europe for the first time
as an infant. He claimed that his earliest memory—from the age two—
was the Napoleonic column of the Place Vendôme in Paris. In 1845 the
James family returned to New York, only to decamp for Europe again in
1855 for three years when Henry James's father declared that America
could not provide a "sensuous education" for his four sons (including
author and philosopher William, the eldest) and daughter Alice. The
family returned to America in 1858, but Europe had made an indelible
impression on Henry and it would be his home for most of his adult life.*

*Henry James wrote travel books, novels, short stories and plays popu-
lated with American characters who are traveling abroad. Probably the
most famous portrayal of nouveau riche Americans on the Grand Tour is*
Daisy Miller *(1879), an unsophisticated girl from Schenectady who is
traveling with her mother. The novel's theme—the confrontation of
American manners and European sensibilities—was repeated often in
James's work including* The American, The Europeans, *and* The
Portrait of a Lady.

*James's friendship with Edith Wharton was the mainstay of his later
years. They met in 1903 and together enjoyed motoring trips through
New England's Berkshire Mountains (on James's first visit to America in
over twenty years) and throughout Europe. Although Wharton was ini-
tially wary of James (critics often compared her work to his), she called
their relationship "the pride and honour of my life." Henry James died
in England in 1916, a year after he became a British citizen.*

Rheims

It was a very little tour, but the charm of the three or four old towns and monuments that it embraced, the beauty of the brilliant October, the pleasure of reminding one's self how much of the interest, strength and dignity of France is to be found outside of that huge pretentious caravansary called Paris (a reminder often needed), these things deserve to be noted. I went down to Rheims to see the famous cathedral, and to reach Rheims I travelled through the early morning hours along the charming valley of the Marne. The Marne is a pretty little green river, the vegetation upon whose banks, otherwise unadorned, had begun to blush with the early frosts in a manner that suggested the autumnal tints of American scenery. The trees and bushes were scarlet and orange; the light was splendid and a trifle harsh; I could have fancied myself immersed in an American "fall," if at intervals some gray old large-towered church had not lifted a sculptured front above a railway station, to dispel the fond illusion. One of these church-fronts (I saw it only from the train) is particularly impressive; the little cathedral of Meaux, of which the great Bossuet was bishop, and along whose frigid nave he set his eloquence rolling with an impetus which it has not wholly lost to this day. It was entertaining, moreover, to enter the country of champagne; for Rheims is in the ancient province whose later fame is syllabled the world over in popping corks. A land of vineyards is not usually accounted sketchable; but the country about Epernay seemed to me to have a charm of its own. It stretched away in soft undulations that were pricked all over with little stakes muffled in leaves. The effect at a distance was that of vast surfaces, long, subdued billows, of pincushion; and yet it was very pretty. The deep blue sky was over the scene; the undulations were half in sun and half in shade; and here and there, among their myriad bristles, were groups of vintagers, who, though they are in reality, doubtless, a prosaic and mercenary body of labourers, yet assumed, to a fancy that glanced at them in the cursory manner permitted by the passage of the train, the appearance of joyous and disinterested votaries of Bacchus. The blouses of the men, the white caps of the women, were gleaming in the sunshine; they moved about crookedly among the tiny vine-poles. I thought them full of a charming suggestiveness. Of all the delightful gifts of France to the world, this was one of the most agreeable—the keen, living liquid in which the finest flower of sociability is usually dipped. It came from these sunny places; this little maze of curling-sticks supplied the world with half the world's gaiety. I call it little only in relation to the immense number of bottles with gilded necks in which this gaiety is annually stored up. The acreage of the champagne seemed to me, in fact, large; the bristling slopes went rolling away to new horizons in a manner that was positively reassuring. Making the handsomest allowance for the wine manufactured from baser elements, it was apparent that this big corner of a province represents a very large number of bottles.

As you draw near to Rheims the vineyards become sparser, and finally disappear, a fact not to be regretted, for there is something incongruous in the juxtaposition of champagne and gothic architecture. It may be said, too, that for the proper appreciation of a structure like the cathedral of Rheims you have need of all your head. As, after my arrival, I sat in my window at the inn, gazing up at the great façade, I found something dizzying in the mere climbing and soaring of one's astonished vision; and later, when I came to wander about in the upper regions of the church, and to peep down through the rugged lacework of the towers at the little streets and the small spots of public places, I found myself musing upon the beauty of soberness. My window at the Lion d'Or was like a proscenium-box at the play; to admire the cathedral at my leisure I had only to perch myself in the casement with a good opera-glass. I sat there for a long time watching the great architectural drama. A drama I may call it, for no church-front that I have seen is more animated, more richly figured. The density of the sculptures, the immense scale of the images, detract, perhaps, at first, in a certain sense, from the impressiveness of the cathedral of Rheims; the absence of large surfaces, of ascending lines, deceives you as to the elevation of the front, and the dimensions of some of the upper statues bring them unduly near the eye. But little by little you perceive that this great figured and storied screen has a mass proportionate to its detail, and that it is the grandest part of a structure which, as a whole, is one of the noblest works of man's hands. Most people remember to have seen some print or some photograph of this heavily-charged façade of Rheims, which is usually put forward as the great example of the union of the purity and the possible richness of gothic. I must first have seen some such print in my earliest years, for I have always thought of Rheims as the typical gothic cathedral. I had vague associations with it; it seemed to me that I had already stood there in the little over-whelmed *place.* One's literary associations with Rheims are indeed very vivid and impressive; they begin with the picture of the steel-clad Maid passing under the deeply-sculptured portal with a banner in her hand which she has no need to lower, and while she stands amid the incense and the chants, the glitter of arms and the glow of coloured lights, asking leave of the young king whom she has crowned to turn away and tend her flocks. And after that there is the sense of all the kings of France having travelled down to Rheims in their splendour to be consecrated; the great groups on the front of the church must have looked down on groups almost as stately—groups full of colour and movement—assembled in the square. (The square of Rheims, it must be confessed, is rather shabby. It is singular that the august ceremony of the *sacre* should not have left its mark upon the disposition of the houses, should not have kept them at a respectful distance. Louis XIV, smoothing his plumage before he entered the church, can

hardly have had space to swing the train of his coronation-robe.)
But when in driving into the town I reached the small precinct,
such as it is, and saw the cathedral lift its spireless towers above
the long rows of its carven saints, the huge wheel of its window,
the three great caverns of its portals, with the high acute pedi-
ments above each arch, and the sides abutting outward like the
beginning of a pyramid; when I looked at all this I felt that I had
carried it in my mind from my earliest years, and that the stately
vision had been implanted there by some forgotten glimpse of an
old-fashioned water-colour sketch, in which the sky was washed
in with expressive splashes, the remoter parts of the church tinted
with a fascinating blueness, and the foundations represented as
encumbered with little gabled and cross-timbered houses, inhab-
ited by women in red petticoats and curious caps.

I shall not attempt any regular enumeration of the great
details of the façade of Rheims; I cannot profess even to have
fully apprehended them. They are a glorious company, and here
and there, on its high-hung pedestal, one of the figures detaches
itself with peculiar effectiveness. Over the central portal sits the
Virgin Mary, meekly submitting her head to the ponderous
crown which her Son prepares to place upon it. The attitude and
movement of Christ are full of a kind of splendid politeness.
The three great doorways are in themselves a museum of imagery,
disposed in each case in five close tiers, the statues in each of the
tiers packed perpendicularly against their comrades. The effect
of these great hollowed and chiselled recesses is extremely strik-
ing; they are a proper vestibule to the dusky richness of the inte-
rior. The cathedral of Rheims, more fortunate than many of its
companions, appears not to have suffered from the iconoclasts of
the Revolution; I noticed no absent heads nor broken noses. It is
very true that these members may have had adventures to which
they do not, as it were, allude. But, like many of its companions,
it is so pressed upon by neighbouring houses that it is not easy to
get a general view of the sides and the rear. You may walk round
it, and note your walk as a long one; you may observe that the

choir of the church travels back almost into another quarter of the city; you may see the far-spreading mass lose itself for a while in parasitic obstructions, and then emerge again with all its buttresses flying; but you miss that wide margin of space and light which should enable it to present itself as a consistent picture. Pictures have their frames, and poems have their margins; a great work of art, such as a gothic cathedral, should at least have elbow-room. You may, however, stroll beneath the walls of Rheims, along a narrow, dark street, and look up at the mighty structure and see its higher parts foreshortened into all kinds of delusive proportions. There is a grand entertainment in the view of the church which you obtain from the farthermost point to which you may recede from it in the rear, keeping it still within sight. I have never seen a cathedral so magnificently buttressed. The buttresses of Rheims are all double; they have a tremendous spring, and are supported upon pedestals surmounted by immense crocketed canopies containing statues of wide-winged angels. A great balustrade of gothic arches connects these canopies one with another, and along this balustrade are perched strange figures of sitting beasts, unicorns and mermaids, griffins and monstrous owls. Huge, terrible gargoyles hang far over into the street, and doubtless some of them have a detail which I afterwards noticed at Laon. The gargoyle represents a grotesque beast—a creature partaking at once of the shape of a bird, a fish, and a quadruped. At Laon, on either side of the main entrance, a long-bellied monster cranes forth into the air with the head of a hippopotamus; and under its belly crouches a little man, hardly less grotesque, making up a rueful grimace and playing some ineffectual trick upon his terrible companion. One of these little figures has plunged a sword, up to the hilt, into the belly of the monster above him, so that when he draws it forth there will be a leak in the great stone gutter; another has suspended himself to a rope that is knotted round the neck of the gargoyle, and is trying in the same manner to interrupt its functions by pulling the cord as tight as possible. There was sure to be a spirit of life in an architectural conception that could range from the combination of clustering towers and opposing fronts to this infinitely minute play of humour.

There is no great play of humour in the interior of Rheims, but there is a great deal of beauty and solemnity. This interior is a spectacle that excites the sensibility, as our forefathers used to say; but it is not an easy matter to describe. It is no description of it to say that it is four hundred and sixty-six feet in length, and that the roof is one hundred and twenty-four feet above the pavement; nor is there any very vivid portraiture in the statement that if there is no coloured glass in the lower windows, there is, *per contra,* a great deal of the most gorgeous and most ancient in the upper ones. The long sweep of the nave, from the threshold to the point where the coloured light-shafts of the choir lose themselves in the gray distance, is a triumph of perpendicular perspective. The white light in the lower part of Rheims really contributes to the picturesqueness of the interior. It makes the gloom above look richer still, and throws that part of the roof which rests upon the gigantic piers of the transepts into mysterious remoteness. I wandered about for a long time; I sat first in one place and then in another; I attached myself to that most fascinating part of every great church, the angle at which the nave and transept divide. It was the better to observe this interesting point, I think, that I passed into the side gate of the choir—the gate that stood ajar in the tall gilded railing. I sat down on a stool near the threshold; I leaned back against the side of one of the stalls; the church was empty, and I lost myself in the large perfection of the place. I lost myself, but the beadle found me; he stood before me, and with a silent, imperious gesture, motioned me to depart. I risked an argumentative glance, whereupon he signified his displeasure, repeated his gesture, and pointed to an old gentleman with a red cape, who had come into the choir softly, without my seeing him, and had seated himself in one of the stalls. This old gentleman seemed plunged in pious thoughts; I was not, after all, very near him, and he did not look as if I disturbed him. A canon is at any time, I imagine, a more merciful man than a beadle. But of course I obeyed the beadle, and eliminated myself from this peculiarly sacred precinct. I found another chair, and I fell to admiring the cathedral again. But this time I think it was with a difference—a difference which may serve as an excuse for the triviality of my anecdote. Sundry other old gentlemen in red capes emerged from the sacristy and went into the choir; presently, when there were half a dozen, they began to chant, and I perceived that the impending vespers had been the reason of my expulsion. This was highly proper, and I forgave the beadle; but I was not so happy as before, for my thoughts had passed out of the architectural channel into— what shall I say?—into the political. Here they found nothing so sweet to feed upon. It was the 5th of October; ten days later the elections for the new Chamber were to take place—the Chamber which was to replace the Assembly dissolved on the 16th of May by Marshal MacMahon, on a charge of "latent" radicalism. Stranger though one was, it was impossible not to be much interested in the triumph of the republican cause; it was impossible not to sympathise with this supreme effort of a brilliant and generous people to learn the lesson of national self-control and self-government. It was impossible, by the same token, not to have noted and detested the alacrity with which the Catholic party had rallied to the reactionary cause, and the unction with which the clergy had converted itself into the go-betweens of Bonapartism. The clergy was giving daily evidence of its devotion to arbitrary rule and to every iniquity that shelters itself behind the mask of "authority." These had been frequent and irritating reflections; they lurked in the folds of one's morning paper. They came back to me in the midst of that tranquil grandeur of Rheims, as I listened to the droning of the old gentlemen in the red capes. Some of the canons, it was painful to observe, had not been punctual; they came hurrying out of the sacristy after the service had begun. They looked like amiable and venerable men; their chanting and droning, as it spread itself under the great arches, was not disagreeable to listen to; I could certainly bear them no grudge. But their presence there was distracting and vexatious; it had spoiled my enjoyment of their church, in which I doubtless had no business. It had set me thinking of the activity and vivacity of the great organisation to which they belonged, and of all the odious things it would have done before the 15th of October. To what base uses do we come at last! It was this same organisation that had erected the magnificent structure around and above me, and which had then seemed an image of generosity and benignant power. Such an edifice might at times make one feel tenderly sentimental toward the Catholic church—make one remember how many of the great achievements of the past we owe to her. To lapse gently into this state of mind seems indeed always, while one strolls about a great cathedral, a proper recognition of its hospitality; but now I had lapsed gently out of it, and it was one of the exasperating elements of the situation that I felt, in a manner, called upon to decide how far such a lapse was unbecoming. I found myself even extending the question a little, and picturing to myself that conflict which must often occur at such a moment as the present—which is actually going on, doubtless, in many thousands of minds—between the actively, practically liberal instinct and what one may call the historic, aesthetic sense, the sense upon which old cathedrals lay a certain palpable obligation. How far should a lover of old cathedrals let his hands be tied by the sanctity of their traditions? How far should he let his imagination bribe him, as it were, from action? This of course is a question for each man to answer for himself; but as I sat listening to the drowsy old canons of Rheims, I was visited, I scarcely know why, by a kind of revelation of the anti-Catholic passion, as it must burn to-day in the breasts of certain radicals. I felt that such persons must be intent upon war to the death; how that must seem the most sacred of all duties. Can anything, in the line of action, for a votary of the radical creed, be more sacred? I asked myself; and can any instruments be too trenchant? I raised my eyes again to the dusky splendour of the upper aisles and measured their enchanting perspective, and it was with a sense of doing them full justice that I gave my fictive liberal my good wishes.

This little operation restored my equanimity, so that I climbed several hundred steps and wandered lightly over the roof of the cathedral. Climbing into cathedral-towers and gaping at the size of the statues that look small from the street has always seemed to me a rather brutal pastime; it is not the proper way to treat a beautiful building; it is like holding one's nose so close to a picture that one sees only the grain of the canvas. But when once I had emerged into the upper wilderness of Rheims the discourse of a very urbane and appreciative old bell-ringer, whom I found lurking behind some gigantic excrescence, gave an aesthetic complexion to what would otherwise have been a rather vulgar fest of gymnastics. It was very well to see what a great cathedral is made of, and in these high places of the immensity of Rheims I found the matter very impressively illustrated. I wandered for half an hour over endless expanses of roof, along the edge of sculptured abysses, through hugely-timbered attics and chambers that were in themselves as high as churches. I stood knee-high to strange images, of unsuspected proportions, and I followed the topmost staircase of one of the towers, which curls upward like the groove of a corkscrew, and gives you at the summit a hint of how a sailor feels at the masthead. The ascent was worth making to learn the fulness of beauty of the church, the solidity and perfection, the mightiness of arch and buttress, the latent ingenuity of detail. At the angles of the balustrade which ornaments the roof of the choir are perched a series of huge sitting eagles, which from below, as you look up at them, produce a great effect. They are immense, grim-looking birds, and the sculptor has given to each of them a pair of very neatly carved human legs, terminating in talons. Why did he give them human legs? Why did he indulge in this ridiculous conceit? I am unable to say, but the conceit afforded me pleasure. It seemed to tell of an imagination always at play, fond of the unexpected and delighting in its labour.

THOMAS JEFFERSON
(1743–1826)

Few Americans could have succeeded the scientist, inventor, statesman, philosopher, publisher Benjamin Franklin as minister to France other than the scientist, architect, inventor, educator, farmer, statesman Thomas Jefferson. By all accounts, Jefferson enjoyed his 1785 appointment to Paris as much as his predecessor. He toured Europe and had a busy social life, often accompanied by an Englishwoman, Maria Cosway.

While in France, Jefferson was witness to many of the events of the Revolution of 1789. Hoping to avoid violence, he even offered a compromise political solution to his old ally Marquis de Lafayette. It was rejected. The king became increasingly intransigent and the mobs more violent, culminating in the storming of the Bastille. Jefferson was convinced of the righteousness of the French people's cause and hosted a meeting of Lafayette and other patriot leaders in his home. His involvement with the French Revolution was cut short by a call to Virginia, and, with his two daughters, he left Paris for what he thought would be just a visit home.

Jefferson did not return to France as minister. While in Virginia he was appointed Secretary of State and, reluctantly, accepted the position. However, he claimed that France was second only to America in his heart. "Ask the traveled inhabitant of any nation in which country on earth would you rather live?" wrote Jefferson. "Certainly my own . . . Which would be your second choice? France."

Property and Natural Right:
A Letter to James Madison

Fontainebleau, Oct. 28, 1780

Dear Sir,

Seven o'clock, and retired to my fireside, I have determined to enter into conversation with you. This is a village of about 15,000 inhabitants when the court is not here, and 20,000 when they are, occupying a valley through which runs a brook and on each side of it a ridge of small mountains, most of which are naked rock. The King comes here, in the fall always, to hunt. His court attend him, as do also the foreign diplomatic corps; but as this is not indispensably required and my finances do not admit the expense of a continued residence here, I propose to come occasionally to attend the King's levees, returning again to Paris, distant forty miles. This being the first trip, I set out yesterday morning to take a view of the place. For this purpose I shaped my course towards the highest of the mountains in sight, to the top of which was about a league.

As soon as I had got clear of the town I fell in with a poor woman walking at the same rate with myself and going the same course. Wishing to know the condition of the laboring poor I entered into conversation with her, which I began by enquiries for the path which would lead me into the mountain: and thence proceeded to enquiries into her vocation, condition and circumstances. She told me she was a day laborer at 8 sous or 4d. sterling the day: that she had two children to maintain, and to pay a rent of 30 livres for her house (which would consume the hire of 75 days), that often she could get no employment and of course was without bread. As we had walked together near a mile and she had so far served me as a guide, I gave her, on parting, 24 sous. She burst into tears of a gratitude which I could perceive was unfeigned because she was unable to utter a word. She had probably never before received so great an aid. This little *attendrissement,* with the solitude of my walk, led me into a train of reflections on that unequal division of property which occasions the numberless instances of wretchedness which I had observed in this country and is to be observed all over Europe.

The property of this country is absolutely concentred in a very few hands, having revenues of from half a million of guineas a year downwards. These employ the flower of the country as servants, some of them having as many as 200 domestics, not laboring. They employ also a great number of manufacturers and tradesmen, and lastly the class of laboring husbandmen. But after all there comes the most numerous of all classes, that is, the poor who cannot find work. I asked myself what could be the reason so many should be permitted to beg who are willing to work, in a country where there is a very considerable proportion of uncultivated lands? These lands are undisturbed only for the sake of game. It should seem then that it must be because of the enormous wealth of the proprietors which places them above attention to the increase of their revenues by permitting these lands to be labored. I am conscious that an equal division of property is impracticable, but the consequences of this enormous inequality producing so much misery to the bulk of mankind, legislators cannot invent too many devices for subdividing property, only taking care to let their subdivisions go hand in hand with the natural affections of the human mind. The descent of property of every kind therefore to all the children, or to all the brothers and sisters, or other relations in equal degree, is a politic measure and a practicable one.

Another means of silently lessening the inequality of property is to exempt all from taxation below a certain point, and to tax the higher portions or property in geometrical progression as they rise. Whenever there are in any country uncultivated lands and unemployed poor, it is clear that the laws of property have been so far extended as to violate natural right. The earth is given as a common stock for man to labor and live on. If for the encouragement of industry we allow it to be appropriated, we must take care that other employment be provided to those excluded from the appropriation. If we do not, the fundamental right to labor the earth returns to the unemployed. It is too soon yet in our country to say that every man who cannot find employment, but who can find uncultivated land, shall be at liberty to cultivate it, paying a moderate rent. But it is not too soon to provide by every possible means that as few as possible shall be without a little portion of land. The small landholders are the most precious part of a state.

The next object which struck my attention in my walk was the deer with which the wood abounded. They were of the kind called "Cerfs," and not exactly of the same species with ours. They are blackish indeed under the belly, and not white as ours, and they are more of the chestnut red; but these are such small differences as would be sure to happen in two races from the same stock breeding separately a number of ages. Their hares are totally different from the animals we call by that name; but their rabbit is almost exactly like him. The only difference is in their manners; the land on which I walked for some time being absolutely reduced to a honey-comb by their burrowing. I think there is no instance of ours burrowing. After descending the hill again I saw a man cutting fern. I went to him under pretence of asking the shortest road to town, and afterwards asked for what use he was cutting fern. He told me that this part of the country furnished a great deal of fruit to Paris. That when packed in straw it acquired an ill taste, but that dry fern preserved it perfectly without communicating any taste at all.

I treasured this observation for the preservation of my apples on my return to my own country. They have no apples here to compare with our Redtown pippin. They have nothing which deserves the name of a peach; there being not sun enough to ripen the plum-peach and the best of their soft peaches being like our autumn peaches. Their cherries and strawberries are fair, but I think lack flavor. Their plums I think are better, so also their gooseberries, and the pears infinitely beyond anything we possess. They have nothing better than our sweet-water; but they have a succession of as good from early in the summer till frost. I am to-morrow to get [to] M. Malsherbes (an uncle of the Chevalier Luzerne's) about seven leagues from hence, who is the most curious man in France as to his trees. He is making for me a collection of the vines from which the Burgundy, Champagne, Bordeaux, Frontignac, and other of the most valuable wines of this country are made. Another gentleman is collecting for me the best eating grapes, including what we call the raisin. I propose also to endeavor to colonize their hare, rabbit, red and grey partridge, pheasants of different kinds, and some other birds. But I find that I am wandering beyond the limits of my walk and will therefore bid you adieu. Yours affectionately.

STANLEY KARNOW
(1925-)

In 1947, Stanley Karnow, an ex-GI with a Harvard diploma, went to Paris for the summer. He stayed ten years. At first he simply toured the sights, stayed in cheap hotels and planned his return to the States. But at the end of the summer he enrolled at the Sorbonne, using his GI bill entitlements of $75 a month to finance his stay. He acquired the language, an understanding of the culture and a French wife, Claude. Karnow needed a job and was hired as a minion in the Paris bureau of Time *magazine. That first job turned into a career and he became a staff correspondent writing on French culture and society, covering personalities and politics. His book* Paris in the Fifties, *from which this excerpt is taken, is in part a memoir and in part a collection of his articles. Although fashion was not part of his regular beat, Karnow captured the frenzy of the Paris spring shows of the 1950s when the French clothing industry—and its titans Givenchy, Balmain, Balenciaga and especially Dior—ruled.*

In 1959 Karnow left Paris for Asia, where he became a correspondent for many magazines and newspapers and wrote several well-received histories of Vietnam. When he returned to Paris in 1968, Karnow dropped into a familiar bar at the Crillon Hotel, a gathering place for the British and American press during the postwar years. Some of his friends were still there. "So was Louis, the bartender, his patent leather hair as slick as ever," recalled Karnow. "Without batting an eye, he extended a limp hand and mumbled, 'Bonjour, M'sieur Karnow, back from vacation?'"

The Glass of Fashion

from PARIS IN THE FIFTIES

The bone-damp chill of winter was lifting, and pale sunlight had begun to etch shadows of the leafless chestnut trees on the cobblestone streets. Children were again playing in the parks, café terraces had started to reopen and lovers could be seen smooching on the banks along the Seine. In the district around the Champs-Élysées, the George V, Prince de Galles and Plaza Athénée lounges were shrill with the shouts of Chicago and Dallas department-store buyers as they cruised from divan to divan, hailing California and Florida dress-chain representatives. At plush restaurants like Lasserre, Ledoyen and Maxim's, stocky, cigar-chomping Seventh Avenue manufacturers in silver ties and white-on-white shirts shared tables with New York designers in jangly bracelets and rhinestone-rimmed glasses. Powder-puff bars were packed with the female editors of women's magazines, photographers, wire service reporters, gossip columnists, press agents, public relations hustlers, titled ladies, rich bourgeois hostesses, stage and screen stars, and the usual celebrities and playboys. This effervescent reunion was a rite of spring—the mystic and sacred moment when the city's top couturiers unveiled to the world the latest variations and dissonances on the theme of the Eternal Feminine.

Though I might drop in on a show once in a while to ogle the mannequins, fashion was not my terrain. In March 1957, however, I was assigned to a mammoth story on the subject. Compared to such industries as food and cars, haute couture contributed little to France's economy. Its income stemmed primarily from serving elite Parisiennes and foreigners, and from exporting designs—especially to America. The thirty or forty *grandes maisons* employed only about seven thousand workers and grossed less than a million dollars a year—in contrast to the four billion dollars' worth of dresses sold annually in the United States. But whatever the balance sheet, Paris fashions swayed the tastes of women everywhere, thereby confirming in the French the conviction that, when it came to producing prestige goods, they were peerless—a belief that, in turn, reinforced their overweening sense of cultural superiority.

Day after day for nearly a month, I crisscrossed the small Right Bank *quartier* where the major fashion houses were clustered. I dutifully viewed the Fath, Balenciaga, Balmain, Castillo, Dessès, Givenchy, Lanvin, Laroche and Patou collections—some of which, for promotional purposes, featured gimmicks like a giraffe-hide coat and a suede bolero lined with alley cat skin. But mainly I focused on Christian Dior, then the preeminent Paris couturier, who was slated to appear on *Time*'s cover.

One morning I took a taxi over to Dior, a baroque granite mansion situated on the Avenue Montaigne, a broad, shaded street between the Rond-Point des Champs-Élysées and the Place de l'Alma. The security reminded me of Fort Knox. Roughly three hundred embossed invitations had been issued to a select list; and, to bar gate-crashers, handsome girls in nondescript black and lockjaw accents guarded the entrance, carefully checking credentials and allocating seats according to a rigid protocol: professional buyers according to their previous purchases, journalists according to the influence of their publications, luminaries according to their current reputations. Punctuality was de rigueur, and absolutely no exceptions. Some months before, the Duchess of Windsor had arrived late, expecting VIP treatment, and she was relegated to a staircase.

The large gold-and-olive salon was a hall of mirrors, the subtle glow of its giant crystal chandeliers overwhelmed by the glare of floodlights. Tucked into alcoves were urns filled with roses, gardenias and carnations whose mélange of fragrances pervaded the chamber. Squeezing into a flimsy gilded chair in the press section, I glanced around. The front rows were crammed with American and European merchandisers cradling pens, notepads and programs. Svelte women in toque hats and pearl chokers leaned forward anxiously; prosperous provincial matrons sat ramrod-upright, clutching stout handbags; a few privileged tourists gazed in awe at the opulence. The mood was as tense and as promising as a Broadway premiere; then the babble subsided as a stereo emitted a medley of waltzes, polkas, ballads and pop tunes—and, in threes and fours, the first of thirteen mannequins glided out from behind a gauze curtain.

Lanky and remote, they seemed to be rapt in an asexual trance as they sashayed up and down the runway in movements and gestures as studiously choreographed as a ballet—hips swiveling, arms akimbo, heads tossing. A woman assistant in basic black, speaking through a microphone, identified their lavish ensembles, tailored sheaths and cocktail casuals in a noncommittal monotone: *"Ariane, trente-trois, zirty-zree," "Chloë, quarante-et-un, fawrty-wan," "Papillon de Printemps, cinquante-cinq, feevty-feeve."* The mannequins would twirl, hover, twirl again, pause, slip off a jacket or a mantle and hand it to an invisible aide, who accepted it silently, like some ancient hetaera. Then yet another pirouette, and they evaporated into the wings. The session lasted three hours, culminating in an array of classic bridal gowns. Most of the audience burst into enthusiastic applause punctuated by cries of *"Magnifique!"* and *"Bravo!"* But, lest the faintest flicker betray their interest in an article to a rival, the pros feigned indifference. Amid it all, a woman reporter for a Fleet Street tabloid nagged me with a torrent of gush: "Isn't that a witty pebble weave?" or "Don't you think that there's a certain je-ne-sais-quoi texture to that velour?"

The frothy pageant was the indispensable prelude to the serious business that began only after the lights had faded. At that juncture, buyers for Henri Bendel, Saks, I. Magnin, Bonwit Teller, Neiman-Marcus and other establishments that catered to the carriage trade huddled with the solemn, black-clad *vendeuses* strategically stationed in the corridors. Every buyer had her personal *vendeuse,* every *vendeuse* her jealously coveted clientele— and, after years of making deals, they trusted each other. Some buyers, enraptured by the models they had just seen, instantly signed contracts, but most of them would shop around and deliberate before deciding. With big bucks at stake, the risks were enormous. An item that glittered in scintillating Paris could bomb in sober Scarsdale.

A spectrum of options was available to wholesalers. I discussed one of them with Sydney Blauner, a chunky man in his fifties whose Manhattan firm turned out a line under the label Suzy Perette. For an ante of two thousand dollars and royalties, he acquired the right to incorporate Dior's notions into dresses that retailed in the United States for fifty or sixty dollars. Thus, on a slim budget, an Atlanta stenographer or a Cleveland nurse could emulate a glamorous Parisienne. As Blauner told me, "If you don't come to Paris, you're missing the boat. There are more ideas in a thimble here than in all of America."

Pirates chronically menaced the couturiers. A case that hit the headlines unfolded in 1948, when a customer complained to Dior that she had paid a whopping sum for an exclusive gown and, at a ritzy nightclub, spotted another woman in exactly the same number. "This is not a joke," she wept, "but a tragedy." Promptly summoned by Dior, the gendarmes launched an investigation that ended six years later in the arrest of a gang of fashion thieves. They had been stealing designs, which they shipped to London, Brussels, Beirut and elsewhere for conversion into cheap facsimiles. Documents compiled by the police divulged their methods. They would bribe a seamstress or a *midinette* to purloin patterns, or coax a mannequin into borrowing a dress for an evening and copy it. Indicted for violating French copyright law, they were convicted and fined. But one couturier, voicing doubts that forgers could ever be stopped, said, "Maybe we ought to take it as a compliment when they rob us."

As I sought to understand fashion, I discovered that it was misty and nebulous—easier described than defined. I reread Proust's passage on Odette Swann: "Attire to her symbolized the delicate and spiritual mechanism of a whole form of civilization." For Jean Cocteau, fertile artist, playwright, filmmaker and aesthetic arbiter, fashion "thrills us briefly with its insolent, enigmatic bouquet—then, like a frail blossom, dies." Cecil Beaton, the chichi English photographer, differed: "Fashions are ephemeral, but fashion is enduring." Over an apéritif at a Saint-Germain-des-Prés café, the sassy Comtesse Louise de Vilmorin discarded all this rhetoric as poppycock: "Fashion is a veneer foisted on naive women by despots. Give me sincere blue jeans."

Late one afternoon I spent an hour or so with Dior in his green-paneled sanctum above his salon. A plump, balding bachelor of fifty-two whose pink cheeks might have been sculpted from marzipan, he resembled an ambassador or a banker in his charcoal double-breasted suit, the rosette in its lapel denoting his grade as an officer of the Légion d'Honneur. Relaxed after the day's grind, he appreciated the chance to talk. His bland, courteous exterior concealed an inner tension, presumably the result of his dedication to a strenuous, competitive field. When I suggested to him that fashion would wither unless women felt compelled to comply with the latest modes, he peered up his aquiline nose at the ceiling, chuckled and replied, "I'm no philosopher, but it seems to me that women—and men too—instinctively yearn to exhibit themselves. In this machine age, which esteems convention and uniformity, fashion is the ultimate refuge of the human, the personal and the inimitable. Even the most outrageous innovations should be welcomed, if only because they shield us against the shabby and the humdrum. Of course fashion is a transient, egotistical indulgence, yet in an era as somber as ours, luxury must be defended centimeter by centimeter." He resented the charge that dressmakers imposed their will on their clients: "It's a calumny to call us dictators. *Le couturier propose, la femme dispose.*"

The following evening Dior invited me for drinks at his *hôtel particulier* in upscale Passy, near the Château de la Muette. His butler uncorked a vintage Dom Pérignon and, enveloped in magenta upholstered armchairs under a stilted Bernard Buffet portrait of him above the fireplace, we sipped a glass or two. Then, realizing that I was there to gather information for my story, he gave me free rein to poke around. The decor was a ragout of the sublime and the grotesque. Tiers of shelves held sets of leather-bound volumes, odd pieces of bric-a-brac and autographed photos of French and foreign dignitaries, famous writers, composers, opera singers, movie directors, actors and actresses. The vermilion damask walls were a quilt of engravings and aquarelles, Impressionists, Neo-Impressionists, Cubists, Surrealists, Dadaists and kitschy fin de siècle paintings of verdant landscapes and beefy nudes. Ancient Greek amphorae and Roman busts, antique Gallic ceramics and Ming porcelains sat on inlaid medieval Spanish and Italian chests alongside such carnival souvenirs as stuffed animals, plastic *poupées* and plaster statuettes. The boudoir was furnished with a crimson-canopied Second Empire bed, a purple Louis XIV *prie-dieu,* mauve draperies and a white bearskin rug. Dior frequently switched clothes three or four times a day; and his closets and drawers, I guessed, contained hundreds of suits, pajamas, ties and pairs of socks and shoes. Peeking into the Florentine-tiled bathroom, I noticed a colossal green marble tub lined in zinc and equipped with swan's-head faucets. "My friends tease me for accumulating this stuff," he said, "but valuable or trashy, it inspires me in some way or other. I regard it as my own flea market."

Unlike many of his fellow couturiers, who publicized themselves by mixing with *le tout Paris* at glittering galas, Dior was a hermit and, prizing his privacy, seldom went to the opera, the cinema or the theater. He preferred to dine quietly at home and perhaps play a rubber of bridge with a few intimates. His domestic staff of six included a cook, and, defying his doctor's orders to curb his weight, he was partial to earthy peasant casseroles accompanied by choice wines and liqueurs, among them a fine framboise bottled at his château in the forest of Fontainebleau, near Paris. A devout Catholic, he rarely skipped Sunday mass, but he was deeply superstitious, regularly consulted an astrologer and swore by her communion with the zodiac.

Pursuing our chat, I asked Dior to explain why fashion thrived in France. "First," he responded, "we inherited a tradition of craftsmanship rooted in the anonymous artisans who constructed the cathedrals and expressed their genius in chiseled stone gargoyles and cherubs. Their descendants—skilled automobile mechanics, cabinetmakers, masons, plumbers, handymen—are proud of their métiers. They feel humiliated if they've done a shoddy job. Similarly, my tailors, seamstresses, even novice *midinettes,* constantly strive for perfection. We also benefit, paradoxically, from having a singularly difficult consumer: the Parisienne. At a fitting she behaves like a contortionist. She stands up, sits down, bends and wriggles around; actually she is testing a dress because, she knows, an unhinged strap or a clasp could mean disaster at a fancy soirée. Often she brings along her husband or her lover, and they fidget as well over stitches, seams and buttonholes. They exasperate us, but we cannot afford to ignore their fussing, however petty it may seem. Unless they leave Chez Dior in complete self-confidence, we have blundered and our image will be tarnished as a consequence."

To create his collections, Dior would seclude himself in his château or soak in his bathtub, drafting thousands of spidery sketches on scraps of paper—a kind of hieroglyphic of silhouettes and contours. "Suddenly," he said, "one of them astounds me, as though I have accidentally encountered an acquaintance on a country lane. I embrace it as my motif for the season and give it a name—the A-line, the H-line, the *haricot-vert* line, whatever. Then I refine and color about seven hundred of these *petites gravures,* and they will make up the core of the collection."

Next he conferred with his principal deputies—three female fashion veterans whose opinions he respected. After much debate, they approved about sixty designs, which were then cut into tulle patterns and modeled by mannequins in Dior's spacious atelier. Wearing a white butcher's smock, perched on a high stool and wielding an ivory-tipped bamboo swagger stick, Dior repeatedly reviewed them for weeks. A stickler for detail, he would point his stick at a mannequin and insist on adjusting a pocket, altering a pleat, revising a collar, moving a belt, shifting a bow. Nothing eluded his sharp eye—purses, necklaces, earrings, stockings, parasols and the myriad other accessories vital to every smart lady's wardrobe. Particularly troublesome for him were so-called Trafalgars, fragile, elaborate ball dresses that easily came unstuck and had to be stiffened without losing their flossiness. He rehearsed the mannequins tirelessly, displaying surprising grace as he stepped onto the floor to demonstrate their routines himself. As the show approached, he toiled around the clock, pushing his team to the brink of exhaustion. Spinster *midinettes,* clinging to custom, would sew a lock of their hair into the hems of the wedding gowns in hopes of snaring a husband during the year ahead.

"After all the horrors of preparing a collection," Dior confided to me, "I wouldn't think of attending a show." One day, however, he authorized me to hang out backstage during a presentation, and it was a zoo. Helpers and apprentices raced around, pushing racks of dresses and bolts of cloth and other paraphernalia. The mannequins, so cool and distant on the runway, were now half nude, disheveled and frenetic as fitters brushed their garments, hairdressers rearranged their coiffures, and cosmeticians freshened their lipstick, rouge and mascara. Sounding like a railroad conductor, a dispatcher brandishing a watch and a schedule gently patted their derrieres as he thrust them into the salon under their pseudonyms: *"Diane, Columbine, Fleur de Lis, Mirabelle . . ."* A supervisor remarked to me as we stood in a corner, *"C'est de l'anarchie, n'est-ce pas, mais ça marche quand même."*

PETER MAYLE

(1939–)

Peter Mayle was an advertising copywriter and executive in his native England before he and his wife moved to Provence in the 1980s. His travails with the renovation of their house and their encounters with the locals became A Year in Provence, *an international bestseller. The memoir's premise: the logical, even-tempered Englishman versus the French peasant's traditions, work ethic, and sense of time. Mayle's enormous stone table became a metaphor for his acclimation to Provence. The table, "a scale model of Stonehenge" roughly five feet square and five feet thick, was delivered and placed near Mayle's garage. "The distance between where it had been delivered and where we wanted it to be was no more than fifteen yards, but it might as well have been fifty miles. The entrance to the courtyard was too narrow for any mechanical transport, and the high wall and tiled half roof that made a sheltered area ruled out the use of a crane." Thus started months of negotiation with various tradesmen to move Stonehenge. Eventually, seven men wrestled Mayle's table into its resting place in the courtyard.*

Mayle's main adversary is the French sense of time. "We learned that time in Provence is a very elastic commodity, even when it is described in clear and specific terms . . . little by little, we reverted to being philosophical and came to terms with the Provençal clock. From now on, we told ourselves, we would assume that nothing would be done when we expected it to be done, the fact that it happened at all would be enough."

Tourists flocked to Provence after reading Mayle's book. His vision of good food, happy people and a slow-paced life seduced many—too many for Mayle. He found himself assailed by enthusiastic fans who stole his privacy and shattered his peace. Mayle now divides his time between Long Island and France.

from **A Year in Provence**

Our friend the London lawyer, a man steeped in English reserve, was watching what he called the antics of the frogs from the Fin de Siècle café in Cavaillon. It was market day, and the pavement was a human traffic jam, slow moving, jostling and chaotic.

"Look over there," he said, as a car stopped in the middle of the street while the driver got out to embrace an acquaintance, "they're always mauling each other. See that? *Men kissing.* Damned unhealthy, if you ask me." He snorted into his beer, his sense of propriety outraged by such deviant behavior, so alien to the respectable Anglo-Saxon.

It had taken me some months to get used to the Provençal delight in physical contact. Like anyone brought up in England, I had absorbed certain social mannerisms. I had learned to keep my distance, to offer a nod instead of a handshake, to ration kissing to female relatives and to confine any public demonstrations of affection to dogs. To be engulfed by a Provençal welcome, as thorough and searching as being frisked by airport security guards, was, at first, a startling experience. Now I enjoyed it, and I was fascinated by the niceties of the social ritual, and the sign language which is an essential part of any Provençal encounter.

When two unencumbered men meet, the least there will be is the conventional handshake. If the hands are full, you will be offered a little finger to shake. If the hands are wet or dirty, you will be offered a forearm or an elbow. Riding a bicycle or driving a car does not excuse you from the obligation to *toucher les cinq sardines,* and so you will see perilous contortions being performed on busy streets as hands grope through car windows and across handlebars to find each other. And this is only at the first and most restrained level of acquaintance. A closer relationship requires more demonstrative acknowledgment.

As our lawyer friend had noticed, men kiss other men. They squeeze shoulders, slap backs, pummel kidneys, pinch cheeks. When a Provençal man is truly pleased to see you, there is a real possibility of coming away from his clutches with superficial bruising.

The risk of bodily damage is less where women are concerned, but an amateur can easily make a social blunder if he miscalculates the required number of kisses. In my early days of *See also* discovery, I would plant a single kiss, only to find that the other cheek was being proffered as I was drawing back. Only snobs kiss once, I was told, or those unfortunates who suffer from congenital *froideur.* I then saw what I assumed to be the correct procedure—the triple kiss, left-right-left, so I tried it on a Parisian friend. Wrong again. She told me that triple-kissing was a low Provençal habit, and that two kisses were enough among civilized people. The next time I saw my neighbor's wife, I kissed her twice. *"Non,"* she said, *"trois fois."*

I now pay close attention to the movement of the female head. If it stops swiveling after two kisses, I am almost sure I've filled my quota, but I stay poised for a third lunge just in case the head should keep moving.

It's a different but equally tricky problem for my wife, who is on the receiving end and has to estimate the number of times she needs to swivel, or indeed if she needs to swivel at all. One morning she heard a bellow in the street, and turned to see Ramon the plasterer advancing on her. He stopped, and wiped his hands ostentatiously on his trousers. My wife anticipated a handshake, and held out her hand. Ramon brushed it aside and kissed her three times with great gusto. You never can tell.

Once the initial greeting is over, conversation can begin. Shopping baskets and packages are put down, dogs are tied to café tables, bicycles and tools are leaned up against the nearest wall. This is necessary, because for any serious and satisfactory discussion both hands must be free to provide visual punctuation, to terminate dangling sentences, to add emphasis, or simply to decorate speech which, as it is merely a matter of moving the mouth, is not on its own sufficiently physical for the Provençal. So the hands and the eternally eloquent shoulders are vital to a quiet exchange of views, and in fact it is often possible to follow the gist of a Provençal conversation from a distance, without hearing the words, just by watching expressions and the movements of bodies and hands.

There is a well-defined silent vocabulary, starting with the hand waggle which had been introduced to us by our builders. They used it only as a disclaimer whenever talking about time or cost, but it is a gesture of almost infinite flexibility. It can describe the state of your health, how you're getting on with your mother-in-law, the progress of your business, your assessment of a restaurant, or your predictions about this year's melon crop. When it is a subject of minor importance, the waggle is perfunctory, and is accompanied by a dismissive raising of the eyebrows. More serious matters—politics, the delicate condition of one's liver, the prospects for a local rider in the Tour de France—are addressed with greater intensity. The waggle is in slow motion, with the upper part of the body swaying slightly as the hand rocks, a frown of concentration on the face.

The instrument of warning and argument is the index finger, in one of its three operational positions. Thrust up, rigid and unmoving, beneath your conversational partner's nose, it signals caution—watch out, *attention,* all is not what it seems. Held just below face level and shaken rapidly from side to side like an agitated metronome, it indicates that the other person is woefully ill informed and totally wrong in what he has just said. The correct opinion is then delivered, and the finger changes from its sideways motion into a series of jabs and prods, either tapping the chest if the unenlightened one is a man or remaining a few discreet centimeters from the bosom in the case of a woman.

Describing a sudden departure needs two hands: the left, fingers held straight, moves upwards from waist level to smack into the palm of the right hand moving downward—a restricted version of the popular and extremely vulgar bicep crunch. (Seen at its best during midsummer traffic jams, when disputing drivers will leave their cars to allow themselves the freedom of movement necessary for a left-arm uppercut stopped short by the right hand clamping on the bicep.)

At the end of the conversation, there is the promise to stay in touch. The middle three fingers are folded into the palm and the hand is held up to an ear, with the extended thumb and little finger imitating the shape of a telephone. Finally, there is a parting handshake. Packages, dogs, and bicycles are gathered up until the whole process starts all over again fifty yards down the street. It's hardly surprising that aerobics never became popular in Provence. People get quite enough physical exercise in the course of a ten-minute chat.

MARY McCARTHY

(1912–1989)

At the age of six Mary McCarthy was orphaned. She and her three brothers were shuttled first to a paternal aunt and then to their maternal grandparents in Seattle. Her upbringing (chronicled in Memories of a Catholic Girlhood *1957) was materially wealthy, but emotionally austere. In 1929 she went to Vassar College, became friends with Muriel Rukeyser, Eleanor Clark and Elizabeth Bishop—and gathered material for her novel* The Group *(1962), a satirical look at women at the Seven Sisters schools.*

In the 1930s McCarthy became a part of the American left and worked as an editor at Covici-Friede Publishers. Her second husband, Edmund Wilson, encouraged her to write, and her first book, The Company She Keeps, *was published in 1942. McCarthy spent the rest of her literary career teaching at universities, writing novels that reflected contemporary (often political) issues and contributing articles to* The New Yorker, Harper's, Partisan Review *and the* Atlantic Monthly.

Critics were never neutral about McCarthy. While most thought her style graceful and precise, one called her "the lady with the switchblade." She was opinionated, forceful and fearless, excoriated by her enemies and lauded by her allies.

In 1960 on a lecture tour of Poland, McCarthy fell in love with a public affairs officer at the U.S. Embassy in Warsaw. Both divorced their respective spouses (McCarthy's third), and married in 1962. From 1961 until her death McCarthy divided her time between an apartment in Paris and a house in Maine. Her novel Birds of America *(1965), from which this selection is taken, is set in both New England and France and tells the story of Peter Levi, an American student who is spending his junior year in Paris. This letter to his mother chronicles his adjustment to life in France.*

Epistle from Mother Carey's Chicken

from BIRDS IN AMERICA

33 rue Monsieur-le-Prince
Paris 6ème
1 Brumaire, CLXXIII

Dear Ma:

I have finally found an apartment. It's on the fifth floor (American sixth), which is good exercise for me. One room, "furnished," plus a separate jakes and a sort of bird bath. I've bought a student lamp, which helps. It has a radiator, but the heat hasn't come on yet; the furnace is in the landlady's apartment, and she doesn't feel the cold. She has let me have some sheets and a so-called blanket, which I took to the cleaner's. Still, it's better than those hotels I've been staying in. Did I write you from the one where they had six Japanese acrobats sleeping on the floor in the room next to me? Contortionists, I assume.

I'm glad to be on my own, making my bed and sweeping. It's good to do a little physical work, and you feel less lonely in your own place, with your stuff unpacked. Also, I never could solve the tipping problem. That was the good part of that military hotel on the rue Littré. But in those other fleabags, where the *service* was *compris* theoretically in the price of the room, I was constantly on the horns of the dilemma. I mean, being an American and getting money from home, I felt I ought to tip the chambermaid even if the other inhabitants didn't. "From each according to his abilities." You know. But then I figured that if I tipped, it was scabbing on the others, who didn't have the dough. Being *prepotente,* the rich American youth. Buying the red carpet. And if I crossed the chambermaid's palm, I did get more service, I found out. In one hotel, every time I started to go to the communal toilet, down the hall, she would rush ahead of me—*"Un instant, monsieur"*—and clean it with one of those filthy hard-rubber brushes they have, all caked with excrement, and when I thanked her, she backed out, curtseying: *"A votre service, monsieur."* It was on account of that I moved. It got so I was lurking in my room, waiting for her to leave the floor so that I wouldn't get this special treatment I seemed to be paying for. If the other inhabitants had to use a dirty, stinking toilet, why should I be the exception? In fact, it was her job to clean the toilet.

On the other hand, when I didn't tip, I felt like a cheapskate. Because of the way I've been brought up, I guess. It's all your fault (ha ha). I tried asking myself what Kant would do in my position: "Behave as if thy maxim could be a universal law." If my maxim was not to tip because the next guy didn't, that would be pretty hard on the chambermaids of Paris, I decided. So, if he was true to his philosophy, Kant would tip. Of course he didn't have to face the issue, never leaving Königsberg. But you could also argue that tipping made it tough on the non-tipper (which I could produce some empirical evidence for), and therefore Kant might be against it. If I understand him, he is saying that an action should be judged by its implications, *i.e.*, if everybody did what you are doing, what would the world be like? Well, a world in which every student gave a five-franc gratuity weekly to the woman who cleaned his room would be OK, but what about a world in which every *other* student did it? Maybe the categorical imperative is not the best guide for Americans abroad. When you think of it, the rule of thumb about tipping is just the opposite of Kant: watch what everybody else does and do the same.

I never could make up my mind whether tipping or not tipping was more cowardly in the circumstances. Maybe any action becomes cowardly once you stop to reason about it. Conscience doth make cowards of us all, eh, *mamma mia?* If you start an argument with yourself, that makes two people at least, and when you have two people, one of them starts appeasing the other.

Anyway, I've found this apartment. It will only cost 30,000 old francs a month, plus the utilities (there's a gas hot-water heater over the bathtub) and a small donation to the concierge at New Year's. The place has its drawbacks but it's a lot better than the *chambres de bonne* a lot of kids rent in the mansards of old buildings. You ought to see those rooms, like a series of doghouses under the eaves, where the maids used to be kept. No heat or running water, the usual foul toilet in the hall, and a common tap with a rusty basin underneath where you go to fill your pitcher and empty your slops. No bathtub or *bidet* on the whole floor; I guess they expected the maids to be dirty. The advantage is that, being high up, you generally have a nice view, through a slanting skylight. There are whole families—mostly Spaniards and Algerians—living in some of those holes.

It's an education, looking for an apartment. Quite a few French families want to rent you a room where you share a bathroom and toilet with them and maybe have the use of the kitchen to make your morning coffee. They call it an apartment. You waste a lot of time that way, answering ads. They won't admit on the telephone that the place doesn't have a separate entrance—*une seule clef.* At first I didn't know how to say that and if I said *une seule porte*—like *una porta sola*—they'd say, *"Oui, oui, monsieur, une seule porte."* Even when they get the idea, they pretend to be surprised, as though a separate entrance was something unheard of and the only reason you could want one was to give orgies or sell your body to French queers.

I got my present pad through the grapevine. The desk clerk at my last hotel knew about it and told the owner I was *per bene.* The putative heating is included in the rent, and there's a two-burner hot plate and a few chipped dishes and a coffeepot. I can wash the dishes in the bathtub. The only thing is, there isn't much light. It looks out on a shaft that goes down to what they call a *courette,* where the garbage cans are kept. But I'll be here mostly in the evenings and anyway the days are getting shorter, as the land-lady pointed out. *I.e.,* when I get up in the morning and come back in the afternoon it will be dark outside anyhow. She had fixed the place up for her son, who was a student; hence the amenities. There are even some home-made bookshelves. It is on a landing, up a few steps from the service entrance of her own apartment. I have to use the service stairs.

At night, the big main door on the ground floor is locked at ten o'clock. If I come in after that, I ring for the concierge to push a button that opens the door. The signal is six short rings; otherwise, she won't open, in case I might be a *clochard* or a burglar. The Parisians spend a lot of time worrying about burglars and prowlers. In those hotels I was staying in, the chambermaid, on receiving a tip, would immediately start warning me about the other denizens—they stole. *"Méfiez-vous, monsieur."* I was urged to be sure to lock my door when I was inside and to put my watch and money under my pillow while I was sleep-ing. I found this quite unpleasant. It made me look at any-body I passed on the stairs with a sort of smutty curiosity, as though they might have it "in them" to be a thief. Like wondering whether a woman you see waiting on a corner could be a prostitute. The French are a suspicious people.

But in fact there's a lot of theft in those Left Bank flops. You would be surprised. In one place I was staying—on the rue St.-André-des-Arts—a kid had his typewriter taken, a new Olivetti. It turned out that it wasn't even his; he'd borrowed it from a girlfriend who typed manuscripts for a living. He reported it to the police, but they just shrugged. Too common an occurrence in that precinct. The way this kid, who was Dutch, reconstructed it, somebody must have lifted his key from the board downstairs, while the desk clerk was elsewhere (half the time in those hotels there's nobody at the desk; you have to ring a hand-bell to get somebody to come), and gone up to his room and helped himself. The Dutchman wanted the police to search all the rooms; he reasoned that it had to be someone in the hotel, who had heard him typing. But the police told him that whoever stole the typewriter would have gone out and sold it right away. They even implied, when he started making a scene, that he might have sold it himself and then reported that he had been robbed.

Then I heard about a Swedish *au pair* girl, in that same hotel, who left her gold watch in the communal bathroom in the soap-dish; when she missed it, ten minutes later, it was gone. An American girl found her crying on the stairs and went with her to the police station. "My golden watch!" she kept saying. You'd think that thieves, being hard up themselves, would have a fellow-feeling; I mean, steal from people who could afford it. But of course people who can afford it stay in hotels where the clientele is "above" stealing watches and typewriters. I guess the world is a vicious circle.

I think I will like Paris better now that I'm no longer a member of its floating population, which can be fairly sordid. The food, at my age level, is fairly sordid too. There are a few *foyers* with a table d'hôte, for students, that are not so bad, but they're crowded and when the novelty wears off they're not a great improvement on eating in commons at home, except that you can have wine. The bread and croissants are great, of course, but the French don't know how to make a sandwich. And I miss salads and orange juice and tuna fish. They hardly ever serve vegetables, except French fries. There's nothing here to compare with the spinach in the Automat, for instance. And I miss the stand-up bars in Italy, where you can have a healthy snack and a *cappuccino*. What I like best in the restaurants here is the *crudités*, but you can't sit down and order *crudités* and a glass of milk; you have to be force-fed with the entire menu. Sometimes I just have a dozen *praires* (which are cheaper than oysters), standing up, on the street, for lunch.

I've started doing my own cooking, with a vegetable binge. No icebox, needless to say, in this apartment, but that doesn't matter with the present room temperature. Besides, the French, like the Italians, only buy what they need for one day. I had a shock, though, yesterday, when I went to do my marketing at the Marché Buci—that big outdoor market, near the Odéon. At one stall, I asked for a carrot, and the *type* refused to sell me one. He said I had to buy a kilo. Like you, dearest Ma, I started to argue. I wanted to know why. How it would damage him to sell me one carrot or one apple or one pear. I explained that I didn't have an icebox and that I was just one person. *"Ça ne me regarde pas,"* he growled. Finally we compromised on a pound. That's quite a lot of carrots for a single man. While he was weighing them, I got into conversation with an Italian, who had been watching me and smiling—very nice, about the *babbo's* age, an intellectual. He said that in Italy not only would they sell you one carrot but divide it in four. According to him, this only proved that Italy is a poor country, while France is a rich country. I said the Ital-

ians had more heart than the French, even if they gyp you
sometimes. The French *grudge* gypping you, Mother.
Maybe, I said, people in poor countries had more heart
than people in rich countries. After all, Poverty used to be
represented as a Virtue. I hadn't noticed any statues of
Poverty on French churches.

By the way, did you know that most of the statues on
the churches here had their heads chopped off? In the
French Revolution. And in the Wars of Religion, this Ital-
ian told me. But he agreed that Dame Poverty was not seen
as a Virtue in France, which he seemed to think was a
good thing.

After I had bought a pound of carrots, three cucum-
bers, a pound of tomatoes, a pound of onions, and a huge
cooked beet, we went to a café around the corner, near the
statue of Danton, and continued the discussion. He thought
it was funny that an American should idealize poverty, and
when I told him that in America you could buy one carrot
even in a supermarket, he seemed skeptical. Perhaps in the
Negro sections, he said. No, I said, anywhere. It was a free
country; you could buy as much or as little as you wanted.
I had to admit, though, that as far as I knew you couldn't
buy one cigarette at a time, the way you can in Italy. And I
realize now I ought to have mentioned those carrots in
plastic bags, which sort of bear out his point. It's odd they
slipped my mind.

Anyway, he explained that in Paris you could buy a sin-
gle carrot or onion or lemon in a *grocery store*. That's differ-
ent from a market. Only in a grocery store you pay more
than you would pay if you bought the carrot at the market.
But since you can't, the point is academic. I said maybe
students who lived in the quarter could get up a pool to
buy a kilo a day of vegetables and fruit at the market and
then divide it up. Take turns doing the shopping. He said I
was defining a co-operative.

It sank me to learn that I'm too small an economic unit to take part in the French way of life. I love those street markets—so colorful—and I'd counted on haunting them every day after school with my *filet*. What's the point of being in Europe if you have to line up in a grocery store, which is usually part of chain, just like at home? This Italian said not to be discouraged: I could still buy fish and meat and cheeses at those market stalls, and in time, if they got to know me, the vegetable- and fruit-sellers might relent; I could become *"l'américain du Marché Buci."*

When we parted, he asked me to come around to his place some evening for dinner; he has kids but much younger than me. If I go (I'm supposed to call him, since I have no phone), it will be the first time I've been in a French household, except that he isn't French. He left Italy under Mussolini, like the *babbo,* and his wife is Russian.

Unfortunately, I haven't made many contacts here. In my course in French civilization, we're all foreigners, obviously. The only student I've had any real talks with is a Norwegian named Dag, who is a sort of Marxist troll. He wants me to go to Poland with him during Christmas vacation. There are some Smith girls I met at a place called Reid Hall where they have supplementary classes, in English, but they stick pretty much together. I asked one to go rowing with me the other day on the lake in the Bois de Boulogne, but her afternoons are all sewed up with her peer group doing art appreciation at the Louvre. On Saturdays and Sundays the lake is too crowded.

I don't see how anybody gets to know any French students, unless they have a letter of introduction. I've tried going to cafés where they're said to hang out, but they're mostly full of Americans who have heard the same rumor. And if they aren't full of Americans, nobody will talk to me. I've actually gone as far as asking for a light. The place to find French students is at the movies. They seem to spend all their time there.

That reminds me. Did you know that you're supposed to tip the usher in a French movie house? I didn't know and got hissed at by the woman the other day when I went to see an Antonioni flick. All the students in the vicinity stopped necking and turned to ogle me as I stumbled into my seat. I gather I was being called a *"sale américain,"* but if she knew I was an American, she might have enlightened me about the local customs. It must happen all the time with foreigners. But I suppose that's what makes her mad. Usually when I'm in some place like a stand-up coffee bar, I watch what the other customers do and follow their example, but in a movie house you're literally in the dark. This little incident wrecked the film for me. I hardly saw Monica Vitti because of the rage I was in. The picture was half over before I finally grasped what my big crime of omission had been. Then it was too late to rectify it—at least without getting stared at some more. Besides, I couldn't see how much the other customers were giving. In case you want to know, it's a franc on the Champs-Elysées and fifty centimes in the little places. The clerk at my hotel told me.

At home I never thought I was much of a conformist. But I now see that I was without knowing it. I did what everybody else did without being aware I was copying them. Here I *mind* being different. Being abroad makes you conscious of the whole imitative side of human behavior. The ape in man. The tourists have it better. I don't sneer any more when I see them being carted around in those double-decker buses with earphones on their ears. I envy them. They've all told each other who they are and where they come from, and to the French they're part of the landscape, like the Tour Eiffel—nobody notices them, except other tourists. Here nobody knows who I am, as a person, which is all right with me, but I can't fade into the foliage either. If I still had Aunt Millie's camera and were willing to carry it, it might make me invisible to the

French. Just another tourist. It occurs to me that that's why, unconsciously, the men are all draped with cameras and light meters and the old women have their glasses slung around their necks—to show they belong to the species, tourist, which allows them to disappear as individuals.

JAN MORRIS

(1926–)

James Humphrey Morris wrote this selection "Trouville: A Town the Artists Loved" in 1964. A well-known foreign correspondent for the London Times *and the* Manchester Guardian, *Morris's pieces on Sir Edmund Hilary's conquest of Mount Everest won international acclaim. He was recognized as an authentic voice in both journalism and travel writing—most notably for* Pax Britannica, *a trilogy on the British Empire.*

Despite his macho image, literary success, and family and four children, James Morris was deeply conflicted. In 1972 James became Jan. As he described in his book Conundrum *(1974), he surgically changed sex, becoming an aunt to his children and partner to his wife. Morris continued a prolific career as a travel writer, but with a decidedly feminine viewpoint. On a trip to Dublin in the mid-1960s, James Morris went to the Half Moon Swimming Club for elderly nudists. One of the members pointed at Morris and said, "That fellow there, the one with the clothes on—surely he can't be a member here, can he?" On Jan Morris's next trip to Dublin in the mid-1970s her clothing issue was finding a suitable dress for the installation of the President of the Irish Republic. ("I congratulate you," said the maid in Morris's hotel, "You have excellent taste.")*

Morris has produced many books of travel literature including Venice, The Matter of Wales, Oxford, Spain, Hong Kong, Journeys, Destinations *and her memoir* Pleasures of a Tangled Life. *One critic wrote that Morris "plays with the conventions of travel writing . . . [and] stands these conventions on their heads—just as travel itself so often plays with our own preconceptions."*

Trouville: A Town the Artists Loved

In 1964 I wrote a series of articles, for the American magazine
Life, about famous European resorts. This happy assignment
introduced me to Trouville, which remains for me still, as it
seemed then, the quintessence of seaside pleasure, and an art form
in itself. You can keep your Acapulcos!

I had to look up Trouville on the map, but when I got there I
knew it at once—not from any specific book or painting, but
from a whole temper or even genre of art. There lay the long
empty foreshore, with only a few shrimp-catchers knee-deep in
its sand pools; and there along the boardwalk strolled a group of
those women that Boudin loved, blurred and shimmery in flow-
ered cottons; and the beach was lined with a gallimaufry of vil-
las, gabled, pinnacled or preposterously half-timbered; and three
fishing boats with riding sails chugged away offshore; and over it
all, over the sands and the estuary and the distant promontory of
Le Havre, there hung a soft impressionist light, summoned out
of moist sunshine, high rolling clouds and the reflection of the
sea. I knew the scene at once, from Monet and Bonnard and
Proust. The English were the modern inventors of the salt-water
resort, and made it fashionable to frequent the beaches; but the
French first saw the beauty of the seaside scene, and transmuted
into art all its perennial sights—the slant of that white sail, the
stoop of that child beside his sand castle, the preen of the great
ladies along the promenade.

This particular aesthetic was born in Trouville. It was among
the earliest of the French seaside resorts, for a time it was the
grandest, and at the back of our minds it is half familiar to us all.

Not far below the Seine estuary a little river called the Touques
arrives unobtrusively at the English Channel, flowing through
the lushly wooded landscape of Normandy, and surrounded at
its mouth by a superb sandy beach. At high tide along this shore
the sea rises to the very edge of the fields and orchards; at low
tide an immense plateau of gold and sea shells is exposed, with
chunks of black rock jutting out to sea, and a million infinitesi-
mal crustaceans hopping about in the shallows. On the right
bank of the Touques, almost at its mouth, there stood at the
beginning of the nineteenth century the isolated village of
Trouville—once a commercial port of some importance, later
overtaken by better situated rivals and reduced to the status of a
minor fishing station. The Channel here abounds in mackerel,
eel, hake, turbot, sole and every kind of shellfish; a packet boat
connected Trouville with Le Havre across the estuary; the vil-
lage pottered along in picturesque modesty, with no great claim
to fame, and not much hope of fortune.

In this condition the artist Charles Mozin discovered it in the
1820s. In a long series of affectionate paintings he portrayed
every detail of Trouville in its pristine days: the few villas beside
the sand, the horsemen plodding across the river at low tide, the
brawny fisherwomen, the bright sails of the boats along the
quays, the colonnaded fish market beside the waterfront, and
above all the limpid hush that seems to have hovered over the lit-
tle town. His pictures, not very distinguished examples of the
romantic school, are mostly forgotten now: but they were
exhibited in Paris, and they introduced the world to the charms
of a coastline hitherto considered bleak, blighted and impossibly
primitive. Other artists followed Mozin to Trouville, and writers
too, and presently the great caravan of fashion found its way to
the Normandy shore, and made the name of Trouville synony-
mous, for a brief but gorgeous heyday, with the pleasures of the
Second Empire.

It was a full-blown sort of climax. Napoleon III's regime began brilliantly, matured lavishly, and died in humiliation. Under its aegis, all the more sumptuous arts flourished. Romanticism flounced through its rich decline. Fashion went in for ribbons, crinolines and massive flowered bonnets. Sainte-Beuve presided over a sparkling school of literary criticism, painters like Courbet and Manet were bringing a daring new splendour to realist art. Led by the Empress Eugénie, herself a creature of infinite sensuality, the Second Empire fell upon Trouville like some overwhelming rich aunt, all scent and furbelows. The boardwalk was laid upon the sands, and above it, beneath the bluffs, a parade of hotels and villas arose—very assured, very opulent, with parasols, and wicker chairs on their verandas, and whirligigs on their eaves. At the point where the river reached the sands, they built a huge casino, a regular monument of a place, with opulent assembly rooms in the latest style, and carriage drives fit for any imperial barouche.

Trouville became a catalyst of the grand and the quaint. Where the fishing quay ended, the village began. The port remained a little port, but to the new resort came the Emperor himself and all of his racy, glamorous but not always very reputable court. The Empire set a seal upon Trouville, and the taste and style it engendered in this place have remained ever since part of the French artistic consciousness. Flaubert, Dumas, Victor Hugo, Boudin, Rossini, Gounod, de Musset and Dufy all felt the spell of the little town. Whistler stayed there with Courbet, Monet with Boudin, and nearly half a century after the fall of the Empire Trouville contributed its elements to the Balbec of Marcel Proust, where the sea looked like a painted fan through the windows of La Raspelière, where Albertine and her friends of the little band idled on the boardwalk, and where the Narrator himself pursued his introspections in "that Pandora's box, the Grand Hotel".

So I recognized it all: the sea and the sand from the painters, the style from the history books, and the very stance of the hotel manager from the pages of *A la Recherche du Temps Perdu*. Trouville has not much grown since Proust's day—or even since Eugénie's. The countryside behind it remains delectably unspoiled, with its famous stud farms hidden away among the elms, and strong emanations of milk, fruit and rough cider. The combination of green grass and sand, meeting at the foreshore, still makes the view from the beaches feel like one of those glimpses you get from the deck of a ship, when the passing landscape seems close but altogether unattainable, as though you are seeing it through plate glass. Across the estuary Le Havre has spread down its peninsula with oil tanks and tall apartment blocks, but its very hint of power and bustle, seen distantly across the water, only heightens Trouville's sense of detachment.

History is kind to pleasure-places, and Trouville has been spared by the wars. Long ago the English corsairs used to raid it, but in modern times nobody has much harmed the town. A plaque in one of the churches gratefully records the fact that the invading Prussian armies of 1871 never came farther than Honfleur, fifteen miles up the coast. In the last war, though the Allies bombed the German defences on the neighbouring hills, and fifty-six citizens of Trouville lost their lives in the Resistance, nevertheless when the liberating Belgians marched in, all was in reasonable order. This impunity means that Trouville, not so far along the shore from Utah Beach or Arromanches, has a curiously preserved or pickled air. It is a period piece, more perfect than most. Its balance of commerce and pleasure has been scrupulously maintained, and you can enjoy today almost the same mixture of sensations that the courtiers and the artists enjoyed a century ago. The core of the town remains the Casino. This has aged a little since its ceremonial opening, and has rather gone down in the world. Part of it is a cinema, part of it a salt-water spa, part a night club, part a waxwork show, part a fire house, part a shabby kind of tenement. As an architectural whole, nevertheless, it is still imposingly snooty, and looks faintly exotic—like a vast Mongol marquee, perhaps, with bobbles and domes and flagstaffs, and its own name in large and ornate letters above the entrance.

———

On my first evening in Trouville I made my way to the steps of this old prodigy and, leaning against a marble pillar, surveyed the town before me. The square outside the Casino, dotted with trees and used as a car park, is asymmetrical, and this splaying of its form makes it look exactly like one of those panoramic post-cards popular among our great-grandmothers, in which several negatives were tacked together, and the view came out peculiarly elongated, smaller at the edges than in the middle. From this distorted apex I could see both halves of Trouville. To my left lay the beach and all it represents, the pride, the old grandeur and the space. To my right, the fishing boats were lined up beside the quay, bright awnings ornamented the shop fronts, and all was cluttered intimacy. Both styles were essential, I realized that evening, to the art form that is Trouville; and it is the confrontation of the two, set against the light and scale of the foreshore, that gives the aesthetic of the seaside its especial tangy charm.

I looked to my right first, towards fisherman's Trouville—still as in the 1820s, any romantic's delight. The tide was high, and the upper works of fishing smacks lined the river boulevard—tangled structures of rope and rigging, hung with flags, buoys, lifebelts, nets and paintpots, and undulating slightly at their moorings. Here and there a crew was unloading its catch in crates upon the quay, while the fish merchant gravely calculated the value, a huddle of housewives knowingly discussed the quality, a few tourists looked on with the glazed fascination that dead fish inspire in almost everyone, and several small boys in their blue school smocks wormed and giggled through the crowd. There were men angling, too, with heavy rods and voluminous canvas satchels. There were porters lounging around the *poissonnerie,* in stained overalls and nautical caps. High-wheeled carts were propped against walls, there was a noise of hammering from a boatyard, and the fish stalls down the street glistened with crabs, lobsters, jumpy things like big water fleas, twitching eels, clams, oysters and mackerel with a cold bluish tinge to their flanks.

For Trouville is still a working town: and behind its water-front, workaday good sense fills the tight mesh of streets at the foot of the hill. There are shops that sell nets and tackle; shops lusciously flowing with the fruits, vegetables and cheeses of Normandy; trim cafés full of mirrors and tobacco smoke; a couple of big chain stores; and up in the grounds of the hospital, overgrown with ivy and embellished with archaic saintly figures, the original church of Trouville, thirteen paces long from door to altar, in whose reverent obscurity the fishing people worshipped for several centuries before the first tourist set eyes upon this place. All the stubborn variety of French provincial life stirs along those streets. Trouville is rich in tough twinkling old ladies, eccentrically dressed and wheeling their groceries on basket trolleys, and in those shabby but courteous old gentlemen of France who might be anything from dukes to retired milkmen, and wear high starched collars in the middle of August. But there are many laughing representatives of the new French generations, taller, gayer and more confident than we have ever known French people before, with beautiful children in the back seats of small family cars, and a sense of bright emancipation from a fusty past—figures from that rich young France which is, as D. W. Brogan has observed, "something that Europe and the world have not seen for a century".

Fisherman's Trouville is never torpid. It admirably illustrates those aspects of the French genius which are unalterably organic—close always to the earth, the sea, the marriage bed and the neighbour's gossip. The Duchesse de Guermantes, the ineffably aristocratic chatelaine of Proust's great novel, loved to tell country anecdotes in a rustic accent: and it is this ancient attachment to earthy things, so vital a part of the French artistic energy, that the right-hand view from the Casino best expresses.

Then I looked to the left, and there lay another France in esplanade. Exuberantly the hotels and villas clustered about the beach—none of them young indeed, but all of them gay, like

jolly old gentlefolk, in lace and grey toppers, out to enjoy them-
selves. It was an elaborate age that made Trouville famous, and
the buildings of this resort are flamboyantly individualist. Some
are gloriously encrusted with coils, domes and flourishes of clas-
sicism. Some are expensively faced in Normandy half-timber,
and stand incongruously beside the sands like farmhouses on
Fifth Avenue. Others go to wilder excess, and are built like cas-
tles, like fairy palaces, even in one case like a Persian caravanserai.
The rooftops of this Trouville are punctuated with golden birds,
pineapples, crescent moons, spindles, metal flowers and urns, and
all the way up the hillside among the trees the mansions stand in
majesty, unabashed by shifts of taste or society, and still looking,
behind their ornamental gates and protective shady gardens,
almost voluptuously comfortable.

Not much has changed since the great days of the resort. The
bright little tents that people put up on the beach are made of
nylon nowadays, but with their suggestion of eastern dalliance
still recall the enthusiasms of Delacroix or Gautier. Cars are not
admitted to the beach, so that the long-celebrated boardwalk,
however crowded it becomes in high summer, is still quiet and
leisurely. Nobody has erected a skyscraper hotel, or built a bowl-
ing alley, and severe instructions affixed to flagstaffs govern the
decorum of the sands. The miniature golf course, beside the
Casino, is a very model of genteel entertainment, admirably
suited to the inhibitions of elastic-sided boots and bustles: with
its painted wooden windmill for knocking balls through, its
tricky inclines and whimsical hazards, it seems to ring perpetu-
ally with the silvery laugh of ladies-in-waiting, and the indul-
gent banter of colonels. As for the unexploded mines and bombs
which occasionally turn up along these shores, Trouville offi-
cially classifies them as *"Objets Bizarres"*—and what a fine old-
school sniff infuses those fastidious syllables!

The Second Empire was scarcely an empire really, but it loved
the imperial trappings, and stamped the grand manner upon
Trouville. Two nineteenth-century churches overshadow the lit-
tle fishermen's chapel, and are full of superior memories. In one,

a large but indistinct painting has nothing to indicate either its subject or its artist, but only a plaque to tell us loftily: "Presented by the Emperor". In the other stands an altar given by the Comte d'Hautpool and his wife the Princesse de Wagram—Napoleonic titles which, for all their splendour, remind us that the ruling class of this extravagant period was never quite the real thing, but rested upon the pedigree of a Corsican adventurer. The florid style of the Empire is everywhere in Trouville, and when the regime collapsed with the defeat of Napoleon III at the Battle of Sedan, the great days of the resort ended too; it was here that the fiery Eugénie stepped aboard an English yacht and sailed away into exile.

Finally I walked behind the great mass of the Casino (looking, as the evening drew on, just as humped and portentous as Bonnard had painted it fifty years before) and across the narrow river I saw another, larger, more glittering city on the other side. The Duc de Morny, half-brother of the Emperor himself, was paradoxically the originator of Trouville's decline. In the 1860s this enterprising speculator cast *his* eye across the Touques, and saw that the sand on the other side was just as golden, the climate just as sparkling, the sea the same stimulating sea—and the landscape entirely empty. Trouville had reached its peak of fashion; the Parisian elite was beginning to hanker for somewhere more exclusive; in a few years, upon the impetus of the duke, there arose on the left bank of the Touques the excruciatingly posh resort of Deauville.

Today it is the smartest watering place in northern France, and it looked to me that evening, from the backside of Trouville's Casino, like a vision of another age. Its clientele nowadays is richer and more cosmopolitan than Trouville's. Its casino has a turnover twice as great. Its street lights come on fifteen minutes earlier. Its race meeting is one of the most important in Europe. No fishermen's cafés soil its elegant promenades, and only yachts and speedboats sail into its basin. It is all resort. Today if you want to explain where Trouville stands, you can best say that it's over the bridge from Deauville.

———

So there is a certain pathos to the prospect from the Casino at Trouville—but pathos of a gentle, amused kind. Trouville does not feel humiliated. It is this small town that the artists loved, its image, variously interpreted down the generations, that has entered all our sensibilities—Trouville's sands and sails we all dimly recognize, Trouville's ludicrous mansions that ornament the album pages, Trouville's bright light that gleams so often, with a tang of Channel air, from the walls of so many galleries. In Trouville the sun, the sea, the fishing folk and the high society became an inspiration, and created a tradition of art.

So I did not mope that evening. I crossed the square to my hotel, accepted the bows of Proust's page boys, left a note inviting Whistler and de Musset to join me for a drink at *Les Vapeurs,* and asked the maid to clean my best shoes, in case I bumped into the Empress at the Casino after dinner.

EZRA POUND
(1885–1972)

In 1958 Ezra Pound, essayist, translator, critic and influential and controversial poet, was sifting through old papers and discovered several small school notebooks, a journal of his hike through southern France in 1912. Pound's daughter, Mary, recalled that the discovery of these early manuscripts—although disorganized and fragmentary—boosted the old poet's spirits. He had just been released from fourteen years in St. Elizabeth's Hospital in Washington, D.C., judged insane after a 1946 trial for treason. Pound was charged with complicity with the Italian Fascist government during World War II; the literary community obtained his release only after years of public pressure. After he left St. Elizabeth's, Pound returned to Europe.

Pound's A Walking Tour in Southern France *is more than juvenilia. He became interested in the French troubadours while at Hamilton College, and his early poetry (which he later dismissed as "stale cream puffs") showed the influence of oral traditions in its lyricism and meter.*

In the introduction to A Walking Tour in Southern France, *Richard Sieburth wrote, "Although of uneven literary quality, the surviving first draft notes of the journey that was to have provided the narrative backbone of* Gironde *nonetheless offer a rare portrait of Pound at a decisive turning point in his career—age twenty-six, no longer the archaizing minstrel of* Canzoni, *but not quite fully at home in the modernist aesthetic."*

Pound's best-known work is the unfinished Cantos, *an epic that addressed commercialism in the arts, world history, economic conditions and his own incarceration. Ezra Pound began them in 1913, published the first group in 1925 and worked on them until his death.*

from A Walking Tour in Southern France

Foix

To Foix by night, for here lived that count who wrote

"Mas qui a flor se vol meschlar"

We are come again to a place where the waters run swiftly & where we have always this chinese background.
  The faint grey of the mountains

The castle of Foix stands as everyone knows on a sharp little rock between the V of 2 rivers, perpendicular above its town & close to a baldish mountain this is shaped like the rump of a very thin, very great elephant & below is fast water, & about are high hills, green, & light green & distant, & there you have it, three towers, a buttress & some bridges & red pink weeds by the way-side if you look back from the rd. to Quilian.
  There was another sharp rock to build on but I dare say Foix is the strongest.

I had at last my plan of starting late in the day so the hills were full of cloud & mist & there were bright & dim colours upon them.
  I went into this Coliseum of hills with Foix like Caesar's stand behind me, but with a veiled light over it & scarcely visible.
  I went out the other end where a great sheet of rock juts thru the quarry, out & into a paler basin that faced me with light emerald & pearlish shadows.

Then you go up & over till the sky shows blue before you. It is not the rd. of the diligence.

One may lie on the earth & possess it & feel the world below one

I took the road again at Foix not from a sense of duty but from a wish to see some Pyrenees, some Pyrenees that is on this side of France, a wish shared by no known troubadour.

"To goon on pilgrimages" is a respectable & ancient habit, it implies a shrine, etc., but to go for mere mts. is decadent, I presume, & modern or at least parvenu & dating from the Ossianic movement.

Of course the quest of adventure is another matter, that also is respectably medieval, but I can not be said to be seeking adventure—a greatly overestimated commodity—for the pleasant ones one can never mention [marginal note: No gallantry in a land smelling of garlic. Impossible.] & the kind that make good telling are usually very fatiguing & uncomfortable while they last, & even then, if one plays anything like a role, a laudable role, this modern, false modern self consciousness keeps one from boasting of it. Assuredly adventure is of little use except to an author, & an author had much better pretend, pretend, I mean, that adventures befell John Donne or Giles Faring or whomsoever.

At any rate I am going the route in sheer truancy.

There is a Mauléon miles to the west which may or may not be *the* Mauléon—at any rate it is said to be a dull place, & up by Castres lies Burlats with a pavilion à Adelaide, at east of it a little is Riquer St. Pons. St. Pons de Tournau [?], but I am heading for Carcassonne with which Troubadours had little to do, & I go by a route that presumably no jongleur ever bothered to climb.

Foix was very right to come to.

Roquefixade

I said this was a route without associations but after one has gone along a ledge of rd. beneath towers & fangs of rock & across a sort of open and up another incline one comes to Rocafixada. I see no reason why this should not have been the hold of a certain little known Q de R.

There is a huge sort of dorsal fin of rock that lifts sharp out of the mtn. One doubts if a man could climb it but there cradled in the sheer mad top of it are the ruins & the arches.

The sky is like a palmer's shell & the herd of hills lies before this.

I mounted the sheer face of rock to this castle & this was as I think of it one of the maddest things I have done in my life & of the sanest. There are chances to break one's neck not only in the ascent to the castle, but from this to the keep, & there in crevasses of ruin. & the land lies below darkening to copper, & the roads like white corals upon it.

Of this place there is nothing in the archives

> walls of keep 12 ft. thick
> went thru alcove of 7.5 ft walls. beyond it terrace. crevice of
>   rock 2 ft. wide.
> weakness–water suffering supply

Sky jap pink & grey when I descended other side—man & oxen. Béziers. S. at Toulouse.

& I went down the darkening valley, & behind me there was light at the base of the rock & the ruined wall acrest it, & I was perhaps foolish for there was an inn in that place & the people were kindly.

But I came down thru pine wood smelling of evening & few stars above me & the mts known only as shadow. O dies et candide lapis, but it was a road to gallop not to walk on & the only

sounds were me & a few tired crickets & one toad & the several
dogs I waked, & gradually the sky brocaded itself, & near Lave-
lanet I met a mason who told me his troubles & so I finished that
journey.

Montségur

I set out the following day with the castle Montségur, which I
had seen from before Roquefixade still in sight on its stilt of a
mountain with a little snow behind it. The road from Lavelanet
lies thru the valley & is devilish hot of mornings with the sun in
ones eyes, & the colour worth next to nothing & the flies thor-
oughly damnable. Were I possessed of any superabundance of
common sense I should have waited for the diligence, for at least
a part of the distance.

I held a late noon at Puivert, however, & proceeded at a saner
hour. One comes to sharp green hummock of mountain with a
false castle of its own rock but this is no second Fixada, tho' the
pines may well give a green name to the peak here.

The fortress of Puivert is on an easy cone in the plateau
beyond this, a stumpy keep, with the proper compliment of
walls, 6 towers, square built like the Scaliger castles.

The town is a remnant, completely hidden.

Quillan

Whether it is a haze of heat or whether it is only the effect of
sunlight & of great distance, I do not know but there come with
these mts, as the sun lowers, a colour at once metallic & oriental,
as of a substance both dim & burnished.

Gaze on a mirrour & you will get something of the quality of
colour, but here are many colours & the mirrour is deeper.

By 4:30 sky is a fine Saracenic blue with charred & blunted
edges.

Above Quillan the rd. leads into Chinese unreality, we enter this & leave Puivert square upon the sky line behind us.

One should descend into Quillan by ladder, the rd. is a waste of time. But the great gates are before you & that may be held repayment.

Quillan has quiet waters & the square stump of a castle. My demons of energy & greed drove me thence straight on that night into Axat. This route is as famous as I am, but then what will you, the reputation is so much older?

The sides of this pass rise higher than the buildings in Wall St. They are not unlike them in colour. It is true that they do not always rise so abruptly and that the gulch is not so narrow at bottom. Still as De Musset has so eloquently said "it is a fine sight for even a New Yorker." Our author is here violently wrong it was not De Musset but *Gautier*

"Ici l'impossible"

It is a mad stack of sheets & spires & obelisks, with a green mass of debris.

Some faces of the rocks are sheer as those of a building & some are low & jutting.

Dwarfed cedars clutch at the crevices at bottom the stream is almost as green as they are. There is a Chinese bridge of poles across this current.

Axat

20 mi. below here is Pradas, but Daude from that place did not amount to much. & beyond there is Figuera. but 2nd rate troubadours were scattered all over this land from Paris to Portugal. One cannot be bothered tracing all of them.

There was likewise a small Pegulhan, but that troubadour was of Tolosa. I have mention of him elsewhere (S.O.R.)

Beyond St. Martin Lys is another less acute defile, a place

more abounding in trees, the rock softer & more broken, the rd. winds thru' the rugged way of the opposing mts.

It is less Ming.

Less like a sport of gods & more like the work of nature.

Twas thru such a pine wood maybe that they hunted mad Peire Vidal. Smith puts Cabaret near Cabestang but I can not so find it.

There seems to be no end to this & similar gorges but I stop at Axat.

47 k. since morning to my credit & the gorges of St. George before me.

DAVID SEDARIS

(1957–)

David Sedaris seems an odd transplant to France. His work, on National Public Radio and in collections of essays including Barrel Fever, Me Talk Pretty One Day *and* Naked, *has the acerbic view of a native New Yorker. Which he is not. Sedaris was raised in North Carolina, the son of a Greek-American father and a mother whose family history of mental and physical health was so poor that their crest was "a bottle of scotch and a tumor." Sedaris claims that he did not read until he graduated from college and then held a series of odd jobs including writing instructor at an art college, floor refinisher and Christmas elf.*

Sedaris relocated to France because his boyfriend Hugh owned a house in Normandy. France intrigued him because it is a "smoker's paradise" ("Tell me again about the ashtrays in the hospital waiting room and don't leave anything out") and has great shopping. Sedaris's purchases ran to taxidermied animals and medical models. His French was limited to the word for "bottleneck."

Sedaris has learned to appreciate other things about France: no one says he is "stressed out," great American movies such as Oklahoma *and* Nashville *are shown in Parisian theaters almost around the clock and French nouns have gender. And then there's the smoking.*

Make That a Double

from ME TALK PRETTY ONE DAY

There are, I have noticed, two basic types of French spoken by Americans vacationing in Paris: the Hard Kind and the Easy Kind. The Hard Kind involves the conjugation of wily verbs and the science of placing them alongside various other words in order to form such sentences as "I go him say good afternoon" and "No, not to him I no go it him say now."

The second, less complicated form of French amounts to screaming English at the top of your lungs, much the same way you'd shout at a deaf person or the dog you thought you could train to stay off the sofa. Doubt and hesitation are completely unnecessary, as Easy French is rooted in the premise that, if properly packed, the rest of the world could fit within the confines of Reno, Nevada. The speaker carries no pocket dictionary and never suffers the humiliation that inevitably comes with pointing to the menu and ordering the day of the week. With Easy French, eating out involves a simple "BRING ME A STEAK."

Having undertaken the study of Hard French, I'll overhear such requests and glare across the room, thinking, "That's *Mister* Steak to you, buddy." Of all the stumbling blocks inherent in learning this language, the greatest for me is the principle that each noun has a corresponding sex that affects both its articles and its adjectives. Because it is a female and lays eggs, a chicken is masculine. *Vagina* is masculine as well, while the word *masculinity* is feminine. Forced by the grammar to take a stand one way or the other, *hermaphrodite* is male and *indecisiveness* female.

I spent months searching for some secret code before I realized that common sense has nothing to do with it. *Hysteria, psychosis, torture, depression:* I was told that if something is unpleasant, it's probably feminine. This encouraged me, but the theory was blown by such masculine nouns as *murder, toothache,* and *Rollerblade.* I have no problem learning the words themselves, it's the sexes that trip me up and refuse to stick.

What's the trick to remembering that a sandwich is masculine? What qualities does it share with anyone in possession of a penis? I'll tell myself that a sandwich is masculine because if left alone for a week or two, it will eventually grow a beard. This works until it's time to order and I decide that because it sometimes loses its makeup, a sandwich is undoubtedly feminine.

I just can't manage to keep my stories straight. Hoping I might learn through repetition, I tried using gender in my everyday English. "Hi, guys," I'd say, opening a new box of paper clips, or "Hey, Hugh, have you seen my belt? I can't find her anywhere." I invented personalities for the objects on my dresser and set them up on blind dates. When things didn't work out with my wallet, my watch drove a wedge between my hairbrush and my lighter. The scenarios reminded me of my youth, when my sisters and I would enact epic dramas with our food. Ketchup-wigged french fries would march across our plates, engaging in brief affairs or heated disputes over carrot coins while burly chicken legs guarded the perimeter, ready to jump in should things get out of hand. Sexes were assigned at our discretion and were subject to change from one night to the next— unlike here, where the corncob and the string bean remain locked in their rigid masculine roles. Say what you like about Southern social structure, but at least in North Carolina a hot dog is free to swing both ways.

Nothing in France is free from sexual assignment. I was leafing through the dictionary, trying to complete a homework assignment, when I noticed the French had prescribed genders for the various land masses and natural wonders we Americans had always thought of as sexless. Niagara Falls is feminine and, against all reason, the Grand Canyon is masculine. Georgia and Florida are female, but Montana and Utah are male. New England is a she, while the vast area we call the Midwest is just one big guy. I wonder whose job it was to assign these sexes in the first place. Did he do his work right there in the sanitarium, or did they rent him a little office where he could get away from all the noise?

There are times when you can swallow the article and others when it must be clearly pronounced, as the word has two different meanings, one masculine and the other feminine. It should be fairly obvious that I cooked an omelette in a frying pan rather than in a wood stove, but it bothers me to make the same mistakes over and over again. I wind up exhausting the listener before I even get to the verb.

My confidence hit a new low when my friend Adeline told me that French children often make mistakes, but never with the sex of their nouns. "It's just something we grow up with," she said. "We hear the gender once, and then think of it as part of the word. There's nothing to it."

It's a pretty grim world when I can't even feel superior to a toddler. Tired of embarrassing myself in front of two-year-olds, I've started referring to everything in the plural, which can get expensive but has solved a lot of my problems. In saying *a melon,* you need to use the masculine article. In saying *the melons,* you use the plural article, which does not reflect gender and is the same for both the masculine and the feminine. Ask for two or ten or three hundred melons, and the number lets you off the hook by replacing the article altogether. A masculine kilo of feminine tomatoes presents a sexual problem easily solved by asking for two kilos of tomatoes. I've started using the plural while shopping, and Hugh has started using it in our cramped kitchen, where he stands huddled in the corner, shouting, "What do we need with four pounds of tomatoes?"

I answer that I'm sure we can use them for something. The only hard part is finding someplace to put them. They won't fit in the refrigerator, as I filled the last remaining shelf with the two chickens I bought from the butcher the night before, forgetting that we were still working our way through a pair of pork roasts the size of Duraflame logs. "We could put them next to the radios," I say, "or grind them for sauce in one of the blenders. Don't get so mad. Having four pounds of tomatoes is better than having no tomatoes at all, isn't it?"

Hugh tells me that the market is off-limits until my French improves. He's pretty steamed, but I think he'll get over it when he sees the CD players I got him for his birthday.

TOBIAS SMOLLETT
(1721–1771)

Tobias Smollett, British novelist and physician, went to the south of France to escape grief. He and his wife, Nancy, lost their only child Elizabeth, a girl of fifteen, three months before their journey. Smollett was "overwhelmed by the sense of a domestic calamity, which it was not in the power of fortune to repair." Smollett's own health was precarious; he had jaundice, asthma and a "complaint of the spleen." His most popular writing—the picaresque novels The Adventures of Roderick Random *and* The Adventures of Peregrine Pickle—*was behind him.*

Smollett was not a happy traveler. Everything about France rankled— the women were dressed like Hottentots, his lodgings were gloomy, the food was inedible and served at odd hours and even Versailles was "dismal." His spirits lightened somewhat as he traveled south, and the Riviera must have reminded him of Jamaica, the place of his wife's birth and where Smollett had spent several years.

Travels in France and Italy *drips with bile and prejudice—which makes it a wicked good read. Smollett gives a brilliant picture of the challenging traveling conditions of the eighteenth century. And here is the author—tired, ill, grieving—but still curious enough to take an arduous journey and record it in vivid prose.*

Letter VIII

Lyons, October 19, 1763

Dear Sir,

I was favoured with yours at Paris, and look upon your reproaches as the proof of your friendship. The truth is, I considered all the letters I have hitherto written on the subject of my travels, as written to your society in general, though they have been addressed to one individual of it; and if they contain any thing that can either amuse or inform, I desire that henceforth all I send may be freely perused by all the members.

With respect to my health, about which you so kindly enquire, I have nothing new to communicate. I had reason to think that my bathing in the sea at Boulogne produced a good effect, in strengthening my relaxed fibres. You know how subject I was to colds in England; that I could not stir abroad after sun-set, nor expose myself to the smallest damp, nor walk till the least moisture appeared on my skin, without being laid up for ten days or a fortnight. At Paris, however, I went out every day, with my hat under my arm, though the weather was wet and cold: I walked in the garden at Versailles even after it was dark, with my head uncovered, on a cold evening, when the ground was far from being dry: nay, at Marli, I sauntered above a mile through damp alleys, and wet grass: and from none of these risques did I feel the least inconvenience.

In one of our excursions we visited the manufacture for porcelain, which the king of France has established at the village of St. Cloud, on the road to Versailles, and which is, indeed, a noble monument of his munificence. It is a very large building, both commodious and magnificent, where a great number of artists are employed, and where this elegant superfluity is carried to as great perfection as it ever was at Dresden. Yet, after all, I know not whether the porcelain made at Chelsea may not vie with the productions either of Dresden, or St. Cloud. If it falls short of either, it is not in the design, painting, enamel, or other ornaments, but only in the composition of the metal, and the method of managing it in the furnace. Our porcelain seems to be a partial vitrification of levigated flint and fine pipe clay, mixed together in a certain proportion; and if the pieces are not removed from the fire in the very critical moment, they will be either too little, or too much vitrified. In the first case, I apprehend they will not acquire a proper degree of cohesion; they will be apt to be corroded, discoloured, and to crumble, like the first essays that were made at Chelsea; in the second case, they will be little better than imperfect glass.

There are three methods of travelling from Paris to Lyons, which, by the shortest road is a journey of about three hundred and sixty miles. One is by the *diligence,* or stage-coach, which performs it in five days; and every passenger pays one hundred livres, in consideration of which, he not only has a seat in the carriage, but is maintained on the road. The inconveniences attending this way of travelling are these. You are crouded into the carriage, to the number of eight persons, so as to sit very uneasy, and sometimes run the risque of being stifled among very indifferent company. You are hurried out of bed, at four, three, nay often at two o'clock in the morning. You are obliged to eat in the French way, which is very disagreeable to an English palate; and, at Chalons, you must embark upon the Saone in a boat, which conveys you to Lyons, so that the two last days of your journey are by water. All these were insurmountable objections to me, who am in such a bad state of health, troubled with an asthmatic cough, spitting, slow fever, and restlessness, which demands a continual change of place, as well as free air, and room for motion. I was this day visited by two young gentlemen, sons of Mr. Guastaldi, late minister from Genoa at London. I had seen them at Paris, at the house of the dutchess of Douglas. They came hither, with their conductor, in the *diligence,* and assured me, that nothing could be more disagreeable than their situation in that carriage.

Another way of travelling in this country is to hire a coach and four horses; and this method I was inclined to take: but when I went to the bureau, where alone these voitures are to be had, I was given to understand, that it would cost me six-and-twenty guineas, and travel so slow that I should be ten days upon the road. These carriages are let by the same persons who farm the *diligence;* and for this they have an exclusive privilege, which makes them very saucy and insolent. When I mentioned my servant, they gave me to understand, that I must pay two loui'dores more for his seat upon the coach box. As I could not relish these terms, nor brook the thoughts of being so long upon the road, I had recourse to the third method, which is going post.

In England you know I should have had nothing to do, but to hire a couple of post-chaises from stage to stage, with two horses in each; but here the case is quite otherwise. The post is farmed from the king, who lays travellers under contribution for his own benefit, and has published a set of oppressive ordonnances, which no stranger nor native dares transgress. The postmaster finds nothing but horses and guides: the carriage you yourself must provide. If there are four persons within the carriage, you are obliged to have six horses, and two postillions; and if your servant sits on the outside, either before or behind, you must pay for a seventh. You pay double for the first stage from Paris, and twice double for passing through Fontainbleau when the court is there, as well as at coming to Lyons, and at leaving this city. These are called royal posts, and are undoubtedly a scandalous imposition.

There are two post roads from Paris to Lyons, one of sixty-five posts, by the way of Moulins; the other of fifty-nine, by the way of Dijon in Burgundy. This last I chose, partly to save sixty livres, and partly to see the wine harvest of Burgundy, which, I was told, was a season of mirth and jollity among all ranks of people. I hired a very good coach for ten loui'dores to Lyons, and set out from Paris on the thirteenth instant, with six horses, two postillions, and my own servant on horseback. We made no stop at Fontainbleau, though the court was there; but lay at Moret, which is one stage further, a very paltry little town; where, however, we found good accommodation.

I shall not pretend to describe the castle or palace of Fontainbleau, of which I had only a glimpse in passing; but the forest, in the middle of which it stands, is a noble chase of great extent, beautifully wild and romantic, well stored with game of all sorts, and abounding with excellent timber. It put me in mind of the New Forest in Hampshire; but the hills, rocks, and mountains, with which it is diversified, render it more agreeable.

The people of this country dine at noon, and travellers always find an ordinary prepared at every *auberge,* or public-house, on the road. Here they sit down promiscuously, and dine at so much a head. The usual price is thirty sols for dinner, and forty for supper, including lodging; for this moderate expence they have two courses and a dessert. If you eat in your own apartment, you pay, instead of forty sols, three, and in some places, four livres a head. I and my family could not well dispense with our tea and toast in the morning, and had no stomach to eat at noon. For my own part, I hate French cookery, and abominate garlic, with which all their ragouts, in this part of the country, are highly seasoned: we therefore formed a different plan of living upon the road. Before we left Paris, we laid in a stock of tea, chocolate, cured neats' tongues, and *saucissons,* or Bologna sausages, both of which we found in great perfection in that capital, where, indeed, there are excellent provisions of all sorts. About ten in the morning we stopped to breakfast at some *auberge,* where we always found bread, butter, and milk. In the mean time, we ordered a *poulard* or two to be roasted, and these, wrapped in a napkin, were put into the boot of the coach, together with bread, wine, and water. About two or three in the afternoon, while the horses were changing, we laid a cloth upon our knees, and producing our store, with a few earthen plates, discussed our short meal without further ceremony. This was followed by a dessert of grapes and other fruit, which we had also provided. I must own I found these transient refreshments much more agreeable than any regular meal I ate upon the road. The wine commonly used in Burgundy is so weak and thin, that you would not drink it in England. The very best which they sell at Dijon, the capital of the province, for three livres a bottle, is in strength, and even in flavour, greatly inferior to what I have drank in London. I believe all the first growth is either consumed in the houses of the noblesse, or sent abroad to foreign markets. I have drank excellent Burgundy at Brussels for a florin a bottle; that is, little more than twenty pence sterling.

The country from the forest of Fontainbleau to the Lyonnois, through which we passed, is rather agreeable than fertile, being part of Champagne and the dutchy of Burgundy, watered by three pleasant pastoral rivers, the Seine, the Yonne, and the Saone. The flat country is laid out chiefly for corn; but produces more rye than wheat. Almost all the ground seems to be ploughed up, so that there is little or nothing lying fallow. There are very few inclosures, scarce any meadow ground, and, so far as I could observe, a great scarcity of cattle. We sometimes found it very difficult to procure half a pint of milk for our tea. In Burgundy I saw a peasant ploughing the ground with a jack-ass, a lean cow, and a he-goat, yoked together. It is generally observed, that a great number of black cattle are bred and fed on the mountains of Burgundy, which are the highest lands in France; but I saw very few. The peasants in France are so wretchedly poor, and so much oppressed by their landlords, that they cannot afford to inclose their grounds, or give a proper respite to their lands; or to stock their farms with a sufficient number of black cattle to produce the necessary manure, without which agriculture can never be carried to any degree of perfection. Indeed, whatever efforts a few individuals may make for the benefit of their own estates, husbandry in France will never be generally improved, until the farmer is free and independent.

From the frequency of towns and villages, I should imagine this country is very populous; yet it must be owned, that the towns are in general thinly inhabited. I saw a good number of country seats and plantations near the banks of the rivers, on each side; and a great many convents, sweetly situated, on rising grounds, where the air is most pure, and the prospect most agreeable. It is surprising to see how happy the founders of those religious houses have been in their choice of situations, all the world over.

In passing through this country, I was very much struck with the sight of large ripe clusters of grapes, entwined with the briars and thorns of common hedges on the wayside. The mountains of Burgundy are covered with vines from the bottom to the top, and seem to be raised by nature on purpose to extend the surface, and to expose it the more advantageously to the rays of the sun. The *vandange* was but just begun, and the people were employed in gathering the grapes; but I saw no signs of festivity among them. Perhaps their joy was a little damped by the bad prospect of their harvest; for they complained that the weather had been so unfavourable as to hinder the grapes from ripening. I thought, indeed, there was something uncomfortable in seeing the vintage thus retarded till the beginning of winter: for, in some parts, I found the weather extremely cold; particularly at a place called Maison-neuve, where we lay, there was a hard frost, and in the morning the pools were covered with a thick crust of ice. My personal adventures on the road were such as will not bear a recital. They consisted of petty disputes with landladies, post-masters, and postillions. The highways seem to be perfectly safe. We did not find that any robberies were ever committed, although we did not see one of the *maréchaussée* from Paris to Lyons. You know the *maréchaussée* are a body of troopers well mounted, maintained in France as safeguards to the public roads. It is a reproach upon England that some such patrol is not appointed for the protection of travellers.

At Sens in Champagne, my servant, who had rode on before to bespeak fresh horses, told me, that the domestic of another company had been provided before him, altho' it was not his turn, as he had arrived later at the post. Provoked at this partiality, I resolved to chide the post-master, and accordingly addressed myself to a person who stood at the door of the *auberge.* He was a jolly figure, fat and fair, dressed in an odd kind of garb, with a gold laced cap on his head, and a cambric handkerchief pinned to his middle. The sight of such a fantastic *petit maître,* in the character of a post-master, increased my spleen. I called to him with an air of authority, mixed with indignation, and when he came up to the coach, asked in a peremptory tone, if he did not understand the king's ordonnance concerning the regulation of the posts? He laid his hand upon his breast;

but before he could make any answer, I pulled out the post-book, and began to read, with great vociferation, the article which orders, that the traveller who comes first shall be first served. By this time the fresh horses being put to the carriage, and the postillions mounted, the coach set off all of a sudden, with uncommon speed. I imagined the post-master had given the fellows a signal to be gone, and, in this persuasion, thrusting my head out at the window, I bestowed some epithets upon him, which must have sounded very harsh in the ears of a Frenchman. We stopped for a refreshment at a little town called Joigne-ville, where (by the bye) I was scandalously imposed upon, and even abused by a virago of a landlady; then proceeding to the next stage, I was given to understand we could not be supplied with fresh horses. Here I perceived at the door of the inn, the same person whom I had reproached at Sens. He came up to the coach, and told me, that notwithstanding what the guides had said, I should have fresh horses in a few minutes. I imagined he was master both of this house and the *auberge* at Sens, between which he passed and repassed occasionally; and that he was now desirous of making me amends for the affront he had put upon me at the other place. Observing that one of the trunks behind was a little displaced, he assisted my servant in adjusting it: then he entered into conversation with me, and gave me to understand, that in a post-chaise, which we had passed, was an English gentleman on his return from Italy. I wanted to know who he was, and when he said he could not tell, I asked him, in a very abrupt manner, why he had not enquired of his servant. He shrugged up his shoulders, and retired to the inn door. Having waited about half an hour, I beckoned to him, and when he approached, upbraided him with having told me that I should be supplied with fresh horses in a few minutes: he seemed shocked, and answered, that he thought he had reason for what he said, observing, that it was as disagreeable to him as to me to wait for a relay. As it began to rain, I pulled up the glass in his face, and he withdrew again to the door, seemingly ruffled at my deportment. In a little time the horses arrived, and three of them were immediately put to a very handsome post-chaise, into which he stepped, and set out, accompanied by a man in a rich livery on horseback. Astonished at this circumstance, I asked the hostler who he was, and he replied, that he was a man of fashion (un seigneur) who lived in the neighbourhood of Auxerre. I was much mortified to find that I had treated a nobleman so scurvily, and scolded my own people for not having more penetration than myself. I dare say he did not fail to descant upon the brutal behaviour of the Englishman; and that my mistake served with him to confirm the national reproach of bluntness, and ill breeding, under which we lie in this country. The truth is, I was that day more than usually peevish, from the bad weather, as well as from the dread of a fit of the asthma, with which I was threatened: and I dare say my appearance seemed as uncouth to him, as his travelling dress appeared to me. I had a grey mourning frock under a wide great coat, a bob wig without powder, a very large laced hat, and a meagre, wrinkled, discontented countenance.

The fourth night of our journey we lay at Macon, and the next day passed through the Lyonnois, which is a fine country, full of towns, villages, and gentlemen's houses. In passing through the Maconnois, we saw a great many fields of Indian corn, which grows to the height of six or seven feet: it is made into flour for the use of the common people, and goes by the name of *Turkey wheat*. Here likewise, as well as in Dauphiné, they raise a vast quantity of very large pompions, with the contents of which they thicken their soup and ragouts.

As we travelled only while the sun was up, on account of my ill health, and the post horses in France are in bad order, we seldom exceeded twenty leagues a day.

I was directed to a lodging-house at Lyons, which being full they shewed us to a tavern, where I was led up three pair of stairs, to an apartment consisting of three paltry chambers, for which the people demanded twelve livres a day: for dinner and supper they asked thirty-two, besides three livres for my servant; so that my daily expence would have amounted to about forty-seven livres, exclusive of breakfast and coffee in the afternoon. I was so provoked at this extortion, that, without answering one word, I drove to another *auberge,* where I now am, and pay at the rate of two-and-thirty livres a day, for which I am very badly lodged, and but very indifferently entertained. I mention these circumstances to give you an idea of the imposition to which strangers are subject in this country. It must be owned, however, that in the article of eating, I might save half the money by going to the public ordinary; but this is a scheme of oeconomy, which (exclusive of other disagreeable circumstances) neither my own health, nor that of my wife permits me to embrace. My journey from Paris to Lyons, including the hire of the coach, and all expences on the road, has cost me, within a few shillings, forty loui'dores. From Paris our baggage (though not plombé) was not once examined till we arrived in this city, at the gate of which we were questioned by one of the searchers, who, being tipt with half a crown, allowed us to proceed without further enquiry.

I purposed to stay in Lyons until I should receive some letters I expected from London, to be forwarded by my banker at Paris: but the enormous expence of living in this manner has determined me to set out in a day or two for Montpellier, although that place is a good way out of the road to Nice. My reasons for taking that route I shall communicate in my next. Mean-while, I am ever,—Dear Sir, Your affectionate and obliged humble servant.

Letter IX

Montpellier, November 5, 1763

Dear Sir,

The city of Lyons has been so often and so circumstantially described, that I cannot pretend to say any thing new on the subject. Indeed, I know very little of it, but what I have read in books; as I had but one day to make a tour of the streets, squares, and other remarkable places. The bridge over the Rhone seems to be so slightly built, that I should imagine it would be one day carried away by that rapid river; especially as the arches are so small, that, after great rains they are sometimes *bouchées,* or stopped up; that is, they do not admit a sufficient passage for the encreased body of the water. In order to remedy this dangerous defect, in some measure, they found an artist some years ago, who has removed a middle pier, and thrown two arches into one. This alteration they looked upon as a masterpiece in architecture, though there is many a common mason in England, who would have undertaken and performed the work, without valuing himself much upon the enterprize. This bridge, as well as that of St. Esprit, is built, not in a strait line across the river, but with a curve, which forms a convexity to oppose the current. Such a bend is certainly calculated for the better resisting the general impetuosity of the stream, and has no bad effect to the eye.

Lyons is a great, populous, and flourishing city; but I am surprised to find it is counted a healthy place, and that the air of it is esteemed favourable to pulmonic disorders. It is situated on the confluence of two large rivers, from which

there must be a great evaporation, as well as from the low
marshy grounds, which these rivers often overflow. This
must render the air moist, frouzy, and even putrid, if it was
not well ventilated by winds from the mountains of Swis-
serland; and in the latter end of autumn, it must be subject
to fogs. The morning we set out from thence, the whole
city and adjacent plains were covered with so thick a fog,
that we could not distinguish from the coach the head of
the foremost mule that drew it. Lyons is said to be very hot
in summer, and very cold in winter; therefore I imagine
must abound with inflammatory and intermittent disor-
ders in the spring and fall of the year.

My reasons for going to Montpellier, which is out of
the strait road to Nice, were these. Having no acquaintance
nor correspondents in the South of France, I had desired
my credit might be sent to the same house to which my
heavy baggage was consigned. I expected to find my bag-
gage at Cette, which is the sea-port of Montpellier; and
there I also hoped to find a vessel, in which I might be
transported by sea to Nice, without further trouble. I
longed to try what effect the boasted air of Montpellier
would have upon my constitution; and I had a great desire
to see the famous monuments of antiquity in and about
the ancient city of Nismes, which is about eight leagues
short of Montpellier.

At the inn where we lodged, I found a return berline,
belonging to Avignon, with three mules, which are the
animals commonly used for carriages in this country. This
I hired for five loui'dores. The coach was large, commodi-
ous, and well-fitted; the mules were strong and in good
order; and the driver, whose name was Joseph, appeared
to be a sober, sagacious, intelligent fellow, perfectly well
acquainted with every place in the South of France. He
told me he was owner of the coach, but I afterwards
learned, he was no other than a hired servant. I likewise
detected him in some knavery, in the course of our jour-

ney; and plainly perceived he had a fellow feeling with the inn-keepers on the road; but, in other respects, he was very obliging, serviceable, and even entertaining. There are some knavish practices of this kind, at which a traveller will do well to shut his eyes, for his own ease and convenience. He will be lucky if he has to do with a sensible knave, like Joseph, who understood his interest too well to be guilty of very flagrant pieces of imposition.

A man, impatient to be at his journey's end, will find this a most disagreeable way of travelling. In summer it must be quite intolerable. The mules are very sure, but very slow. The journey seldom exceeds eight leagues, about four and twenty miles a day: and as those people have certain fixed stages, you are sometimes obliged to rise in a morning before day; a circumstance very grievous to persons in ill health. These inconveniences, however, were over-balanced by other *agreemens*. We no sooner quitted Lyons, than we got into summer weather, and travelling through a most romantic country, along the banks of the Rhone, had opportunities (from the slowness of our pace) to contemplate its beauties at leisure.

The rapidity of the Rhone is, in a great measure, owing to its being confined within steep banks on each side. These are formed almost through its whole course, by a double chain of mountains, which rise with an abrupt ascent from both banks of the river. The mountains are covered with vineyards, interspersed with small summer-houses, and in many places they are crowned with churches, chapels, and convents, which add greatly to the romantic beauty of the prospect. The highroad, as far as Avignon, lies along the side of the river, which runs almost in a straight line, and affords great convenience for inland commerce. Travellers, bound to the southern parts of France, generally embark in the *diligence* at Lyons, and glide down this river with great velocity, passing a great number of towns and villages on each side, where they find ordinaries every day at dinner and supper. In good weather, there is no danger in this method of travelling, 'till you come to the Pont St. Esprit, where the stream runs through the arches with such rapidity, that the boat is sometimes overset. But those passengers who are under any apprehension are landed above-bridge, and taken in again, after the boat has passed, just in the same manner as at London Bridge. The boats that go up the river are drawn against the stream by oxen, which swim through one of the arches of this bridge, the driver sitting between the horns of the foremost beast. We set out from Lyons early on Monday morning, and as a robbery had been a few days before committed in that neighbourhood I ordered my servant to load my musquetoon with a charge of eight balls. By the bye, this piece did not fail to attract the curiosity and admiration of the people in every place through which we passed. The carriage no sooner halted, than a crowd immediately surrounded the man to view the blunderbuss, which they dignified with the title of *petit canon*. At Nuys in Burgundy, he fired it in the air, and the whole mob dispersed, and scampered off like a flock of sheep. In our journey hither, we generally set out in a morning at eight o'clock, and travelled 'till noon, when the mules were put up and rested a couple of hours. During this halt, Joseph went to dinner, and we went to breakfast, after which we ordered provision for our refreshment in the coach, which we took about three or four in the afternoon, halting for that purpose, by the side of some transparent brook, which afforded excellent water to mix with our wine. In this country I was almost poisoned with garlic, which they mix in their ragouts, and all their sauces; nay, the smell of it perfumes the very chambers, as well as every person you approach. I was also very sick of *beca ficas, grives,* or thrushes, and other little birds, which are served up twice a day at all ordinaries on the road. They make their appearance in vine-leaves, and are always half raw, in which condition the French choose to eat them, rather than run the risque of losing the juice by over-roasting.

The peasants on the South of France are poorly clad, and look as if they were half-starved, diminutive, swarthy, and meagre; and yet the common people who travel, live luxuriously on the road. Every carrier and mule-driver has two meals a day, consisting each of a couple of courses and a dessert, with tolerable small wine.—That which is called *hermitage,* and grows in this province of Dauphiné, is sold on the spot for three livres a bottle. The common draught, which you have at meals in this country, is remarkably strong, though in flavour much inferior to that of Burgundy. The accommodation is tolerable, though they demand (even in this cheap country) the exorbitant price of four livres a head for every meal, of those who choose to eat in their own apartments. I insisted, however, upon paying them with three, which they received, though not without murmuring and seeming discontented. In this journey, we found plenty of good mutton, pork, poultry, and game, including the red partridge, which is near twice as big as the partridge of England. Their hares are likewise surprisingly large and juicy. We saw great flocks of black turkeys feeding in the fields, but no black cattle; and milk was so scarce, that sometimes we were obliged to drink our tea without it.

One day perceiving a meadow on the side of the road, full of a flower which I took to be the crocus, I desired my servant to alight and pull some of them. He delivered the musquetoon to Joseph, who began to tamper with it, and off it went with a prodigious report, augmented by an echo from the mountains that skirted the road. The mules were so frightened, that they went off at the gallop; and Joseph, for some minutes, could neither manage the reins, nor open his mouth. At length he recollected himself, and the cattle were stopt, by the assistance of the servant, to whom he delivered the musquetoon, with a significant shake of the head. Then alighting from the box, he examined the heads of his three mules, and kissed each of them in his turn. Finding they had received no damage, he came up to the coach, with a pale visage and staring eyes, and said it was God's mercy he had not killed his beasts. I answered, that it was a greater mercy he had not killed his passengers; for the muzzle of the piece might have been directed our way as well as any other, and in that case Joseph might have been hanged for murder. "I had as good be hanged (said he) for murder, as be ruined by the loss of my cattle." This adventure made such an impression upon him, that he recounted it to every person we met; nor would he ever touch the blunderbuss from that day. I was often diverted with the conversation of this fellow, who was very arch and very communicative. Every afternoon, he used to stand upon the foot-board, at the side of the coach, and discourse with us an hour together. Passing by the gibbet of Valencia, which stands very near the high-road, we saw one body hanging quite naked, and another lying broken on the wheel. I recollected, that Mandrin had suffered in this place, and calling to Joseph to mount the foot-board, asked if he had ever seen that famous adventurer. At mention of the name of Mandrin, the tear started in Joseph's eye, he discharged a deep sigh, or rather groan, and told me he was his dear friend. I was a little startled at this declaration; however, I concealed my thoughts, and began to ask questions about the character and exploits of a man who had made such noise in the world.

He told me, Mandrin was a native of Valencia, of mean extraction: that he had served as a soldier in the army, and afterwards acted as *maltotier,* or tax-gatherer: that at length he turned *contrebandier,* or smuggler, and by his superior qualities, raised himself to the command of a formidable gang, consisting of five hundred persons well armed with carbines and pistols. He had fifty horses for his troopers, and three hundred mules for the carriage of his merchandize. His head-quarters were in Savoy: but he made incursions into Dauphiné, and set the *maréchaussée* at defiance. He maintained several bloody skirmishes with these troopers, as well as with other regular detachments, and in all those actions signalized himself by his courage and conduct. Coming up at one time with fifty of the *maréchaussée*, who were in quest of him, he told them very calmly, he had occasion for their horses and acoutrements, and desired them to dismount. At that instant his gang appeared, and the troopers complied with his request, without making the least opposition. Joseph said he was as generous as he was brave, and never molested travellers, nor did the least injury to the poor; but, on the contrary, relieved them very often. He used to oblige the gentlemen in the country to take his merchandize, his tobacco, brandy, and muslins, at his own price; and, in the same manner, he laid the open towns under contribution. When he had no merchandize, he borrowed money off them upon the credit of what he should bring when he was better provided. He was at last betrayed, by his wench, to the colonel of a French regiment, who went with a detachment in the night to the place where he lay in Savoy, and surprized him in a wood-house, while his people were absent in different parts of the country. For this intrusion, the court of France made an apology to the king of Sardinia, in whose territories he was taken. Mandrin being conveyed to Valencia, his native place, was for some time permitted to go abroad, under a strong guard, with chains upon his legs; and here he conversed freely with all sorts of people, flattering himself with the hopes of a pardon, in which, however, he was disappointed. An order came from court to bring him to his trial, when he was found guilty, and condemned to be broke on the wheel. Joseph said he drank a bottle of wine with him the night before his execution. He bore his fate with great resolution, observing that if the letter which he had written to the King had been delivered, he certainly should have obtained his Majesty's pardon. His executioner was one of his own gang, who was pardoned on condition of performing this office. You know, that criminals broke upon the wheel are first strangled, unless the sentence imports, that they shall be broke alive. As Mandrin had not been guilty of cruelty in the course of his delinquency, he was indulged with this favour. Speaking to the executioner, whom he had formerly commanded, *"Joseph (dit il), je ne veux pas que tu me touche, jusqu'à ce que je sois roid mort,"* "Joseph," said he, "thou shalt not touch me till I am quite dead."—Our driver had no sooner pronounced these words, than I was struck with a suspicion, that he himself was the executioner of his friend Mandrin. On that suspicion, I exclaimed, "Ah! ah! Joseph!" The fellow blushed up to the eyes, and said, *Oui, son nom etoit Joseph aussi bien que le mien,* "Yes, he was called *Joseph,* as I am." I did not think proper to prosecute the inquiry; but did not much relish the nature of Joseph's connexions. The truth is, he had very much the looks of a ruffian; though, I must own, his behaviour was very obliging and submissive.

On the fifth day of our journey, in the morning, we passed the famous bridge at St. Esprit, which to be sure is a great curiosity, from its length, and the number of its arches: but these arches are too small: the passage above is too narrow; and the whole appears to be too slight, considering the force and impetuosity of the river. It is not comparable to the bridge at Westminster, either for beauty or solidity. Here we entered Languedoc, and were stopped to have our baggage examined; but the searcher, being tipped with a three-livre piece, allowed it to pass. Before we leave Dauphiné, I must observe, that I was not a little surprized to see figs and chestnuts growing in the open fields, at the discretion of every passenger. It was this day I saw the famous Pont du Garde; but as I cannot possibly include, in this letter, a description of that beautiful bridge, and of the other antiquities belonging to Nismes, I will defer it until the next opportunity, being, in the mean time, with equal truth and affection,—Dear Sir, Your obliged humble Servant.

GERTRUDE STEIN
(1874–1946)

Gertrude Stein counted among her many friends Hemingway, the Fitz-geralds, Picasso, Braque, Matisse, Sherwood Anderson, Mabel Dodge, and Ford Maddox Ford. In his book A Moveable Feast, Hemingway credits Stein with the term "The Lost Generation." "'That's what you are,' Miss Stein said, 'that's what you all are. All of you young people who served in the war. You are a lost generation.' 'Really?' I said. 'You are,' she insisted. 'You have no respect for anything. You drink yourselves to death . . .'"

Stein was born in Pennsylvania, raised in California and went to Radcliffe College in Boston, where her philosophy teacher was William James, brother of Henry. In 1904 she moved to Paris and did not return to the States for thirty years. She, her brother Leo, and eventually her life partner Alice B. Toklas took up residence at 27 rue de Fleurus and hosted a salon for writers and artists. Stein wrote, "Paris was the place that suited those of us that were to create the twentieth century art and litera-ture." After her guests left for the evening, Stein began to write. Although her literary style was not popular with the general public, she is now recognized as an experimental abstract writer who played with sentence structure and words; some called her a "literary cubist." Her most famous work, The Autobiography of Alice B. Toklas (1933) from which this excerpt is taken, brought her wealth and celebrity.

Stein and Toklas remained in Paris for most of World War I. As wit-nesses to the devastation of the First World War, they refused to believe that humanity would tolerate a second in two decades. That miscalcula-tion almost cost them dearly; Stein and Toklas, both of Jewish descent, barely escaped internment in a concentration camp. Nearly destitute, they *sold some of their paintings to avoid starvation. Stein died in 1946 and Toklas survived her by thirty years. Hemingway once wrote to Stein, "It was a vital day for me when I stumbled upon you."*

My Arrival in Paris

from THE AUTOBIOGRAPHY OF ALICE B. TOKLAS

This was the year 1907. Gertrude Stein was just seeing through the press Three Lives which she was having privately printed, and she was deep in The Making of Americans, her thousand page book. Picasso had just finished his portrait of her which nobody at that time liked except the painter and the painted and which is now so famous, and he had just begun his strange complicated picture of three women. Matisse had just finished his Bonheur de Vivre, his first big composition which gave him the name of fauve or a zoo. It was the moment Max Jacob has since called the heroic age of cubism. I remember not long ago hearing Picasso and Gertrude Stein talking about various things that had happened at that time, one of them said but all that could not have happened in that one year, oh said the other, my dear you forget we were young then and we did a great deal in a year.

There are a great many things to tell of what was happening then and what had happened before, which led up to then, but now I must describe what I saw when I came.

The home at 27 rue de Fleurus consisted then as it does now of a tiny pavillon of two stories with four small rooms, a kitchen and bath, and a very large atelier adjoining. Now the atelier is attached to the pavillon by a tiny hall passage added in 1914 but at that time the atelier had its own entrance, one rang the bell of the pavillon or knocked at the door of the atelier, and a great many people did both, but more knocked at the atelier. I was privileged to do both. I had been invited to dine on Saturday evening which was the evening when everybody came, and indeed everybody did come. I went to dinner. The dinner was cooked by Hélène. I must tell a little about Hélène.

Hélène had already been two years with Gertrude Stein and her brother. She was one of those admirable bonnes in other words excellent maids of all work, good cooks thoroughly occupied with the welfare of their employers and of themselves, firmly convinced that everything purchasable was far too dear. Oh but it is dear, was her answer to any question. She wasted nothing and carried on the household at the regular rate of eight francs a day. She even wanted to include guests at that price, it was her pride, but of course that was difficult since she for the honour of her house as well as to satisfy her employers always had to give every one enough to eat. She was a most excellent cook and she made a very good soufflé. In those days most of the guests were living more or less precariously, no one starved, some one always helped but still most of them did not live in abundance. It was Braque who said about four years later when they were all beginning to be known, with a sigh and a smile, how life has changed we all now have cooks who can make a soufflé.

Hélène had her opinions, she did not for instance like Matisse. She said a frenchman should not stay unexpectedly to a meal particularly if he asked the servant beforehand what there was for dinner. She said foreigners had a perfect right to do these things but not a frenchman and Matisse had once done it. So when Miss Stein said to her, Monsieur Matisse is staying for dinner this evening, she would say, in that case I will not make an omelette but fry the eggs. It takes the same number of eggs and the same amount of butter but it shows less respect, and he will understand.

Hélène stayed with the household until the end of 1913. Then her husband, by that time she had married and had a little boy, insisted that she work for others no longer. To her great regret she left and later she always said that life at home was never as amusing as it had been at the rue de Fleurus. Much later, only about three years ago, she came back for a year, she and her husband had fallen on bad times and her boy had died. She was as cheery as ever and enormously interested. She said isn't it extraordinary, all those people whom I knew when they were nobody are now always mentioned in the newspapers, and the other night over the radio they mentioned the name of Monsieur Picasso. Why they even speak in the newspapers of Monsieur Braque, who used to hold up the big pictures to hang because he was the strongest, while the janitor drove the nails, and they are putting into the Louvre, just imagine it, into the Louvre, a picture by that little poor Monsieur Rousseau, who was so timid he did not even have courage enough to knock at the door. She was terribly interested in seeing Monsieur Picasso and his wife and child and cooked her very best dinner for him, but how he has changed, she said, well, said she, I suppose that is natural but then he has a lovely son. We thought that really Hélène had come back to give the young generation the once over. She had in a way but she was not interested in them. She said they made no impression on her which made them all very sad because the legend of her was well known to all Paris. After a year things were going better again, her husband was earning more money, and she once more remains at home. But to come back to 1907.

Before I tell about the guests I must tell what I saw. As I said being invited to dinner I rang the bell of the little pavillon and was taken into the tiny hall and then into the small dining room lined with books. On the only free space, the doors, were tacked up a few drawings by Picasso and Matisse. As the other guests had not yet come Miss Stein took me into the atelier. It often rained in Paris and it was always difficult to go from the little pavillon to the atelier door in the rain in evening clothes, but you were not to mind such things as the hosts and most of the guests did not. We went into the atelier, which opened with a yale key the only yale key in the quarter at that time, and this was not so much for safety, because in those days the pictures had no value, but because the key was small and could go into a purse instead of being enormous as french keys were. Against the walls were several pieces of large italian renaissance furniture and in the middle of the room was a big renaissance table, on it a lovely inkstand, and at one end of it note-books neatly arranged, the kind of note-books french children use, with pictures of earth-quakes and explorations on the outside of them. And on all the walls right up to the ceiling were pictures. At one end of the room was a big cast iron stove that Hélène came in and filled with a rattle, and in one corner of the room was a large table on which were horseshoe nails and pebbles and little pipe cigarette holders which one looked at curiously but did not touch, but which turned out later to be accumulations from the pockets of Picasso and Gertrude Stein. But to return to the pictures. The pictures were so strange that one quite instinctively looked at any-thing rather than at them just at first. I have refreshed my mem-ory by looking at some snap shots taken inside the atelier at that time. The chairs in the room were also all italian renaissance, not very comfortable for short-legged people and one got the habit of sitting on one's legs. Miss Stein sat near the stove in a lovely high-backed one and she peacefully let her legs hang, which was a matter of habit, and when any one of the many visitors came to ask her a question she lifted herself up out of this chair and usually replied in french, not just now. This usually referred to something they wished to see, drawings which were put away, some german had once spilled ink on one, or some other not to be fulfilled desire. But to return to the pictures. As I say they completely covered the white-washed walls right up to the top of the very high ceiling. The room was lit at this time by high gas fixtures. This was the second stage. They had just been put in. Before that there had only been lamps, and a stalwart guest held up the lamp while the others looked. But gas had just been put in and an ingenious american painter named Sayen, to divert his mind from the birth of his first child, was arranging some mechanical contrivance that would light the high fixtures by themselves. The old landlady extremely conservative did not allow electricity in her houses and electricity was not put in until 1914, the old landlady by that time too old to know the difference, her house agent gave permission. But this time I am really going to tell about the pictures.

It is very difficult now that everybody is accustomed to everything to give some idea of the kind of uneasiness one felt when one first looked at all these pictures on these walls. In those days there were pictures of all kinds there, the time had not yet come when they were only Cézannes, Renoirs, Matisses and Picassos, nor as it was even later only Cézannes and Picassos. At that time there was a great deal of Matisse, Picasso, Renoir, Cézanne but there were also a great many other things. There were two Gauguins, there were Manguins, there was a big nude by Valloton that felt like only it was not like the Odalisque of Manet, there was a Toulouse-Lautrec. Once about this time Picasso looking at this and greatly daring said, but all the same I do paint better than he did. Toulouse-Lautrec had been the most important of his early influences. I later bought a little tiny picture by Picasso of that epoch. There was a portrait of Gertrude Stein by Valloton that might have been a David but was not, there was a Maurice Denis, a little Daumier, many Cézanne water colours, there was in short everything, there was even a little Delacroix and a moderate sized Greco. There were enormous Picassos of the Harlequin period, there were two rows of Matisses, there was a big portrait of a woman by Cézanne and some little Cézannes, all these pictures had a history and I will soon tell them. Now I was confused and I looked and I looked and I was confused. Gertrude Stein and her brother were so accustomed to this state of mind in a guest that they payed no attention to it.

Then there was a sharp tap at the atelier door. Gertrude Stein opened it and a little dark dapper man came in with hair, eyes, face, hands and feet all very much alive. Hullo Alfy, she said, this is Miss Toklas. How do you do Miss Toklas, he said very solemnly. This was Alfy Maurer, an old habitué of the house. He had been there before there were these pictures, when there were only japanese prints, and he was among those who used to light matches to light up a little piece of the Cézanne portrait. Of course you can tell it is a finished picture, he used to explain to the other american painters who came and looked dubiously, you can tell because it has a frame, now whoever heard of anybody framing a canvas if the picture isn't finished. He had followed, followed, followed always humbly always sincerely, it was he who selected the first lot of pictures for the famous Barnes collection some years later faithfully and enthusiastically. It was he who when later Barnes came to the house and waved his cheque-book said, so help me God, I didn't bring him. Gertrude Stein who has an explosive temper, came in another evening and there were her brother, Alfy and a stranger. She did not like the stranger's looks. Who is that, said she to Alfy. I didn't bring him, said Alfy. He looks like a Jew, said Gertrude Stein, he is worse than that, says Alfy. But to return to that first evening. A few minutes after Alfy came in there was a violent knock at the door and, dinner is ready, from Hélène. It's funny the Picassos have not come, said they all, however we won't wait at least Hélène won't wait. So we went into the court and into the pavillon and dining room and began dinner. It's funny, said Miss Stein, Pablo is always promptness itself, he is never early and he is never late, it is his pride that punctuality is the politeness of kings, he even makes Fernande punctual. Of course he often says yes when he has no intention of doing what he says yes to, he can't say no, no is not in his vocabulary and you have to know whether his yes means yes and or means no, but when he says a yes that means yes and he did about to-night he is always punctual. These were the days before automobiles and nobody worried about accidents. We had just finished the first course when there was a quick patter of footsteps in the court and Hélène opened the door before the bell rang. Pablo and Fernande as everybody called them at that time walked in. He, small, quick moving but not restless, his eyes having a strange faculty of opening wide and drinking in what he wished to see. He had the isolation and movement of the head of a bull-fighter at the head of their procession. Fernande was a tall beautiful woman with a wonderful big hat and a very evidently new dress, they were both very fussed. I am very upset, said Pablo, but you know very well Gertrude I am never late but Fernande had ordered a dress for the vernissage to-morrow and it didn't come. Well here you are anyway, said Miss Stein, since it's you Hélène won't mind. And we all sat down. I was next to Picasso who was silent and then gradually became peaceful. Alfy paid compliments to Fernande and she was soon calm and placid. After a little while I murmured to Picasso that I liked his portrait of Gertrude Stein. Yes, he said, everybody says that she does not look like it but that does not make any difference, she will, he said. The conversation soon became lively it was all about the opening day of the salon indépendant which was the great event of the year. Everybody was interested in all the scandals that would or would not break out. Picasso never exhibited but as his followers did and there were a great many stories connected with each follower the hopes and fears were vivacious.

While we were having coffee footsteps were heard in the court quite a number of footsteps and Miss Stein rose and said, don't hurry, I have to let them in. And she left.

When we went into the atelier there were already quite a number of people in the room, scattered groups, single and couples all looking and looking. Gertrude Stein sat by the stove talking and listening and getting up to open the door and go up to various people talking and listening. She usually opened the door to the knock and the usual formula was, de la part de qui venez-vous, who is your introducer. The idea was that anybody could come but for form's sake and in Paris you have to have a

formula, everybody was supposed to be able to mention the
name of somebody who had told them about it. It was a mere
form, really everybody could come in and as at that time these
pictures had no value and there was no social privilege attached
to knowing any one there, only those came who really were
interested. So as I say anybody could come in, however, there
was the formula. Miss Stein once in opening the door said as she
usually did by whose invitation do you come and we heard an
aggrieved voice reply, but by yours, madame. He was a young
man Gertrude Stein had met somewhere and with whom she
had had a long conversation and to whom she had given a cor-
dial invitation and then had as promptly forgotten.

The room was soon very very full and who were they all.
Groups of hungarian painters and writers, it happened that some
hungarian had once been brought and the word had spread from
him throughout all Hungary, any village where there was a
young man who had ambitions heard of 27 rue de Fleurus and
then he lived but to get there and a great many did get there. They
were always there, all sizes and shapes, all degrees of wealth and
poverty, some very charming, some simply rough and every now
and then a very beautiful young peasant. Then there were quan-
tities of germans, not too popular because they tended always to
want to see anything that was put away and they tended to break
things and Gertrude Stein has a weakness for breakable objects,
she has a horror of people who collect only the unbreakable. Then
there was a fair sprinkling of americans, Mildred Aldrich would
bring a group or Sayen, the electrician, or some painter and occa-
sionally an architectural student would accidentally get there and
then there were the habitués, among them Miss Mars and Miss
Squires whom Gertrude Stein afterwards immortalised in her
story of Miss Furr and Miss Skeene. On that first night Miss
Mars and I talked of a subject then entirely new, how to make
up your face. She was interested in types, she knew that there
were femme décorative, femme d'intérieur and femme intrig-
ante; there was no doubt that Fernande Picasso was a femme
décorative, but what was Madame Matisse, femme d'intérieur, I

said, and she was very pleased. From time to time one heard the high spanish whinnying laugh of Picasso the gay contralto outbreak of Gertrude Stein, people came and went, in and out. Miss Stein told me to sit with Fernande. Fernande was always beautiful but heavy in hand. I sat, it was my first sitting with a wife of a genius.

Before I decided to write this book my twenty-five years with Gertrude Stein, I had often said that I would write, The wives of geniuses I have sat with. I have sat with so many. I have sat with wives who were not wives, of geniuses who were real geniuses. I have sat with real wives of geniuses who were not real geniuses. I have sat with wives of geniuses, of near geniuses, of would be geniuses, in short I have sat very often and very long with many wives and wives of many geniuses.

As I was saying Fernande, who was then living with Picasso and had been with him a long time that is to say they were all twenty-four years old at that time but they had been together a long time, Fernande was the first wife of a genius I sat with and she was not the least amusing. We talked hats. Fernande had two subjects hats and perfumes. This first day we talked hats. She liked hats, she had the true french feeling about a hat, if a hat did not provoke some witticism from a man on the street the hat was not a success. Later on once in Montmartre she and I were walking together. She had on a large yellow hat and I had on a much smaller blue one. As we were walking along a workman stopped and called out, there go the sun and the moon shining together. Ah, said Fernande to me with a radiant smile, you see our hats are a success.

Miss Stein called me and said she wanted to have me meet Matisse. She was talking to a medium sized man with a reddish beard and glasses. He had a very alert although slightly heavy presence and Miss Stein and he seemed to be full of hidden meanings. As I came up I heard her say, Oh yes but it would be more difficult now. We were talking, she said, of a lunch party we had in here last year. We had just hung all the pictures and we asked all the painters. You know how painters are, I wanted to make them happy so I placed each one opposite his own picture, and they were happy so happy that we had to send out twice for more bread, when you know France you will know that that means that they were happy, because they cannot eat and drink without bread and we had to send out twice for bread so they were happy. Nobody noticed my little arrangement except Matisse and he did not until just as he left, and now he says it is a proof that I am very wicked, Matisse laughed and said, yes I know Mademoiselle Gertrude, the world is a theatre for you, but there are theatres and theatres, and when you listen so carefully to me and so attentively and do not hear a word I say then I do say that you are very wicked. Then they both began talking about the vernissage of the independent as every one else was doing and of course I did not know what it was all about. But gradually I knew and later on I will tell the story of the pictures, their painters and their followers and what this conversation meant.

Later I was near Picasso, he was standing meditatively. Do you think, he said, that I really do look like your president Lincoln. I had thought a good many things that evening but I had not thought that. You see, he went on, Gertrude, (I wish I could convey something of the simple affection and confidence with which he always pronounced her name and with which she always said, Pablo. In all their long friendship with all its sometimes troubled moments and its complications this has never changed.) Gertrude showed me a photograph of him and I have been trying to arrange my hair to look like his, I think my forehead does. I did not know whether he meant it or not but I was sympathetic. I did not realise then how completely and entirely american was Gertrude Stein. Later I often teased her, calling her a general, a civil war general of either or both sides. She had a series of photographs of the civil war, rather wonderful photographs and she and Picasso used to pore over them. Then he would suddenly remember the spanish war and he became very spanish and very bitter and Spain and America in their persons could say very bitter things about each other's country. But at this my first evening I knew nothing of all this and so I was polite and that was all.

And now the evening was drawing to a close. Everybody was leaving and everybody was still talking about the vernissage of the independent. I too left carrying with me a card of invitation for the vernissage. And so this, one of the most important evenings of my life, came to an end.

ROBERT LOUIS
STEVENSON
(1850–1894)

"We are all travelers in what John Bunyan calls the wilderness of the world," wrote Robert Louis Stevenson *in his introduction to* Travels with a Donkey *written in 1879 when he was twenty-nine. "All, too, travelers with a donkey; and the best that we find in our travels is an honest friend. He is a fortunate voyager who finds many."*

Born in Scotland, Stevenson was an inveterate traveler despite ill health. He studied both civil engineering and law, but practiced neither. Instead, he set off to Europe, a trip that supplied the material for both An Inland Voyage *(1878) and* Travels with a Donkey. *In France he met Mrs. Fanny Osborne, pursued her to California and married her. In 1883 he wrote his most famous work* Treasure Island *for his young stepson Lloyd. Both Fanny and Lloyd later collaborated with Stevenson on a series of (unsuccessful) plays.*

In 1888 Stevenson left England to find a more hospitable climate. He settled in Samoa, bought an estate and for six years enjoyed relative good health. He also had a productive literary period, writing novellas about the South Seas in which he condemned European influence and colonization of the island culture. Stevenson died suddenly of a brain hemorrhage and was buried on Samoa. He was called Tusitala (The Teller of Tales) by the native people.

from Travels with a Donkey

"Many are the mighty things, and nought is more mighty than man. . . . He masters by his devices the tenant of the fields."
ANTIGONE

"Who hath loosed the bands of the wild ass?"
JOB

The Donkey, The Pack, and The Pack-Saddle

In a little place called Le Monastier, in a pleasant highland valley fifteen miles from Le Puy, I spent about a month of fine days. Monastier is notable for the making of lace, for drunkenness, for freedom of language, and for unparalleled political dissension. There are adherents of each of the four French parties—Legitimists, Orleanists, Imperialists, and Republicans—in this little mountain-town; and they all hate, loathe, decry, and calumniate each other. Except for business purposes, or to give each other the lie in a tavern brawl, they have laid aside even the civility of speech. 'Tis a mere mountain Poland. In the midst of this Babylon I found myself a rallying-point; every one was anxious to be kind and helpful to the stranger. This was not merely from the natural hospitality of mountain people, nor even from the surprise with which I was regarded as a man living of his own free will in Monastier, when he might just as well have lived anywhere else in this big world; it arose a good deal from my projected excursion southward through the Cévennes. A traveller of my sort was a thing hitherto unheard of in that district. I was looked upon with contempt, like a man who should project a journey to the moon, but yet with a respectful interest, like one setting forth for the inclement Pole. All were ready to help in my preparations; a crowd of sympathizers supported me at the critical moment of a bargain; not a step was taken but was heralded by glasses round and celebrated by a dinner or a breakfast.

It was already hard upon October before I was ready to set forth, and at the high altitudes over which my road lay there was no Indian summer to be looked for. I was determined, if not to camp out, at least to have the means of camping out in my possession; for there is nothing more harassing to an easy mind than the necessity of reaching shelter by dusk, and the hospitality of a village inn is not always to be reckoned sure by those who trudge on foot.

A tent, above all for a solitary traveller, is troublesome to pitch, and troublesome to strike again; and even on the march it forms a conspicuous feature in your baggage. A sleeping-sack, on the other hand, is always ready—you have only to get into it; it serves a double purpose—a bed by night, a portmanteau by day; and it does not advertise your intention of camping out to every curious passer-by. This is a huge point. If the camp is not secret, it is but a troubled resting-place; you become a public character; the convivial rustic visits your bedside after an early supper; and you must sleep with one eye open, and be up before the day. I decided on a sleeping-sack; and after repeated visits to Le Puy, and a deal of high living for myself and my advisers, a sleeping-sack was designed, constructed, and triumphally brought home.

This child of my invention was nearly six feet square, exclusive of two triangular flaps to serve as a pillow by night and as the top and bottom of the sack by day. I call it "the sack," but it was never a sack by more than courtesy: only a sort of long roll or sausage, green waterproof cart cloth without and blue sheep's fur within. It was commodious as a valise, warm and dry for a bed. There was luxurious turning-room for one; and at a pinch the thing might serve for two. I could bury myself in it up to the neck; for my head I trusted to a fur cap, with a hood to fold down over my ears and a band to pass under my nose like a respirator; and in case of heavy rain I proposed to make myself a little tent, or tentlet, with my waterproof coat, three stones, and a bent branch.

It will readily be conceived that I could not carry this huge package on my own, merely human, shoulders. It remained to choose a beast of burthen. Now, a horse is a fine lady among animals, flighty, timid, delicate in eating, of tender health; he is too valuable and too restive to be left alone, so that you are chained to your brute as to a fellow galley-slave; a dangerous road puts him out of his wits; in short, he's an uncertain and exacting ally, and adds thirty-fold to the troubles of the voyager. What I required was something cheap and small and hardy, and of a stolid and peaceful temper; and all these requisites pointed to a donkey.

There dwelt an old man in Monastier, of rather unsound intellect according to some, much followed by street-boys, and known to fame as Father Adam. Father Adam had a cart, and to draw the cart a diminutive she-ass, not much bigger than a dog, the color of a mouse, with a kindly eye and a determined under-jaw. There was something neat and high-bred, a quakerish elegance, about the rogue that hit my fancy on the spot. Our first interview was in Monastier market-place. To prove her good temper, one child after another was set upon her back to ride, and one after another went head over heels into the air; until a want of confidence began to reign in youthful bosoms, and the experiment was discontinued from a dearth of subjects. I was already backed by a deputation of my friends; but as if this were not enough, all the buyers and sellers came round and helped me in the bargain; and the ass and I and Father Adam were the centre of a hubbub for near half an hour. At length she passed into my service for the consideration of sixty-five francs and a glass of brandy. The sack had already cost eighty francs and two glasses of beer; so that Modestine, as I instantly baptized her, was upon all accounts the cheaper article. Indeed, that was as it should be; for she was only an appurtenance of my mattress, or self-acting bedstead on four castors.

I had a last interview with Father Adam in a billiard-room at the witching hour of dawn, when I administered the brandy. He professed himself greatly touched by the separation, and declared he had often bought white bread for the donkey when he had been content with black bread for himself; but this, according to the best authorities, must have been a flight of fancy. He had a name in the village for brutally misusing the ass; yet it is certain that he shed a tear, and the tear made a clean mark down one cheek.

By the advice of a fallacious local saddler, a leather pad was made for me with rings to fasten on my bundle; and I thoughtfully completed my kit and arranged my toilette. By way of armory and utensils, I took a revolver, a little spirit-lamp and pan, a lantern and some halfpenny candles, a jack-knife and a large leather flask. The main cargo consisted of two entire changes of warm clothing—besides my traveling wear of country velveteen, pilot-coat, and knitted spencer—some books, and my railway-rug, which, being also in the form of a bag, made me a double castle for cold nights. The permanent larder was represented by cakes of chocolate and tins of Bologna sausage. All this, except what I carried about my person, was easily stowed into the sheepskin bag; and by good fortune I threw in my empty knapsack, rather for convenience of carriage than from any thought that I should want it on my journey. For more immediate needs, I took a leg of cold mutton, a bottle of Beaujolais, an empty bottle to carry milk, an egg-beater, and a considerable quantity of black bread and white, like Father Adam, for myself and donkey, only in my scheme of things the destinations were reversed.

Monastrians, of all shades of thought in politics, had agreed in threatening me with many ludicrous misadventures, and with sudden death in many surprising forms. Cold, wolves, robbers, above all the nocturnal practical joker, were daily and eloquently forced on my attention. Yet in these vaticinations, the true, patent danger was left out. Like Christian, it was from my pack I suffered by the way. Before telling my own mishaps, let me, in two words, relate the lesson of my experience. If the pack is well strapped at the ends, and hung at full length—not doubled, for your life—across the pack-saddle, the traveller is safe. The saddle will certainly not fit, such is the imperfection of our transitory life; it will assuredly topple and tend to overset; but there are stones on every roadside, and a man soon learns the art of correcting any tendency to overbalance with a well-adjusted stone.

On the day of my departure I was up a little after five; by six, we began to load the donkey; and ten minutes after, my hopes were in the dust. The pad would not stay on Modestine's back for half a moment. I returned it to its maker, with whom I had so contumelious a passage that the street outside was crowded from wall to wall with gossips looking on and listening. The pad changed hands with much vivacity; perhaps it would be more descriptive to say that we threw it at each other's heads; and, at any rate, we were very warm and unfriendly, and spoke with a deal of freedom.

I had a common donkey pack-saddle—a *barde,* as they call it—fitted upon Modestine; and once more loaded her with my effects. The double sack, my pilot-coat (for it was warm, and I was to walk in my waistcoat), a great bar of black bread, and an open basket containing the white bread, the mutton, and the bottles, were all corded together in a very elaborate system of knots, and I looked on the result with fatuous content. In such a monstrous deck-cargo, all poised above the donkey's shoulders, with nothing below to balance, on a brand-new pack-saddle that had not yet been worn to fit the animal, and fastened with brand-new girths that might be expected to stretch and slacken by the way, even a very careless traveller should have seen disaster brewing. That elaborate system of knots, again, was the work of too many sympathizers to be very artfully designed. It is true they tightened the cords with a will; as many as three at a time would have a foot against Modestine's quarters, and be hauling with clenched teeth; but I learned afterwards that one thoughtful person, without any exercise of force, can make a more solid job than half-a-dozen heated and enthusiastic grooms. I was then but a novice; even after the misadventure of the pad nothing could disturb my security, and I went forth from the stable-door as an ox goeth to the slaughter.

The Green Donkey-Driver

The bell of Monastier was just striking nine as I got quit of these preliminary troubles and descended the hill through the common. As long as I was within sight of the windows, a secret shame and the fear of some laughable defeat withheld me from tampering with Modestine. She tripped along upon her four small hoofs with a sober daintiness of gait; from time to time she shook her ears or her tail; and she looked so small under the bundle that my mind misgave me. We got across the ford without difficulty—there was no doubt about the matter, she was docility itself—and once on the other bank, where the road begins to mount through pinewoods, I took in my right hand the unhallowed staff, and with a quaking spirit applied it to the donkey. Modestine brisked up her pace for perhaps three steps, and then relapsed into her former minuet. Another application had the same effect, and so with the third. I am worthy the name of an Englishman, and it goes against my conscience to lay my hand rudely on a female. I desisted, and looked her all over from head to foot; the poor brute's knees were trembling and her breathing was distressed; it was plain that she could go no faster on a hill. God forbid, thought I, that I should brutalize this innocent creature; let her go at her own pace, and let me patiently follow.

What that pace was, there is no word mean enough to describe, it was something as much slower than a walk as a walk is slower than a run; it kept me hanging on each foot for an incredible

length of time; in five minutes it exhausted the spirit and set up
a fever in all the muscles of the leg. And yet I had to keep close at
hand and measure my advance exactly upon hers; for if I dropped
a few yards into the rear, or went on a few yards ahead, Modestine
came instantly to a halt and began to browse. The thought that
this was to last from here to Alais nearly broke my heart. Of all
conceivable journeys, this promised to be the most tedious. I tried
to tell myself it was a lovely day; I tried to charm my foreboding
spirit with tobacco; but I had a vision ever present to me of the
long, long roads, up hill and down dale, and a pair of figures ever
infinitesimally moving, foot by foot, a yard to the minute, and,
like things enchanted in a nightmare, approaching no nearer to
the goal.

In the meantime there came up behind us a tall peasant, per-
haps forty years of age, of an ironical snuffy countenance, and
arrayed in the green tail-coat of the country. He overtook us
hand over hand, and stopped to consider our pitiful advance.

"Your donkey," says he, "is very old?"

I told him, I believed not.

Then, he supposed, we had come far.

I told him, we had but newly left Monastier.

"Et vous marchez comme ça!" cried he; and, throwing back his
head, he laughed long and heartily. I watched him, half prepared
to feel offended, until he had satisfied his mirth; and then, "You
must have no pity on these animals," said he; and, plucking a
switch out of a thicket, he began to lace Modestine about the
stern-works, uttering a cry. The rogue pricked up her ears and
broke into a good round pace, which she kept up without flag-
ging, and without exhibiting the least symptom of distress, as
long as the peasant kept beside us. Her former panting and shak-
ing had been, I regret to say, a piece of comedy.

My *deus ex machina,* before he left me, supplied some excel-
lent, if inhumane, advice; presented me with the switch, which
he declared she would feel more tenderly than my cane; and
finally taught me the true cry or masonic word of donkey-
drivers, "Proot!" All the time, he regarded me with a comical

incredulous air, which was embarrassing to confront; and smiled over my donkey-driving, as I might have smiled over his orthography, or his green tail-coat. But it was not my turn for the moment.

I was proud of my new lore, and thought I had learned the art to perfection. And certainly Modestine did wonders for the rest of the forenoon, and I had a breathing space to look about me. It was Sabbath; the mountain-fields were all vacant in the sunshine; and as we came down through St. Martin de Frugères, the church was crowded to the door, there were people kneeling without upon the steps, and the sound of the priest's chanting came forth out of the dim interior. It gave me a home feeling on the spot; for I am a countryman of the Sabbath, so to speak, and all Sabbath observances, like a Scotch accent, strike in me mixed feelings, grateful and the reverse. It is only a traveller, hurrying by like a person from another planet, who can rightly enjoy the peace and beauty of the great ascetic feast. The sight of the resting country does his spirit good. There is something better than music in the wide unusual silence; and it disposes him to amiable thoughts like the sound of a little river or the warmth of sunlight.

In this pleasant humor I came down the hill to where Goudet stands in the green end of a valley, with Château Beaufort opposite upon a rocky steep, and the stream, as clear as crystal, lying in a deep pool between them. Above and below, you may hear it wimpling over the stones, an animal stripling of a river, which it seems absurd to call the Loire. On all sides, Goudet is shut in by mountains; rocky foot-paths, practicable at best for donkeys, join in to the outer world of France; and the men and women drink and swear, in their green corner, or look up at the snow-clad peaks in winter from the threshold of their homes, in isolation, you would think, like that of Homer's Cyclops. But it is not so; the postman reaches Goudet with the letter-bag; the aspiring youth of Goudet are within a day's walk of the railway at Le Puy; and here in the inn you may find an engraved portrait of the host's nephew, Règis Senac, "Professor of Fencing and

Champion of the two Americas," a distinction gained by him, along with the sum of five hundred dollars, at Tammany Hall, New York, on the 10th April, 1876.

I hurried over my midday meal, and was early forth again. But, alas, as we climbed the interminable hill upon the other side, "Proot!" seemed to have lost its virtue. I prooted like a lion, I prooted mellifluously like a sucking-dove; but Modestine would be neither softened nor intimidated. She held doggedly to her pace; nothing but a blow would move her, and that only for a second. I must follow at her heels, incessantly belaboring. A moment's pause in this ignoble toil, and she relapsed into her own private gait. I think I never heard of any one in as mean a situation. I must reach the lake of Bouchet, where I meant to camp, before sundown, and, to have even a hope of this, I must instantly maltreat this uncomplaining animal. The sound of my own blows sickened me. Once, when I looked at her, she had a faint resemblance to a lady of my acquaintance who formerly loaded me with kindness; and this increased my horror of my cruelty.

To make matters worse, we encountered another donkey, ranging at will upon the roadside; and this other donkey chanced to be a gentleman. He and Modestine met nickering for joy, and I had to separate the pair and beat down their young romance with a renewed and feverish bastinado. If the other donkey had had the heart of a male under his hide, he would have fallen upon me tooth and hoof; and this was a kind of consolation—he was plainly unworthy of Modestine's affection. But the incident saddened me, as did everything that spoke of my donkey's sex.

It was blazing hot up the valley, windless, with vehement sun upon my shoulders; and I had to labor so consistently with my stick that the sweat ran into my eyes. Every five minutes, too, the pack, the basket, and the pilot-coat would take an ugly slew to one side or the other; and I had to stop Modestine, just when I had got her to a tolerable pace of about two miles an hour, to tug, push, shoulder, and readjust the load. And at last, in the village of Ussel, saddle and all, the whole hypothec turned round and grovelled in the dust below the donkey's belly. She, none better pleased, incontinently drew up and seemed to smile; and a party of one man, two women, and two children came up, and, standing round me in a half-circle, encouraged her by their example.

I had the devil's own trouble to get the thing righted; and the instant I had done so, without hesitation, it toppled and fell down upon the other side. Judge if I was hot! And yet not a hand was offered to assist me. The man, indeed, told me I ought to have a package of a different shape. I suggested, if he knew nothing better to the point in my predicament, he might hold his tongue. And the good-natured dog agreed with me smilingly. It was the most despicable fix. I must plainly content myself with the pack for Modestine, and take the following items for my own share of the portage: a cane, a quart flask, a pilot-jacket heavily weighted in the pockets, two pounds of black bread, and an open basket full of meats and bottles. I believe I may say I am not devoid of greatness of soul; for I did not recoil from this infamous burthen. I disposed it, Heaven knows how, so as to be mildly portable, and then proceeded to steer Modestine through the village. She tried, as was indeed her invariable habit, to enter every house and every courtyard in the whole length; and, encumbered as I was, without a hand to help myself, no words can render an idea of my difficulties. A priest, with six or seven others, was examining a church in process of repair, and he and his acolytes laughed loudly as they saw my plight. I remembered having laughed myself when I had seen good men struggling with adversity in the person of a jackass, and the recollection filled me with penitence. That was in my old light days, before this trouble came upon me. God knows at least that I shall never laugh again, thought I. But O, what a cruel thing is a farce to those engaged in it!

A little out of the village, Modestine, filled with the demon, set her heart upon a by-road, and positively refused to leave it. I dropped all my bundles, and, I am ashamed to say, struck the poor sinner twice across the face. It was pitiful to see her lift up her head with shut eyes, as if waiting for another blow. I came very near crying; but I did a wiser thing than that, and sat squarely down by the roadside to consider my situation under the cheerful influence of tobacco and a nip of brandy. Modestine, in the meanwhile, munched some black bread with a contrite hypocritical air. It was plain that I must make a sacrifice to the gods of shipwreck. I threw away the empty bottle destined to carry milk; I threw away my own white bread, and, disdaining to act by general average, kept the black bread for Modestine; lastly, I threw away the cold leg of mutton and the egg-whisk, although this last was dear to my heart. Thus I found room for everything in the basket, and even stowed the boating-coat on the top. By means of an end of cord I slung it under one arm; and although the cord cut my shoulder and the jacket hung almost to the ground, it was with a heart greatly lightened that I set forth again.

I had now an arm free to thrash Modestine, and cruelly I chastised her. If I were to reach the lakeside before dark, she must bestir her little shanks to some tune. Already the sun had gone down into a windy-looking mist; and although there were still a few streaks of gold far off to the east on the hills and the black fir-woods, all was cold and grey about our onward path. An infinity of little country by-roads led hither and thither among the fields. It was the most pointless labyrinth. I could see my destination overhead, or rather the peak that dominates it; but choose as I pleased, the roads always ended by turning away from it, and sneaking back towards the valley, or northward along the margin of the hills. The failing light, the waning color, the naked, unhomely, stony country through which I was travelling, threw me into some despondency. I promise you, the stick was not idle; I think every decent step that Modestine took must have cost me at least two emphatic blows. There was not another sound in the neighborhood but that of my unwearying bastinado.

Suddenly, in the midst of my toils, the load once more bit the dust, and, as by enchantment, all the cords were simultaneously loosened, and the road scattered with my dear possessions. The packing was to begin again from the beginning; and as I had to invent a new and better system, I do not doubt but I lost half an hour. It began to be dusk in earnest as I reached a wilderness of turf and stones. It had the air of being a road which should lead everywhere at the same time; and I was falling into something not unlike despair when I saw two figures stalking towards me over the stones. They walked one behind the other like tramps, but their pace was remarkable. The son led the way, a tall, ill-made, sombre, Scotch-looking man; the mother followed, all in her Sunday's best, with an elegantly-embroidered ribbon to her cap, and a new felt hat atop and proffering, as she strode along with kilted petticoats, a string of obscene and blasphemous oaths.

I hailed the son and asked him my direction. He pointed loosely west and north-west, muttered an inaudible comment, and, without slackening his pace for an instant, stalked on, as he was going, right athwart my path. The mother followed without so much as raising her head. I shouted and shouted after them, but they continued to scale the hillside, and turned a deaf ear to my outcries. At last, leaving Modestine by herself, I was constrained to run after them, hailing the while. They stopped as I drew near, the mother still cursing; and I could see she was a handsome, motherly, respectable-looking woman. The son once more answered me roughly and inaudibly, and was for setting out again. But this time I simply collared the mother, who was nearest me, and, apologizing for my violence, declared that I could not let them go until they had put me on my road. They were neither of them offended—rather mollified than otherwise; told me I had only to follow them; and then the mother asked me what I wanted by the lake at such an hour. I replied, in the Scotch manner, by inquiring if she had far to go herself. She told me, with another oath, that she had an hour and a half's road before her. And then, without salutation, the pair strode forward again up the hillside in the gathering dusk.

I returned for Modestine, pushed her briskly forward, and, after a sharp ascent of twenty minutes, reached the edge of a plateau. The view, looking back on my day's journey, was both wild and sad. Mount Mézenc and the peaks beyond St. Julien stood out in trenchant gloom against a cold glitter in the east; and the intervening field of hills had fallen together into one broad wash of shadow, except here and there the outline of a wooded sugar-loaf in black, here and there a white irregular patch to represent a cultivated farm, and here and there a blot where the Loire, the Gazeille, or the Lausonne wandered in a gorge.

Soon we were on a highroad, and surprise seized on my mind as I beheld a village of some magnitude close at hand; for I had been told that the neighborhood of the lake was uninhabited except by trout. The road smoked in the twilight with the children driving home cattle from the fields; and a pair of mounted stride-legged women, hat and cap and all, dashed past me at a hammering trot from the canton where they had been to church and market. I asked one of the children where I was. At Bouchet St. Nicolas, he told me. Thither, about a mile south of my destination, and on the other side of a respectable summit, had these confused roads and treacherous peasantry conducted me. My shoulder was cut, so that it hurt sharply; my arm ached like a toothache from perpetual beating; I gave up the lake and my design to camp, and asked for the *auberge*.

PAUL THEROUX
(1941–)

Paul Theroux grew up in a large New England family. "A big family isn't just a nest of love," Theroux said. "It's like a whole society that's contending for attention." Theroux craved solitude and found it in writing. After graduating from the University of Massachusetts, he taught in Italy and then Africa, where he met the writer V. S. Naipaul, a strong personal and literary influence.

Since 1971 Theroux has written full-time and his first great success in travel writing was The Great Railway Bazaar, *an account of his train trip from Europe to Asia. Theroux has produced over forty books, both fiction and nonfiction, and many articles and short stories. He said, "Mark Twain was a great traveler and he wrote three or four great travel books. I wouldn't say I'm a travel novelist, but rather a novelist who travels—and who uses travel as a background for finding stories of places."*

The word most often used to describe Theroux is "dyspeptic." But he prefers to think of himself as a misunderstood ironist. "I think that the people who read my books and like them, and there are plenty of them, wouldn't read me if I were merely a bad-tempered person," he said. Theroux finds travel itself often tedious, repetitive, and uncomfortable, but he finds the lure of the road as strong now as when he was young. "The travel impulse is mental and physical curiosity. It's a passion. And I can't understand people who don't want to travel."

"Le Grand Sud" to Nice

from THE PILLARS OF HERCULES

What threw me was the sameness of the sea. The penetrating blue this winter day and the pale sky and the lapping of water on the shore, continuous and unchanging, the simultaneous calm in eighteen countries, and those aqueous and indistinct borders, made it seem like a small world of nations, cheek by jowl, with their chins in the water. And it was so calm I could imagine myself trespassing, from one to the other, in a small boat, or even swimming. So much for the immutable sea.

On land, the station at Port-Bou, the edge of Spain, was like a monument to Franco. Fascism shows more clearly in the facades of buildings than in the faces of people. This one was self-consciously monumental, austere to the point of ugliness, very orderly and uncomfortable, under the Chaine des Arberes, a gray range of mountains. The train rattled, and it moved slowly on squeaky wheels through the gorge to the station at Cerbère, the beginning of France.

There were no passport formalities, the bright winter light did not change, and yet there was a distinct sense of being in another country. And that was odd because all we had done was jog a short way along the shore. Gibraltar is a marvel of nature— it looks like a different place. But the border between Spain and France (and France and Italy, and so on) looks arbitrary, vague in reality and distinct only on a map. But some aspects of it spoke of a frontier: the different angle of the mountains, especially the way the lower slopes were covered in cactuses, plump little plants, sprouting from every crevice and ledge on the rock face and cliffs that overlooked the harbor at Cerbère, an odor, too—disinfectant and the sea and the cigarette smoke; but most of all the Arabs. There had been none in the small port towns over the border, but there was a sudden arabesque of lounging cab drivers, porters, travelers, lurkers.

"There are a lot of them in Marseilles," a young man said in English. He was sitting just ahead of me, with his friend, and holding a guitar case on his lap, he was addressing two Japanese travelers, still saying "them."

He was referring to the Arabs without using the word.

"We're going there," one of the Japanese said.

"That's a real rough place."

"What? You mean we'll get ripped off?"

"Worse."

That stopped them. What was worse than being robbed?

"Like I got robbed on the subway train," the first American said. "And then they tried to steal my guitar. There are gangs."

"Gangs," the Japanese man said.

"Lots of them," the American said.

"Where do you think we should stay?"

"Not in Marseilles. Arles, maybe. Van Gogh? The painter? That Arles. Like you could always take a day trip to Marseilles."

"Is it that bad?"

The second American said, "I'd go to Marseilles again if I could leave my stuff behind. That's why I didn't go to Morocco. What would I do with my guitar?"

"You speak French?" the Japanese traveler asked.

"I can read it. Do you know any other languages?"

"Japanese."

"Your English is great."

"I grew up in New Jersey," the Japanese man said.

At this point I took out my notebook, and on the pretext of reading my newspaper wrote down the conversation. The Japanese man was talking about Fort Lee, New Jersey, his childhood, the schools. The man with the guitar was also from New Jersey.

"Fort Lee's not that nice," the man with the guitar said. It seemed a harsh judgment of the Japanese fellow's hometown.

"It used to be," the Japanese man said. "But I'd be freaking out when I went to New York."

"My brother loves sports, but he's too scared to go to New York and watch the games."

"Like, I never took the subway in ten years."

"I don't have a problem with the subway."

"Except, like, you might get dead there."

The Japanese man was silent. Then he said, "How did these guys attempt to rob you?"

"Did I say 'attempt'?"

"Okay, how did they do it?"

"The way they always do. They crowd you. They get into your pockets. One guy went for me. I kicked him in the legs. He tried to kick me when he got off the train."

"That's it. I'm not going to Marseilles," the Japanese man said.

I got tired of transcribing this conversation, which was repetitious, the way fearful people speak when they require reassurance. It all sounded convincing to me, and it made me want to go to Marseilles.

The landscape had begun to distract me. Almost immediately a greater prosperity had become apparent—in the houses, the way they were built, the trees, the towns, the texture of the land, the well-built retaining walls, the sturdy fences, even the crops, the blossoms, the way the fields are squared off, from Banyuls-sur-Mer to bourgeoisified Perpignan.

With this for contrast, I saw Spain as a place that was struggling to keep afloat. It had something to do with tourism. The Spanish towns from the Costa Brava south are dead in the low season; the French towns just a few miles along looked as though they were booming even without tourists. They did not have that soulless appearance of apprehension and abandonment that tourist towns take on in the winter: the empty streets, the wind-swept beach, the promises on signs and posters, the hollow-eyed hotels.

The train was traveling next to the sea—or, rather, more precisely, next to the great lagoon-like ponds called *étangs:* Étang de

Leucate, Étang de Lapalme, and into Narbonne, the Étang de Bages et de Sigean, the railway line between Étang de l'Ayrolle—like a low-lying Asiatic landscape feature, the traverse between fish farms or paddy fields.

Towards Narbonne there were fruit trees in bloom—apples, cherries, peach blossoms. And shore birds in the marshes, and at the edges of the flat attenuated beach. There were Dalí-esque details in all this—I put this down to my recent visit to the crack-pot museum. The first was a chateau in the middle of nowhere, with vineyards around it, turrets and towers and pretty windows, a smug little absurdity in the seaside landscape, a little castle, like a grace note in a painting. There was no reason for it to be there. And much stranger than that, what looked like an enormous flock of pink flamingos circling over the étang a few miles before the tiny station of Gruissan-Tourebelle. I made a note of the name because I felt I was hallucinating. *Flamingos? Here?*

That night, in Narbonne, in Languedoc, I was wondering about those flamingos I thought I had seen flying out of the salty lagoons by the sea on the way into the city. Having a cup of coffee in the cool blossom-scented air of Mediterranean midwinter I struck up a conversation with Rachel, at the next table. A student at the university of Montpellier, she was spending a few days at home with her family. She was twenty, a native of Narbonne.

"They are flamingos, yes—especially at Étang de Leucate," Rachel said.

The tall pink birds had not been a hallucination of mine; yet it was February, fifty degrees Fahrenheit. What was the story?

"All the étangs have flamingos"—the word is the same in French—"but in the summer when there are a lot of people around they sometimes fly off and hide in the trees."

Rachel did not know more than that.

She said, "The étangs are very salty, very smelly at low tide, but there are fish in them and lots of mussels."

"I associate flamingos with Africa," I said.

Rachel shrugged. "I have not traveled. You are traveling now?"

"To Arles, and then Marseilles."

"I have never been to Arles," she said.

It was thirty miles beyond her college dorm at Montpellier.

"Or Marseilles, or Nice," she went on. "I went to Spain once. And to Brittany once. I prefer the sea in Brittany—it is rough and beautiful."

"What about the Mediterranean?"

"It is not exciting," she said.

I could have told her that the Mediterranean extended to the shores of Syria, was sucked into Trieste, formed a torrent at Messina, hugged the delta of the Nile, and even wetted a strip of Bosnia.

"And will you stay in Nice?" she said.

"For a few days. Then I'll take the ferry to Corsica."

"I have a friend from Corsica. He told me that the people are very traditional there. The women are suppressed—not free as they are here."

"Is his family traditional?"

"Yes. In fact, when they heard that he was talking about life there they got really angry. Corsicans think it's bad to repeat these things. I feel bad that I am telling you."

So to change the subject, I asked her about her studies.

"I am studying psychology. It's a six-year course. I chose it because I want to work with autistic children after I graduate."

"Have you ever worked with autistic children?"

"In the summer, yes, several times," she said. "Ever since I was twelve I knew I wanted to work with handicapped people. I knew it would be my life."

"That's hard work, isn't it?"

"Yes, it's hard. You give a lot. You don't get back very much. But I don't mind. Not many people want to do it."

Such idealism seemed rare to me. These were not sentiments I had heard expressed very often, and they lifted my spirits.

The next day was sunny, and Arles was not far. I left my bag at Narbonne railway station and went for a walk along the étangs, and watched the flamingos feeding and flying.

This Mediterranean sunshine was like a world of warmth and light, and it was inspirational, too. It was easy to understand the feelings of T. E. Lawrence, who took a dip there in 1908 and wrote to his mother, "I felt I had at last reached the way to the South, and all the glorious East; Greece, Carthage, Egypt, Tyre, Syria, Italy, Spain, Sicily, Crete, . . . they were all there, and all within reach of me."

I had thought that I had left Narbonne in plenty of time, but the early darkness of winter fell upon Arles just as the train pulled into the station. I had wanted to arrive in daylight. It was the seventeenth of February; Vincent Van Gogh had first arrived in Arles on the twentieth (in 1888), and because of that timing his life was changed.

"You know, I feel I am in Japan," he wrote to his brother Theo.

It was the light, the limpid colors. It was, most of all, the trees in bloom. And strangely that February was very cold and snowy. To see branches covered in snowflakes and white blossoms thrilled Van Gogh—and this in a low Hollandaise landscape of flat fields and windbreaks by the Rhône. They were almond blossoms mostly, but also cherry, peach, plum and apricot. Van Gogh painted the almond flowers on the branches, a Japanese-style picture that resembled a floral design that he had seen before on a screen panel.

Even in the dark I could see some blossoms, and in the glary light of streetlamps the almond petals were like moths clustered on the black branches and twisted twigs.

Arles had three or four large luxury hotels, but I was put off by their ridiculous prices. I had found the name of a twenty-dollar hotel in a guidebook. This was called La Gallia. It was apparently a cafe and pizza joint.

The man at the coffee machine said, "Go outside, turn right, go around to the back and up the stairs. Use this key. The light switch is on the wall. Your room is on the second floor. You can't miss it."

"Do you want me to sign anything?"

"No name needed. No signature. Just the money in advance. No passport. Sleep well!"

"Is there a toilet?"

"It's in the hall. But you have a sink."

It was a medieval tenement on a backstreet, with a cobblestone courtyard and a winding staircase. I was halfway up the stairs when everything went black; the timer on the light ran out. I struggled in the dark to the landing, where I fumbled my flashlight out of my bag. I used this to find the light switch on the next landing. It seemed so difficult contriving to enter and leave this odd empty building that I stayed in my room and went out at the first sign of dawn.

That morning there was an old man with a wooden leg trying to climb the stairs.

"Softly," I said.

There was only room for one person at a time on these precipitous stairs.

"This wooden leg of mine is heavy," he panted. "It was the war."

"My uncle was here in the war."

Cpl. Arthur Theroux of Stoneham, Massachusetts.

"Fighting?"

"Running a blood bank. He was a medic. Thirty-third Station Hospital."

We had to throw most of the French blood away, Paulie. They all had syphilis. The American whole blood was the stuff we used.

In the watery morning light I saw a profusion of almond blossoms. But I would have noticed them without the suggestion of Van Gogh; there was no subtlety. It was an explosion of flowers, the trees frothing with blossoms. The cherry blossoms of early spring in London and on Cape Cod always indicated to me that winter was almost over, and there is something magical about their appearing before the trees were in leaf.

Walking towards the river, a man—American—asked me directions to the railway station. He was Jim, from Connecticut, relieved to be in Arles after a harrowing trip—so he said—through Portugal and Spain.

"I hated Spain. I almost got robbed in Madrid."

He was a recent graduate of Bucknell. Philosophy major.

"Ever heard of Philip Roth? He went to Bucknell," Jim said. "We had to study him. Everyone at Bucknell reads him. I hated that stuff."

I asked him whether he was on vacation.

"No. I quit my job. I hate the job market. I worked a little while for Cadbury-Schweppes. They were developing a home soft-drink dispenser. The whole bit. Syrup, gas, water—your own soft drinks on tap. It was like a coffee machine."

"What were you doing?"

"Test-marketing it."

"Did it fly?"

"It was a failure. It was too expensive—and who needs it?" He kicked along beside me. "They weren't open to new ideas, so I quit."

"I'm sure you did the right thing—and here you are, a free man, seeing the world."

"What are you doing?"

His lack of interest in writing or reading encouraged me, and so I said, "I'm a publisher."

"What do you look for in a novel?" he asked suddenly. It was a good question.

"Originality, humor, subtlety. The writing itself. A sense of place. A new way of seeing. Lots of things. I like to believe the things I read."

I pulled a novel, *The Rock Pool,* by Cyril Connolly, out of my back pocket and waved it at him.

"This has some of those qualities, but not enough."

"What's it about?"

"People going to pieces on the Riviera."

"Another one of those!"

True enough, I thought. "Do you do any writing?"

"No. I'm planning to go to art school, but at the moment I'm heading for Bratislava."

"Any particular reason?"

"Supposed to be a pretty nice place."

With that, he jogged off to the railway station, and I continued strolling through the backstreets of Arles to the river. In many respects this was much the same place that Van Gogh saw; many of the same buildings still stand, the same streets and squares and boulevards. There is a vast Roman arena in the town, a splendid hippodrome the size of a small football stadium, used at certain seasons for bullfights. One series had just been held, another, the Easter Feria (*Feria de Paque*), was coming soon.

Not far from here, the town of Nîmes was the center of French bullfighting and had been for a decade or so, since the revival of the nauseating—what? recreation? pastime?—you could hardly call it a sport. It had been dying out, but Nîmes's right-wing backward-looking mayor, Jean Bousquet, provided guidance and enthusiasm. There are three bullfighting festivals a year in Nîmes, one attracting almost a million people. Of course French bullfighting had been denounced by animal-rights activists and foreigners, but nothing encourages the French so much as disapproval, especially from aliens.

"Do you go to the bullfights?" I asked a man walking a dog along the river.

"Sometimes. But you know these special events are to bring in the tourists," he said. "I prefer football."

Arles was a small town and it had the two disfigurements of pretty French towns in the provinces, dog merdes and graffiti. The sidewalks were so fouled they were almost impassable because of the merdes. As for the graffiti, there was something particularly depressing about spray-painted scrawls on the stone of ancient facades. *Up your ass, Paris (Paris-t'on cule)* and *Gilly = a whore and a slut (Gilly = pute et salope)* were two of the more picturesque obscenities.

The town had prepared itself for tourists, but on this winter day it looked especially empty: too many brasseries, hotels, gift shops, and stores; in July it would be packed, the people said. But Arles had an off-season friendliness and lack of urgency. The waiters were not surly. One explained the drinks available and laughed with me over the odd names Foetus Whisky, Delirium Tremens Beer ("It's from Belgium") and the blue cordial liqueur called "Fun Blue."

I eavesdropped in Arles, though it annoyed me when people were talking and I could not understand them, because of the intrusive background music or other voices. It was like looking at something interesting while someone intruded on my line of vision. I felt stifled and frustrated.

Some of the snippets tantalized me:

A man said, "Let's do in Italy what we did in France, back at the hotel—"

A woman said, "I am not going to go to another place like that again, because, one, it's too complicated, and two, what if we got sick? And three, the other people look really strange—"

There were almond blossoms everywhere, which gave a great freshness to Arles and all its fields and made it seem still rural, picturesque and even inspirational. I liked the provinciality of the place, and its clear light.

But Arles was not all floral, and tweeting with sparrows. The mailman was doing his rounds, a hardworking housewife with big red hands down at the grocer's was complaining about the high price of morel mushrooms. This so-called cup fungus was selling at 168 francs for a hundred grams, which worked out at $126 a pound. And even in the early morning there were drinkers leaning on bars. It was never too early for a drink in provincial France. Two ladies were tippling Pernod. And down the street a florid blowzy woman was nursing a beer. This was at seven in the morning in an Arles backstreet.

To verify that Arles is a seaport, I walked along the east bank of the Rhône, in a southerly direction for a day of sunshine and sweet air. There were windbreaks of twigs and boughs, and the wide flat fields. There had been floods a few months before which showed on the banks of the river. Some sections of it had been fortified, sections of the retaining wall and the embankment filled in.

In the late afternoon I walked back to town to take the train the short distance to Marseilles. At the small railway station at Arles there were almond trees on each platform and they were in blossom. Such a pretty station! Such lovely trees! And then the TGV was announced. The TGV is the French high-speed train, much too fast and too grand to stop at a little station like Arles. It screamed past the platforms with such speed and backdraft that a special yellow TGV line was painted on the platform, so that people would stand at a safe distance, giving the train six feet of leeway. It howled like an earthbound jet, doing about 160 miles an hour, and with such a rush of air that petals were blown from the almond trees. The sight, the sound, the rush of air, made it a deafening event, the train slicing the day in half and leaving such a vacuum that I had the sense that my brain was being sucked out of my ears.

Anyone who hankers for the romance of railways, of the branch lines jogging through Provence, ought to consider the fact that the newest trains are nearly as obnoxious—as noisy and intrusive—as jets.

GILLIAN TINDALL
(1938–)

Versatile British writer Gillian Tindall is the author of fiction, urban history and literary biography. The common element in her work is insatiable curiosity, whether she is writing a social history of a London suburb (The Fields Beneath, *a sociological history of Kentish Town), the biography of a romance writer* (Rosamond Lehmann: An Appreciation) *or her novels, including* Fly Away Home, To the City *and* The Traveller and His Child. *One reviewer wrote, "Where she is content to let her heart lead her, Tindall's work comes alive."*

Tindall stumbled across the story of Célestine after she and her husband bought a house in the French village of Chassignolles. Inside their cottage they found several carefully preserved letters to a former occupant, Célestine Chaumette, born in 1844 and the daughter of a local innkeeper. "One is from a schoolmaster, another from a salesman traveling for a local wine merchant. Others came from a bakery, from a village where rural iron foundries then were, and from another known for its annual cattle fair . . . Some sentences sprang fresh as flowers from the pages; others seemed for the moment impenetrable." The letters were marriage proposals—each one rejected—and set Tindall on a search for more information about Célestine's life and times. The result is a study of life in nineteenth century rural France. W. S. Merwin wrote in the New York Times Book Review *that* Célestine: Voices from a French Village *is "a narrative of enigmatic beauty, a glimpse of time and mortality and of a quite earthly unearthly light.*

from **Célestine**

I had come to the village some dozen years earlier on just such
an evening of unearthly light. I arrived there by chance, with
my husband and our then small son, driving south on minor
roads, hesitating before obscure signposts by fields where white
Charolais cattle drifted in ghostly herds and mistletoe hung in
swags from the trees. It was a relief when we saw a church spire
and a water-tower ahead and at last drove into an irregular square
with a café and two petrol pumps and a tree. We stayed the night
in one of the café's four hotel rooms, ate a home-cooked meal,
went for a brief walk round unknowable houses in the starry
dark that surprised us by its sudden cold. In the hot May sun
of the following morning we played ball with our child in the
hotel yard, packed up the car and drove off, mentally rolling up
behind us like a map this unremarkable village. However, by
chance we returned, in a different season. And then returned
again. The place's situation near the geographical centre of
France, an area crossed by many itineraries yet generally con-
signed by the French themselves to that unexplored and appar-
ently unexplorable region *la France profonde,* began to speak to us.

On our fourth or fifth visit we asked the owner of the café-
hotel, Suzanne Calvet, who had inherited it from her father
when it was a plain village inn, if she knew of any houses for
sale? It was 1972, the autumn before the Common Market was
due to include Britain in its reluctant embrace.

'I'll go and ask the men in the bar,' she said.

These, since it was morning, were a coterie of elderly citizens
all wearing the striped trousers and black alpaca jackets that had
indicated respectability in their youth. The consensus was that
there were two possible houses for us. One was a pretty but large

and dilapidated property by the cemetery. (It was later bought by a local faith-healer and teller of fortunes, but good fortune it did not bring him.) The other house was agreed by all to be extremely tiny but in good condition. Georges Bernardet, who had acquired it in 1938 for the widowed aunt who had brought him up, was known to be a conscientious owner. 'The Proprietor' was his village nickname.

'Bought it for her out of what he saved when he was doing his military service, he did.'

'How he managed to save beats me. But that's him all over.' Comfortable, slightly malicious chuckles. They were café-frequenters; Georges Bernardet was not.

'Ah, it's so small, it wouldn't have cost much then. Doesn't cost much now, come to that. Same price as a small car.' To me: 'You buy it, Madame, you won't regret it, the roof's sound . . . Well, go and look at it anyway. Last house in the village on the Séchère road, the corner by the cross. Its garden's all down to cabbages this year. Georges never leaves land idle . . . You can't miss it.'

Four months later, on a day when January hoar-frost was petrifying every leaf, blade of grass and spider's web, the house became ours. Or, more accurately, it became mine, since I was the one able to be present in the attorney's office in La Châtre for the ceremonial signing of documents that French law requires.

Bernardet had ridden in on his mobylette. I did not then know, but came later to understand, what an exceptional event it had to be to bring him into the town. Tall, heavy, battered-looking but wearing his sixty years well, he was ill at ease, constantly resetting his cap on his thick grey hair. He was mistrustful of the lawyer, the traditional enemy. Some months later, when it became apparent that an extra and wrong land registry number had been put in by mistake on the purchase document, Bernardet was not so much annoyed as grimly triumphant to have his suspicions vindicated, and gave the attorney a piece of his mind.

That day he was circumspect, however; disposed to be amiable to me but on his guard, sizing me up over an exceptional, ceremonial drink in the café afterwards. Was I going to like his house—understand how to live in it? Would I and my husband really be happy for the time being with the earth closet he had rashly agreed to construct for us at the bottom of the garden? He spoke carefully in his elegant, Sunday-best French, which was different from the tongue he employed at home. When the subject of the cabbage-patch garden came up, however, he became more animated, even gallant.

'I myself will do the garden for you, Madame, as I mentioned to you when you first looked at the house. That's good earth you've got there. I like to see it put to proper use.'

The next summer, and for sixteen summers after, the garden in late summer was a neat vision of potatoes, carrots, leeks, lettuces, haricot beans and tomatoes. Once in a while there was a coolness from him if we failed to be there at the right time to harvest everything he provided. We would beg him to use the stuff himself, but this was not part of his plan. He never entirely came to terms with our itinerant habits, but after many years he relented so far as to regard these as our fate and our misfortune rather than our own foolish choice. Once or twice, coming upon me with papers spread out on the table, he expressed sympathy for me—it must be hard on the brain, I ought to take care not to overdo it—and general relief that he himself had never been constrained by a Higher Authority to take up book-work.

Choice and free will were things of which life had provided him with little experience, yet he had turned his own fate to good advantage. Born into a large and poor family, bred to labour on the land of others, he set himself to acquire territory of his own. Over many years, intelligently and persistently, he worked his way into a position of modest comfort and universal respect: this was the real drama in his life.

Its one great adventure was a different matter. Called up at the beginning of the Second World War, he was taken prisoner at the fall of France along with half a million other Frenchmen. He was sent to a transit camp on the borders of Belgium, where his job was to get requisitioned horses ready for transport to

Germany. It was clear to him that soon it would be men who were being deported thence, and having established an image of himself as a trusty, he made his plans to escape and did so. How he managed, without papers, money or civilian clothes, to make his way over hundreds of miles of occupied France was something I never entirely understood. Once, in conversation alone with me, he mentioned that *une personne* had been of crucial assistance at one point. French uses the female form to describe any person, so the word was opaque, but I felt that if his helper had been a man he would have said *quelqu'un* or *un type* (a chap). At other times he said that whenever he sensed a German patrol might be near he would take to the fields and pretend to be tending the crops, a role in which he presumably looked so convincing that he was never questioned. Once he hastily joined a family who were digging up potatoes, muttering to them 'I'm your cousin . . .' Potatoes, cabbages and turnips—the main crops at that season in the chilly north—also provided his food. The motorized and provisioned troops of 1940 covered territory at speed; half of France was in German hands almost before the distraught populace had grasped the scale of the defeat. But stragglers, deserters, escaped prisoners, and refugees were back to the pace of foot-soldiers living off the land, as in the days when France was 'sixteen days wide and twenty-two days long.'

His keenest anxiety during that journey was that he did not know whether his home country, that *pays* to which he was pertinaciously, almost instinctively making his way, was now in the Occupied Zone or in Pétain's nominally Free one. In fact the Department of the Indre was just within the Free Zone: the line of demarcation was the River Cher, which bisects the old province of the Berry into two Napoleonic Departments, each named after its river. Bernardet only discovered the position of the frontier when he reached its banks. There he wandered for hours, avoiding the bridges which were now equipped with gun posts, gazing morosely at the farther shore. From any deserted water-meadow a swimmer could have made it easily to the other side. However, the rivers that criss-cross Bernardet's landlocked native countryside are all smaller than the Cher. The Indre there is easily fordable; the larger Creuse is twenty miles away. So Bernardet had never learnt to swim.

His saviour, who appeared at last as night was falling, was that classic figure of French folk-tale, a small boy herding cows. The child showed him where he could wade across, armpit deep. Some sixteen hours later, having walked in exhilaration all through the night, he strode into his own village. He went straight to his aunt, in the house that is now ours.

He never travelled again after that. He had done it, and that was enough. Why should he wander in other people's kingdoms when his own, so intimately known to him in all its rises and descents, its variations in soil, its pastures and crop fields, vine-yards, copses and vegetable gardens, was there demanding his attention?

Late in life, he did occasionally get on the train to visit his daughter, established in the suburbs of Paris, but this was on the understanding that her garden needed expert attention which her garage-mechanic husband could not be expected to provide. Each to his own skill. I believe that in his seventies, also, he did once relent so far as to accompany his wife on a day trip to the Atlantic coast, but till then it had been almost a matter of pride to him that he had never seen the sea.

After the war, when the aged, limiting structure of French rural life was at last cracking open a little, one or two friends suggested to him that a man of his acknowledged capabilities might aspire now to a different job. The local Gendarmerie, per-haps, where a good friend was established? Or the railways? His army sergeant, in civilian life a railway worker, would put in a good word for him there. Bernardet considered these proposi-tions but turned them down: the thought of a life unencum-bered by the demands of either the fields or the animals that meant so much to him did not, after all, appeal.

He grumbled furiously at times, but that is a general trait in farmers, subject as they are to forces of God and Government perpetually beyond their control. Not that he believed much in God, and he had a covert contempt for all forms of organized government from the Élysée Palace to the village municipal council. His ethic and his passion was work; it was his pride that, apart from all his farming skills, both current and remembered, he could turn his hand to a whole range of other things: he made gates, ladders and wheelbarrows, chicken coops and pigsties, he retiled roofs, laid hedges.

His great model in life, his personal version of the admired grown-up that is internalized within us, was his maternal grandfather. 'Ah, my grandfather could have told you that,' he would say, when I sought some piece of knowledge about the village's past. This man, whom I eventually discovered to have been a contemporary of Célestine Chaumette, grew up within a mile of her. They must have been acquainted: in those days the inhabitants of a rural area hardly ever encountered a face to which they were unable to put a name. But socially there would have been a gap between them. He was the son of a day-labourer, while the daughter of the innkeeper was almost a member of the bourgeoisie. The word originally indicated no more than those who lived *au bourg*—that is, within a little town or village however rural, as opposed to those who lived on a more remote farm or hamlet among the fields—but certain social differences tended to follow from these different circumstances, and still exist today. In the last century the differences would have been more marked. Clearly, Célestine could read and write herself (so, as we shall see, could her father) whereas Bernardet's grandfather was completely illiterate. He is said, however, to have been able to 'calculate anything in his head.' When still in his teens and working long days on someone else's farm, he took to fetching stone in the evenings from a local quarry with a hand-made cart and a borrowed mule. He fetched lime, too, from a river-bank, sawed wood and seasoned it. With infinite labour in snatched hours, he built a two-roomed house for himself and his future wife outside the village. It is standing to this day.

From the vantage-point of the present Bernardet himself now seems a figure from another era, one of those people who are irreplaceable because they can no longer be made: the mould is broken. It is a comfort, of a sort, to realize that the idea that the modern world has invaded and destroyed an ageless, unchanging peasant culture at some recent date (1950? 1939? 1914?) is to some extent an optical illusion. Moulds have repeatedly been broken over the previous centuries; peasant cultures, however apparently static, have often before been in a state of deep-seated change: otherwise, paradoxically, they could not have survived. Bernardet, in his turn, regarded his grandfather as a representative of the world he felt had slipped away already by his own youth: the world of the reaping hook, the wolves, the fairies and the all-night *veillées* where nuts were shelled for oil and wool was carded, and where the folk memories of unlettered men and women went back before the Revolution.

In old age, when he had retired from the heaviest farm labours, Bernardet softened his work ethic to the extent of adding a few flowers among the regimented vegetables in our garden. He had always, till then, regarded flowers as 'the wife's department.' A hedge of pink escallonia that we planted ourselves particularly took his fancy, and in the early summer of 1988 we received a letter from him that for once conveyed no practical message but simply told us: 'your primroses [*vos prime verts*] are a marvel to see.'

It was to be the last year he saw them.

CALVIN TRILLIN
(1935–)

Calvin Trillin wrote that he always referred to his wife as the Principessa or, in the rare instances that she lowered her restaurant and hotel standards, the Contessa. Alice Trillin was her husband's culinary foil, ready to call a halt to his order of, say, lobster with a fried chicken chaser. In his books on food and travel (American Fried; Travels with Alice; Alice, Let's Eat; *and* Third Helpings) *Alice is such a rational presence that Trillin claims that people "expect her to be a nutritionist in sensible shoes, hair in a bun."*

Trillin's writing is not limited to food and travel. He is a regular contributor to both The Nation *and* The New Yorker *and appeared in two one-man shows "Calvin Trillin's Uncle Sam" (1988) and "Calvin Trillin's Words, No Music" (1990). His most recent novel* Tepper Isn't Going Out *is about that great Manhattan tradition of holding a parking space by colonizing it for hours.*

Despite his identification with New York, Trillin was born in Kansas City, Missouri (which explains his fondness for barbecued backribs and chicken-fried steak). "It's true that when you talk about being from Kansas City—people assume you're a Methodist." Trillin is Jewish, the son of a father who spoke Yiddish, but also used expressions like "haven't had so much fun since the hogs ate my sister." Trillin inherited his father's duality—he appreciates regional American cuisine and five-star French restaurants, his humor has both the dry understatement of the Midwest and the punch line of the Borscht Belt, and his writing includes doggerel and Remembering Denny, *a highly acclaimed book about a Yale classmate who committed suicide.*

Alice Trillin died in Manhattan on September 11, 2001, of natural causes.

Hanging Around in Uzès

from T R A V E L S   W I T H   A L I C E

I suppose I could say that we decided to take a house in the South of France for a month because it would give Abigail an opportunity to improve her French, but that would be like a newly rich businessman saying that he decided to buy a brand-new Cadillac El Dorado because a heavy car sticks to the road: it's true, but it's not the whole story.

Everyone in the family had some pleasant extraeducational daydreams of what life in the South of France might be like. In the one I most often clicked on in the months preceding our trip, I am sitting in an outdoor café on the town square sipping a drink, having somehow found some alcoholic beverage in a French café that does not taste like cough medicine. I am staring down at my drink in the significant way French intellectuals stare down at their drinks in cafés—either because they have just thought of something profoundly ironic or because they are wondering why they drink things that taste like cough medicine. Meanwhile, Abigail, then a tenth-grader with a couple of years of French under her belt, is scampering around the shops of the town to gather ingredients for the afternoon *pique-nique*—a French word I taught her myself, nearly exhausting my vocabulary in the process, on the theory that there are some things one cannot learn in school.

Sarah is with her, absorbing enough of that musical shopkeeper French (*Bonjour, madame; Merci, madame; Au revoir, madame*) to become the outstanding beginning French student in the next fall's seventh grade. Alice—who has just paid a visit to the local museum and made dinner reservations at a nearby two-star restaurant that happens to specialize in fish soup and done some window shopping (in my daydream, the only expensive women's clothing store in town happens to have an annual vacation closing that coincides precisely with the dates of our visit) and picked up some fresh *chèvre* from a wandering goat farmer—is about to join me at the café and to assure me that we are going to have the finest *pique-nique* in the history of the Republic, heavy on the *saucisson*. I, having at last thought of something profoundly ironic (perhaps the dates of the annual closing of the clothing store), lift my head and say, *"Quelle ironie!"* The other drinkers look up, nod, and draw up their lower lips in that French gesture of acknowledgment ("Well, the foreign-looking fellow is an intellectual after all"). Then we all go back to staring down at our drinks.

Until the trip was announced—we had found a house in a town called Uzès, about twenty miles from Avignon—Abigail and Sarah must have been pretty much resigned to seeing France only in daydreams. They had heard us say any number of times that children are ready to take a trip to France about the time they are ready to eat mushrooms. It was an opinion formed over the years by observing children who were being subjected to the Grand Tour of Europe—children who sat in formal hotel dining rooms doodling on the tablecloth with their butter knives, looking as if they were wondering whether there was any reason to hold out hope that they might be spared the second of tomorrow's scheduled cathedrals by a sudden downpour or perhaps a nuclear attack. We had not changed our view that staggering from hotel to sight to hotel to sight with the girls would be painful folly, but it had occurred to us that simply renting a house in a small town might be a sensible alternative—a way to be with the girls in

France even before they were of an age to go through the Mush-
room Passage.

By the time the plane landed in France, I was considering some
arguments on the other side. During the flight across the
Atlantic, the vision of the outdoor café had faded away, and in
its place was a vision of me trying to deal with a particularly
obdurate French plumber. The plumber is speaking very rapidly
in French I don't understand. Abigail is consulting two different
French-English dictionaries, and I am thumbing desperately
through a phrase book that goes into great detail about how to
send a cable from the post office but does not trouble to include
the French for "stopped up."

Aside from the language barrier, my experiences in France
had, to put it as politely as possible, not persuaded me that the
French have a particularly strong tradition of friendliness and
helpfulness toward visitors—even visitors with serious plumbing
problems. So far, no scholar of Franco-American relations has
attempted to refute the theory I once offered that some of the
problems American visitors have with the French can be traced
to the Hollywood movies of Maurice Chevalier. According to
the theory, meeting a surly bureaucrat or a rude taxi driver is
bound to be particularly disappointing if you've arrived with the
expectation that every Frenchman you encounter will be a
charming, debonair old gent who at any moment might start
singing, "Sank Evan for leetle gerls."

Also, I realized almost immediately upon our arrival—it was
at dinner on the terrace of a lovely country hotel we were
spending the night in before driving on to our house—that my
daydreams about life in France might have included the occa-
sional two-star restaurant without including any information
about what the girls were supposed to eat there. Quickly I fast-
forwarded through the daydreams, searching for eating scenes. I
found a scene of Abigail and Sarah going in the morning to the
local bakery for croissants and *pains au chocolat*. There was a

scene showing all of us gathered around a dinner table in the garden of our house to eat whatever we had collected at the stalls of the local market. But I couldn't find a scene that included Sarah, then a figure of some repute among fussy eaters, sitting in a grand restaurant.

As I snapped back into real time, I happened to glance at Sarah across the table. She seemed to be waiting in quiet trepidation, as if she expected at any moment to be required to consume a live asparagus. The expression on her face was the sort of expression associated with someone who might answer a question about whether he was enjoying his meal by saying, "Well, yes, warden, under the circumstances I am, and I do appreciate the effort you folks have made to make this meal special." Could it be, I wondered, that in an attempt at family togetherness we were about to turn our own daughter into a tablecloth doodler?

It had also occurred to me by then that American parents might be risking a serious guilt attack by bringing their children to Europe—at the cost of at least the extras on a brand-new Cadillac El Dorado—without injecting them with a full dose of what used to be called "cultural enrichment." I had seen the danger on the drive over, when we stopped for lunch at a village that happened to have a rather distinguished little church in it. After lunch we strolled into the church and gave the girls what I believe French intellectuals call "the Romanesque-Gothic rap." We spent a pleasant few minutes in the church, but after we emerged I happened to notice in the Michelin green guide that the time allotted for a viewing of the church interior was forty-five minutes. Forty-five minutes! We had just arrived, and we were already way behind.

I had figured that just living in a French town—getting the croissants every morning, searching out a parent who had absent-mindedly lingered in the café past dinnertime, maybe even dealing with an obdurate plumber—might qualify as culturally enriching, but I wasn't sure it measured up to the standards expected from the sort of American parents who wouldn't even bother with a village church as they ticked off the Big

Sights. I envisioned a scene at JFK one month in the future as we presented ourselves to the immigration officer:

"You must have loved the Tower of London, little lady," the officer says to Sarah in a disarmingly friendly tone.

"We didn't actually go there," Sarah says.

"Well," he says, turning to Abigail with that same friendly air, "the Colosseum in Rome must have been pretty exciting."

"We were mainly just in this one town," Abigail says. Then, sensing trouble, she adds, "It was a very nice town."

The immigration officer turns to me, his voice coldly polite. "I'm afraid I'll have to hold on to this passport of yours for a while, sir," he says. "Just routine."

Uzès was indeed a very nice town—a market center of about seven thousand people in French farmland bearing an uncanny resemblance to a wine label. Best known as the site of the first duchy established in France, it still has a ducal palace with a multicolored roof that I rather admired even after I read in some Tweediesque guidebook that it was a "nineteenth-century error." Apparently, a ducal palace is not the sort of attraction that can deflect an overwhelming number of tourists who are bent on seeing the Palace of the Popes in Avignon and the Palace of the Grimaldis in Monte Carlo on the same day, so Uzès is a relatively peaceful place. In the still of the early evening, a visitor could have a drink in one of the cafés on the Place des Herbes, a vast and beautiful plaza right in the middle of town, and muse (at least in my case) on how his trepidations about taking a house in France were unfounded.

Our lack of fluency in French turned out not to be a problem: among four people, someone is bound to come up with the right word or gesture, and great command of the language is not required in order to point to a display of fluffy croissants and say, "Fourteen, please." After a couple of meals in good restaurants, we realized that even what seems to be the stuffiest French restaurant will always arrange to split a set meal between two children or to do up a simple piece of sole or even to produce, with some flourish, a ham sandwich. Sarah relaxed, as if there had been a last-minute reprieve from the governor.

Abigail and Sarah were, in fact, able to walk to the bakery every morning for croissants, since it was only three or four doors down the street. Our house was small and simple—a restored mid-nineteenth-century row house on an otherwise ungentrified block just off the main street of Uzès—but it turned out to be splendid. It had thick stone walls and a first-rate kitchen and precisely the garden I had imagined our having supper in every evening—a private little place, with a table underneath an arbor. The plumbing held up admirably—something I'll remember next time I get in one of those geopolitical discussions about whether the French can be depended on.

My concerns about providing sufficient cultural enrichment turned out to be the easiest to deal with. Every afternoon I simply informed the girls of what they were missing that day by not being on the Grand Tour. "It's Rome today, *jeunes filles*," I would say as we sat next to one of our favorite swimming spots on the Gard River, just after a splendid picnic (heavy on the *saucission*). "The Trevi Fountain! There it is—excellent fountain, excellent. The Spanish Steps. Watch it there, mister, don't shove. Plenty of room for everybody, at least there would be if you people didn't travel in regiments in those damn tour buses. Okay, girls, we'll want to take in the Colosseum while it's still there. On to the Vatican. Whoops! A lot of traffic around the Vatican. Awfully hot in Rome this time of year, particularly with the traffic. I don't think I've ever been so hot."

"In that case, Daddy," one of the girls would say, "maybe we should just get in the water."

By switching swimming holes one day, I was able to present a real rather than imaginary sight of Grand Tour proportions. "Look above you," I said, pointing up at the Pont du Gard. "That's the best-preserved Roman aqueduct in the world, seen from the authentic angle of a Roman slave who fell off it during construction."

I don't mean to imply that we ignored the sights in our vicinity that were not observable from a backstroke. On a sunny morning we might take a drive that combined an outdoor lunch and a stroll with a visit to, say, the Palace of the Popes in Avignon or a castle we had been admiring in Tarascon or the Roman arena in Nîmes or the medieval village of Les Baux. "Life is not all *pain au chocolat,* ladies," I would announce at breakfast. "We are about to endeavor to stuff a little culture down you."

I also don't mean to imply that my notion about the cultural enrichment of simply living in a French town proved to be one of those brilliantly simple theories that work without qualification. There is a fuzzy line, it turns out, between an experience that seems interesting in the French version ("Isn't it interesting to see a French supermarket?" I would say, ecstatic at the sight of bins full of ninety-cent wine) and experiences that may best be described in the remark "You didn't come all the way to France to play miniature golf." Where the line is drawn obviously depends on who does the drawing—a fact brought home to me one day as we were walking past a line of gumball machines and Sarah said, "Wouldn't it be interesting to try French bubble gum!"

"Uh-oh," I thought. "She's broken the code."

Instead of miniature golf, we played what the French call *baby-foot,* a two-franc soccer game in which you drive the ball toward your opponent's goal by flipping miniature players attached to rods. Our approach to being in France carried with it, I suppose, a bias toward doing things rather than seeing things, toward being in places where something was happening rather than being in places where something once happened. We liked the splendidly preserved Roman arena of Nîmes when we strolled through it almost alone one quiet Sunday. We liked it even better when we sat in it a few days later to watch a traveling European circus that had an American theme—including a troupe of knockabout acrobats who were dressed in double-breasted blue suits and were constantly shooting blanks at each other from snub-nosed revolvers and were called Le Chicago. The acrobatic act may have been the inspiration for the device I found myself using to strike terror into the heart of any shopkeeper or minor official who displeased me: I'd make a pistol out of my thumb and forefinger, cock my thumb, say "She-ca-go," and walk away.

Our approach meant spending a lot of time at the morning market, checking to see which farmer had brought in the best tomatoes. It involved going to any local event that sounded at all intriguing—including a Saturday-night jollity called *taureaux piscine,* which struck me as impossible to describe to an immigration officer who was expecting youthful impressions of Big Ben and Versailles and the Colosseum. ("Yes, that's what I'm saying—sort of a plastic swimming pool right in the middle of the bullring . . .") It meant taking a lot of evening strolls that didn't have any particular destination, and lingering in the garden over suppers that reflected more shopping than cooking—salad and cheese from the market, and the local wine, and, for the girls, those French versions of pizza that in the South of France seem to be turned out in every bakery and even a few butcher shops. In other words, we hung around.

When we visited nearby towns, I realized that hanging around is not an activity covered well by guidebooks. I don't mean that I'm not interested in the sort of information offered by guidebooks that emphasize history and architecture. The scenes of van Gogh's paintings were somehow more interesting to me after I read that when van Gogh cut off his ear, he knocked on the door of a woman he knew in Arles, presented her with the ear, said, "Guard this precious item," and disappeared into the night. I'm also interested, though, in a lot of information guidebooks don't seem to have—when the town has its market day and whether there's a good annual celebration and where you can find the best street for strolling. I'd like to know which of the town cafés caters to soccer fans and which to *boules* players and which to the cycling crowd and which to intellectuals who

stare significantly down at their cough medicine. The guide-
book we could have used for our day trips from Uzès would be
called *The Hanging Around Guide to France,* first in a series.

In Uzès itself, of course, we eventually found the best
strolling streets and the best *babyfoot* game—in the soccer fans'
café, where middle-aged men sat quietly enjoying a drink or
playing cards and the walls were decorated with league schedules
and group pictures of the Uzès squad. Once found, our favorite
places became part of a routine. One of the essential differences
between the Grand Tour and the Hanging Around approaches
to being in Europe is the attitude toward repeat visits. On the
Grand Tour, you go once. You don't go back to Notre Dame
once you've seen Notre Dame. Once you've seen Notre Dame,
you go to the Louvre. In Hanging Around, repetition is part of
the pleasure. If you find a nice local museum—like the Museon
Arlaten in Arles—you go back now and then. If you find a
pommes frites stand that reminds you why French fries were
named after the French, you make it a regular stop on the
evening stroll. In a few days it becomes natural to say, "I'll meet
you at our *pommes frites* stand."

There came a time in Uzès when it became natural to think
of a lot of things around town as our things. Saturday is the mar-
ket day in the Place des Herbes, and we had been there enough
Saturdays to decide which was our *saucisson* stand and which was
our baker. Thanks to some local kids Abigail and Sarah met at
the river, we had discovered what would obviously be our
swimming hole. Our evening routine had become pretty well
set. We stopped at our *pommes frites* stand, got two orders to go,
and then adjourned to a place on the Place des Herbes that
made fruit drinks in a blender—our fruit-drink place. We would
have supper in the garden and then, maybe, a game of *babyfoot* at
the soccer bar. Over the *babyfoot* game one evening toward the
end of our stay—Alice had remained at the house to finish a
book, and I was playing against Abigail and Sarah—it occurred
to me that things had worked out more like the daydreams of
the spring than the horrifying visions on the day of our arrival.

Abigail had been chattering away in French to the kids at the river and had taken charge of making restaurant reservations over the telephone in French. Sarah knew every word in French that could be used to describe a flavor of ice cream, as she demonstrated later in the summer when, during a North American picnic lunch at which raspberry Kool-Aid was being served, she said, "Please pass the *framboise*." In the subtle negotiations that occur when time is up for grabs rather than strictly allotted, Alice had got her share of scenic drives and the girls had got their share of swims and I had got my share of fish soup.

The other way to look at it, I realized at almost the same moment, was that we had brought our children to France to hang out in bars and live on French fries and take-out pizza. At that moment Sarah drilled one past my goalie, giving her and Abigail the game. Hanging out in bars and beating their elders at two-franc soccer games! I looked up from the goal. *"Quelle ironie!"* I said.

MARK TWAIN
(1835–1910)

The author of Tom Sawyer, Huckleberry Finn, The Prince and the Pauper *and* Life on the Mississippi *was a terrible businessman. Samuel Clemens aka Mark Twain failed at every investment. His books made him a fortune and his wife, Livy, came from a wealthy family—yet Twain never managed to hang on to money. His inevitable financial pattern was to pay off his hounding creditors and then invest in another highly speculative (and ultimately doomed) venture.*

From his earliest days as a newspaperman, Twain found that he could travel and write profitable articles. Eventually, he added lecturing to his travel repertoire. After his marriage, Twain and Livy moved abroad, often for years at a time, to save money. In the United States they lived in their very expensive, architecturally fanciful mansion in Hartford, Connecticut, with their three daughters.

Twain's financial situation reached a crisis in 1896 when he and Livy lost collectively nearly $200,000. Twain also realized that he had failed to secure his most valuable asset, the copyright to his writing. To pay off his creditors, he began a round-the-world lecture tour that lasted more than a year. His writings were collected in Following the Equator *(1897).*

Twain's travel writing was as acerbic as his fiction. He wrote, "I offer no apologies for any departures from the usual style of travel-writing that may be charged against me—for I think I have seen with impartial eyes, and I am sure I have written at least honestly, whether wisely or not."

Aix-les-Bains

Certainly Aix-les-Bains is an enchanting place. It is a strong word, but I think the facts justify it. True, there is a rabble of nobilities, big and little, here all the time, and often a king or two, but as these behave quite nicely and also keep mainly to themselves, they are little or no annoyance. And then a king makes the best advertisement there is, and the cheapest. All he costs is a reception at the station by the Mayor and the police in their Sunday uniforms, shop-front decorations along the route from station to hotel, brass band at the hotel, fireworks in the evening, free bath in the morning. This is the whole expense; and in return for it he goes away from here with the broad of his back metaphorically stenciled over with display ads, which shout to all the nations of the earth, assisted by the telegraph:

RHEUMATISM ROUTED AT AIX-LES-BAINS!
GOUT ADMONISHED, NERVES BRACED UP!
ALL DISEASES WELCOMED, AND SATISFACTION
GIVEN, OR THE MONEY REFUNDED AT THE DOOR.

We leave nature's noble cliffs and crags undefiled and unin-sulted by the advertiser's paint-brush. We use the back of a king, which is better and properer, and more effective, too, for the cliff stays still and few see it, but the king moves across the fields of the world, and is visible from all points like a constellation. We are out of kings this week, but one will be along soon—possibly his Satanic Majesty of Russia. There's a colossus for you! A mysterious and terrible form that towers up into unsearchable space and casts a shadow across the universe like a planet in eclipse. There will be but one absorbing spectacle in this world when we stencil him and start him out.

This is an old valley, this of Aix, both in the history of man and the geological records of its rocks. Its little Lake of Bourget carries the human history back to the lake dwellers, furnishing seven groups of their habitations, and Dr. William Wakefield says in his interesting local guide-book that the mountains round about furnish "geologically, a veritable epitome of the globe." The stratified chapters of the earth's history are clearly and permanently written on the sides of the roaring bulk of the Dent du Chat, but many of the layers of race, religion, and government, which in turn have flourished and perished here between the lake dweller of several thousand years ago and the French Republican of today, are ill-defined and uninforming by comparison. There were several varieties of pagans. They went their way, one after the other, down into night and oblivion, leaving no account of themselves, no memorials. The Romans arrived 2,300 years ago; other parts of France are rich with remembrances of their eight centuries of occupation, but not many are here. Other pagans followed the Romans. By and by Christianity arrived, some 400 years after the time of Christ. The long procession of races, languages, religions, and dynasties demolished each other's monuments and obliterated each other's records—it is a man's way always.

As a result, nothing is left of the handiwork of the remoter inhabitants of the region except the constructions of the lake dwellers and some Roman odds and ends. There is part of a small Roman temple, there is part of a Roman bath, there is a graceful and battered Roman arch. It stands on a turfy level over the way from the present great bathhouse, is surrounded by magnolia trees, and is both a picturesque and suggestive object. It has stood there some 1,600 years. Its nearest neighbor, not twenty steps away, is a Catholic church. They are symbols of the two chief eras in the history of Aix. Yes, and of the European world. I judge that the venerable arch is held in reverent esteem by everybody, and that this esteem is its sufficient protection from insult, for it is the only public structure I have yet seen in France which lacks the sign, "It is forbidden to post bills here." Its neighbor, the church, has that sign on more than one of its sides, and other signs, too, forbidding certain other sorts of desecration.

The arch's next nearest neighbor—just at its elbow, like the church—is the telegraph office. So there you have the three great eras bunched together—the era of war, the era of theology, the era of business. You pass under the arch, and the buried Caesars seem to rise from the dust of the centuries and flit before you; you pass by that old battered church, and are in touch with the middle ages, and with another step you can put down ten francs and shake hands with Oshkosh under the Atlantic.

It is curious to think what changes the last of the three symbols stands for; changes in men's ways and thoughts, changes in material civilization, changes in the Deity—or in men's conception of the Deity, if that is an exacter way of putting it. The second of the symbols arrived in the earth at a time when the Deity's possessions consisted of a small sky freckled with mustard seed stars, and under it a patch of landed estate not so big as the holdings of the Czar today, and all his time was taken up in trying to keep a handful of Jews in some sort of order—exactly the same number of them that the Czar has lately been dealing with in a more abrupt and far less loving and long-suffering way. At a later time—a time within all old men's memories—the Deity was otherwise engaged. He was dreaming his eternities away on his great white throne, steeped in the soft bliss of hymns of praise wafted aloft without ceasing from choirs of ransomed souls, Presbyterians and the rest. This was a Deity proper enough to the size and condition of things, no doubt a provincial Deity with provincial tastes. The change since has been inconceivably vast. His empire has been unimaginably enlarged. Today he is master of a universe made up of myriads upon myriads of gigantic suns, and among them, lost in that limitless sea of light, floats that atom, his earth, which once seemed so good and satisfactory and cost so many days of patient labor to build, a mere cork adrift in the waters of a shoreless Atlantic. This is the business era, and no doubt he is governing his huge empire now, not by dreaming the time away in the buzz of hymning choirs, with occasional explosions of arbitrary power disproportioned to the size of the annoyance, but, by applying laws of a sort proper and necessary to the sane and successful management of a complex and prodigious establishment, and by seeing to it that the exact and constant operation of these laws is not interfered with for the accommodation of any individual or political or religious faction or nation.

Mighty has been the advance of the nations and the liberalization of thought. A result of it is a changed Deity, a Deity of a dignity and sublimity proportioned to the majesty of his office and the magnitude of his empire, a Deity who has been freed from a hundred fretting chains and will in time be freed from the rest by the several ecclesiastical bodies who have these matters in charge. It was, without doubt, a mistake and a step backward when the Presbyterian Synods of America lately decided, by vote, to leave him still embarrassed with the dogma of infant damnation. Situated as we are, we cannot at present know with how much of anxiety he watched the balloting, nor with how much of grieved disappointment he observed the result.

Well, all these eras above spoken of are modern, they are of last week, they are of yesterday, they are of this morning, so to speak. The springs, the healing waters that gush up from under this hillside village, indeed are ancient; they, indeed, are a genuine antiquity; they antedate all those fresh human matters by processions of centuries; they were born with the fossils of the Dent du Chat, and they have been always limpid and always abundant. They furnished a million gallons a day to wash the lake dwellers with, the same to wash the Cæsars with, no less to wash the Balzac with, and have not diminished on my account. A million gallons a day—for how many days? Figures cannot set forth the number. The delivery, in the aggregate, has amounted to an Atlantic. And there is still an Atlantic down in there. By Dr. Wakefield's calculation that Atlantic is three-quarters of a mile down in the earth. The calculation is based upon the temperature of the water, which is 114° to 117° Fahrenheit, the natural law being that below a certain depth heat augments at the rate of one degree for every sixty feet of descent.

Aix is handsome and handsomely situated, too, on its hill slope, with its stately prospect of mountain range and plain spread out before it and about it. The streets are mainly narrow, and steep, and crooked, and interesting, and offer considerable variety in the way of names; on the corner of one of them you read this: Rue du Puits d'Enfer—pit of Hell street. Some of the sidewalks are only eighteen inches wide; they are for the cats probably. There is a pleasant park, and there are spacious and beautiful grounds connected with the two great pleasure resorts— the Cercle and the Villa des Fleurs. The town consists of big hotels, little hotels, and pensions. The season lasts about six months, beginning with May. When it is at is height there are thousands of visitors here, and in the course of the season as many as 20,000 in the aggregate come and go.

These are not all here for the baths; some come for the gambling facilities and some for the climate. It is a climate where the field strawberry flourishes through the spring, summer, and fall. It is hot in the summer, and hot in earnest; but this is only in the daytime; it is not hot at night. The English season is May and June; they get a good deal of rain then, and they like that. The Americans take July and the French take August. By the 1st of July the open air music and the evening concerts and operas and plays are fairly under way, and from that time onward the rush of pleasure has a steadily increasing boom. It is said that in August the great grounds and the gambling-rooms are crowded all the time and no end of ostensible fun going on.

It is a good place for rest and sleep and general recuperation of forces. The book of Dr. Wakefield says there is something about this atmosphere which is the deadly enemy of insomnia, and I think this must be true, for, if I am any judge, this town is at times the noisiest one in Europe, and yet a body gets more sleep here than he could at home, I don't care where his home is. Now we are living at a most comfortable and satisfactory pension, with a garden of shade trees and flowers and shrubs, and a convincing air of quiet and repose. But just across the little narrow street is the little market square, and at a corner of that is that church that is neighbor to the Roman arch, and that narrow street, and that billiard-table of a market place, and that church are able, on a bet, to turn out more noise to the cubic yard at the wrong time than any other similar combination in the earth or out of it. In the street you have the skull bursting thunder of the passing hack, a volume of sound not producible by six hacks anywhere else; on the hack is a lunatic with a whip, which he cracks to notify the public to get out of his way. This crack is as keen and sharp and penetrating and ear-splitting as a pistol shot at close range, and the lunatic delivers it in volleys, not single shots. You think you will not be able to live till he gets by, and when he does get by he only leaves a vacancy for the bandit who sells *Le Petit Journal* to fill with his strange and awful yell. He arrives with the early morning and the market people, and there is a dog that arrives at about the same time and barks steadily at nothing till he dies, and they fetch another dog just like him. The bark of this breed is the twin of the whip volley, and stabs like a knife. By and by, what is left of you the church-bell gets. There are many bells, and apparently 6,000 or 7,000 town clocks, and as they are all five minutes apart—probably by law—there are no intervals. Some of them are striking all the time—at least, after you go to bed they are. There is one clock that strikes the hour, and then strikes it over again to see if it was right. Then for evenings and Sundays there is a chime—a chime that starts in pleasantly and musically, then suddenly breaks into a frantic roar, and boom, and crash of warring sounds that make you think Paris is up and the revolution come again. And yet, as I have said, one sleeps here—sleeps like the dead. Once he gets his grip on his sleep neither hack, nor whip, nor news fiend, nor dog, nor bell-cyclone, nor all of them together can wrench it loose or mar its deep and tranquil continuity. Yes, there is indeed something in this air that is death to insomnia.

The buildings of the Cercle and the Villa des Fleurs are huge in size and each has a theater in it and a great restaurant, also conveniences for gambling and general and variegated entertainment. They stand in ornamental grounds of great extent and beauty. The multitudes of fashionable folk sit at refreshment tables in the open air afternoons and listen to the music, and it is there that they mainly go to break the Sabbath.

To get the privilege of entering these grounds and buildings you buy a ticket for a few francs which is good for the whole season. You are then free to go and come at all hours, attend the plays and concerts free, except on special occasions, gamble, buy refreshments, and make yourself symmetrically comfortable.

Nothing could be handier than those two little theaters. The curtain doesn't rise until 8:30. Then between the acts one can idle for half an hour in the other departments of the building, damaging his appetite in the restaurants or his pocket in the baccarat room. The singers and actors are from Paris and their performance is beyond praise.

I was never in a fashionable gambling hall until I came here. I had read several millions of descriptions of such places, but the reality was new to me. I very much wanted to see this animal, especially the now historic game of baccarat, and this was a good place, for Aix ranks next to Monte Carlo for high play and plenty of it. But the result was what I might have expected—the interest of the looker-on perishes with the novelty of the spectacle—that is to say, in a few minutes. A permanent and intense interest is acquirable in baccarat or in any other game, but you have to buy it. You don't get it by standing around looking on.

The baccarat table is covered with green cloth and is marked off in divisions with chalk or something. The banker sits in the middle, the croupier opposite. The customers fill all the chairs at the table, and the rest of the crowd are massed at their backs and leaning over them to deposit chips or gold coins. Constantly money and chips are flung upon the table, and the game seems to consist in the croupier's reaching for those things with a flexible sculling oar and raking them home. It appeared to be a rational enough game for him, and if I could have borrowed his oar I would have stayed, but I didn't see where the entertainment of the others came in. This was because I saw without perceiving and observed without understanding. For the widow and the orphan and the others do win money there. Once an old gray mother from Israel or elsewhere pulled out, and I heard her say to her daughter or her granddaughter as they passed me: "There, I've won six louis, and I'm going to quit while I'm ahead." Also there was this statistic. A friend pointed to a young man with the dead stub of a cigar in his mouth, which he kept munching nervously all the time and pitching hundred-dollar chips on the board while two sweet young girls reached down over his shoulders to deposit modest little gold pieces, and said: "He's only funning now; wasting a few hundred to pass the time—waiting for the 'gold room' to open, you know, which won't be till well after midnight—then you'll see him bet! He won £14,000 there last night. They don't bet anything there but big money."

The thing I chiefly missed was the haggard people with the intense eye, the hunted look, the desperate mien, candidates for suicide and the pauper's grave. They are in the descriptions, as a rule, but they were off duty that night. All the gamblers, male and female, old and young, looked abnormally cheerful and prosperous.

However, all the nations were there, clothed richly, and speaking all the languages. Some of the women were painted and were evidently shaky as to character. These items tallied with the descriptions well enough.

The etiquette of the place was difficult to master. In the brilliant and populous halls and corridors you don't smoke, and you wear your hat, no matter how many ladies are in the thick throng of drifting humanity; but the moment you cross the sacred threshold and enter the gambling hell, off the hat must come, and everybody lights his cigar and goes to suffocating the ladies.

But what I came here for, five weeks ago, was the baths. My right arm was disabled with rheumatism. To sit at home in America and guess out the European bath best fitted for a particular ailment or combination of ailments, it is not possible, and it would not be a good idea to experiment in that way, anyhow. There are a great many curative baths on the continent, and some are good for one disease but bad for another. So it is necessary to let a physician name your bath for you. As a rule, Americans go to London to get this advice, and South Americans go to Paris for it. Now and then an economist chooses his bath himself and does a thousand miles of railroading to get to it, and then the local physicians tell him he has come to the wrong place. He sees that he has lost time and money and strength, and almost the minute that he realizes this he loses his temper. I had the rheumatism and was advised to go to Aix, not so much because I had that disease as because I had the promise of certain others. What they were was not explained to me, but they are either in the following menu or I have been sent to the wrong place. Dr. Wakefield's book says:

"We know that the class of maladies benefited by the water and baths at Aix are those due to defect of nutrition, debility of the nervous system, or to a gouty, rheumatic, herpetic, or scrofulous diathesis—all diseases extremely debilitating and requiring a tonic, and not a depressing action of the remedy. This it seems to find here, as recorded experience and daily action can testify. . . . According to the line of treatment, followed particularly with due regard to the temperature, the action of the Aix waters can be made sedative, exciting, derivative, or alterative and tonic."

The "Establishment" is the property of France, and all the officers and servants are employés of the French Government.

The bath-house is a huge and massive pile of white marble masonry, and looks more like a temple than anything else. It has several floors, and each is full of bath cabinets. There is every kind of bath—for the nose, the ears, the throat, vapor baths, tube baths, swimming baths, and all people's favorite, the douche. It is a good building to get lost in when you are not familiar with it. From early morning until nearly noon people are streaming in and streaming out without halt. The majority come afoot, but great numbers are brought in sedan chairs, a sufficiently ugly contrivance whose cover is a steep little tent made of striped canvas. You see nothing of the patient in this diving-bell as the bearers tramp along, except a glimpse of his ankles bound together and swathed around with blankets or towels to that generous degree that the result suggests a sore piano leg. By attention and practice the pallbearers have got so that they can keep out of step all the time—and they do it. As a consequence their veiled churn goes rocking, tilting, swaying along like a bell-buoy in a ground swell. It makes the oldest sailor sea-sick to look at that spectacle.

The "course" is usually fifteen douche baths and five tub baths. You take the douche three days in succession, then knock off and take a tub. You keep up this distribution through the course. If one course does not cure you, you take another one after an interval. You seek a local physician and he examines your case and prescribes the kind of bath required for it, with various other particulars; then you buy your course tickets and pay for them in advance—$9. With the tickets you get a memorandum book with your dates and hours all set down in it. The doctor takes you into the bath the first morning and gives some instructions to the two doucheurs who are to handle you through the course. The pour boires are about 10 cents to each of the men for each bath, payable at the end of the course. Also, at the end of the course, you pay three or four francs to the superintendent of your department of the bath house. These are useful particulars to know, and are not to be found in the books.

A servant of your hotel carries your towels and sheet to the bath daily and brings them away again. They are the property of the hotel; the French Government doesn't furnish these things.

You meet all kinds of people at a place like this, and if you give them a chance they will submerge you under their experiences, for they are either glad or sorry they came, and they want to spread their feelings out and enjoy them. One of these said to me:

"It's great, these baths. I didn't come here for my health—I only came to find out if there was anything the matter with me. The doctor told me if there was the symptoms would soon appear. After the first douche I had sharp pains in all my muscles. The doctor said it was different varieties of rheumatism, and the best varieties there were, too. After my second bath I had aches in my bones, and skull, and around. The doctor said it was different varieties of neuralgia, and the best in the market—anybody would tell me so. I got many new kinds of pains out of my third douche. These were in my joints. The doctor said it was gout, complicated with heart disease, and encouraged me to go on. Then we had the fourth douche, and I came out on a stretcher that time and fetched with me one vast, diversified, undulating, continental kind of pain, with horizons to it and zones and parallels of latitude and meridians of longitude and isothermal belts and variations of the compass—O, everything tidy and right up to the latest developments, you know. The doctor said it was inflammation of the soul, and just the very thing. Well, I went right on gathering them in—toothache, liver complaint, softening of the brain, nostalgia, bronchitis, osteology, fits, coleoptera, hydrangea, cyclopedia britannica, delirium tremens, and a lot of other things that I've got down in my list that I'll show you, and you can keep it if you like and tally off the bric-à-brac as you lay it in.

"The doctor said I was a grand proof of what these baths could do; said I had come here as innocent of disease as a grindstone, and inside of these three weeks these baths had sluiced out of me every important ailment known to medical science, along with considerable more that were entirely new and patentable. Why he wanted to exhibit me in his bay window."

There seems to be a good many liars this year. I began to take the baths, and found them most enjoyable; so enjoyable that if I hadn't had a disease I would have borrowed one, just to have a pretext for going on. They took me into a stone-floored basin about fourteen feet square, which had enough strange-looking pipes and things in it to make it look like a torture chamber. The two half-naked men seated me on a pine stool, and kept a couple of warm-water jets as thick as one's wrist playing upon me while they kneaded me, stroked me, twisted me, and applied all the other details of the scientific massage to me for seven or eight minutes. Then they stood me up and played a powerful jet upon me all around for another minute. The cool shower bath came next, and the thing was over. I came out of the bath-house a few minutes later feeling younger and fresher and finer than I have felt since I was a boy. The spring and cheer and delight of this exhalation lasted three hours, and the same uplifting effect has followed the twenty douches which I have taken since.

After my first douche I went to the chemist's on the corner, as per instructions, and asked for a half a glass of Challe water. It comes from a spring sixteen miles from here. It was furnished to me, but, perceiving that there was something the matter with it, I offered to wait till they could get some that was fresh, but they said it always smelt that way. They said that the reason that this was so much ranker than the sulfur water of the bath was that this contained thirty-two times as much sulfur as that. It may be true, but in my opinion that water comes from a cemetery, and not a fresh cemetery, either. History says that one of the early Roman Generals lost an army down there somewhere. If he could come back now I think this water would help him find it again. However, I drank the Challe, and have drank it once or twice every day since. I suppose it is all right, but I wish I knew what was the matter with those Romans.

My first baths developed plenty of pain, but the subsequent

ones removed almost all of it. I have got back the use of my arm these last few days, and I am going away now.

There are many beautiful drives about Aix, many interesting places to visit, and much pleasure to be found in paddling around the little Lake Bourget on the small steamers, but the excursion which satisfied me best was a trip to Annecy and its neighborhood. You go to Annecy in an hour by rail, through a garden land that has not had its equal for beauty, perhaps, since Eden; and certainly Eden was not cultivated as this garden is. The charm and loveliness of the whole region are bewildering. Picturesque rocks, forest-clothed hills, slopes richly bright in the cleanest and greenest grass, fields of grain without fleck or flaw, dainty of color, and as shiny and shimmery as silk, old gray mansions and towers half buried in foliage and sunny eminences, deep chasms with precipitous walls, and a swift stream of pale blue water between, with now and then a tumbling cascade, and always noble mountains in view, with vagrant white clouds curling about their summits.

Then at the end of an hour you come to Annecy and rattle through its old crooked lanes, built solidly up with curious old houses that are a dream of the middle ages, and presently you come to the main object of your trip—Lake Annecy. It is a revelation, it is a miracle. It brings the tears to a body's eyes it is so enchanting. That is to say, it affects you just as all things that you instantly recognize as perfect affect you—perfect music, perfect eloquence, perfect art, perfect joy, perfect grief. It stretches itself out there in the caressing sunlight, and away towards its border of majestic mountains, a crisped and radiant plain of water of the divinest blue that can be imagined. All the blues are there, from the faintest shoal water suggestion of the color, detectable only in the shadow of some overhanging object, all the way through, a little blue and a little bluer still, and again a shade bluer till you strike the deep, rich Mediterranean splendor which breaks the heart in your bosom, it is so beautiful.

And the mountains, as you skim along on the steamboat, how stately their forms, how noble their proportions, how green their velvet slopes, how soft the mottlings of sun and shadow that play about the rocky ramparts that crown them, how opaline the vast upheavals of snow banked against the sky in the remoteness beyond—Mont Blanc and the others—how shall anybody describe? Why, not even the painter can quite do it, and the most the pen can do is to suggest.

Up the lake there is an old abbey—Talloires—relic of the middle ages. We stopped there; stepped from the sparkling water and the rush and boom and fret and fever of the nineteenth century into the solemnity and the silence and the soft gloom and the brooding mystery of a remote antiquity. The stone step at the water's edge had the traces of a worn-out inscription on it; the wide flight of stone steps that led up to the front door was polished smooth by the passing feet of forgotten centuries, and there was not an unbroken stone among them all. Within the pile was the old square cloister with covered arcade all around it where the monks of the ancient times used to sit and meditate, and now and then welcome to their hospitalities the wandering knight with his tin breeches on, and in the middle of the square court (open to the sky) was a stone well curb, cracked and slick with age and use, and all about it were weeds, and among the weeds moldy brickbats that the Crusaders used to throw at each other. A passage at the further side of the cloister led to another weedy and roofless little inclosure beyond, where there was a ruined wall clothed to the top with masses of ivy and flanking it was a battered and picturesque arch. All over the building there were comfortable rooms and comfortable beds, and clean plank floors with no carpets on them. In one bedroom up-stairs were half a dozen portraits, dimming relics of the vanished centuries—portraits of abbots who used to be as grand as princes in their old day, and very rich and much worshiped and very holy; and in the next room there was a howling chromo and an electric bell. Downstairs there was an ancient wood carving with a Latin word commanding silence, and there was a spang new piano close by. Two elderly French women, with the kindest and honestest and sincerest faces, have the abbey now, and they board and lodge people who are tired of the roar of cities and want to be where the dead silence and serenity and peace of this old nest will heal their blistered spirits and patch up their ragged minds. They fed us well, they slept us well, and I wish I could have stayed there a few years and got a solid rest.

EDITH WHARTON
(1862–1937)

Edith Newbold was born to a socially prominent Manhattan family, and spent most of her childhood in Europe. She married Edward Wharton in 1885 and the young couple split their time between America and the Continent. The union disintegrated in the wake of mutual infidelities and nervous collapses, and the Whartons finally divorced in 1913. In the nearly thirty years of her marriage, Wharton wrote numerous articles on garden and home design, short stories and several novels, including the masterpieces Ethan Frome *and* The House of Mirth.

After the dissolution of her marriage, Wharton spent almost all of her time in France. Undeterred by the outbreak of World War I, she threw herself into the French effort and organized the American Hostels for Refugees, which assisted nearly 10,000 refugees, providing food, shelter, clothing and medical care. In 1915 she made half a dozen visits to the front (and described them in articles for Scribner's*). For her efforts Wharton was awarded the Legion of Honor by the French government in 1918. Her last great novel,* The Age of Innocence, *for which she was awarded the Pulitzer Prize, was published in 1918.*

This excerpt is from one of Wharton's lesser-known novels, The Reef *(1912), which concerns the double standards of sexuality imposed on men and women. George Darrow falls into an affair with young Sophy Viner, who, in a classic Victorian turn of events, becomes the fiancée of his future wife's stepson. Darrow and Viner are both caught in Paris—and fall in love with the city and each other.*

from The Reef

The girl was there, in the room next to him. That had been the first point in his waking consciousness. The second was a sense of relief at the obligation imposed on him by this unexpected turn of events. To wake to the necessity of action, to postpone perforce the fruitless contemplation of his private grievance, was cause enough for gratitude, even if the small adventure in which he found himself involved had not, on its own merits, roused an instinctive curiosity to see it through.

When he and his companion, the night before, had reached the Farlows' door in the rue de la Chaise, it was only to find, after repeated assaults on its panels, that the Farlows were no longer there. They had moved away the week before, not only from their apartment but from Paris; and Miss Viner's breach with Mrs. Murrett had been too sudden to permit her letter and telegram to overtake them. Both communications, no doubt, still reposed in a pigeon-hole of the *loge;* but its custodian, when drawn from his lair, sulkily declined to let Miss Viner verify the fact, and only flung out, in return for Darrow's bribe, the statement that the Americans had gone to Joigny.

To pursue them there at that hour was manifestly impossible, and Miss Viner, disturbed but not disconcerted by this new obstacle, had quite simply acceded to Darrow's suggestion that she should return for what remained of the night to the hotel where he had sent his luggage.

The drive back through the dark hush before dawn, with the nocturnal blaze of the Boulevard fading around them like the false lights of a magician's palace, had so played on her impressionability that she seemed to give no farther thought to her own predicament. Darrow noticed that she did not feel the beauty and mystery of the spectacle as much as its pressure of human significance, all its hidden implications of emotion and adventure. As they passed the shadowy colonnade of the Français, remote and temple-like in the paling lights, he felt a clutch on his arm, and heard the cry: "There are things *there* that I want so desperately to see!" and all the way back to the hotel she continued to question him, with shrewd precision and an artless thirst for detail, about the theatrical life of Paris. He was struck afresh, as he listened, by the way in which her naturalness eased the situation of constraint, leaving to it only a pleasant savour of good fellowship. It was the kind of episode that one might, in advance, have characterized as "awkward", yet that was proving, in the event, as much outside such definitions as a sunrise stroll with a dryad in a dew-drenched forest; and Darrow reflected that mankind would never have needed to invent tact if it had not first invented social complications.

It had been understood, with his good-night to Miss Viner, that the next morning he was to look up the Joigny trains, and see her safely to the station; but, while he breakfasted and waited for a time-table, he recalled again her cry of joy at the prospect of seeing Cerdine. It was certainly a pity, since that most elusive and incalculable of artists was leaving the next week for South America, to miss what might be a last sight of her in her greatest part; and Darrow, having dressed and made the requisite excerpts from the time-table, decided to carry the result of his deliberations to his neighbour's door.

It instantly opened at his knock, and she came forth looking as if she had been plunged into some sparkling element which had curled up all her drooping tendrils and wrapped her in a shimmer of fresh leaves.

"Well, what do you think of me?" she cried; and with a hand at her waist she spun about as if to show off some miracle of Parisian dress-making.

"I think the missing trunk has come—and that it was worth waiting for!"

"You *do* like my dress?"

"I adore it! I always adore new dresses—why, you don't mean to say it's *not* a new one?"

She laughed out her triumph.

"No, no, no! My trunk hasn't come, and this is only my old rag of yesterday—but I never knew the trick to fail!" And, as he stared: "You see," she joyously explained, "I've always had to dress in all kinds of dreary left-overs, and sometimes, when everybody else was smart and new, it used to make me awfully miserable. So one day, when Mrs. Murrett dragged me down unexpectedly to fill a place at dinner, I suddenly thought I'd try spinning around like that, and say to everyone: *'Well, what do you think of me?'* And, do you know, they were all taken in, including Mrs. Murrett, who didn't recognize my old turned and dyed rags, and told me afterward it was awfully bad form to dress as if I were somebody that people would expect to know! And ever since, whenever I've particularly wanted to look nice, I've just asked people what they thought of my new frock; and they're always, always taken in!"

She dramatized her explanation so vividly that Darrow felt as if his point were gained.

"Ah, but this confirms your vocation—of course," he cried, "you must see Cerdine!" and, seeing her face fall at this reminder of the change in her prospects, he hastened to set forth his plan. As he did so, he saw how easy it was to explain things to her. She would either accept his suggestion, or she would not: but at least she would waste no time in protestations and objections, or any vain sacrifice to the idols of conformity. The conviction that one could, on any given point, almost predicate this of her, gave him the sense of having advanced far enough in her intimacy to urge his arguments against a hasty pursuit of her friends.

Yes, it would certainly be foolish—she at once agreed—in the case of such dear indefinite angels as the Farlows, to dash off after them without more positive proof that they were established at Joigny, and so established that they could take her in.

She owned it was but too probable that they had gone there to "cut down", and might be doing so in quarters too contracted to receive her; and it would be unfair, on that chance, to impose herself on them unannounced. The simplest way of getting farther light on the question would be to go back to the rue de la Chaise, where, at that more conversable hour, the *concierge* might be less chary of detail; and she could decide on her next step in the light of such facts as he imparted.

Point by point, she fell in with the suggestion, recognizing, in the light of their unexplained flight, that the Farlows might indeed be in a situation on which one could not too rashly intrude. Her concern for her friends seemed to have effaced all thought of herself, and this little indication of character gave Darrow a quite disproportionate pleasure. She agreed that it would be well to go at once to the rue de la Chaise, but met his proposal that they should drive by the declaration that it was a "waste" not to walk in Paris; so they set off on foot through the cheerful tumult of the streets.

The walk was long enough for him to learn many things about her. The storm of the previous night had cleared the air, and Paris shone in morning beauty under a sky that was all broad wet washes of white and blue; but Darrow again noticed that her visual sensitiveness was less keen than her feeling for what he was sure the good Farlows—whom he already seemed to know—would have called "the human interest". She seemed hardly conscious of sensations of form and colour, or of any imaginative suggestion, and the spectacle before them—always, in its scenic splendour, so moving to her companion—broke up, under her scrutiny, into a thousand minor points: the things in the shops, the types of character and manner of occupation shown in the passing faces, the street signs, the names of the hotels they passed, the motley brightness of the flower-carts, the identity of the churches and public buildings that caught her eye. But what she liked best, he divined, was the mere fact of being free to walk abroad in the bright air, her tongue rattling on as it pleased, while her feet kept time to the mighty orchestration of the city's sounds. Her delight in the fresh air, in the freedom, light and sparkle of the morning, gave him a sudden insight into her stifled past; nor was it indifferent to him to perceive how much his presence evidently added to her enjoyment. If only as a sympathetic ear, he guessed what he must be worth to her. The girl had been dying for some one to talk to, some one before whom she could unfold and shake out to the light her poor little shut-away emotions. Years of repression were revealed in her sudden burst of confidence; and the pity she inspired made Darrow long to fill her few free hours to the brim.

She had the gift of rapid definition, and his questions as to the life she had led with the Farlows, during the interregnum between the Hoke and Murrett eras, called up before him a queer little corner of Parisian existence. The Farlows themselves—he a painter, she a "magazine writer"—rose before him in all their incorruptible simplicity: an elderly New England couple, with vague yearnings for enfranchisement, who lived in Paris as if it were a Massachusetts suburb, and dwelt hopefully on the "higher side" of the Gallic nature. With equal vividness she set before him the component figures of the circle from which Mrs. Farlow drew the "Inner Glimpses of French Life" appearing over her name in a leading New England journal: the Roumanian lady who had sent them tickets for her tragedy, an elderly French gentleman who, on the strength of a week's stay at Folkestone, translated English fiction for the provincial press, a lady from Wichita, Kansas, who advocated free love and the abolition of the corset, a clergyman's widow from Torquay who had written an "English Ladies' Guide to Foreign Galleries" and a Russian sculptor who lived on nuts and was "almost certainly" an anarchist. It was this nucleus, and its outer ring of musical, architectural and other American students, which posed successively to Mrs. Farlow's versatile fancy as a centre of "University Life", a "Salon of the Faubourg St. Germain", a group of Parisian "Intellectuals" or a "Cross-section of Montmartre"; but even her faculty for extracting from it the most varied literary effects had not sufficed to create a permanent demand for the "Inner Glimpses", and there were days when—Mr. Farlow's landscapes being equally unmarketable—a temporary withdrawal to the country (subsequently utilized as "Peeps into Château Life") became necessary to the courageous couple.

Five years of Mrs. Murrett's world, while increasing Sophy's tenderness for the Farlows, had left her with few illusions as to their power of advancing her fortunes; and she did not conceal from Darrow that her theatrical projects were of the vaguest. They hung mainly on the problematical goodwill of an ancient comédienne, with whom Mrs. Farlow had a slight acquaintance (extensively utilized in "Stars of the French Footlights" and "Behind the Scenes at the Français"), and who had once, with signs of approval, heard Miss Viner recite the Nuit de Mai.

"But of course I know how much that's worth," the girl broke off, with one of her flashes of shrewdness. "And besides, it isn't likely that a poor old fossil like Mme. Dolle could get anybody to listen to her now, even if she really thought I had talent. But she might introduce me to people; or at least give me a few tips. If I could manage to earn enough to pay for lessons I'd go straight to some of the big people and work with them. I'm rather hoping the Farlows may find me a chance of that kind—an engagement with some American family in Paris who would want to be 'gone round' with like the Hokes, and who'd leave me time enough to study."

In the rue de la Chaise they learned little except the exact address of the Farlows, and the fact that they had sub-let their flat before leaving. This information obtained, Darrow proposed to Miss Viner that they should stroll along the quays to a little restaurant looking out on the Seine, and there, over the *plat du jour*, consider the next step to be taken. The long walk had given her cheeks a glow indicative of wholesome hunger, and she made no difficulty about satisfying it in Darrow's company. Regaining the river they walked on in the direction of Notre Dame, delayed now and again by the young man's irresistible tendency to linger over the bookstalls, and by his ever-fresh

response to the shifting beauties of the scene. For two years his
eyes had been subdued to the atmospheric effects of London, to
the mysterious fusion of darkly-piled city and low-lying bitumi-
nous sky; and the transparency of the French air, which left the
green gardens and silvery stones so classically clear yet so softly
harmonized, struck him as having a kind of conscious intelli-
gence. Every line of the architecture, every arch of the bridges,
the very sweep of the strong bright river between them, while
contributing to this effect, sent forth each a separate appeal to
some sensitive memory; so that, for Darrow, a walk through the
Paris streets was always like the unrolling of a vast tapestry from
which countless stored fragrances were shaken out.

It was a proof of the richness and multiplicity of the spectacle
that it served, without incongruity, for so different a purpose as
the background of Miss Viner's enjoyment. As a mere drop-scene
for her personal adventure it was just as much in its place as in
the evocation of great perspectives of feeling. For her, as he
again perceived when they were seated at their table in a low
window above the Seine, Paris was "Paris" by virtue of all its
entertaining details, its endless ingenuities of pleasantness. Where
else, for instance, could one find the dear little dishes of *hors
d'oeuvre*, the symmetrically-laid anchovies and radishes, the thin
golden shells of butter, or the wood strawberries and brown jars
of cream that gave to their repast the last refinement of rusticity?
Hadn't he noticed, she asked, that cooking always expressed the
national character, and that French food was clever and amusing
just because the people were? And in private houses, every-
where, how the dishes always resembled the talk—how the very
same platitudes seemed to go into people's mouths and come out
of them? Couldn't he see just what kind of menu it would
make, if a fairy waved a wand and suddenly turned the conver-
sation at a London dinner into joints and pudding? She always
thought it a good sign when people liked Irish stew; it meant
that they enjoyed changes and surprises, and taking life as it
came; and such a beautiful Parisian version of the dish as the
navarin that was just being set before them was like the very best

kind of talk—the kind when one could never tell before-hand just what was going to be said!

Darrow, as he watched her enjoyment of their innocent feast, wondered if her vividness and vivacity were signs of her calling. She was the kind of girl in whom certain people would instantly have recognized the histrionic gift. But experience had led him to think that, except at the creative moment, the divine flame burns low in its possessors. The one or two really intelligent actresses he had known had struck him, in conversation, as either bovine or primitively "jolly". He had a notion that, save in the mind of genius, the creative process absorbs too much of the whole stuff of being to leave much surplus for personal expression; and the girl before him, with her changing face and flexible fancies, seemed destined to work in life itself rather than in any of its counterfeits.

The coffee and liqueurs were already on the table when her mind suddenly sprang back to the Farlows. She jumped up with one of her subversive movements and declared that she must telegraph at once. Darrow called for writing materials, and room was made at her elbow for the parched ink-bottle and saturated blotter of the Parisian restaurant; but the mere sight of these jaded implements seemed to paralyze Miss Viner's faculties. She hung over the telegraph-form with anxiously-drawn brow, the tip of the pen-handle pressed against her lip; and at length she raised her troubled eyes to Darrow's.

"I simply can't think how to say it."

"What—that you're staying over to see Cerdine?"

"But *am* I—am I, really?" The joy of it flamed over her face.

Darrow looked at his watch. "You could hardly get an answer to your telegram in time to take a train to Joigny this afternoon, even if you found your friends could have you."

She mused for a moment, tapping her lip with the pen. "But I must let them know I'm here. I must find out as soon as possible if they *can* have me." She laid the pen down despairingly. "I never *could* write a telegram!" she sighed.

"Try a letter, then, and tell them you'll arrive tomorrow."

This suggestion produced immediate relief, and she gave an energetic dab at the ink-bottle; but after another interval of uncertain scratching she paused again.

"Oh, it's fearful! I don't know what on earth to say. I wouldn't for the world have them know how beastly Mrs. Murrett's been."

Darrow did not think it necessary to answer. It was no business of his, after all. He lit a cigar and leaned back in his seat, letting his eyes take their fill of indolent pleasure. In the throes of invention she had pushed back her hat, loosening the stray lock which had invited his touch the night before. After looking at it for a while he stood up and wandered to the window.

Behind him he heard her pen scrape on.

"I don't want to worry them—I'm so certain they've got bothers of their own." The faltering scratches ceased again. "I wish I weren't such an idiot about writing: all the words get frightened and scurry away when I try to catch them."

He glanced back at her with a smile as she bent above her task like a school-girl struggling with a "composition". Her flushed cheek and frowning brow showed that her difficulty was genuine and not an artless device to draw him to her side. She was really powerless to pull her thoughts into writing, and the inability seemed characteristic of her quick impressionable mind, and of the incessant come-and-go of her sensations. He thought of Anna Leath's letters, or rather of the few he had received, years ago, from the girl who had been Anna Summers. He saw the slender firm strokes of the pen, recalled the clear structure of the phrases, and, by an abrupt association of ideas, remembered that, at that very hour, just such a document might be awaiting him at the hotel.

What if it were there, indeed, and had brought him a complete explanation of her telegram? The revulsion of feeling produced by this thought made him look at the girl with sudden impatience. She struck him as positively stupid, and he wondered how he could have wasted half his day with her, when all the while Mrs. Leath's letter might be lying on his table. At that moment, if he could have chosen, he would have left his companion on the spot; but he had her on his hands, and must accept the consequences.

Some odd intuition seemed to make her conscious of his change of mood, for she sprang from her seat, crumpling the letter in her hand.

"I'm too stupid; but I won't keep you any longer. I'll go back to the hotel and write there."

Her colour deepened, and for the first time, as their eyes met, he noticed a faint embarrassment in hers. Could it be that his nearness was, after all, the cause of her confusion? The thought turned his vague impatience with her into a definite resentment toward himself. There was really no excuse for his having blundered into such an adventure. Why had he not shipped the girl off to Joigny by the evening train, instead of urging her to delay, and using Cerdine as a pretext? Paris was full of people he knew, and his annoyance was increased by the thought that some friend of Mrs. Leath's might see him at the play, and report his presence there with a suspiciously good-looking companion. The idea was distinctly disagreeable: he did not want the woman he adored to think he could forget her for a moment. And by this time he had fully persuaded himself that a letter from her was awaiting him, and had even gone so far as to imagine that its contents might annul the writer's telegraphed injunction, and call him to her side at once . . .

RICHARD WILBUR
(1921–)

*"Poems are not addressed to anybody in particular," wrote poet Richard Wilbur. "They are conflicts with disorder, not messages from one person to another." Initially, Wilbur wrote poetry in response to the chaos of World War II. The Amherst graduate found himself a soldier in the battles for Europe, first in Italy and then in the amphibious landing in France and finally in the push north to Germany. "Poetry being the organizing art which one can practice in a foxhole, I and countless other soldiers have made use of it. A lot of apprentice efforts, as you suppose, were excluded from my first book (*The Beautiful Changes, 1947*) and I've tended not to borrow from them, though I recall what gave them rise."*

After the war, Wilbur went to graduate school at Harvard and began a career as a poet and translator of Racine and Molière. His poetry is usually metrically regular and rhymed, and he is thought of as a traditionalist in the school of Wallace Stevens and Andrew Marvell. Wilbur often includes translations and original poetry in one volume. This selection "Place Pigalle" is from New and Collected Poems *published in 1988. Richard Wilbur, a former poet laureate, has been awarded, among many honors, the Pulitzer Prize and the Ordre des Palmes Academiques.*

Place Pigalle

Now homing tradesmen scatter through the streets
Toward suppers, thinking on improved conditions,
While evening, with a million simple fissions,
Takes up its warehouse watches, storefront beats,
By nursery windows its assigned positions.

Now at the corners of the Place Pigalle
Bright bars explode against the dark's embraces;
The soldiers come, the boys with ancient faces,
Seeking their ancient friends, who stroll and loll
Amid the glares and glass: electric graces.

The puppies are asleep, and snore the hounds;
But here wry hares, the soldier and the whore,
Mark off their refuge with a gaudy door,
Brazen at bay, and boldly out of bounds:
The puppies dream, the hounds superbly snore.

Ionized innocence: this pair reclines,
She on the table, he in a tilting chair,
With Arden ease; her eyes as pale as air
Travel his priestgoat face; his hand's thick tines
Touch the gold whorls of her Corinthian hair.

"Girl, if I love thee not, then let me die;
Do I not scorn to change my state with kings?
Your muchtouched flesh, incalculable, which wrings
Me so, now shall I gently seize in my
Desperate soldier's hands which kill all things."

WILLIAM CARLOS
WILLIAMS
(1883–1963)

For nearly all of his eighty years William Carlos Williams lived, wrote poetry and several novels, and practiced medicine within one mile of his birthplace: Rutherford, New Jersey. He earned his medical degree at the University of Pennsylvania, where he met his lifelong friend, Ezra Pound. While Pound left the United States for Europe, Williams returned to Rutherford to set up a practice. They exchanged letters across the Atlantic; Pound entreated Williams to come to Europe. "You'd better come across and broaden your mind." And Williams accused Pound of "unconstrained vagabondism." Pound wrote, "I don't really believe you want to leave the U.S. permanently. I think you are suffering from nerve; that you are really afraid to leave Rutherford. I think you ought to take a year or a six months' vacation in Europe."

In 1924 Williams, on sabbatical from his practice, left for Europe with his wife. The trip became the framework for A Voyage from Pagany (dedicated to Pound). Williams described Pagany as "my first (limping) novel" even though it was largely autobiographical, less a travelogue and more an impressionistic ramble. Throughout his trip, Williams's sensibilities remain firmly American. It was this "Americanness" that separated him from his fellow imagists, Pound and T. S. Eliot. Shunning academia and European aesthetics, Williams's poetry was rooted in the ordinary and everyday. Late in life he became a champion of younger poets, especially Allen Ginsberg from nearby Paterson, New Jersey. Williams wrote the introduction to Howl, Ginsberg's first book of poetry.

Paris Again

from A   V O Y A G E   T O   P A G A N Y

Paris! where notable Englishmen come to see their illegitimate daughters.

Paris, a place abandoned and serious. What is its touted frivolity? The froth of serious waves?—In this way, it being now full evening, Evans had been composing apostrophes to Paris for the last twenty minutes of his ride—Paris! Its frivolity, its frantic milling about for pleasure—that's America, not France—*"Jenseits des Lust-prinzips."* These are the evidences of a seriousness foreign to us; this rock sets us spinning as dry land does feet after a ship. From the small cities of the whole world, frivolous from their bedrooms to the ornate corridors of the minds of their—to every little chamber where men and women hide themselves to do business of whatever sort—and no business without first the gesture of hiding—in Paris it bursts out to become serious—

Paris as a serious city, the beloved of men; Paris that releases what there is in men—the frivolity that means a knife cut through self-deception.

He also thought of Paris as a woman watching for a lover. Paris is a stitched-up woman watching the international array that constantly deploys about the Eiffel Tower and goes frantically about its streets in the squealing taxis—hunting a lover.

It must be a lover. He must come of machines, he must break through. Nothing will subdue him.

Yes, that is Paris. Nothing will subdue him. Finally he grows serious, finally clear. It expects lovers out of the hearts of machines. Out of the felted chamber of boredom you must come clean. Somehow you must have saved, must have built up a great seriousness.

Good God, Paris—He remembered how he had hated it; just an opportunity to shed the nerves; the cast-off of international malady, like the crutches at Lourdes.

They were passing through the city now. And Evans began to think of the stern morality of certain legendary great French families, the rigid discipline, the cold aloofness from the loose life of Montmartre, bespeaking a solidity of character which permits liberties no other nature could afford. He remembered his mother's stories. And her brother's.

And they are dextrous. To that he added "argus-eyed."

Paris wipes all frivolity aside and stares in. What are you made of? What are you made of? What are you made of? It coincided with the slowing rhythm of the train. Then try it, try it then, try it then.

This is the secret of Paris—and, that if it be a lover, *here* is the reward.

Come, you incestuous,
Bald and uxorious.

In the crowd at the Gare St. Lazare the porter was drunk and started to put up a scene. What! only two francs. What! for the boat train!—Evans gave him five and demanded the two in return. The porter gave them back grumbling, and the dilapidated taxi started out madly into the rain in the disordered whirl about the station front. At his time of life Evans was less inclined to stop the parade to think than formerly. He was always straining out of windows. And now for the third time in Paris he stared and stared into the gloom of the rue du Havre in an excited frame of mind. Had it changed?

Had it changed since as a boy Trufley had taken him to the

Catacombs and on the great boulevards fed him *syrop de Groseille* while he himself slowly sipped absinthe and smiled and smiled? Had it changed since that day when, a schoolboy from great America, he had sat playing with others on the third floor of an apartment house on rue la Bruyère, and one of the little devils had tried to push him out of the low French window? *Coup de poing américain!* He smiled. Had it changed since he had come from Germany reading Heine; from London where he had seen the literary world just before the war?

What would Jack be like now? And he was anxious to meet his sister. No one had come to the station. Well, so much the better. He wondered what luck he would have on this trip. And always he kept saying: Perhaps this is the time. Something may happen and I shall not return.

But what to do? and what to do next?

Bess, his sister, was in Paris ostensibly to sing. She had the available cash of the family that their mother had left them when she died. Evans wanted none of it; he could work. Bess was twelve years her brother's junior. They had sided together against the old man. Evans was like his mother. "Bess is like the old man— purged," her brother sometimes said.

Marvelous to be in Paris, the air is different; feel it at once. Even that night he had to go out for a walk—anywhere—to the Boulevards.

You must not be afraid.—But Evans was uncertain—and American—and this and that and careless—and amused and lazy and more than a little critical and no drunkard at any time and— hard to crack, a sparrow in short. He wanted to write—that was all, and not to have written, but to be writing. He got his whisky that way, he got all he ever got from that. To be feeling it in his mind and his fingers as it flowed out. And there in secret he lived.

What a life! But Paris understands that too. It did not seem to Evans that he was afraid; it was that he had to discard so much to get at what he wanted that he never arrived anywhere. The whole world is built to keep it from being said. And so he walked admiring the fabric of it—the hateful fabric.—No, he laughed, not hateful, but in the repulsive phase. Every discovery is only a discovery to hide it deeper.—How shall I talk to Jack for instance, when I see him?

Permissions Acknowledgments